THE ILIAD

THE ILIAD

Homer

WORDSWORTH CLASSICS

This edition published 1995 by Wordsworth Editions Limited
Cumberland House, Crib Street, Ware, Hertfordshire SG12 9ET

ISBN 1 85326 242 0

Printed and bound in Greast Britain by
Mackays of Chatham plc, Chatham, Kent

INTRODUCTION

The Iliad which appears here in prose translation for ease of use, is widely regarded as being the earliest extant example of ancient Greek literature. It was originally written as an epic poem comprising twenty-four books of approximately sixteen thousand lines in dactylic hexameter and, although scholarly opinion is divided on its authorship, it is usually ascribed to the great Greek poet, Homer, who is thought to have dictated the poem having first composed it orally. The story is set in the final year of the epic Trojan War and centres on the Greek hero, Achilles, who leaves the field of battle in high dudgeon to sulk famously in his tent, after his Commander-in-Chief, Agamemnon, confiscates his prize of war, the lovely maid, Briseis. Denied Achilles' prowess as a warrior, the fortunes of the Greek army suffer a reverse. Achilles is only persuaded to rejoin the fray following the death of his great friend, Patroclus, who is slain in battle wearing Achilles' armour by the mighty Trojan prince, Hector. The scene is then set for the final battle between the Greek hero Achilles and Hector, the outcome of which contest will decide the victor of the Trojan War and set the seal on the fate of Troy. The compassion shown by Achilles to the aged Priam is one of the most moving parts of the story. *The Iliad* is a story of war in which heroism and compassion rise above the sinister futility of the destructive power of conflict to the glory of the valiant human spirit of the heroic and often tragic Mycenaean age.

The identity of the Ionian poet, Homer, remains unknown. Seven cities claimed him as their own; tradition has it that he was blind and a modern theory supposes Homer to have been a woman. The modern consensus is that The Iliad and The Odyssey were each the work of single but different poets. Textual analysis shows that both poems, as they have come down to us, date from the eighth century BC, though the diction and language of *The Odyssey* indicate that it is a slightly later work. It is likely that both works represent a drawing together of several oral traditions. They are the first truly great works of Western literature, and hold a place more central to the Greek tradition even than Shakespeare in the

English tradition, since they provided so much basic education and information, however flawed, for the ancient Greek civilisation.

FURTHER READING

K. J. Atchity, *Homer's Iliad* 1978
C. R. Beye, *The Iliad, The Odyssey and the Epic Tradition* 1966
C. M. Bowra, *Homer* 1972
P. Vivante, *The Homeric Imagination* 1970
M. M. Wilcox (Ed.), *The Iliad of Homer* 1984

THE ILIAD

BOOK I

How Agamemnon and Achilles fell out at the siege of Troy; and Achilles withdrew himself from battle, and won from Zeus a pledge that his wrong should be avenged on Agamemnon and the Achaians.

SING, goddess, the wrath of Achilles Peleus' son, the ruinous wrath that brought on the Achaians woes innumerable, and hurled down into Hades many strong souls of heroes, and gave their bodies to be a prey to dogs and all winged fowls; and so the counsel of Zeus wrought out its accomplishment from the day when first strife parted Atreides king of men and noble Achilles

Who then among the gods set the twain at strife and variance? Even the son of Leto and of Zeus; for he in anger at the king sent a sore plague upon the host, that the folk began to perish, because Atreides had done dishonour to Chryses the priest. For he had come to the Achaians' fleet ships to win his daughter's freedom, and brought a ransom beyond telling; and bare in his hands the fillet of Apollo the Far-darter upon a golden staff; and made his prayer unto all the Achaians, and most of all to the two sons of Atreus, orderers of the host: 'Ye sons of Atreus and all ye well-greaved Achaians now may the gods that dwell in the mansions of Olympus grant you to lay waste the city of Priam, and to fare happily homeward; only set ye my dear child free, and accept the ransom in reverence to the son of Zeus, far-darting Apollo.'

Then all the other Achaians cried assent, to reverence the priest and accept his goodly ransom; yet the thing pleased not the heart of Agamemnon son of Atreus, but he roughly sent him away, and laid stern charge upon him, saying: 'Let me not find thee, old man, amid the hollow ships, whether tarrying now or returning again hereafter, lest the staff and fillet of the god avail thee naught. And her will I not set free; nay, ere that shall old age come on her in our house, in Argos, far from her native land, where she shall ply the loom and serve my couch. But depart, provoke me not, that thou mayest the rather go in peace.'

So said he, and the old man was afraid and obeyed his word, and fared silently along the shore of the loud-sounding sea. Then went that aged man apart and prayed aloud to king Apollo, whom Leto of the fair locks bare: 'Hear me, god of the silver bow, that standest over Chryse and holy Killa, and rulest Tenedos with might, O Smintheus! If ever I built a temple gracious in thine eyes, or if ever I burnt to thee fat flesh of thighs of bulls or goats, fulfil thou this my desire; let the Danaans pay by thine arrows for my tears.'

So spake he in prayer, and Phoebus Apollo heard him, and came down from the peaks of Olympus wroth at heart, bearing on his shoulders his bow and covered quiver. And the arrows clanged upon his shoulders in his wrath, as the god moved; and he descended like to night. Then he sate him aloof from the ships, and let an arrow fly; and there was heard a dread clanging of the silver bow. First did he assail the mules and fleet dogs, but afterward, aiming at the men his piercing dart, he smote; and the pyres of the dead burnt continually in multitude.

Now for nine days ranged the god's shafts through the host; but on the tenth Achilles summoned the folk to assembly, for in his mind did goddess Hera of the white arms put the thought, because she had pity on the Danaans when she beheld them perishing. Now when they had gathered and were met in assembly, then Achilles fleet of foot stood up and spake among them: 'Son of Atreus, now deem I that we shall return wandering home again – if verily we might escape death – if war at once and pestilence must indeed ravage the Achaians. But come, let us now inquire of some soothsayer or priest, yea, or an interpreter of dreams – seeing that a dream too is of Zeus – who shall say wherefore Phoebus Apollo is so wroth, whether he blame us by reason of vow or hecatomb; if perchance he would accept the savour of lambs or unblemished goats, and so would take away the pestilence from us.'

So spake he and sate him down; and there stood up before them Kalchas son of Thestor, most excellent far of augurs, who knew both things that were and that should be and that had been before, and guided the ships of the Achaians to Ilios by his soothsaying that Phoebus Apollo bestowed on him. He of good intent made harangue and spake amid them: 'Achilles, dear to Zeus, thou biddest me tell the wrath of Apollo, the king that smiteth afar. Therefore will I speak; but do thou make covenant with me, and swear that verily with all thy heart thou wilt aid me both by word and deed. For of a truth I deem that I shall provoke one that ruleth all the Argives with might, and whom the Achaians obey. For a king is more of might when he is wroth with a meaner man; even though for the one day he swallow his anger, yet doth he still keep his displeasure thereafter in his breast till he accomplish it. Consider thou, then, if thou wilt hold me safe.'

And Achilles fleet of foot made answer and spake to him: 'Yea, be of good courage, speak whatever soothsaying thou knowest; for by Apollo dear to Zeus, him by whose worship thou, O Kalchas, declarest thy soothsaying to the Danaans, no man while I live and behold light on earth shall lay violent hands upon thee amid the hollow ships; no man of all the Danaans, not even if thou mean Agamemnon, that now avoweth him to be greatest far of the Achaians.'

Then was the noble seer of good courage, and spake: 'Neither by reason of a vow is he displeased, nor for any hecatomb, but for his priest's sake to whom Agamemnon did despite, and set not his daughter free and accepted not the ransom; therefore hath the Far-darter brought woes upon us, yea, and will bring. Nor will he ever remove the loathly pestilence from the Danaans till we have given the bright-eyed damsel to her father, unbought, unransomed, and carried a holy hecatomb to Chryse; then might we propitiate him to our prayer.'

So said he and sate him down, and there stood up before them the hero son of Atreus, wide-ruling Agamemnon, sore displeased; and his dark heart within him was greatly filled with anger, and his eyes were like flashing fire. To Kalchas first spake he with look of ill: 'Thou seer of evil, never yet hast thou told me the thing that is pleasant. Evil is ever the joy of thy heart to prophesy, but never yet didst thou tell any good matter nor bring it to pass. And now with soothsaying thou makest harangue among the Danaans, how that the Far-darter bringeth woes upon them because, forsooth, I would not take the goodly ransom of the damsel Chryseis, seeing I am the rather fain to keep her own self within mine house. Yea, I prefer her before Klytaimnestra my wedded wife; in no wise is she lacking beside her, neither in favour nor stature, nor wit nor skill Yet for all this will I give her back, if that is better; rather would I see my folk whole than perishing. Only make ye me ready a prize of honour forthwith, lest I alone of all the Argives be disprized, which thing beseemeth not; for ye all behold how my prize is departing from me.'

To him then made answer fleet-footed goodly Achilles: 'Most noble son of Atreus, of all men most covetous, how shall the great-hearted Achaians give thee a meed of honour? We know naught of any wealth of common store, but what spoil soe'er we took from captured cities hath been apportioned, and it beseemeth not to beg all this back from the folk. Nay, yield thou the damsel to the god, and we Achaians will pay thee back threefold and fourfold, if ever Zeus grant us to sack some well-walled town of Troy-land.'[1]

To him lord Agamemnon made answer and said: 'Not in this wise, strong as thou art, O godlike Achilles, beguile thou me by craft; thou shalt not outwit me nor persuade me. Dost thou wish, that thou mayest keep thy meed of honour, for me to sit idle in bereavement, and biddest me give her back? Nay, if the great-hearted Achaians will give me a meed suited to my mind, that the recompense be equal – but if they give it not, then I myself will go and take a meed of honour, thine be it or Aias', or Odysseus' that I will take unto me; wroth shall he be to whomsoever I come. But for this we will take counsel hereafter; now let us launch a black ship on the great sea, and gather picked oarsmen, and set therein a hecatomb, and embark Chryseis of the fair cheeks herself, and let one of our counsellors be captain, Aias or Idomeneus or goodly Odysseus, or thou, Peleides, most redoubtable of men, to do sacrifice for us and propitiate the Far-darter.'

Then Achilles fleet of foot looked at him scowling and said: 'Ah me, thou clothed in shamelessnes, thou of crafty mind, how shall any Achaian hearken to thy bidding with all his heart, be it to go a journey or to fight the foe amain? Not by reason of the Trojan spearmen came I hither to fight, for they have not wonged me; never did they harry mine oxen nor my horses, nor ever waste my harvest in deep-soiled Phthia, the nurse of men; seeing there lieth between us long space of shadowy mountains and sounding sea; but thee, thou shameless one, followed we hither to make thee glad, by earning recompense at the Trojans' hands for Menelaos and for thee, thou dog-face! All this thou reckonest not nor takest thought thereof; and now thou threatenest thyself to take my meed of honour, wherefor I travailed much, and the sons of the Achaians gave it me. Never win I meed like unto thine, when the Achaians sack any populous citadel of Trojan men; my hands bear the brunt of furious war, but when the apportioning cometh then is thy meed far ampler, and I betake me to the ships with some small thing, yet mine own, when I have fought to weariness. Now will I depart to Phthia, seeing it is far better to return home on my beaked ships; nor am I minded here in dishonour to draw thee thy fill of riches and wealth.'

Then Agamemnon king of men made answer to him.

[1]Reading with Cobet Τρωην for Τροίην.

'Yea, flee, if thy soul be set thereon. It is not I that beseech thee to tarry for my sake; I have others by my side that shall do me honour, and above all Zeus lord of counsel. Most hateful art thou to me of all kings, fosterlings of Zeus; thou ever lovest strife and wars and fightings. Though thou be very strong, yet that I ween is a gift to thee of God. Go home with thy ships and company and lord it among thy Myrmidons; I reck not aught of thee nor care I for thine indignation; and this shall be my threat to thee: seeing Phoebus Apollo bereaveth me of Chryseis, her with my ship and my company will I send back; and mine own self will I go to thy hut and take Briseis of the fair cheeks, even that thy meed of honour, that thou mayest well know how far greater I am than thou, and so shall another hereafter abhor to match his words with mine and rival me to my face.'

So said he, and grief came upon Peleus' son, and his heart within his shaggy breast was divided in counsel, whether to draw his keen blade from his thigh and set the company aside and so slay Atreides, or to assuage his anger and curb his soul. While yet he doubted thereof in heart and soul, and was drawing his great sword from his sheath, Athene came to him from heaven, sent forth of the white-armed goddess Hera, whose heart loved both alike and had care for them. She stood behind Peleus' son and caught him by his golden hair, to him only visible, and of the rest no man beheld her. Then Achilles marvelled, and turned him about, and straightway knew Pallas Athene; and terribly shone her eyes. He spake to her winged words, and said: 'Why now art thou come hither, thou daughter of aegis-bearing Zeus? Is it to behold the insolence of Agamemnon, son of Atreus? Yea, I will tell thee that I deem shall even be brought to pass: by his own haughtinesses shall he soon lose his life.'

Then the bright-eyed goddess Athene spake to him again: 'I came from heaven to stay thine anger, if perchance thou wilt hearken to me, being sent forth of the white-armed goddess Hera, that loveth you twain alike and careth for you. Go to now, cease from strife, and let not thine hand draw the sword; yet with words indeed revile him, even as it shall come to pass. For thus will I say to thee, and so it shall be fulfilled; hereafter shall goodly gifts come to thee, yea in threefold measure, by reason of this despite; hold thou thine hand, and hearken to us.'

And Achilles fleet of foot made answer and said to her: 'Goddess, needs must a man observe the saying of you twain, even though he be very wroth at heart; for so is the better way. Whosoever obeyeth the gods, to him they gladly hearken.'

He said, and stayed his heavy hand on the silver hilt, and thrust the great sword back into the sheath, and was not disobedient to the saying of Athene; and she forthwith was departed to Olympus, to the other gods in the palace of aegis-bearing Zeus.

Then Peleus' son spake again with bitter words to Atreus' son, and in no wise ceased from anger: 'Thou heavy with wine, thou with face of dog and heart of deer, never didst thou take courage to arm for battle among thy folk or to lay ambush with the princes of the Achaians; that to thee were even as death. Far better booteth it, forsooth, to seize for thyself the meed of honour of every man through the wide host of the Achaians that speaketh contrary to thee. Folk-devouring king! Seeing thou rulest men of naught; else were this despite, thou son of Atreus, thy last. But I will speak my word to thee, and swear a mighty oath therewith: verily by this staff that shall no more put forth leaf or twig, seeing it hath for ever left its trunk among the hills, neither shall it grow green again, because the axe hath stripped it of leaves and bark; and now the sons of the Achaians that exercise judgment bear it in their hands, even they that by Zeus' command watch over the traditions – 50 shall this be a mighty oath in thine eyes – verily shall longing for Achilles come hereafter upon the sons of the Achaians one and all; and then wilt thou in no wise avail to save them, for all thy grief, when multitudes fall dying before manslaying Hector. Then shalt thou tear thy heart within thee for anger that thou didst in no wise honour the best of the Achaians.'

So said Peleides and dashed to earth the staff studded with golden nails, and himself sat down; and over against him Atreides waxed furious. Then in their midst rose up Nestor, pleasant of speech, the clear-voiced orator of the Pylians, he from whose tongue flowed discourse sweeter than honey. Two generations of mortal men already had he seen perish, that had been of old time born and nurtured with him in goodly Pylos, and he was king among the third. He of good intent made harangue to them and said: 'Alas, of a truth sore lamentation cometh upon the land of Achaia. Verily Priam would be glad and Priam's sons, and all the Trojans would have great joy of heart, were they to hear all this tale of strife between you twain that are chiefest of the Danaans in counsel and chiefest in battle. Nay, hearken to me; ye are younger both than I. Of old days held I converse with better men even than you, and never did they make light of me. Yea, I never beheld such warriors, nor shall behold, as were Peirithoos and Dryas shepherd of the host and Kaineus and Exadios and godlike Polyphemos [and Theseus son of

Aigeus, like to the immortals]. Mightiest of growth were they of all men upon the earth; mightiest they were and with the mightiest fought they, even the wild tribes of the mountain caves, and destroyed them utterly. And with these held I converse, being come from Pylos, from a distant land afar; for of themselves they summoned me. So I played my part in fight; and with them could none of men that are now on earth do battle. And they laid to heart my counsels and hearkened to my voice. Even so hearken ye also, for better is it to hearken. Neither do thou, though thou art very great, seize from him his damsel but leave her as she was given at the first by the sons of the Achaians to be a meed of honour; nor do thou, son of Peleus, think to strive with a king, might against might; seeing that no common honour pertaineth to a sceptred king to whom Zeus apportioneth glory. Though thou be strong, and a goddess mother bare thee, yet his is the greater place, for he is king over more. And thou, Atreides, abate thy fury; nay, it is even I that beseech thee to let go thine anger with Achilles, who is made unto all the Achaians a mighty bulwark of evil war.'

Then lord Agamemnon answered and said: 'Yea verily, old man, all this thou sayest is according unto right. But this fellow would be above all others, he would be lord of all and king among all and captain to all; wherein I deem none will hearken to him. Though the immortal gods made him a spearman, do they therefore put revilings in his mouth for him to utter?'

Then goodly Achilles brake in on him and answered: 'Yea, for I should be called coward and man of naught, if I yield to thee in every matter, howsoe'er thou bid To others give now thine orders, not to me [play master; for thee I deem that I shall no more obey]. This, moreover, will I say to thee, and do thou lay it to thy heart. Know that not by violence will I strive for the damsel's sake, neither with thee nor any other; ye gave and ye have taken away. But of all else that is mine beside my fleet black ship, thereof shalt thou not take anything or bear it away against my will. Yea, go to now, make trial, that all these may see; forthwith thy dark blood shall gush about my spear.'

Now when the twain had thus finished the battle of violent words, they stood up and dissolved the assembly beside the Achaian ships Peleides went his way to his huts and trim ships with Menoitios' son[1] and his company; and Atreides launched a fleet ship on the sea, and picked twenty oarsmen therefor, and embarked the

[1]Patroklos

hecatomb for the god and brought Chryseis of the fair cheeks and set her therein; and Odysseus of many devices went to be their captain.

So these embarked and sailed over the wet ways; and Atreides bade the folk purify themselves So they purified themselves, and cast the defilements into the sea and did sacrifice to Apollo, even unblemished hecatombs of bulls and goats, along the shore of the unvintaged sea; and the sweet savour arose to heaven eddying amid the smoke.

Thus were they busied throughout the host; but Agamemnon ceased not from the strife wherewith he threatened Achilles at the first; he spake to Talthybios and Eurybates that were his heralds and nimble squires: 'Go ye to the tent of Achilles Peleus' son, and take Briseis of the fair cheeks by the hand and lead her hither; and if he give her not, then will I myself go, and more with me, and seize her; and that will be yet more grievous for him.'

So saying he sent them forth, and laid stem charge upon them. Unwillingly went they along the beach of the unvintaged sea, and came to the huts and ships of the Myrmidons Him found they sitting beside his hut and black ship; nor when he saw them was Achilles glad. So they in dread and reverence of the king stood, and spake to him no word nor questioned him. But he knew in his heart, and spake to them: 'All hail, ye heralds, messengers of Zeus and men, come near; ye are not guilty in my sight, but Agamemnon that sent you for the sake of the damsel Briseis. Go now, heaven-sprung Patroklos bring forth the damsel, and give them her to lead away. Moreover, let the twain themselves be my witnesses before the face of the blessed gods and mortal men, yea and of him, that king untoward, against the day when there cometh need of me hereafter to save them all from shameful wreck. Of a truth he raveth with baleful mind, and hath not knowledge to look before and after, that so his Achaians might battle in safety beside their ships.'

So said he, and Patroklos hearkened to his dear comrade, and led forth from the hut Briseis of the fair cheeks, and gave them her to lead away. So these twain took their way back along the Achaians' ships, and with them went the woman all unwilling. Then Achilles wept anon, and sat him down apart, aloof from his comrades on the beach of the grey sea, gazing across the boundless main; he stretched forth his hands and prayed instantly to his dear mother: 'Mother, seeing thou didst of a truth bear me to so brief span of life, honour at the least ought the Olympian to have granted me, even Zeus that thundereth on high; but now doth he not honour me, no, not one whit. Verily Atreus' son, wide-ruling Agamemnon, hath done me dishonour; for he hath taken away my meed of honour and keepeth her of his own violent deed.'

So spake he weeping, and his lady mother heard him as she sate in the sea-depths beside her aged sire. With speed arose she from the grey sea, like a mist, and sate her before the face of her weeping son, and stroked him with her hand, and spake and called on his name: 'My child, why weepest thou? What sorrow hath entered into thy heart? Speak it forth, hide it not in thy mind, that both may know it.'

Then with heavy moan Achilles fleet of foot spake to her: 'Thou knowest it; why should I tell this to thee that knowest all! We had fared to Thebe, the holy city of Eëtion, and laid it waste and carried hither all the spoils. So the sons of the Achaians divided among them all aright; and for Atreides they set apart Chryseis of the fair cheeks. But Chryses, priest of Apollo the Far-darter, came unto the fleet ships of the mail-clad Achaians to win his daughter's freedom, and brought a ransom beyond telling, and bare in his hands the fillet of Apollo the Far-darter upon a golden staff, and made his prayer unto all the Achaians, and most of all to the two sons of Atreus, orderers of the host. Then all the other Achaians cried assent, to reverence the priest and accept his goodly ransom; yet the thing pleased not the heart of Agamemnon son of Atreus, but he roughly sent him away and laid stern charge upon him. So the old man went back in anger; and Apollo heard his prayers, seeing he loved him greatly, and he aimed against the Argives his deadly darts. So the people began to perish in multitudes, and the god's shafts ranged everywhither throughout the wide host of the Achaians. Then of full knowledge the seer declared to us the oracle of the Far-darter. Forthwith I first bade propitiate the god; but wrath gat hold upon Atreus' son thereat, and anon he stood up and spake a threatening word, that hath now been accomplished Her the glancing-eyed Achaians are bringing on their fleet ship to Chryse, and bear with them offerings to the king; and the other but now the heralds went and took from my hut, even the daughter of Briseus, whom the sons of the Achaians gave me. Thou therefore, if indeed thou canst, guard thine own[1] son; betake thee to Olympus and beseech Zeus by any deed or word whereby thou ever didst make glad his heart. For oft have I heard thee proclaiming in my father's halls and telling that thou alone amid the immortals didst save the

[1]Reading δοῖε.

son of Kronos, lord of the storm-cloud, from shameful wreck, when all the other Olympians would have bound him, even Hera and Poseidon and Pallas Athene. Then didst thou, O goddess, enter in and loose him from his bonds, having with speed summoned to high Olympus him of the hundred arms whom gods call Briareus, but all men call Aigaion; for he is mightier even than his father – so he sate him by Kronion's side rejoicing in his triumph, and the blessed gods feared him withal and bound not Zeus. This bring thou to his remembrance and sit by him and clasp his knees, if perchance he will give succour to the Trojans; and for the Achaians, hem them among their ships' sterns about the bay, given over to slaughter; that they may make trial of their king, and that even Atreides, wide-ruling Agamemnon, may perceive his blindness, in that he honoured not at all the best of the Achaians.'

Then Thetis weeping made answer to him: 'Ah me, my child, why reared I thee, cursed in my motherhood? Would thou hadst been left tearless and griefless amid the ships, seeing thy lot is very brief and endureth no long while; but now art thou made short-lived alike and lamentable beyond all men; in an evil hour I bare thee in our halls. But I will go myself to snow-clad Olympus to tell this thy saying to Zeus, whose joy is in the thunder,[1] if perchance he may hearken to me. But tarry thou now amid thy fleet-faring ships, and continue wroth with the Achaians, and refrain utterly from battle: for Zeus went yesterday to Okeanos, unto the noble Ethiopians for a feast, and all the gods followed with him; but on the twelfth day will he return to Olympus, and then will I fare to Zeus' palace of the bronze threshold, and will kneel to him and think to win him.'

So saying she went her way and left him there, vexed in spirit for the fair-girdled woman's sake, whom they had taken perforce despite his will: and meanwhile Odysseus came to Chryse with the holy hecatomb. When they were now entered within the deep haven, they furled their sails and laid them in the black ship, and lowered the mast by the forestays and brought it to the crutch with speed, and rowed her with oars to the anchorage. Then they cast out the mooring stones and made fast the hawsers, and so themselves went forth on to the sea-beach, and forth they brought the hecatomb for the Far-darter Apollo, and forth came Chryseis withal from the seafaring ship. Then Odysseus of many counsels brought her to the altar and gave her into her father's arms, and spake unto

[1]Perhaps rather, 'hurler of the thunderbolt.'

him: 'Chryses, Agamemnon king of men sent me hither to bring thee thy daughter, and to offer to Phoebus a holy hecatomb on the Danaans' behalf, wherewith to propitiate the king that hath now brought sorrow and lamentation on the Argives.'

So saying he gave her to his arms, and he gladly took his dear child; and anon they set in order for the god the holy hecatomb about his well-builded altar; next washed they their hands and took up the barley meal. Then Chryses lifted up his hands and prayed aloud for them: 'Hearken to me, god of the silver bow that standest over Chryse and holy Killa, and rulest Tenedos with might; even as erst thou heardest my prayer, and didst me honour, and mightily afflictedst the people of the Achaians, even so now fulfil me this my desire: remove thou from the Danaans forthwith the loathly pestilence.'

So spake he in prayer, and Phoebus Apollo heard him. Now when they had prayed and sprinkled the barley meal, first they drew back the victims' heads and slaughtered them and flayed them, and cut slices from the thighs and wrapped them in fat, making a double fold, and laid raw collops thereon, and the old man burnt them on cleft wood and made libation over them of gleaming wine; and at his side the young men in their hands held five-pronged forks. Now when the thighs were burnt and they had tasted the vitals, then sliced they all the rest and pierced it through with spits, and roasted it carefully, and drew all off again. So when they had rest from the task and had made ready the banquet, they feasted, nor was their heart aught stinted of the fair banquet. But when they had put away from them the desire of meat and drink, the young men crowned the bowls with wine, and gave each man his portion after the drink-offering had been poured into the cups. So all day long worshipped they the god with music, singing the beautiful paean, the sons of the Achaians making music to the Far-darter[1]; and his heart was glad to hear. And when the sun went down and darkness came on them, they laid them to sleep beside the ship's hawsers; and when rosy-fingered Dawn appeared, the child of morning, then set they sail for the wide camp of the Achaians; and Apollo the Far-darter sent them a favouring gale. They set up their mast and spread the white sails forth, and the wind filled the sail's belly and the dark wave sang loud about the stem as the ship made way, and she sped across the wave, accomplishing her journey. So when they were now come to the wide camp of the Achaians, they drew up their black ship to

[1] Or, 'the Averter' (of pestilence).

land high upon the sands, and set in line the long props beneath her; and themselves were scattered amid their huts and ships.

But he sat by his swift-faring ships, still wroth, even the heaven-sprung son of Peleus, Achilles fleet of foot; he betook him neither to the assembly that is the hero's glory, neither to war, but consumed his heart in tarrying in his place, and yearned for the war-cry and for battle.

Now when the twelfth morn thereafter was come, then the gods that are for ever fared to Olympus all in company, led of Zeus. And Thetis forgat not her son's charge, but rose up from the sea-wave, and at early morn mounted up to great heaven and Olympus. There found she Kronos' son of the far-sounding voice sitting apart from all on the topmost peak of many-ridged Olympus. So she sat before his face and with her left hand clasped his knees, and with her right touched him beneath his chin, and spake in prayer to king Zeus son of Kronos: 'Father Zeus, if ever I gave thee aid amid the immortal gods, whether by word or deed, fulfil thou this my desire: do honour to my son, that is doomed to earliest death of all men: now hath Agamemnon king of men done him dishonour, for he hath taken away his meed of honour and keepeth her of his own violent deed. But honour thou him, Zeus of Olympus, lord of counsel; grant thou victory to the Trojans the while, until the Achaians do my son honour and exalt him with recompense.'

So spake she; but Zeus the cloud-gatherer said no word to her, and sat long time in silence. But even as Thetis had clasped his knees, so held she by him clinging, and questioned him yet a second time: 'Promise me now this thing verily, and bow thy head thereto; or else deny me, seeing there is naught for thee to fear; that I may know full well how I among all gods am least in honour.'

Then Zeus the cloud-gatherer, sore troubled, spake to her: 'Verily it is a sorry matter, if thou wilt set me at variance with Hera, whene'er she provoketh me with taunting words. Even now she upbraideth me ever amid the immortal gods, and saith that I aid the Trojans in battle. But do thou now depart again, lest Hera mark aught; and I will take thought for these things to fulfil them. Come now, I will bow my head to thee, that thou mayest be of good courage; for that, of my part, is the surest token amid the immortals; no word of mine is revocable nor false nor unfulfilled when he bowing of my head hath pledged it.'

Kronion spake, and bowed his dark brow, and the ambrosial locks waved from the king's immortal head; and he made great Olympus quake.

Thus the twain took counsel and parted; she leapt therewith into the deep sea from glittering Olympus, and Zeus fared to his own palace. All the gods in company arose from their seats before their father's face; neither ventured any to await his coming, but they stood up all before him. So he sate him there upon his throne; but Hera saw, and was not ignorant now that the daughter of the Ancient of the sea, Thetis the silver-footed, had devised counsel with him. Anon with taunting words spake she to Zeus the son of Kronos: 'Now who among the gods, thou crafty of mind, hath devised counsel with thee? It is ever thy good pleasure to hold aloof from me and in secret meditation to give thy judgments, nor of thine own good will hast thou ever brought thyself to declare unto me the thing thou purposest.'

Then the father of gods and men made answer to her: 'Hera, think not thou to know all my sayings; hard they are for thee, even though thou art my wife. But whichsoever it is seemly for thee to hear, none sooner than thou shall know, be he god or man. Only when I will to take thought aloof from the gods, then do not thou ask of every matter nor make question.'

Then Hera the ox-eyed queen made answer to him. 'Most dread son of Kronos, what word is this thou hast spoken? Yea, surely of old I have not asked thee nor made question, but in very quietness thou devisest all thou wilt. But now is my heart sore afraid lest thou have been won over by silver-footed Thetis, daughter of the Ancient of the sea, for she at early morn sat by thee and clasped thy knees. To her I deem thou gavest a sure pledge that thou wilt do honour to Achilles, and lay many low beside the Achaians' ships.'

To her made answer Zeus the cloud-gatherer: 'Lady, Good lack! ever art thou imagining, nor can I escape thee; yet shalt thou in no wise have power to fulfil, but wilt be the further from my heart; that shall be even the worse for thee. And if it be so, then such must my good pleasure be. Abide thou in silence and hearken to my bidding, lest all the gods that are in Olympus keep not off from thee my visitation, when I put forth my hands unapproachable against thee.'

He said, and Hera the ox-eyed queen was afraid, and sat in silence, curbing her heart; but throughout Zeus' palace the gods of heaven were troubled Then Hephaistos the famed craftsman began to make harangue among them, to do kindness to his dear mother, white-armed Hera: 'Verily this will be a sorry matter, neither any more endurable, if ye twain thus fight for mortals' sakes, and bring wrangling among the gods; neither will there any more be joy of the goodly feast, seeing that evil triumpheth. So I give counsel to my mother, though herself is wise, to do kindness to our dear father Zeus, that our father upbraid us not again and cast the banquet in confusion. What if the Olympian, the lord of the lightning, will to dash us from our seats! for he is strongest far. Nay, approach thou him with gentle words, then will the Olympian forthwith be gracious unto us.'

So speaking he rose up and set in his dear mother's hand the twy-handled cup, and spake to her: 'Be of good courage, mother mine, and endure, though thou art vexed, lest I behold thee, that art so dear, chastised before mine eyes, and then shall I not be able for all my sorrow to save thee; for the Olympian is a hard foe to face. Yea, once ere this, when I was fain to save thee, he caught me by my foot and hurled me from the heavenly threshold; all day I flew, and at the set of sun I fell in Lemnos, and little life was in me. There did the Sintian folk forthwith tend me for my fall.'

He spake, and the white-armed goddess Hera smiled, and smiling took the cup at her son's hand. Then he poured wine to all the other gods from right to left, ladling the sweet nectar from the bowl. And laughter unquenchable arose amid the blessed gods to see Hephaistos bustling through the palace.

So feasted they all day till the setting of the sun; nor was their soul aught stinted of the fair banquet, nor of the beauteous lyre that Apollo held, and the Muses singing alternately with sweet voice.

Now when the bright light of the sun was set, these went each to his own house to sleep, where each one had his palace made with cunning device by famed Hephaistos the lame god; and Zeus the Olympian, the lord of lightning, departed to his couch where he was wont of old to take his rest, whenever sweet sleep visited him. There went he up and slept, and beside him was Hera of the golden throne.

BOOK II

How Zeus beguiled Agamemnon by a dream; and of the assembly of the Achaians and their marching forth to battle. And of the names and numbers of the hosts of the Achaians and the Trojans.

NOW ALL OTHER GODS and chariot-driving men slept all night long, only Zeus was not holden of sweet sleep; rather was he pondering in his heart how he should do honour to Achilles and destroy many beside the Achaians' ships. And this design seemed to his mind the best, to wit, to send a baneful dream upon Agamemnon son of Atreus. So he spake, and uttered to him winged words: 'Come now, thou baneful Dream, go to the Achaians' fleet ships, enter into the hut of Agamemnon son of Atreus, and tell him every word plainly as I charge thee. Bid him call to arms the flowing-haired Achaians with all speed, for that now he may take the wide-wayed city of the Trojans. For the immortals that dwell in the halls of Olympus are no longer divided in counsel, since Hera hath turned the minds of all by her beseeching, and over the Trojans sorrows hang.'

So spake he, and the Dream went his way when he had heard the charge. With speed he came to the Achaians' fleet ships, and went to Agamemnon son of Atreus, and found him sleeping in his hut, and ambrosial slumber poured over him. So he stood over his head in seeming like unto the son of Neleus, even Nestor, whom most of all the elders Agamemnon honoured; in his likeness spake to him the heavenly Dream:

'Sleepest thou, son of wise Atreus tamer of horses. To sleep all night through beseemeth not one that is a counsellor, to whom peoples are entrusted and so many cares belong. But now hearken straightway to me, for I am a messenger to thee from Zeus, who though he be afar yet hath great care for thee and pity. He biddeth thee call to arms the flowing-haired Achaians with all speed, for that now thou mayest take the wide-wayed city of the Trojans. For the immortals that dwell in the halls of Olympus are no longer divided in counsel, since Hera hath turned the minds of all by her beseeching, and over the Trojans sorrows hang by the will of Zeus. But do thou keep this in thy heart, nor let forgetfulness come upon thee when honeyed sleep shall leave thee.'

So spake the Dream, and departed and left him there, deeming in his mind things that were not to be fulfilled. For indeed he thought to take Priam's city that very day; fond man, in that he knew not the plans that Zeus had in mind, who was willed to bring yet more grief and wailing on Trojans alike and Danaans throughout the course of stubborn fights. Then woke he from sleep, and the heavenly voice was in his ears. So he rose up sitting, and donned his soft tunic, fair and bright, and cast around him his great cloak, and beneath his glistering feet he bound his fair sandals, and over his shoulder cast his silver-studded sword, and grasped his sires' sceptre, imperishable for ever, wherewith he took his way amid the mail-clad Achaians' ships.

Now went the goddess Dawn to high Olympus, foretelling daylight to Zeus and all the immortals; and the king bade the clear-voiced heralds summon to the assembly the flowing-haired Achaians. So did those summon, and these gathered with speed.

But first the council of the great-hearted elders met beside the ship of king Nestor the Pylos-born. And he that had assembled them framed his cunning counsel: 'Hearken, my friends. A dream from heaven came to me in my sleep through the ambrosial night, and chiefly to goodly Nestor was very like in shape and bulk and stature. And it stood over my head and charged me saying: "Sleepest thou, son of wise Atreus tamer of horses? To sleep all night through beseemeth not one that is a counsellor, to whom peoples are entrusted and so many cares belong. But now hearken straightway to me, for I am a messenger to thee from Zeus, who though he be afar yet hath great care for thee and pity. He biddeth thee call to arms the flowing-haired Achaians with all speed, for that now thou mayest take the wide-wayed city of the Trojans. For the immortals that dwell in the palaces of Olympus are no longer divided in counsel, since Hera hath turned the minds of all by her beseeching, and over the Trojans sorrows hang by the will of Zeus. But keep thou this in thy heart." So spake the dream and was flown away, and sweet sleep left me. So come, let us now call to arms as we may the sons of the Achaians. But first I will speak to make trial of them as is fitting, and will bid them flee with their benched ships; only do ye from this side and from that speak to hold them back.'

So spake he and sate him down; and there stood up among them Nestor, who was king of sandy Pylos. He of good intent made harangue to them and said: 'My friends, captains and rulers of the Argives, had any other of the Achaians told us this dream we might deem it a false thing, and rather turn away therefrom; but now he hath seen it who of all Achaians avoweth himself far greatest. So come, let us call to arms as we may the sons of the Achaians.'

So spake he, and led the way forth from the council, and all the other sceptred chiefs rose with him and obeyed the shepherd of the host; and the people hastened to them. Even as when the tribes of thronging bees issue from some hollow rock, ever in fresh procession, and fly clustering among the flowers of spring, and some on this hand and some on that fly thick; even so from ships and huts before the low beach marched forth their many tribes by companies to the place of assembly. And in their midst blazed forth Rumour, messenger of Zeus, urging them to go; and so they gathered. And the place of assemblage was in an uproar, and the earth echoed again as the hosts sate them down, and there was turmoil. Nine heralds restrained them with shouting, if perchance they might refrain from clamour, and hearken to their kings, the fosterlings of Zeus. And hardly at the last would the people sit, and keep them to their benches and cease from noise. Then stood up lord Agamemnon bearing his sceptre, that Hephaistos had wrought curiously. Hephaistos gave it to king Zeus son of Kronos, and then Zeus gave it to the messenger-god the slayer of Argus[1]; and king Hermes gave it to Pelops the charioteer, and Pelops again gave it to Atreus shepherd of the host. And Atreus dying left it to Thyestes rich in flocks, and Thyestes in his turn left it to Agamemnon to bear, that over many islands and all Argos he should be lord. Thereon he leaned and spake his saying to the Argives:

'My friends, Danaan warriors, men of Ares' company, Zeus Kronos' son hath bound me with might in grievous blindness of soul; hard of heart is he, for that erewhile he promised me and pledged his nod that not till I had wasted well-walled Ilios should I return; but now see I that he planned a cruel wile and biddeth me return to Argos dishonoured, with the loss of many of my folk. So meseems it pleaseth most mighty Zeus, who hath laid low the head of many a city, yea, and shall lay low; for his is highest power. Shame is this even for them that come after to hear; how so goodly and great a folk of the Achaians thus vainly warred a bootless war, and fought scantier enemies, and no end thereof is yet seen. For if perchance we were minded, both Achaians and Trojans, to swear a solemn truce, and to number ourselves, and if the Trojans should gather together all that have their dwellings in the city, and we Achaians should marshal ourselves by tens, and every company

[1]Or, possibly, 'the swift-appearing.'

choose a Trojan to pour their wine, then would many tens lack a
cup-bearer: so much, I say, do the sons of the Achaians outnumber
the Trojans that dwell within the city. But allies from many cities,
even warriors that wield the spear, are therein, and they hinder me
perforce, and for all my will suffer me not to waste the populous
citadel of Ilios. Already have nine years of great Zeus passed away,
and our ships' timbers have rotted and the tackling is loosed; while
there our wives and little children sit in our halls awaiting us; yet is
our task utterly unaccomplished wherefor we came hither. So come,
even as I shall bid let us all obey. Let us flee with our ships to our
dear native land; for now shall we never take wide-wayed Troy.'

So spake he, and stirred the spirit in the breasts of all throughout
the multitude, as many as had not heard the council. And the
assembly swayed like high sea-waves of the Icarian Main that east
wind and south wind raise, rushing upon them from the clouds of
father Zeus; and even as when the west wind cometh to stir a deep
cornfield with violent blast, and the ears bow down, so was all the
assembly stirred, and they with shouting hasted toward the ships;
and the dust from beneath their feet rose and stood on high. And
they bade each man his neighbour to seize the ships and drag them
into the bright salt sea, and cleared out the launching-ways, and the
noise went up to heaven of their hurrying homewards; and they
began to take the props from beneath the ships.

Then would the Argives have accomplished their return against
the will of fate, but that Hera spake a word to Athene: 'Out on it,
daughter of aegis-bearing Zeus, unwearied maiden! Shall the
Argives thus indeed flee homeward to their dear native land over
the sea's broad back? But they would leave to Priam and the Trojans their boast, even Helen of Argos, for whose sake many an
Achaian hath perished in Troy, far away from his dear native land.
But go thou now amid the host of the mail-clad Achaians; with thy
gentle words refrain thou every man, neither suffer them to draw
their curved ships down to the salt sea.'

So spake she, and the bright-eyed goddess Athene disregarded
not; but went darting down from the peaks of Olympus, and came
with speed to the fleet ships of the Achaians. There found she
Odysseus standing, peer of Zeus in counsel, neither laid he any
hand upon his decked black ship, because grief had entered into his
heart and soul. And bright-eyed Athene stood by him and said:
'Heaven-sprung son of Laertes, Odysseus of many devices, will ye
indeed fling yourselves upon your benched ships to flee homeward
to your dear native land? But ye would leave to Priam and the Tro-

jans their boast, even Helen of Argos, for whose sake many an Achaian hath perished in Troy, far from his dear native land. But go thou now amid the host of the Achaians, and tarry not; and with thy gentle words refrain every man, neither suffer them to draw their curved ships down to the salt sea.'

So said she, and he knew the voice of the goddess speaking to him, and set him to run, and cast away his mantle, the which his herald gathered up, even Eurybates of Ithaca, that waited on him. And himself he went to meet Agamemnon son of Atreus, and at his hand received the sceptre of his sires, imperishable for ever, wherewith he took his way amid the ships of the mail-clad Achaians.

Whenever he found one that was a captain and a man of mark, he stood by his side, and refrained him with gentle words: 'Good sir, it is not seemly to affright thee like a coward, but do thou sit thyself and make all thy folk sit down. For thou knowest not yet clearly what is the purpose of Atreus' son; now is he but making trial, and soon he will afflict the sons of the Achaians. And heard we not all of us what he spake in the council? Beware lest in his anger he evilly entreat the sons of the Achaians. For proud is the soul of heaven-fostered kings; because their honour is of Zeus, and the god of counsel loveth them.'[1]

But whatever man of the people he saw and found him shouting, him he drave with his sceptre and chode him with loud words: 'Good sir, sit still and hearken to the words of others that are thy betters; but thou art no warrior, and a weakling, never reckoned whether in battle or in council. In no wise can we Achaians all be kings here. A multitude of masters is no good thing; let there be one master, one king, to whom the son of crooked-counselling Kronos hath granted it, [even the sceptre and judgments, that he may rule among you'].

So masterfully ranged he the host; and they hasted back to the assembly from ships and huts, with noise as when a wave of the loud-sounding sea roareth on the long beach and the main resoundeth.

Now all the rest sat down and kept their place upon the benches, only Thersites still chattered on, the uncontrolled of speech, whose mind was full of words many and disorderly, wherewith to strive against the chiefs idly and in no good order, but even as he deemed that he should make the Argives laugh. And he was ill-favoured beyond all men that came to Ilios. Bandy-legged was he, and lame of

---

[1] Reading διοτρεφέων βασιλήων with Zenodotos.

one foot, and his two shoulders rounded, arched down upon his chest; and over them his head was warped, and a scanty stubble sprouted on it. Hateful was he to Achilles above all and to Odysseus, for them he was wont to revile. But now with shrill shout he poured forth his upbraidings upon goodly Agamemnon. With him the Achaians were sore vexed and had indignation in their souls. But he with loud shout spake and reviled Agamemnon: 'Atreides, for what art thou now ill content and lacking? Surely thy huts are full of bronze and many women are in thy huts, the chosen spoils that we Achaians give thee first of all, whene'er we take a town. Can it be that thou yet wantest gold as well, such as some one of the horse-taming Trojans may bring from Ilios to ransom his son, whom I per-chance or some other Achaian have led captive; or else some young girl, to know in love, whom thou mayest keep apart to thyself? But it is not seemly for one that is their captain to bring the sons of the Achaians to ill. Soft fools, base things of shame, ye women of Achaia and men no more, let us depart home with our ships, and leave this fellow here in Troy-land to gorge him with meeds of honour, that he may see whether our aid avail him aught or no; even he that hath now done dishonour to Achilles, a far better man than he; for he hath taken away his meed of honour and keepeth it by his own vio-lent deed. Of a very surety is there no wrath at all in Achilles' mind, but he is slack; else this despite, thou son of Atreus, were thy last.'

So spake Thersites reviling Agamemnon shepherd of the host. But goodly Odysseus came straight to his side, and looking sternly at him with hard words rebuked him: 'Thersites, reckless in words, shrill orator though thou art, refrain thyself, nor aim to strive singly against kings. For I deem that no mortal is baser than thou of all that with the sons of Atreus came before Ilios. Therefore were it well that thou shouldest not have kings in thy mouth as thou talkest, and utter revilings against them and be on the watch for departure. We know not yet clearly how these things shall be, whether we sons of the Achaians shall return for good or for ill. Therefore now dost thou revile continually Agamemnon son of Atreus, shepherd of the host, because the Danaan warriors give him many gifts, and so thou talkest tauntingly. But I will tell thee plain, and that I say shall even be brought to pass: if I find thee again raving as now thou art, then may Odysseus' head no longer abide upon his shoulders, nor may I any more be called father of Telemachos, if I take thee not and strip from thee thy garments, thy mantle and tunic that cover thy naked-ness, and for thyself send thee weeping to the fleet ships and beat thee out of the assembly with shameful blows'

So spake he, and with his staff smote his back and shoulders: and he bowed down and a big tear fell from him, and a bloody weal stood up from his back beneath the golden sceptre. Then he sat down and was amazed, and in pain with helpless look wiped away the tear. But the rest, though they were sorry, laughed lightly at him, and thus would one speak looking at another standing by: 'Go to, of a truth Odysseus hath wrought good deeds without number ere now, standing foremost in wise counsels and setting battle in array, but now is this thing the best by far that he hath wrought among the Argives, to wit, that he hath stayed this prating railer from his harangues. Never again, forsooth, will his proud soul henceforth bid him revile the kings with slanderous words.'

So said the common sort; but up rose Odysseus waster of cities, with the sceptre in his hand. And by his side bright-eyed Athene in the likeness of a herald bade the multitude keep silence, that the sons of the Achaians, both the nearest and the farthest, might hear his words together and give heed to his counsel. He of good intent made harangue to them and said: 'Atreides, now surely are the Achaians for making thee, O king, most despised among all mortal men, nor will they fulfil the promise that they pledged thee when they still were marching hither from horse-pasturing Argos; that thou shouldest not return till thou hadst laid well-walled Ilios waste. For like young children or widow women do they wail each to the other of returning home. Yea, here is toil to make a man depart disheartened. For he that stayeth away but one single month far from his wife in his benched ship fretteth himself when winter storms and the furious sea imprison him; but for us, the ninth year of our stay here is upon us in its course. Therefore do I not marvel that the Achaians should fret beside their beaked ships; yet nevertheless is it shameful to wait long and to depart empty. Be of good heart, my friends, and wait a while, until we learn whether Kalchas be a true prophet or no. For this thing verily we know well in our hearts, and ye all are witnesses thereof, even as many as the fates of death have not borne away. It was as it were but yesterday or the day before that the Achaians' ships were gathering in Aulis, freighted with trouble for Priam and the Trojans; and we round about a spring were offering on the holy altars unblemished hecatombs to the immortals, beneath a fair plane-tree whence flowed bright water, when there was seen a great portent: a snake blood-red on the back, terrible, whom the god of Olympus himself had sent forth to the light of day, sprang from beneath the altar and darted to the plane-tree. Now there were there the brood of a sparrow, tender little ones, upon the topmost branch, nestling beneath the leaves; eight were they and the mother of the little ones was the ninth, and the snake swallowed these cheeping pitifully. And the mother fluttered around wailing for her dear little ones; but he coiled himself and caught her by the wing as she screamed about him. Now when he had swallowed the sparrow's little ones and the mother with them, the god who revealed him made of him a sign; for the son of crooked-counselling Kronos turned him to stone, and we stood by and marvelled to see what was done. So when the dread portent brake in upon the hecatombs of the gods, then did Kalchas forthwith prophesy, and said: "Why hold ye your peace, ye flowing-haired Achaians? To us hath Zeus the counsellor shown this great sign, late come, of late fulfilment, the fame whereof shall never perish. Even as he swallowed the sparrow's little ones and herself, the eight wherewith the mother that bare the little ones was the ninth, so shall we war there so many years, but in the tenth year shall we take the wide-wayed city." So spake the seer; and now are all these things being fulfilled. So come, abide ye all, ye well-greaved Achaians, even where ye are, until we have taken the great city of Priam.'

So spake he, and the Argives shouted aloud, and all round the ships echoed terribly to the voice of the Achaians as they praised the saying of god-like Odysseus. And then spake among them knightly Nestor of Gerenia: 'Out on it; in very truth ye hold assembly like silly boys that have no care for deeds of war. What shall come of our covenants and our oaths? Let all counsels be cast into the fire and all devices of warriors and the pure drink-offerings and the right hands of fellowship wherein we trusted. For we are vainly striving with words nor can we find any device at all, for all our long tarrying here. Son of Atreus, do thou still, as erst, keep steadfast purpose and lead the Argives amid the violent fray; and for these, let them perish, the one or two Achaians that take secret counsel – though fulfilment shall not come thereof – to depart to Argos first, before they know whether the promise of aegis-bearing Zeus be a lie or no. Yea, for I say that most mighty Kronion pledged us his word that day when the Argives embarked upon their fleet ships, bearing unto the Trojans death and fate; for by his lightning upon our right he manifested signs of good. Therefore let no man hasten to depart home till each have lain by some Trojan's wife and paid back his strivings and groans for Helen's sake. But if any man is overmuch desirous to depart homewards, let him lay his hand upon his decked black ship, that before all men he may encounter death and fate. But do thou, my king, take good counsel thyself, and hearken to another that shall give it; the word that I speak, whate'er it be, shall not be cast away. Separate thy warriors by tribes and by clans, Agamemnon, that clan may give aid to clan and tribe to tribe. If thou do thus and the Achaians hearken to thee, then wilt thou know who among thy captains and who of the common sort is a coward, and who too is brave; for they will fight each after their sort. So wilt thou know whether it is even by divine command that thou shalt not take the city, or by the baseness of thy warriors and their ill skill in battle.'

And lord Agamemnon answered and said to him: 'Verily hast thou again outdone the sons of the Achaians in speech, old man. Ah, father Zeus and Athene and Apollo, would that among the Achaians I had ten such councillors; then would the city of king Priam soon bow beneath our hands, captive and wasted. But aegis-bearing Zeus, the son of Kronos, hath brought sorrows upon me, in that he casteth my lot amid fruitless wranglings and strifes. For in truth I and Achilles fought about a damsel with violent words, and I was first to be angry; but if we can only be at one in council, then will there no more be any putting off the day of evil for the Trojans, no not for an instant. But now go ye to your meal that we may join battle. Let each man sharpen well his spear and bestow well his shield, and let him well give his fleet-footed steeds their meal, and look well to his chariot on every side and take thought for battle, that all day long we may contend in hateful war. For of respite shall there intervene no, not a whit, only that the coming of night shall part the fury of warriors. On each man's breast shall the baldrick of his covering shield be wet with sweat, and his hand shall grow faint about the spear, and each man's horse shall sweat as he draweth the polished chariot. And whomsoever I perceive minded to tarry far from the fight beside the beaked ships, for him shall there be no hope hereafter to escape the dogs and birds of prey.'

So spake he, and the Argives shouted aloud, like to a wave on a steep shore, when the south wind cometh and stirreth it; even on a jutting rock, that is never left at peace by the waves of all winds that rise from this side and from that. And they stood up and scattered in haste throughout the ships, and made fires in the huts and took their meal. And they did sacrifice each man to one of the everlasting gods, praying for escape from death and the tumult of battle. But Agamemnon king of men slew a fat bull of five years to most mighty Kronion, and called the elders, the princes of the Achaian host, Nestor first and king Idomeneus, and then the two Aiantes and

Tydeus' son, and sixthly Odysseus peer of Zeus in counsel. And Menelaos of the loud war-cry came to him unbidden, for he knew in his heart how his brother toiled. Then stood they around the bull and took the barley-meal. And Agamemnon made his prayer in their midst and said: 'Zeus, most glorious, most great, god of the storm-cloud, that dwellest in the heaven, vouchsafe that the sun set not upon us nor the darkness come near, till I have laid low upon the earth Priam's palace smirched with smoke, and burnt the doorways thereof with consuming fire, and rent on Hector's breast his doublet cleft with the blade; and about him may full many of his comrades prone in the dust bite the earth.'

So spake he, but not as yet would Kronion grant him fulfilment; he accepted the sacrifice, but made toil to wax unceasingly.

Now when they had prayed and sprinkled the barley-meal they first drew back the bull's head and cut his throat and flayed him, and cut slices from the thighs and wrapped them in fat, making a double fold, and laid raw collops thereon. And these they burnt on cleft wood stript of leaves, and spitted the vitals and held them over Hephaistos' flame. Now when the thighs were burnt and they had tasted the vitals, then sliced they all the rest and pierced it through with spits, and roasted it carefully and drew all off again. So when they had rest from the task and had made ready the banquet, they feasted nor was their heart aught stinted of the fair banquet. But when they had put away from them the desire of meat and drink, then did knightly Nestor of Gerenia open his saying to them: 'Most noble son of Atreus, Agamemnon king of men, let us not any more hold long converse here, nor for long delay the work that god putteth in our hands; but come, let the heralds of the mail-clad Achaians make proclamation to the folk and gather them throughout the ships; and let us go thus in concert through the wide host of the Achaians, that the speedier we may arouse keen war.'

So spake he and Agamemnon king of men disregarded not. Straightway he bade the clear-voiced heralds summon to battle the flowing-haired Achaians. So those summoned and these gathered with all speed. And the kings, the fosterlings of Zeus that were about Atreus' son, eagerly marshalled them, and bright-eyed Athene in the midst, bearing the holy aegis that knoweth neither age nor death, whereon wave an hundred tassels of pure gold, all deftly woven and each one an hundred oxen worth. Therewith she passed dazzling through the Achaian folk, urging them forth; and in every man's heart she roused strength to battle without ceasing and to fight. So was war made sweeter to them than to depart in their hollow ships to their dear native land. Even as ravaging fire kindleth a boundless forest on a mountain's peaks, and the blaze is seen from afar, even so as they marched went the dazzling gleam from the innumerable bronze through the sky even unto the heavens.

And as the many tribes of feathered birds, wild geese or cranes or long-necked swans, on the Asian mead by Kaystrios' stream, fly hither and thither joying in their plumage, and with loud cries settle ever onwards, and the mead resounds, even so poured forth the many tribes of warriors from ships and huts into the Skamandrian plain. And the earth echoed terribly beneath the tread of men and horses. So stood they in the flowery Skamandrian plain, unnumbered as are leaves and flowers in their season. Even as the many tribes of thick flies that hover about a herdsman's steading in the spring season, when milk drencheth the pails, even in like number stood the flowing-haired Achaians upon the plain in face of the Trojans, eager to rend them asunder. And even as the goatherds easily divide the ranging flocks of goats when they mingle in the pasture, so did their captains marshal them on this side and on that, to enter into the fray, and in their midst lord Agamemnon, his head and eyes like unto Zeus whose joy is in the thunder,[1] and his waist like unto Ares and his breast unto Poseidon. Even as a bull standeth out far foremost amid the herd, for he is pre-eminent amid the pasturing kine, even such did Zeus make Atreides on that day, pre-eminent among many and chief amid heroes.

Tell me now, ye Muses that dwell in the mansions of Olympus – seeing that ye are goddesses and are at hand and know all things, but we hear only a rumour and know not anything – who were the captains of the Danaans and their lords. But the common sort could I not number nor name, nay, not if ten tongues were mine and ten mouths, and a voice unwearied, and my heart of bronze within me, did not the Muses of Olympus, daughters of aegis-bearing Zeus, put into my mind all that came to Ilios. So will I tell the captains of the ships and all the ships in order.

Of the Boiotians Peneleos and Leitos were captains, and Arkesilaos and Prothoënor and Klonios; these were they that dwelt in Hyria and rocky Aulis and Schoinos and Skolos and Eteonos full of ridges, Thespeia and Graia and Mykalessos with wide lawns; and that dwelt about Harma and Eilesion and Erythrai, and they that possessed Eleon and Peteon and Hyle, Okalea and the stablished fortress of Medeon, Kopai and Eutresis and Thisbe haunt of doves;

[1] See note on p. 14

and they of Koroneia and grassy Haliartos, and that possessed Plataia and that dwelt in Glisas, and that possessed the stablished fortress of lesser Thebes and holy Onchestos, Poseidon's bright grove; and that possessed Arne rich in vineyards, and Mideia and sacred Nisa and Anthedon on the furthest borders. Of these there came fifty ships, and in each one embarked young men of the Boiotians an hundred and twenty. And they that dwelt in Aspledon and Orchomenos of the Minyai were led of Askalaphos and Ialmenos, sons of Ares, whom Astyoche conceived of the mighty god in the palace of Aktor son of Azeus, having entered her upper chamber, a stately maiden; for mighty Ares lay with her privily. And with them sailed thirty hollow ships.

And the Phokians were led of Schedios and Epistrophos, sons of great-hearted Iphitos son of Naubolos; these were they that possessed Kyparissos and rocky Pytho and sacred Krisa and Daulis and Panopeus, and they that dwelt about Anemoreia and Hyampolis, yea, and they that lived by the goodly river Kephisos and possessed Lilaia by Kephisos' springs. And with them followed forty black ships. So they marshalled the ranks of the Phokians diligently, and had their station hard by the Boiotians on the left.

And of the Lokrians the fleet son of Oileus was captain, Aias the less, that was not so great as was the Telamonian Aias but far less. Small was he, with linen corslet, but with the spear he far outdid all the Hellenes and Achaians. These were they that dwelt in Kynos and Opus and Kalliaros and Bessa and Skarphe and lovely Augeiai and Tarphe and Thronion, about the streams of Boagrios. And with Aias followed forty black ships of the Lokrians that dwell over against holy Euboia.

And the Abantes breathing fury, they that possessed Euboia and Chalkis and Eiretria and Histiaia rich in vines, and Kerinthos by the sea and the steep fortress of Dios, and they that possessed Karystos, and they that dwelt in Styra, all these again were led of Elephenor of the stock of Ares, even the son of Chalkodon, and captain of the proud Abantes. And with him followed the fleet Abantes with hair flowing behind, spearmen eager with ashen shafts outstretched to tear the corslets on the breasts of the foes. And with him forty black ships followed.

And they that possessed the goodly citadel of Athens, the domain of Erechtheus the high-hearted, whom erst Athene daughter of Zeus fostered when Earth, the grain-giver, brought him to birth; — and she gave him a resting-place in Athens in her own rich sanctuary; and there the sons of the Athenians worship him with bulls and rams as the years turn in their courses – these again were led of Menestheus son of Peteos. And there was no man upon the face of earth that was like him for the marshalling of horsemen and warriors that bear the shield. Only Nestor rivalled him, for he was the elder by birth. And with him fifty black ships followed.

And Aias led twelve ships from Salamis, [and brought them and set them where the battalions of the Athenians stood].

And they that possessed Argos and Tiryns of the great walls, Hermione and Asine that enfold the deep gulf, Troizen and Eïonai and Epidauros full of vines, and the youths of the Achaians that possessed Aigina and Mases, these were led of Diomedes of the loud war-cry and Sthenelos, dear son of famous Kapaneus. And the third with them came Euryalos, a godlike warrior, the son of king Mekisteus son of Talaos. But Diomedes of the loud war-cry was lord over all. And with them eighty black ships followed.

And of them that possessed the stablished fortress of Mykene and wealthy Corinth and stablished Kleonai, and dwelt in Orneiai and lovely Araithyrea and Sikyon, wherein Adrestos was king at the first; and of them that possessed Hyperesie and steep Gonoessa and Pellene, and dwelt about Aigion and through all the coast-land and about broad Helike, of them did lord Agamemnon son of Atreus lead an hundred ships. With him followed most and goodliest folk by far; and in their midst himself was clad in flashing bronze, all glorious, and was pre-eminent amid all warriors, because he was goodliest and led folk far greatest in number.

And of them that possessed Lakedaimon lying low amid the rifted hills, and Pharis and Sparta and Messe, the haunt of doves, and dwelt in Bryseiai and lovely Augeiai, and of them too that possessed Amyklai and the sea-coast fortress of Helos, and that possessed Laas and dwelt about Oitylos, of these was the king's brother leader, even Menelaos of the loud war-cry, leader of sixty ships, and these were arrayed apart. And himself marched among them confident in his zeal, urging his men to battle: and his heart most of all was set to take vengeance for his strivings and groans for Helen's sake.[1]

And of them that dwelt in Pylos and lovely Arene and Thryon the fording-place of Alpheios, and in stablished Aipy, and were inhabitants of Kyparisseis and Amphigeneia and Pteleos and Helos and Dorion – where the Muses met Thamyris the Thracian, and made an end of his singing, as he was faring from Oichalia, from Eurytos the Oichalian; for he averred with boasting that he would conquer,

[1]Or, 'for Helen's searchings of heart and groans.'

even did the Muses themselves sing against him, the daughters of aegis-bearing Zeus; but they in their anger maimed him, moreover they took from him the high gift of song and made him to forget his harping – of all these was knightly Nestor of Gerenia leader, and with him sailed ninety hollow ships.

And of them that possessed Arkadia beneath the steep mountain of Kyllene, beside the tomb of Aipytos, where are warriors that fight hand to hand; and of them that dwelt in Pheneos and Orchomenos abounding in flocks, and Rhipe and Stratie and windy Enispe, and that possessed Tegea and lovely Mantineia, and possessed Stymphelos and dwelt in Parrhasie, of these was Ankaios' son lord Agapenor leader, even of sixty ships; and in each ship embarked many Arkadian warriors skilled in fight. For Agamemnon king of men himself gave them benched ships wherewith to cross the wine-dark sea, even he the son of Atreus; for matters of seafaring concerned them not.

And they too that inhabited Bouprasion and goodly Elis, so much thereof as Hyrmine and Myrsinos upon the borders and the Olenian rock and Aleision bound between them, of these men there were four captains, and ten swift ships followed each one, and many Epeians embarked thereon. So some were led of Amphimachos and Thalpios, of the lineage of Aktor, sons one of Kteatos and one of Eurytos; and of some was stalwart Diores captain, son of Amarynkes; and of the fourth company godlike Polyxeinos was captain, son of king Agasthenes Augeias' son.

And them of Doulichion and the holy Echinean Isles that stand beyond the sea over against Elis, even these did Meges lead, the peer of Ares, Phyleides to wit, for he was begotten of knightly Phyleus dear to Zeus, him that erst changed his habitation to Doulichion for anger against his father.[1] And with him followed forty black ships.

And Odysseus led the great-hearted Kephallenians, them that possessed Ithaka and Neriton with quivering leafage, and dwelt in Krokyleia and rugged Aigilips, and them that possessed Zakynthos and that dwelt in Samos, and possessed the mainland and dwelt in the parts over against the isles. Them did Odysseus lead, the peer of Zeus in counsel, and with him followed twelve ships with vermilion prow.

And of the Aitolians Thoas was captain, the son of Andraimon, even of them that dwelt in Pleuron and Olenos and Pylene, and

[1]Note 1

Chalkis on the sea-shore and rocky Kalydon For the sons of great-hearted Oineus were no more, neither did he still live, and golden-haired Meleagros was dead, to whose hands all had been committed, for him to be king of the Aitolians. And with Thoas there followed forty black ships.

And of the Cretans Idomeneus the famous spearman was leader, even of them that possessed Knosos and Gortys of the great walls, Lyktos and Miletos and chalky Lykastos and Phaistos and Rhytion, stablished cities all; and of all others that dwelt in Crete of the hundred cities. Of these men was Idomeneus the famous spearman leader, and Meriones peer of the man-slaying war-god. With these followed eighty black ships.

And Tlepolemos, Herakles' son goodly and tall, led from Rhodes nine ships of the lordly Rhodians, that dwelt in Rhodes in threefold ordering, in Lindos and Ialysos and chalky Kameiros. These were led of Tlepolemos the famous spearman, that was born to great Herakles by Astyocheia, whom he had brought away from Ephyre by the river Selleëis, when he laid waste many cities of strong men, fosterlings of Zeus. Now when Tlepolemos had grown to manhood within the strong palace walls, anon he slew his own father's dear uncle, an old man now, Likymnios of the stock of Ares. Then with speed built he ships and gathered much folk together, and went fleeing across the deep, because the other sons and grandsons of great Herakles threatened him. So he came to Rhodes a wanderer, enduring hardships, and his folk settled by kinship in three tribes, and were loved of Zeus that is king among gods and men; and Kronion poured upon them exceeding great wealth.

Nireus, moreover, led three trim ships from Syme, Nireus son of Aglaia and king Charopos, Nireus the most beauteous man that came up under Ilios of all the Danaans, after the noble son of Peleus. Howbeit he was a weakling, and a scanty host followed him.

And of them that possessed Nisyros and Krapathos and Kasos and Kos the city of Eurypylos, and the Kalydnian Isles, of them Pheidippos and Antiphos were leaders, the two sons of king Thessalos son of Herakles. With them were arrayed thirty hollow ships.

Now all moreover that dwelt in the Pelasgian Argos and inhabited Alos and Alope and Trachis and possessed Phthia and Hellas the home of fair women, and were called Myrmidons and Hellenes and Achaians; of all these, even fifty ships, Achilles was captain. But these took no thought of noisy war; for there was no man to array them in line of battle. For fleet-footed goodly Achilles lay idle amid the ships, wroth for the sake of a damsel, Briseis of the lovely hair, whom he had won from Lyrnessos with much travail, what time he laid waste Lyrnessos and the walls of Thebe, and overthrew Mynes and Epistrophos, warriors that bare the spear, sons of king Euenos Selepos' son. For her sake lay Achilles sorrowing; but soon was he to arise again.

And of them that possessed Phylake and flowery Pyrasos, Demeter's sanctuary, and Iton mother of flocks, and Antron by the seashore and Pteleos couched in grass, of all these was warlike Protesilaos leader while yet he lived; but now ere this the black earth held him fast. His wife with marred visage was left alone in Phylake, yea, and his bridal chamber half builded; for a Dardanian warrior slew him as he leapt from his ship far first of the Achaians. Yet neither were his men leaderless, though they sorrowed for their leader; for Podarkes of the stock of Ares marshalled them, son of Phylakos' son Iphiklos was he, the lord of many flocks, own brother of great-hearted Protesilaos, and younger-born than he: but the other was alike the elder and the braver, even Protesilaos, that mighty man of war. Yet did not the host lack at all a leader, only they yearned for the noble dead. With him followed forty black ships.

And of them that dwelt in Pherai by the Boibeian mere, in Boibe and Glaphyre and stablished Iolkos, of them, even eleven ships, Admetos' dear son was leader, Eumelos whom Alkestis, fair among women, bare to Admetos, she that was most beauteous to look upon of the daughters of Pelias.

And of them that dwelt in Methone and Thaumakie, and possessed Meliboia and rugged Olizon, of these, even seven ships, was Philoktetes leader, the cunning archer; and in each ship sailed fifty oarsmen skilled to fight amain with the bow. But their captain lay enduring sore pain in the isle of goodly Lemnos, where the sons of the Achaians left him sick of a grievous wound from a deadly watersnake. There lay he pining; yet were the Argives soon to bethink them beside their ships of king Philoktetes. Yet neither were his men leaderless, only they sorrowed for their leader; but Medon marshalled them, Oileus' bastard son, whom Rhene bare to Oileus waster of cities.

And of them that possessed Trikke and terraced Ithome and that possessed Oichalia city of Eurytos the Oichalian, of these again Asklepios' two sons were leaders, the cunning leeches Podaleirios and Machaon. And with them were arrayed thirty hollow ships.

And of them that possessed Ormenios and the fountain of Hypereia, and possessed Asterion and the white crests of Titanos, of these was Eurypylos leader, Euaimon's glorious son; and with him forty black ships followed.

And of them that possessed Argissa and dwelt in Gyrtona, Orthe and Elone and the white city of Oloosson, of these was captain unflinching Polypoites, son of Peirithoos that immortal Zeus begat: and Polypoites did famed Hippodameia conceive of Peirithoos on that day when he took vengeance of the shaggy wild folk, and thrust them forth from Pelion and drave them to the Aithikes. And Poly-poites ruled not alone, but with him was Leonteus of the stock of Ares, son of high-hearted Koronos Kaineus's son. And with them forty black ships followed.

And Gouneus from Kyphos led two-and-twenty ships, and with him followed the Enienes and unflinching Peraibians that had pitched their homes about wintry Dodona, and dwelt on the tilth about lovely Titaresios that poureth his fair-flowing stream into Peneios. Yet doth he not mingle with the silver eddies of Peneios, but floweth on over him like unto oil, seeing that he is an offspring from the water of Styx, the dread river of the oath.

And the Magnetes were led of Prothoos son of Tenthredon, even they that dwelt about Peneios and Pelion with trembling leafage. These did fleet Prothoos lead, and with him forty black ships fol-lowed.

So these were the leaders of the Danaans and their captains. Now tell me, O Muse, who among them was first and foremost, of war-riors alike and horses that followed the sons of Atreus. Of horses they of Pheres' son were far goodliest, those that Eumelos drave, swift as birds, like of coat, like of age, matched to the measure of a levelling line across their backs. These were reared in Peraia by Apollo of the silver bow, two mares carrying onward the terror of battle. But of warriors far best was the Telamonian Aias, while the wrath of Achilles yet endured; for he was greatest of all, he and his horses that bore him, even Peleus' noble son. But he lay idle among his seafaring ships, in sore wrath against Agamemnon Atreus' son, shepherd of the host; and his folk along the sea-shore sported with quoits and with casting of javelins and archery; and the horses each beside his own chariot stood idle, champing clover and parsley of the marsh, and their lords' chariots lay well covered up within the huts, while the men yearned for their warrior chief, and wandered hither and thither through the camp and fought not.

So marched they then as though all the land were consuming with fire; and the earth groaned beneath them as at the wrath of Zeus whose joy is in the thunder, when he lasheth the earth about

Typhoeus in the country of the Arimoi, where men say is Typhoeus' couch. Even so groaned the earth aloud at their tread as they went: and with speed advanced they across the plain.

Now fleet Iris the wind-footed went to the Trojans, a messenger from aegis-bearing Zeus, with a grievous message. These were holding assembly at Priam's gate, being gathered all together both young men and old. And fleet-footed Iris stood hard by and spake to them; and she made her voice like to the voice of Polites son of Priam, who was the sentinel of the Trojans and was wont to sit trusting in his fleetness upon the barrow of Aisyetes of old, and on the top thereof wait the sallying of the Achaians forth from their ships. Even in his likeness did fleet-footed Iris speak to Priam: 'Old man, words beyond number are still pleasant to thee as erst in the days of peace; but war without respite is upon us. Of a truth have I very oft ere now entered into battles of the warriors, yet have I never seen so goodly a host and so great; for in the very likeness of the leaves of the forest or the sands of the sea are they marching along the plain to fight against the city. But Hector, thee do I charge beyond all to do even as I shall say. Seeing that the allies are very many throughout Priam's great city, and diverse men, being scattered abroad, have diverse tongues; therefore let each one give the word to those whose chieftain he is, and them let him lead forth and have the ordering of his countrymen.'

So spake she, and Hector failed not to know the voice of the goddess, and straightway dismissed the assembly, and they rushed to arms. And the gates were thrown open wide, and the host issued forth, footmen and horsemen, and mighty din arose.

Now there is before the city a certain steep mound apart in the plain, with a clear way about it on this side and on that; and men indeed call this 'Batieia,' but the immortals call it 'The tomb of lithe Myrine.' There did the Trojans and their allies divide their companies.

Amid the Trojans great Hector of the glancing helm was leader, the son of Priam; with him the greatest hosts by far and the goodliest were arrayed, eager warriors of the spear.

But the Dardanians were led of the princely son of Anchises, Aineias, whom bright Aphrodite conceived to Anchises amids the spurs of Ida, a goddess wedded to a mortal. Neither was he alone; with him were Antenor's two sons, Archelochos and Akamas, well skilled in all the ways of war.

And of them that dwelt in Zeleia beneath the nethermost foot of Ida, the men of substance that drink the dark waters of Aisepos, even the Troes; of these Lykaon's glorious son was leader, Pan-daros, to whom Apollo himself gave the bow.

And of them that possessed Adresteia and the land of Apaisos and possessed Pityeia and the steep hill of Tereia, of these Adrestos was captain, and Amphios of the linen corslet, the two sons of Merops of Perkote, that beyond all men knew soothsaying, and would have hindered his children marching to murderous war. But they gave him no heed, for the fates of black death led them on.

And they that dwelt about Perkote and Praktios and possessed Sestos and Abydos and bright Arisbe, these were led of Hyrtakos' son Asios, a prince of men, Asios son of Hyrtakos, whom his tall sorrel steeds brought from Arisbe, from the river Selleëis.

And Hippothoos led the tribes of the Pelasgians that fight with spears, them that inhabited deep-soiled Larisa These were led of Hippothoos and Pylaios of the stock of Ares, twain sons of Pelasgian Lethos son of Teutamos.

And the Thracians were led of Akamas and hero Peiroos, even all they that the strong stream of Hellespont shutteth in. And Euphemos was captain of the Kikonian spearmen, the son of Troizenos Keos' son, fosterling of Zeus.

But Pyraichmes led the Paionians with curving bows, from far away in Amydon, from the broad stream of Axios, Axios whose water is the fairest that floweth over the face of the earth.

And Pylaimenes of rugged heart led the Paphlagonians from the land of the Eneti, whence is the breed of wild mules This folk were they that possessed Kytoros and dwelt about Sesamon, and inhabited their famed dwellings round the river Parthenios and Kromna and Aigialos and lofty Erythini.

And the Alizones were led of Odios and Epistrophos, from far away in Alybe, where is the birthplace of silver.

And the Mysians were led of Chromis and Ennomos the augur, yet with all his auguries warded he not black fate from him, but was vanquished by the hand of fleet-footed Aiakides in the river, when he made havoc of the Trojans there and of the rest.

And Phorkys and godlike Askanios led the Phrygians from far Askania, and these were eager to fight in the battle-throng.

And the Maionians were commanded of Mesthles and Antiphos, Talaimenes' two sons, whose mother was the Gygaian mere. So these led the Maionians, whose birthplace was under Tmolos.

But Nastes led the Karians, uncouth of speech, that possessed Miletos and the mountain of Phthires, of leafage numberless, and the streams of Maiandros and the steep crest of Mykale. These were led of Amphimachos and Nastes: Nastes and Amphimachos the glorious children of Nomion. And he came, forsooth, to battle with golden attire like a girl – fond man: that held not back in any wise grievous destruction, but he was vanquished by the hands of fleet-footed Aiakides in the river, and wise-hearted Achilles carried away his gold.

And Sarpedon and blameless Glaukos led the Lykians from far away in Lykia by eddying Xanthos.

BOOK III

How Menelaos and Paris fought in single combat; and Aphrodite rescued Paris. And how Helen and Priam beheld the Achaian host from the walls of Troy.

NOW WHEN THEY WERE ARRAYED, each company with their captains, the Trojans marched with clamour and with shouting like unto birds, even as when there goeth up before heaven a clamour of cranes which flee from the coming of winter and sudden rain, and fly with clamour towards the streams of ocean, bearing slaughter and fate to the Pigmy men, and in early morn offer cruel battle. But on the other side marched the Achaians in silence breathing courage, eager at heart to give succour man to man.

Even as when the south wind sheddeth mist over the crests of a mountain, mist unwelcome to the shepherd, but to the robber better than night, and a man can see no further than he casteth a stone; even so thick arose the gathering dust-clouds at their tread as they went; and with all speed they advanced across the plain.

So when they were now come nigh in onset on each other, godlike Alexandros played champion to the Trojans, wearing upon his shoulders panther-skin and curved bow and sword; and he brandished two bronze-headed spears and challenged all the chieftains of the Argives to fight him man to man in deadly combat. But when Menelaos dear to Ares marked him coming in the forefront of the multitude with long strides, then even as a lion is glad when he lighteth upon a great carcase, a horned stag, or a wild goat that he hath found, being an hungered; and so he devoureth it amain, even though the fleet hounds and lusty youths set upon him; even thus was Menelaos glad when his eyes beheld godlike Alexandros; for he thought to take vengeance upon the sinner. So straightway he leapt in his armour from his chariot to the ground.

But when godlike Alexandros marked him appear amid the champions, his heart was smitten, and he shrank back into the host of his comrades, avoiding death. And even as a man that hath seen a serpent in a mountain glade starteth backward and trembling seizeth his feet beneath him, and he retreateth back again, and paleness hath hold of his cheeks, even so did godlike Alexandros for fear of Atreus' son shrink back into the throng of lordly Trojans. But

Hector beheld and upbraided him with scornful words: 'Ill Paris, most fair in semblance, thou deceiver woman-mad, would thou hadst been unborn and died unwed. Yea, that were my desire, and it were far better than thus to be our shame and looked at askance of all men. I ween that the flowing-haired Achaians laugh, deeming that a prince is our champion only because a goodly favour is his; but in his heart is there no strength nor any courage. Art thou indeed such an one that in thy seafaring ships thou didst sail over the deep with the company of thy trusty comrades, and in converse with strangers didst bring back a fair woman from a far country, one that was by marriage daughter to warriors that bear the spear, that she might be a sore mischief to thy father and city and all the realm, but to our foes a rejoicing, and to thyself a hanging of the head? And canst thou not indeed abide Menelaos dear to Ares? Thou mightest see what sort of warrior is he whose lovely wife thou hast. Thy lyre will not avail thee nor the gifts of Aphrodite, those thy locks and fair favour, when thou grovellest in the dust. But the Trojans are very cowards: else ere this hadst thou donned a robe of stone[1] for all the ill thou hast wrought.'

And godlike Alexandros made answer to him again: 'Hector, since in measure thou chidest me and not beyond measure – thy heart is ever keen, even as an axe that pierceth a beam at the hand of a man that shapeth a ship's timber with skill, and thereby is the man's blow strengthened; even such is thy heart undaunted in thy breast. Cast not in my teeth the lovely gifts of golden Aphrodite; not to be flung aside are the gods' glorious gifts that of their own good will they give; for by his desire can no man win them. But now if thou wilt have me do battle and fight, make the other Trojans sit down and all the Achaians, and set ye me in the midst, and Menelaos dear to Ares, to fight for Helen and all her wealth. And whichsoever shall vanquish and gain the upper hand, let him take all the wealth aright, and the woman, and bear them home. And let the rest pledge friendship and sure oaths; so may ye dwell in deep-soiled Troy, and let them depart to Argos pasture-land of horses, and Achaia home of fair women.'

So spake he, and Hector rejoiced greatly to hear his saying, and went into the midst and restrained the battalions of the Trojans, with his spear grasped by the middle; and they all sate them down. But the flowing-haired Achaians kept shooting at him, aiming with arrows and casting stones. But Agamemnon king of men cried

[1] *i.e.* been stoned by the people.

aloud: 'Refrain, ye Argives; shoot not, ye sons of the Achaians; for Hector of the glancing helm hath set himself to say somewhat.'

So spake he, and they refrained from battle and made silence speedily. And Hector spake between the two hosts 'Hear of me, Trojans and well-greaved Achaians, the saying of Alexandros, for whose sake strife hath come about. He biddeth the other Trojans and all the Achaians to lay down their goodly armour on the boun-teous earth, and himself in the midst and Menelaos dear to Ares to fight alone for Helen and all her wealth. And whichsoever shall van-quish and gain the upper hand, let him take all the wealth aright, and the woman, and bear them home; but let all of us pledge friend-ship and sure oaths.'

So spake he, and they all kept silence and were still. Then in their midst spake Menelaos of the loud war-cry: 'Hearken ye now to me, too; for into my heart most of all is grief entered; and I deem that the parting of Argives and Trojans hath come at last; seeing ye have endured many ills because of my quarrel and the first sin of Alexan-dros. And for whichsoever of us death and fate are prepared, let him lie dead: and be ye all parted with speed. Bring ye two lambs, one white ram and one black ewe, for earth and sun; and let us bring one for Zeus. And call hither great Priam, that he may pledge the oath himself, seeing he hath sons that are overweening and faithless, lest any by transgression do violence to the oath of Zeus; for young men's hearts are ever lifted up. But wheresoever an old man entereth in, he looketh both before and after, whereby the best issue shall come for either side.'

So spake he, and Achaians and Trojans were glad, deeming that they should have rest from grievous war. So they refrained their chariots to the ranks, and themselves alighted and doffed their arms. And these they laid upon the earth each close to each, and there was but small space between. And Hector sent two heralds to the city with all speed, to bring the lambs, and to call Priam And lord Agamemnon sent forth Talthybios to go to the hollow ships, and bade him bring a ram; and he was not disobedient to noble Agamemnon.

Now Iris went with a message to white-armed Helen in the like-ness of her husband's sister, the spouse of Antenor's son, even her that lord Helikaon Antenor's son had to wife, Laodike fairest favoured of Priam's daughters. And in the hall she found Helen weaving a great purple web of double fold, and embroidering thereon many battles of horse-taming Trojans and mail-clad Acha-ians, that they had endured for her sake at the hands of Ares. So

fleet-footed Iris stood by her side and said: 'Come hither, dear
sister, that thou mayest see the wondrous doings of horse-taming
Trojans and mail-clad Achaians. They that erst waged tearful war
upon each other in the plain, eager for deadly battle, even they sit
now in silence, and the battle is stayed, and they lean upon their
shields, and the tall spears are planted by their sides. But Alexandros
and Menelaos dear to Ares will fight with their tall spears for thee;
and thou wilt be declared the dear wife of him that conquereth.'

So spake the goddess, and put into her heart sweet longing for
her former husband and her city and parents.

Forthwith she veiled her face in shining linen, and hastened from
her chamber, letting fall a round tear; not unattended, for there followed with her two handmaidens, Aithre daughter of Pittheus and
ox-eyed Klymene. Then came she straightway to the place of the
Skaian gates. And they that were with Priam and Panthoos and
Thymoites and Lampos and Klytios and Hiketaon of the stock of
Ares, Oukalegon withal and Antenor, twain sages, being elders of
the people, sat at the Skaian gates. These had now ceased from
battle for old age, yet were they right good orators, like grasshop-
pers that in a forest sit upon a tree and utter their lily-like[1] voice;
even so sat the elders of the Trojans upon the tower. Now when
they saw Helen coming to the tower they softly spake winged words
one to the other: 'Small blame is it that Trojans and well-greaved
Achaians should for such a woman long time suffer hardships; marvellously like is she to the immortal goddesses to look upon. Yet
even so, though she be so goodly, let her go upon their ships and
not stay to vex us and our children after us.'

So said they, and Priam lifted up his voice and called to Helen:
'Come hither, dear child, and sit before me, that thou mayest see
thy former husband and thy kinsfolk and thy friends. I hold thee not
to blame; nay, I hold the gods to blame who brought on me the
dolorous war of the Achaians – so mayest thou now tell me who is
this huge hero, this Achaian warrior so goodly and great. Of a truth
there are others even taller by a head; yet did mine eyes never
behold a man so beautiful nor so royal; for he is like unto one that is
a king.'

And Helen, fair among women, spake and answered him: 'Rev-
erend art thou to me and dread, dear father of my lord; would that
sore death had been my pleasure when I followed thy son hither,
and left my home and my kinsfolk and my daughter in her girlhood

[1]Supposed to mean 'delicate' or 'tender.'

and the lovely company of mine age-fellows. But that was not so, wherefore I pine with weeping. Now will I tell thee that whereof thou askest me and enquirest. This is Atreides, wide-ruling Agamemnon, one that is both a goodly king and mighty spearman. And he was husband's brother to me, ah shameless me; if ever such an one there was.'

So said she, and the old man marvelled at him, and said: 'Ah, happy Atreides, child of fortune, blest of heaven; now know I that many sons of the Achaians are subject to thee. Erewhile fared I to Phrygia, the land of vines, and there saw I that the men of Phrygia, they of the nimble steeds, were very many, even the hosts of Otreus and godlike Mygdon, that were then encamped along the banks of Sangarios. For I too being their ally was numbered among them on the day that the Amazons came, the peers of men. Yet were not even they so many as are the glancing eyed Achaians.'

And next the old man saw Odysseus, and asked: 'Come now, tell me of this man too, dear child, who is he, shorter by a head than Agamemnon son of Atreus, but broader of shoulder and of chest to behold? His armour lieth upon the bounteous earth, and himself like a bell-wether rangeth the ranks of warriors. Yea, I liken him to a thick-fleeced ram ordering a great flock of white ewes.'

Then Helen sprung of Zeus made answer to him: 'Now this is Laertes' son, crafty Odysseus, that was reared in the realm of Ithaka, rugged though it be, and is skilled in all the ways of wile and cunning device.'

Then sage Antenor made answer to her: 'Lady, verily the thing thou sayest is true indeed, for erst came goodly Odysseus hither also on an embassage for thee, in the company of Menelaos dear to Ares; and I gave them entertainment and welcomed them in my halls, and learnt the aspect of both and their wise devices. Now when they mingled with the Trojans in the assembly, while all stood up Menelaos overpassed them all by the measure of his broad shoulders; but when both sat down, Odysseus was the more stately. And when they began to weave the web of words and counsel in the face of all, then Menelaos harangued fluently, in few words, but very clearly, seeing he was not long of speech, neither random, though in years he was the younger. But whenever Odysseus full of wiles rose up, he stood and looked down, with eyes fixed upon the ground, and waved not his staff whether backwards or forwards, but held it stiff, like to a man of no understanding; one would deem him to be churlish, and naught but a fool. But when he uttered his great voice from his chest, and words like unto the snowflakes of winter, then could no mortal man contend with Odysseus; then marvelled we not thus to behold Odysseus' aspect.'

And thirdly the old man saw Aias, and asked: 'Who then is this other Achaian warrior, goodly and great, pre-eminent among the Argives by the measure of his head and broad shoulders?'

And long-robed Helen, fair among women, answered: 'This is huge Aias, bulwark of the Achaians. And on the other side amid the Cretans standeth Idomeneus like a god, and about him are gathered the captains of the Cretans. Oft did Menelaos dear to Ares entertain him in our house whene'er he came from Crete. And now behold I all the other glancing-eyed Achaians, whom well I could discern and tell their names; but two captains of the host can I not see, even Kastor tamer of horses and Polydeukes the skilful boxer, mine own brethren, whom the same mother bare. Either they came not in the company from lovely Lakedaimon; or they came hither indeed in their seafaring ships, but now will not enter into the battle of the warriors, for fear of the many scornings and revilings that are mine.'

So said she; but them the life-giving earth held fast there in Lakedaimon, in their dear native land.

Meanwhile were the heralds bearing through the city the holy oath-offerings, two lambs and strong-hearted wine, the fruit of the earth, in a goat-skin bottle. And the herald Idaios bare the shining bowl and golden cups; and came to the old man and summoned him and said: 'Rise, thou son of Laomedon. The chieftains of the horse-taming Trojans and mail-clad Achaians call on thee to go down into the plain, that ye may pledge a trusty oath. But Alexandros and Menelaos dear to Ares will fight with their long spears for the lady's sake; and let lady and treasure go with him that shall conquer. And may we that are left pledge friendship and trusty oaths and dwell in deep-soiled Troy, and they shall depart to Argos pasture-land of horses and Achaia home of fair women.'

So said he, and the old man shuddered and bade his companions yoke the horses; and they with speed obeyed. Then Priam mounted and drew back the reins, and by his side Antenor mounted the splendid chariot. So the two drave the fleet horses through the Skaian gates to the plain. And when they had come even to the Trojans and Achaians, they went down from the chariots upon the bounteous earth, and marched into the midst of Trojans and Achaians. Then forthwith rose up Agamemnon king of men, and up rose Odysseus the man of wiles; and the lordly heralds gathered together the holy oath-offerings of the gods, and mingled the wine in a bowl, and poured water over the princes' hands. And Atreides put forth his hand and drew his knife that hung ever beside his sword's great sheath, and cut the hair from off the lambs' heads; and then the heralds portioned it among the chief of the Trojans and Achaians. Then in their midst Atreus' son lifted up his hands and prayed aloud: 'Father Zeus, that rulest from Ida, most glorious, most great, and thou Sun that seest all things and hearest all things, and ye Rivers and thou Earth, and ye that in the underworld punish men outworn, whosoever sweareth falsely; be ye witnesses, and watch over the faithful oath. If Alexandros slay Menelaos, then let him have Helen to himself and all her possessions; and we will depart on our seafaring ships But if golden-haired Menelaos slay Alexandros, then let the Trojans give back Helen and all her possessions and pay the Argives the recompense that is seemly, such as shall live among men that shall be hereafter. But if so be that Priam and Priam's sons will not pay the recompense unto me when Alexandros falleth, then will I fight on thereafter for the price of sin, and abide here till I compass the end of war.'

So said he, and cut the lambs' throats with the pitiless knife. Them he laid gasping upon the ground, failing of breath, for the knife had taken their strength from them; and next they drew the wine from the bowl into the cups, and poured it forth and prayed to the gods that live for ever. And thus would say many an one of Achaians and Trojans: 'Zeus most glorious, most great, and all ye immortal gods, which folk soe'er be first to sin against the oaths, may their brains be so poured forth upon the earth even as this wine, theirs and their children's; and let their wives be made subject unto strangers.'

So spake they, but the son of Kronos vouchsafed not yet fulfilment. And in their midst Priam of the seed of Dardanos uttered his saying: 'Hearken to me, Trojans and well-greaved Achaians. I verily will return back to windy Ilios, seeing that I can in no wise bear to behold with mine eyes my dear son fighting with Menelaos dear to Ares. But Zeus knoweth, and all the immortal gods, for whether of the twain the doom of death is appointed.'

So spake the godlike man, and laid the lambs in his chariot, and entered in himself, and drew back the reins; and by his side Antenor mounted the splendid chariot. So they departed back again to Ilios; and Hector son of Priam and goodly Odysseus first meted out a space, and then they took the lots, and shook them in a bronze-bound helmet, to know whether of the twain should first cast his spear of bronze. And the people prayed and lifted up their hands to the gods; and thus would say many an one of Achaians and Trojans: 'Father Zeus, that rulest from Ida, most glorious, most great;

whichsoe'er it be that brought this trouble upon both peoples, vouchsafe that he may die and enter the house of Hades; that so for us peace may be assured and trusty oaths.'

So said they; and great Hector of the glancing plume shook the helmet, looking behind him; and quickly leapt forth the lot of Paris. Then the people sat them down by ranks where each man's high-stepping horses and inwrought armour lay. And upon his shoulders goodly Alexandros donned his beauteous armour, even he that was lord to Helen of the lovely hair. First upon his legs set he his greaves, beautiful, fastened with silver ankle-clasps; next upon his breast he donned the corslet of his brother Lykaon, and fitted it upon himself. And over his shoulders cast he his silver-studded sword of bronze, and then a shield great and sturdy. And on his mighty head he set a wrought helmet of horse-hair crest, whereover the plume nodded terribly, and he took him a strong spear fitted to his grasp. And in like wise warlike Menelaos donned his armour.

So when they had armed themselves on either side in the throng, they strode between Trojans and Achaians, fierce of aspect, and wonder came on them that beheld, both on the Trojans tamers of horses and on the well-greaved Achaians. Then took they their stand near together in the measured space, brandishing their spears in wrath each against other. First Alexandros hurled his far shadow-ing spear, and smote on Atreides' round shield; but the bronze brake not through, for its point was turned in the stout shield. Next Menelaos son of Atreus lifted up his hand to cast, and made prayer to father Zeus: 'King Zeus, grant me revenge on him that was first to do me wrong, even on goodly Alexandros, and subdue thou him at my hands; so that many an one of men that shall be hereafter may shudder to wrong his host that hath shown him kindness.'

So said he, and poised his far-shadowing spear, and hurled, and smote on the round shield of the son of Priam. Through the bright shield went the ponderous spear and through the inwrought breast-plate it pressed on; and straight beside his flank the spear rent the tunic, but he swerved and escaped black death. Then Atreides drew his silver-studded sword and lifted up his hand and smote the helmet-ridge; but the sword shattered upon it into three, yea four, and fell from his hand Thereat Atreides looked up to the wide heaven and cried: 'Father Zeus, surely none of the gods is crueller than thou. Verily I thought to have gotten vengeance on Alexandros for his wickedness, but now my sword breaketh in my hand, and my spear sped from my grasp in vain, and I have not smitten him.'

So saying, he leapt upon him and caught him by his horse-hair crest, and swinging him round dragged him towards the well-greaved Achaians; and he was strangled by the embroidered strap beneath his soft throat, drawn tight below his chin to hold his helm. Now would Menelaos have dragged him away and won glory unspeakable, but that Zeus' daughter Aphrodite was swift to mark, and tore asunder for him the strap of slaughtered ox's hide; so the helmet came away empty in his stalwart hand. Thereat Menelaos cast it with a swing toward the well-greaved Achaians, and his trusty comrades took it up; and himself sprang back again eager to slay him with spear of bronze. But Aphrodite snatched up Paris, very easily as a goddess may, and hid him in thick darkness, and set him down in his fragrant perfumed chamber; and herself went to summon Helen. Her she found on the high tower, and about her the Trojan women thronged. So with her hand she plucked her perfumed raiment and shook it and spake to her in the likeness of an aged dame, a woolcomber that was wont to work for her fair wool when she dwelt in Lakedaimon, whom too she greatly loved. Even in her likeness fair Aphrodite spake: 'Come hither; Alexandros summoneth thee to go homeward. There is he in his chamber and inlaid bed, radiant in beauty and vesture; nor wouldst thou deem him to be come from fighting his foe, but rather to be faring to the dance, or from the dance to be just resting and set down.'

So said she, and stirred Helen's soul within her breast; and when now she marked the fair neck and lovely breast and sparkling eyes of the goddess, she marvelled straightway and spake a word and called upon her name: 'Strange queen, why art thou desirous now to beguile me? Verily thou wilt lead me further on to some one of the peopled cities of Phrygia or lovely Maionia, if there too thou hast perchance some other darling among mortal men, because even now Menelaos hath conquered goodly Alexandros, and will lead me, accursed me, to his home. Therefore thou comest hither with guileful intent. Go and sit thou by his side, and depart from the way of the gods; neither let thy feet ever bear thee back to Olympus, but still be vexed for his sake and guard him till he make thee his wife or perchance his slave. But thither will I not go – that were a sinful thing – to array the bed of him; all the women of Troy will blame me hereafter; and I have griefs untold within my soul.'

Then in wrath bright Aphrodite spake to her: 'Provoke me not, rash woman, lest in mine anger I desert thee, and hate thee even as now I love thee beyond measure, and lest I devise grievous enmities between both, even betwixt Trojans and Achaians, and so thou perish in evil wise.'

So said she, and Helen sprung of Zeus was afraid, and went wrapped in her bright radiant vesture, silently, and the Trojan women marked her not; and the goddess led the way.

Now when they were come to the beautiful house of Alexandros the handmaidens turned straightway to their tasks, and the fair lady went to the high-roofed chamber; and laughter-loving Aphrodite took for her a chair and brought it, even she the goddess, and set it before the face of Paris. There Helen took her seat, the child of aegis-bearing Zeus, and with eyes turned askance spake and chode her lord: 'Thou comest back from battle; would thou hadst perished there, vanquished of that great warrior that was my former husband. Verily it was once thy boast that thou wast a better man than Menelaos dear to Ares, in the might of thine arm and thy spear. But go, now, challenge Menelaos dear to Ares to fight thee again face to face. Nay, but I, even I, bid thee refrain, nor fight a fight with golden-haired Menelaos man to man, neither attack him recklessly, lest perchance thou fall to his spear anon.'

And Paris made answer to her and said: 'Chide not my soul, lady, with cruel taunts. For now indeed hath Menelaos vanquished me with Athene's aid, but another day may I do so unto him; for we too have gods with us. But come now, let us have joy of love upon our couch; for never yet hath love so enwrapped my heart – not even then when first I snatched thee from lovely Lakedaimon and sailed with thee on my seafaring ships, and in the isle of Kranaë had converse with thee upon thy couch in love – as I love thee now and sweet desire taketh hold upon me.' So saying he led the way to the couch, and the lady followed with him.

Thus laid they them upon their fretted couch; but Atreides the while strode through the host like to a wild beast, if anywhere he might set eyes on godlike Alexandros. But none of the Trojans or their famed allies could discover Alexandros to Menelaos dear to Ares. Yet surely did they in no wise hide him for kindliness, could any have seen him; for he was hated of all even as black death. So Agamemnon king of men spake among them there: 'Hearken to me, Trojans and Dardanians and allies. Now is victory declared for Menelaos dear to Ares; give ye back Helen of Argos and the possessions with her, and pay ye the recompense such as is seemly, that it may live even among men that shall be hereafter.' So said Atreides, and all the Achaians gave assent.

BOOK IV

How Pandaros wounded Menelaos by treachery; and Agamemnon exhorted his chief captains to battle.

NOW THE GODS sat by Zeus and held assembly on the golden floor, and in the midst the lady Hebe poured them their nectar: they with golden goblets pledged one another, and gazed upon the city of the Trojans. Then did Kronos son essay to provoke Hera with vexing words, and spake maliciously: 'Twain goddesses hath Menelaos for his helpers, even Hera of Argos and Alalkomenean Athene. Yet these sit apart and take their pleasure in beholding; but beside that other ever standeth laughter-loving Aphrodite and wardeth off fate from him, and now hath she saved him as he thought to perish. But of a truth the victory is to Menelaos dear to Ares; so let us take thought how these things shall be; whether once more we shall arouse ill war and the dread battle-din, or put friendship between the foes. Moreover if this were welcome to all and well pleasing, may the city of king Priam yet be an habitation, and Menelaos take back Helen of Argos.'

So said he, but Athene and Hera murmured thereat, who were sitting by him and devising ills for the Trojans. Now Athene held her peace and said not anything, for wrath at father Zeus, and fierce anger gat hold upon her: but Hera's breast contained not her anger, and she spake: 'Most dread son of Kronos, what word is this thou hast spoken? How hast thou the will to make my labour void and of none effect, and the sweat of my toil that I sweated, when my horses were wearied with my summoning of the host, to be the plague of Priam and his sons? Do as thou wilt; but we other gods do not all approve thee.'

Then in sore anger Zeus the cloud-gatherer spake to her: 'Good lack, how have Priam and Priam's sons done thee such great wrong that thou art furiously minded to sack the stablished citadel of Ilios? Perchance wert thou to enter within the gates and long walls and devour Priam raw, and Priam's sons and all the Trojans, then mightest thou assuage thine anger. Do as thou art minded, only let not this quarrel hereafter be to me and thee a sore strife between us both. And this moreover will I say to thee, and do thou lay it to thy heart; whene'er I too be of eager mind to lay waste a city where is the race of men that are dear to thee, hinder thou not my wrath, but let me be, even as I yield to thee of free will, yet with soul unwilling. For of all cities beneath sun and starry heaven that are the dwelling of mortal men, holy Ilios was most honoured of my heart, and Priam and the folk of Priam of the good ashen spear. For never did mine altar lack the seemly feast, even drink-offering and burnt-offering, the worship that is our due.'

Then Hera the ox-eyed queen made answer to him: 'Of a surety three cities are there that be dearest far to me, Argos and Sparta and wide-wayed Mykene; these lay thou waste whene'er they are found hateful to thy heart; not for them will I stand forth, nor do I grudge thee them. For even if I be jealous and would forbid thee to overthrow them, yet will my jealousy not avail, seeing that thou art stronger far than I. Still must my labour too not be made of none effect; for I also am a god, and my lineage is even as thine, and Kronos the crooked counsellor begat me to the place of honour in double wise, by birthright, and because I am named thy spouse, and thou art king among all the immortals. Let us indeed yield each to other herein, I to thee and thou to me, and the rest of the immortal gods will follow with us; and do thou with speed charge Athene to betake her to the fierce battle din of Trojans and Achaians, and to essay that the Trojans may first take upon them to do violence to the Achaians in their triumph, despite the oaths.'

So said she, and the father of men and gods disregarded not; forthwith he spake to Athene winged words: 'Betake thee with all speed to the host, to the midst of Trojans and Achaians, and essay that the Trojans may first take upon them to do violence to the Achaians in their triumph, despite the oaths.'

So spake he, and roused Athene that already was set thereon; and from Olympus' heights she darted down. Even as the son of Kronos the crooked counsellor sendeth a star, a portent for mariners or a wide host of men, bright shining, and therefrom are scattered sparks in multitude; even in such guise sped Pallas Athene to earth, and leapt into their midst; and astonishment came on them that beheld, on horse-taming Trojans and well-greaved Achaians. And thus would many an one say, looking at his neighbour: 'Of a surety either shall sore war and the fierce battle din return again; or else Zeus doth stablish peace between the foes, even he that is men's dispenser of battle.'

Thus would many an one of Achaians and Trojans say. Then the goddess entered the throng of Trojans in the likeness of a man, even Antenor's son Laodokos, a stalwart warrior, and sought for godlike Pandaros, if haply she might find him. Lykaon's son found she, the noble and stalwart standing, and about him the stalwart ranks of the shield-bearing host that followed him from the streams of Aisepos. So she came near and spake winged words: 'Wilt thou now hearken to me, thou wise son of Lykaon? Then wouldst thou take heart to shoot a swift arrow at Menelaos, and wouldst win favour and glory before all the Trojans, and before king Alexandros most of all. Surely from him first of any wouldst thou receive glorious gifts, if perchance he see Menelaos, Atreus' warrior son, vanquished by thy dart and brought to the grievous pyre. Go to now, shoot at glorious Menelaos, and vow to Apollo, the son of light,[1] the lord of archery, to sacrifice a goodly hecatomb of firstling lambs when thou art returned to thy home, in the city of holy Zeleia'

So spake Athene, and persuaded his fool's heart. Forthwith he unsheathed his polished bow of horn of a wild ibex that he himself had erst smitten beneath the breast as it came forth from a rock, the while he awaited in a lurking-place; and had pierced it in the chest, so that it fell backward on the rock. Now from its head sprang there horns of sixteen palms; these the artificer, even the worker in horn, joined cunningly together, and polished them all well and set the tip of gold thereon. So he laid it down when he had well strung it, by resting it upon the ground; and his staunch comrades held their shields before him, lest the warrior sons of the Achaians should first set on them, ere Menelaos, Atreus' warrior son, were smitten. Then opened he the lid of his quiver and took forth a feathered arrow, never yet shot, a source of grievous pangs; and anon he laid the bitter dart upon the string and vowed to Apollo, the son of light, the lord of archery, to sacrifice a goodly hecatomb of firstling lambs when he should have returned to his home in the city of holy Zeleia. Then he took the notch and string of oxes' sinew together, and drew, bringing to his breast the string, and to the bow the iron head. So when he had now bent the great bow into a round, the horn twanged, and the string sang aloud, and the keen arrow leapt eager to wing his way amid the throng.

But the blessed gods immortal forgat not thee, Menelaos; and before all the daughter of Zeus, the driver of the spoil, who stood before thee and warded off the piercing dart. She turned it just aside from the flesh, even as a mother driveth a fly from her child that lieth in sweet slumber; and with her own hand guided it where the

[1]Or, perhaps, 'the Wolf-born.'

golden buckles of the belt were clasped and the doubled breastplate met them. So the bitter arrow lighted upon the firm belt; through the inwrought belt it sped and through the curiously wrought breastplate it pressed on and through the taslet[1] he wore to shield his flesh, a barrier against darts; and this best shielded him, yet it passed on even through this. Then did the arrow graze the warrior's outermost flesh, and forthwith the dusky blood flowed from the wound.

As when some woman of Maionia or Karia staineth ivory with purple, to make a cheek-piece for horses, and it is laid up in the treasure chamber, and many a horseman prayeth for it to wear; but it is laid up to be a king's boast, alike an adornment for his horse and a glory for his charioteer; even in such wise, Menelaos, were thy shapely thighs stained with blood and thy legs and thy fair ankles beneath.

Thereat shuddered Agamemnon king of men when he saw the black blood flowing from the wound. And Menelaos dear to Ares likewise shuddered; but when he saw how thread[2] and barbs were without, his spirit was gathered in his breast again. Then lord Agamemnon moaned deep, and spake among them, holding Menelaos by the hand; and his comrades made moan the while: 'Dear brother, to thy death, meseemeth, pledged I these oaths, setting thee forth to fight the Trojans alone before the face of the Achaians; seeing that the Trojans have so smitten thee, and trodden under foot the trusty oaths. Yet in no wise is an oath of none effect, and the blood of lambs and pure drink-offerings and the right hands of fellowship wherein we trusted. For even if the Olympian bring not about the fulfilment forthwith, yet doth he fulfil at last, and men make dear amends, even with their own heads and their wives and little ones. Yea of a surety I know this in heart and soul; the day shall come for holy Ilios to be laid low, and Priam and the folk of Priam of the good ashen spear; and Zeus the son of Kronos enthroned on high, that dwelleth in the heaven, himself shall brandish over them all his lowring aegis, in indignation at this deceit. Then shall all this not be void; yet shall I have sore sorrow for thee, Menelaos, if thou die and fulfil the lot of life. Yea in utter shame should I return to thirsty Argos, seeing that the Achaians will forthwith bethink them of their native land, and so should we leave to Priam and the Trojans their boast, even Helen of Argos. And the

[1] An apron or belt set with metal, worn below the corslet.
[2] By which the iron head was attached to the shaft.

earth shall rot thy bones as thou liest in Troy with thy task unfin-
ished: and thus shall many an over-weening Trojan say as he
leapeth upon the tomb of glorious Menelaos: "Would to God
Agamemnon might so fulfil his wrath in every matter, even as now
he led hither the host of the Achaians for naught, and hath gone
home again to his dear native land with empty ships, and hath left
noble Menelaos behind." Thus shall men say hereafter: in that day
let the wide earth gape for me.'

But golden-haired Menelaos encouraged him and said 'Be of
good courage, neither dismay at all the host of the Achaians. The
keen dart lighted not upon a deadly spot; my glistering belt in front
stayed it, and the kirtle of mail beneath, and the taslet that the cop-
persmiths fashioned.'

Then lord Agamemnon answered him and said: 'Would it may be
so, dear Menelaos. But the leech shall feel the wound, and lay
thereon drugs that shall assuage thy dire pangs.'

So saying he spake to godlike Talthybios, his herald: 'Talthybios,
with all speed call Machaon hither, the hero son of Asklepios the
noble leech, to see Menelaos, Atreus' warrior son, whom one well
skilled in archery, some Trojan or Lykian, hath wounded with a
bow-shot, to his glory and our grief.'

So said he, and the herald heard him and disregarded not, and
went his way through the host of mail-clad Achaians to spy out the
hero Machaon. Him he found standing, and about him the stalwart
ranks of the shield-bearing host that followed him from Trike, pasture land of horses. So he came near and spake his winged words:
'Arise, thou son of Asklepios. Lord Agamemnon calleth thee to see
Menelaos, captain of the Acnaians, whom one well skilled in
archery, some Trojan or Lykian, hath wounded with a bow-shot, to
his glory and our grief.'

So saying he aroused his spirit in his breast, and they went their
way amid the throng, through the wide host of the Achaians. And
when they were now come where was golden-haired Menelaos
wounded, and all as many as were chieftains gathered around him in
a circle, the godlike hero came and stood in their midst, and anon
drew forth the arrow from the clasped belt; and as it was drawn
forth the keen barbs were broken backwards. Then he loosed the
glistering belt and the kirtle of mail beneath and taslet that the cop-
persmiths fashioned; and when he saw the wound where the bitter
arrow had lighted, he sucked out the blood and cunningly spread
thereon soothing drugs, such as Cheiron of his good will had
imparted to his sire.

While these were tending Menelaos of the loud war-cry, the ranks of shield-bearing Trojans came on; so the Achaians donned their arms again, and bethought them of the fray. Now wouldest thou not see noble Agamemnon slumbering, nor cowering, nor unready to fight, but very eager for glorious battle. He left his horses and his chariot adorned with bronze; and his squire, even Eurymedon son of Ptolemaios Peiraieus' son, kept apart the snorting steeds; and he straitly charged him to have them at hand whenever weariness should come upon his limbs with marshalling so many; and thus on foot ranged he through the ranks of warriors. And whomsoever of all the fleet-horsed Danaans he found eager, he stood by them and by his words encouraged them: 'Ye Argives, relax not in any wise your impetuous valour; for father Zeus will be no helper of liars, but as these were first to transgress against the oaths, so shall their own tender flesh be eaten of the vultures, and we shall bear away their dear wives and little children in our ships, when once we take the stronghold.'

But whomsoever he found shrinking from hateful battle, these he chode sore with angry words: 'Ye Argives, warriors of the bow, ye men of dishonour, have ye no shame? Why stand ye thus dazed like fawns that are weary with running over the long plain and so stand still, and no valour is found in their hearts at all? Even thus stand ye dazed, and fight not. Is it that ye wait for the Trojans to come near where your good ships' sterns are drawn up on the shore of the grey sea, to see if Kronion will stretch his arm over you indeed?'

So masterfully ranged he through the ranks of warriors Then came he to the Cretans as he went through the throng of warriors; and these were taking arms around wise Idomeneus; Idomeneus amid the foremost, valiant as a wild boar, and Meriones the while was hastening his hindermost battalions Then Agamemnon king of men rejoiced to see them, and anon spake to Idomeneus with kindly words: 'Idomeneus, more than all the fleet-horsed Danaans do I honour thee, whether in war or in task of other sort or in the feast, when the chieftains of the Argives mingle in the bowl the gleaming wine of the counsellors. For even though all the other flowing-haired Achaians drink one allotted portion, yet thy cup standeth ever full even as mine, to drink as oft as thy soul biddeth thee. Now arouse thee to war like such an one as thou avowest thyself to be of old.'

And Idomeneus the captain of the Cretans made answer to him: 'Atreides, of very truth will I be to thee a trusty comrade even as at the first I promised and gave my pledge; but do thou urge on all the flowing-haired Achaians, that we may fight with all speed, seeing the Trojans have disannulled the oaths. But for all that death and sorrow hereafter shall be their lot, because they were the first to transgress against the oaths.'

So said he, and Agamemnon passed on glad at heart. Then came he to the Aiantes as he went through the throng of warriors; and these twain were arming, and a cloud of footmen followed with them. Even as when a goatherd from a place of outlook seeth a cloud coming across the deep before the blast of the west wind; and to him being afar it seemeth ever blacker, even as pitch, as it goeth along the deep, and bringeth a great whirlwind, and he shuddereth to see it and driveth his flock beneath a cave; even in such wise moved the serried battalions of young men, the fosterlings of Zeus, by the side of the Aiantes into furious war, battalions dark of line, bristling with shields and spears. And lord Agamemnon rejoiced to see them and spake to them winged words, and said: 'Aiantes, leaders of the mail-clad Argives, to you twain, seeing it is not seemly to urge you, give I no charge; for of your own selves ye do indeed bid your folk to fight amain. Ah, father Zeus and Athene and Apollo, would that all had like spirit in their breasts; then would king Priam's city soon bow captive and wasted beneath our hands.'

So saying he left them there, and went to others. Then found he Nestor, the clear-voiced orator of the Pylians, arraying his comrades, and urging them to fight, around great Pelagon and Alastor and Chromios and lord Haimon and Bias shepherd of the host. And first he arrayed the horse-men with horses and chariots, and behind them the footmen many and brave, to be a bulwark of battle; but the cowards he drave into the midst, that every man, even though he would not, yet of necessity must fight. First he laid charge upon the horsemen; these he bade hold in their horses nor be entangled in the throng. 'Neither let any man, trusting in his horsemanship and manhood, be eager to fight the Trojans alone before the rest, nor yet let him draw back, for so will ye be enfeebled. But whensoever a warrior from the place of his own car can come at a chariot of the foe, let him thrust forth with his spear; even so is the far better way. Thus moreover did men of old time lay low cities and walls, because they had this mind and spirit in their breasts.'

So did the old man charge them, being well skilled of yore in battles. And lord Agamemnon rejoiced to see him, and spake to him winged words, and said: 'Old man, would to god that, even as thy spirit is in thine own breast, thy limbs might obey and thy strength be unabated. But the common lot of age is heavy upon thee; would that it had come upon some other man, and thou wert amid the young.'

Then knightly Nestor of Gerenia answered him: 'Atreides, I verily, even I too, would wish to be as on the day when I slew noble Ereuthalion. But the gods in no wise grant men all things at once. As I was then a youth, so doth old age now beset me. Yet even so will I abide among the horsemen and urge them by counsel and words; for that is the right of elders. But the young men shall wield the spear, they that are more youthful than I and have confidence in their strength'

So spake he, and Atreides passed on glad at heart. He found Menestheus the charioteer, the son of Peteos, standing still, and round him were the Athenians, masters of the battle-cry. And hard by stood crafty Odysseus, and round about him the ranks of Kephallenians, no feeble folk, stood still; for their host had not yet heard the battle-cry, seeing the battalions of horse-taming Trojans and Achaians had but just bestirred them to move; so these stood still tarrying till some other column of the Achaians should advance to set upon the Trojans and begin the battle. But when Agamemnon king of men saw it, he upbraided them, and spake to them winged words, saying: 'O son of king Peteos fosterling of Zeus, and thou skilled in evil wiles, thou cunning of mind, why stand ye shrinking apart, and tarry for others? You beseemeth it to stand in your place amid the foremost and to front the fiery battle; for ye are the first to hear my bidding to the feast, as oft as we Achaians prepare a feast for the counsellors. Then are ye glad to eat roast meat and drink your cups of honey-sweet wine as long as ye will. But now would ye gladly behold it, yea, if ten columns of Achaians in front of you were fighting with the pitiless sword.'

But Odysseus of many counsels looked fiercely at him and said: 'Atreides, what word is this that hath escaped the barrier of thy lips? How sayest thou that we are slack in battle? When once our[1] Achaians launch furious war on the Trojans, tamers of horses, then shalt thou, if thou wilt, and if thou hast any care therefor, behold Telemachos' dear father mingling with the champions of the Trojans, the tamers of horses. But that thou sayest is empty as air.'

Then lord Agamemnon spake to him smiling, seeing how he was wroth, and took back his saying: 'Heaven-sprung son of Laertes, Odysseus full of devices, neither do I chide thee beyond measure

---

[1] Or, 'that we are slack in battle, when once we Achaians,' putting the note of interrogation after 'tamers of horses.'

nor urge thee; for I know that thy heart within thy breast is kindly disposed; for thy thoughts are as my thoughts. Go to, we will make amends hereafter, if any ill word hath been spoken now; may the gods bring it all to none effect.'

So saying he left them there and went on to others. The son of Tydeus found he, high-hearted Diomedes, standing still with horses and chariot well compact; and by him stood Sthenelos son of Kapaneus. Him lord Agamemnon saw and upbraided, and spake to him winged words, and said. 'Ah me, thou son of wise Tydeus tamer of horses, why shrinkest thou, why gazest thou at the highway, of the battle? Not thus was Tydeus wont to shrink, but rather to fight his enemies far in front of his dear comrades, as they say that beheld him at the task; for never did I meet him nor behold him, but men say that he was pre-eminent amid all. Of a truth he came to Mykene, not in enmity, but as a guest with godlike Polyneikes, to raise him an army for the war that they were levying against the holy walls of Thebes; and they besought earnestly that valiant allies might be given them, and our folk were fain to grant them and made assent to their entreaty, only Zeus showed omens of ill and turned their minds. So when these were departed and were come on their way, and had attained to Asopos deep in rushes, that maketh his bed in grass, there did the Achaians appoint Tydeus to be their ambassador. So he went and found the multitude of the sons of Kadmos feasting in the palace of mighty Eteokles. Yet was knightly Tydeus, even though a stranger, not afraid, being alone amid the multitude of the Kadmeians, but challenged them all to feats of strength, and in every one vanquished he them easily; so present a helper was Athene unto him. But the Kadmeians, the urgers of horses, were wroth, and as he fared back again they brought and set a strong ambush, even fifty young men, whose leaders were twain, Maion son of Haimon, like to the immortals, and Autophonos' son Polyphontes staunch in battle. Still even on these Tydeus brought shameful death; he slew them all, save one that he sent home alone; Maion to wit he sent away in obedience to the omens of heaven. Such was Tydeus of Aitolia; but he begat a son that in battle is worse than he; only in harangue is he the better.'

So said he, and stalwart Diomedes made no answer, but had respect to the chiding of the king revered. But the son of glorious Kapaneus answered him: 'Atreides, utter not falsehood, seeing thou knowest how to speak truly. We avow ourselves to be better men by far than our fathers were: we did take the seat of Thebes the seven gated, though we led a scantier host against a stronger wall, because we followed the omens of the gods and the salvation of Zeus; but they perished by their own iniquities. Do not thou therefore in any wise have our fathers in like honour with us.'

But stalwart Diomedes looked sternly at him, and said: 'Brother, sit silent and obey my saying. I grudge not that Agamemnon shepherd of the host should urge on the well-greaved Achaians to fight; for him the glory will attend if the Achaians lay the Trojans low and take holy Ilios; and his will be the great sorrow if the Achaians be laid low. Go to now, let us too bethink us of impetuous valour.'

He spake and leapt in his armour from the chariot to earth, and terribly rang the bronze upon the chieftain's breast as he moved; thereat might fear have come even upon one stout-hearted.

As when on the echoing beach the sea-wave lifteth up itself in close array before the driving of the west wind; out on the deep doth it first raise its head, and then breaketh upon the land and belloweth aloud and goeth with arching crest about the promontories, and speweth the foaming brine afar; even so in close array moved the battalions of the Danaans without pause to battle. Each captain gave his men the word, and the rest went silently; thou wouldest not deem that all the great host following them had any voice within their breasts; in silence feared they their captains. On every man glittered the inwrought armour wherewith they went clad. But for the Trojans, like sheep beyond number that stand in the courtyard of a man of great substance, to be milked of their white milk, and bleat without ceasing to hear their lambs' cry, even so arose the clamour of the Trojans through the wide host. For they had not all like speech nor one language, but their tongues were mingled, and they were brought from many lands. These were urged on of Ares, and those of bright-eyed Athene, and Terror and Rout, and Strife whose fury wearieth not, sister and friend of murderous Ares; her crest is but lowly at the first, but afterward she holdeth up her head in heaven and her feet walk upon the earth. She now cast common discord in their midst, as she fared through the throng and made the lamentation of men to wax.

Now when they were met together and come unto one spot, then clashed they targe and spear and fury of bronze-clad warrior; the bossed shields pressed each on each and mighty din arose. Then were heard the voice of groaning and the voice of triumph together of the slayers and the slain, and the earth streamed with blood. As when two winter torrents flow down the mountains to a watersmeet and join their furious flood within the deep ravine from their great springs, and the shepherd heareth the roaring far off among the

hills: even so from the joining of battle came there forth shouting
and travail. Antilochos first slew a Trojan warrior in full array,
valiant amid the champions, Echepolos son of Thalysios; him was
he first to smite upon the ridge of his crested helmet, and he drave
the spear into his brow and the point of bronze passed within the
bone; darkness clouded his eyes, and he crashed like a tower amid
the press of fight. As he fell lord Elephenor caught him by the foot,
Chalkodon's son, captain of the great-hearted Abantes, and dragged
him from beneath the darts, eager with all speed to despoil him of
his armour. Yet but for a little endured his essay; great-hearted
Agenor saw him haling away the corpse, and where his side was left
uncovered of his buckler as he bowed him down, there smote he
him with bronze-tipped spear-shaft and unstrung his limbs So his
life departed from him, and over his corpse the task of Trojans and
Achaians grew hot; like wolves leapt they one at another, and man
lashed at man.

Next Telamonian Aias smote Anthemion's son, the lusty stripling
Simoeisios, whom erst his mother bare beside the banks of Simoeis
on the way down from Ida whither she had followed with her parents to see their flocks. Therefore they called him Simoeisios, but
he repaid not his dear parents the recompense of his nurture; scanty
was his span of life by reason of the spear of great-hearted Aias that
laid him low. For as he went he first was smitten on his right breast
beside the pap; straight through his shoulder passed the spear of
bronze, and he fell to the ground in the dust like a poplar-tree, that
hath grown up smooth in the lowland of a great marsh, and its
branches grow upon the top thereof; this hath a wainwright felled
with gleaming steel, to bend him a felloe for a goodly chariot, and
so it lies drying by a river's banks. In such fashion did heaven-
sprung Aias slay Simoeisios son of Anthemion; then at him
Antiphos of the glancing corslet, Priam's son, made a cast with his
keen javelin across the throng. Him he missed, but smote Odysseus'
valiant comrade Leukos in the groin as he drew the corpse his way,
so that he fell upon it and the body dropped from his hands. Then
Odysseus was very wroth at heart for the slaying of him, and strode
through the forefront of the battle harnessed in flashing bronze,
and went and stood hard by and glanced around him, and cast his
bright javelin; and the Trojans shrank before the casting of the
hero. He sped not the dart in vain, but smote Demokoon, Priam's
bastard son that had come to him from tending his fleet mares in
Abydos. Him Odysseus, being wroth for his comrade's sake, smote
with his javelin on one temple; and through both temples passed the

point of bronze, and darkness clouded his eyes, and he fell with a crash and his armour clanged upon him. Then the forefighters and glorious Hector yielded, and the Argives shouted aloud, and drew the bodies unto them, and pressed yet further onward. But Apollo looked down from Pergamos, and had indignation, and with a shout called to the Trojans: 'Arise, ye Trojans, tamers of horses; yield not to the Argives in fight; not of stone nor iron is their flesh, that it should resist the piercing bronze when they are smitten. Moreover Achilles, son of Thetis of the fair tresses, fighteth not, but amid the ships broodeth on his bitter anger.'

So spake the dread god from the city; and the Achaians likewise were urged on of Zeus' daughter the Triton-born, most glorious, as she passed through the throng wheresoever she beheld them slackening.

Next was Diores son of Amarynkeus caught in the snare of fate; for he was smitten by a jagged stone on the right leg hard by the ankle, and the caster thereof was captain of the men of Thrace, Peiroös son of Imbrasos that had come from Ainos. The pitiless stone crushed utterly the two sinews and the bones; back fell he in the dust, and stretched out both his hands to his dear comrades, gasping out his soul. Then he that smote him, even Peiroös, sprang at him and pierced him with a spear beside the navel; so all his bowels gushed forth upon the ground, and darkness clouded his eyes. But even as Peiroös departed from him Thoas of Aitolia smote with a spear his chest above the pap, and the point fixed in his lung. Then Thoas came close, and plucked out from his breast the ponderous spear, and drew his sharp sword, wherewith he smote his belly in the midst, and took his life. Yet he stripped not off his armour; for his comrades, the men of Thrace that wear the topknot, stood around, their long spears in their hands, and albeit he was great and valiant and proud they drave him off from them and he gave ground reeling. So were the two captains stretched in the dust side by side, he of the Thracians and he of the mail-clad Epeians; and around them were many others likewise slain.

Now would none any more enter in and make light of the battle, could it be that a man yet unwounded by dart or thrust of keen bronze might roam in the midst, being led of Pallas Athene by the hand, and by her guarded from the flying shafts. For many Trojans that day and many Achaians were laid side by side upon their faces in the dust.

BOOK V

How Diomedes by his great valour made havoc of the Trojans, and wounded even Aphrodite and Ares by the help of Athene.

BUT NOW TO TYDEUS' son Diomedes Pallas Athene gave might and courage, for him to be pre-eminent amid all the Argives and win glorious renown. She kindled flame unwearied from his helmet and shield, like to the star of summer that above all others glittereth bright after he hath bathed in the ocean stream. In such wise kindled she flame from his head and shoulders and sent him into the midst, where men thronged the thickest.

Now there was amid the Trojans one Dares, rich and noble, priest of Hephaistos; and he had two sons, Phegeus and Idaios, well skilled in all the art of battle. These separated themselves and assailed him face to face, they setting on him from their car and he on foot upon the ground. And when they were now come near in onset on each other, first Phegeus hurled his far-shadowing spear; and over Tydeides' left shoulder the spear point passed, and smote not his body. Then next Tydeides made a spear-cast, and the javelin sped not from his hand in vain, but smote his breast between the nipples, and thrust him from the chariot. So Idaios sprang away, leaving his beautiful car, and dared not to bestride his slain brother; else had neither be himself escaped black fate: but Hephaistos guarded him and saved him in a veil of darkness, that he might not have his aged priest all broken with sorrow. And the son of great-hearted Tydeus drave away the horses and gave them to his men to take to the hollow ships. But when the great-hearted Trojans beheld the sons of Dares, how one was fled, and one was slain beside his chariot, the spirit of all was stirred. But bright-eyed Athene took impetuous Ares by the hand and spake to him and said: 'Ares, Ares, blood-stained bane of mortals, thou stormer of walls, can we not now leave the Trojans and Achaians to fight, on whichsoever it be that father Zeus bestoweth glory? But let us twain give place, and escape the wrath of Zeus.'

So saying she led impetuous Ares from the battle. Then she made him sit down beside loud Skamandros, and the Danaans pushed the Trojans back. Each one of the captains slew his man; first Agamemnon king of men thrust from his chariot the lord of the Halizonians,

great Odios; for as he first turned to flight Agamemnon thrust his
dart into his back between his shoulders, and drave it through his
breast. And he fell with a crash, and his armour clanged upon him.

And Idomeneus slew Phaistos son of Boros the Maïonian, that
came from deep-soiled Tarne. Him in the act to mount upon his
car spear-famed Idomeneus pierced with his long dart through his
right shoulder; and he fell from the car and hateful darkness gat
hold of him.

Him then Idomeneus' squires despoiled; and Skamandrios, son of
Strophios, cunning in the chase, fell to the keen-pointed spear of
Menelaos son of Atreus; even he the mighty hunter, whom Artemis
herself had taught to shoot all manner of wild things that the mountain forest breedeth. But now did Archer Artemis avail him naught
nor all his marksmanship wherein of old time he excelled; but spear
famed Menelaos son of Atreus smote him with his dart as he fled
before him, in his back [between his shoulders, and pierced through
his breast]. So he fell prone and his armour clanged upon him.

And Meriones slew Phereklos, son of Tekton Harmon's son,
whose hands were cunning to make all manner of curious work; for
Pallas Athene loved him more than all men. He likewise built
Alexandros the trim ships, source of ills, that were made the bane of
all the Trojans and of himself, because he knew not the oracles of
heaven. Him Meriones pursued and overtaking him smote him in
the right buttock, and right through passed the point straight to the
bladder beneath the bone; and he fell to his knees with a cry, and
death overshadowed him.

Then Meges slew Pedaios Antenor's son, that was a bastard; yet
goodly Theano nurtured him carefully like to her own children, to
do her husband pleasure. To him Phyleus' spear-famed son came
near, and with keen dart smote him upon the sinew of the head; and
right through amid the teeth the point of bronze cleft the tongue's
root. So he fell in the dust, and bit the cold bronze with his teeth.

And by Eurypylos, Euaimon's son, noble Hypsenor son of high-
hearted Dolopion that was appointed Skamandros' priest and like to
a god was held in honour of the folk – by Eurypylos Euaimon's glorious son, he as he fled before him was pursued and smitten on the
shoulder with a sword-thrust, and his heavy arm was shorn away.
All bleeding the arm fell upon the earth; and over his eyes came
gloomy death and forceful fate.

So laboured these in the violent mellay; but of Tydeides man
could not tell with whom he were joined, whether he consorted
with Trojans or with Achaians. For he stormed across the plain like

a winter torrent at the full, that in swift course scattereth the causeys; neither can the long lines of[1] causeys hold it in, nor the fences of fruitful orchards stay its sudden coming when the rain of heaven driveth it; and so before it perish in multitudes the fair works of the sons of men. Thus before Tydeides the serried battalions of the Trojans were overthrown, and they abode him not for all they were so many.

But when Lykaon's glorious son marked him storming across the plain, overthrowing battalions before him, anon he bent his crooked bow against Tydeides, and smote him as he sped onwards, hitting hard by his right shoulder the plate of his corslet; the bitter arrow flew through and held straight upon its way, and the corslet was dabbled with blood. Over him then loudly shouted Lykaon's glorious son: 'Bestir you, great-hearted Trojans, urgers of horses; the best man of the Achaians is wounded, and I deem that he shall not for long endure the violent dart, if verily the king, the son of Zeus,[2] sped me on my way from Lykia.'

So spake he boasting; yet was the other not vanquished of the swift dart, only he gave place and stood before his horses and his chariot and spake to Sthenelos son of Kapaneus: 'Haste thee, dear son of Kapaneus; descend from thy chariot, to draw me from my shoulder the bitter arrow.'

So said he, and Sthenelos leapt from his chariot to earth and stood beside him and drew the swift shaft right through, out of his shoulder; and the blood darted up through the pliant tunic. Then Diomedes of the loud war-cry prayed thereat: 'Hear me, daughter of aegis-bearing Zeus, unwearied maiden! If ever in kindly mood thou stoodest by my father in the heat of battle, even so now be thou likewise kind to me, Athene. Grant me to slay this man, and bring within my spear-cast him that took advantage to shoot me, and boasteth over me, deeming that not for long shall I see the bright light of the sun.'

So spake he in prayer, and Pallas Athene heard him, and made his limbs nimble, his feet and his hands withal, and came near and spake winged words: 'Be of good courage now, Diomedes, to fight the Trojans; for in thy breast I have set thy father's courage undaunted, even as it was in knightly Tydeus, wielder of the buckler. Moreover I have taken from thine eyes the mist that erst was on them, that thou mayest well discern both god and man. Therefore if

---

[1] Reading ἐεϱμέναι, with Aristarchos.
[2] Apollo.

any god come hither to make trial of thee, fight not thou face to face with any of the immortal gods; save only if Aphrodite daughter of Zeus enter into the battle, her smite thou with the keen bronze.'

So saying bright-eyed Athene went her way and Tydeides returned and entered the forefront of the battle; even though erst his soul was eager to do battle with the Trojans, yet now did three-fold courage come upon him, as upon a lion whom some shepherd in the field guarding his fleecy sheep hath wounded, being sprung into the fold, yet hath not vanquished him; he hath roused his might, and then cannot beat him back, but lurketh amid the steading, and his forsaken flock is affrighted; so the sheep are cast in heaps, one upon the other, and the lion in his fury leapeth out of the high fold; even so in fury mingled mighty Diomedes with the Trojans.

There slew he Astynoos and Hypeiron shepherd of the host; the one he pierced above the nipple with his bronze-shod dart, the other with his great sword upon the collar-bone beside the shoulder he smote, and severed the shoulder from neck and back. Them left he there, and pursued after Abas and Polyidos, sons of old Eury-damas dreamer of dreams; yet discerned he no dreams for them when they went,[1] but stalwart Diomedes despoiled them. Then went he after Xanthos and Thoon, sons of Phainops, striplings both; but their father was outworn of grievous age, and begat no other son for his possessions after him. Then Diomedes slew them and bereft the twain of their dear life, and for their father left only lamentation and sore distress, seeing he welcomed them not alive returned from battle; and kinsmen divided his substance.

Then caught he two sons of Priam of the seed of Dardanos, riding in one chariot, Echemmon and Chromios. As a lion leapeth among the kine and breaketh the neck of cow or heifer grazing in a woodland pasture, so Tydeus' son thrust in ill wise from their char-iot both of them unwilling, and thereafter despoiled them of their arms; and the horses gave he to his comrades to drive them to the ships.

Him Aineias beheld making havoc of the ranks of warriors, and went his way along the battle and amid the hurtling of spears, seek-ing godlike Pandaros, if haply he might find him. Lykaon's son he found, the noble and stalwart, and stood before his face, and spake a word unto him 'Pandaros, where now are thy bow and thy winged arrows, and the fame wherein no man of this land rivalleth thee, nor

[1]Or, 'yet came they not home for him to discern dreams for them.'

any in Lykia boasteth to be thy better? Go to now, lift thy hands in prayer to Zeus and shoot thy dart at this fellow, whoe'er he be that lordeth it here and hath already wrought the Trojans much mischief, seeing he hath unstrung the knees of many a brave man; if indeed it be not some god wroth with the Trojans, in anger by reason of sacrifices; the wrath of god is a sore thing to fall on men.'[2]

And Lykaon's glorious son made answer to him: 'Aineias, counsellor of the mail-clad Trojans, in everything liken I him to the wise son of Tydeus; I discern him by his shield and crested helmet, and by the aspect of his horses; yet know I not surely if it be not a god. But if it be the man I deem, even the wise son of Tydeus, then not without help of a god is he thus furious, but some immortal standeth beside him with a cloud wrapped about his shoulders and turned aside from him my swift dart even as it lighted. For already have I shot my dart at him and smote his right shoulder right through the breastplate of his corslet, yea and I thought to hurl him headlong to Aidoneus, yet I vanquished him not; surely it is some wrathful god. And I have no steeds at hand nor any chariot whereon to mount – yet in Lykaon's halls are eleven fair chariots, new wrought, with gear all fresh, and cloths spread over them; and beside each standeth a yoke of horses, champing white barley and spelt. Moreover Lykaon the aged spearman at my departing laid instant charge upon me in our well-builded house; he bade me mount horse and chariot to lead the Trojans in the violent mellay; but I obeyed him not – far better had that been! – but spared the horses lest in the great crowd of men they should lack fodder that had been wont to feed their fill. Therefore I left them and am come on foot to Ilios, trusting to my bow; and now must my bow not help me! Already have I aimed at two princes, Tydeus' and Atreus' sons, and both I smote and surely drew forth blood, yet only roused them the more. Therefore in an evil hour I took from the peg my curved bow on that day when I led my Trojans to lovely Ilios, to do noble Hector pleasure. But if I return and mine eyes behold my native land and wife and great palace lofty-roofed, then may an alien forthwith cut my head from me if I break not this bow with mine hands and cast it upon the blazing fire; worthless is its service to me as air.'

Then Aineias captain of the Trojans answered him: 'Nay, talk not thus; naught shall be mended before that we with horses and chariot have gone to face this man, and made trial of him in arms. Come

[2]Or, 'and the wrath of the gods be heavy upon us.'

then, mount upon my car that thou mayest see of what sort are the steeds of Tros, well skilled for following or for fleeing hither or thither very fleetly across the plain; they will e'en bring us to the city safe and sound, even though Zeus hereafter give victory to Diomedes son of Tydeus. Come therefore, take thou the lash and shining reins, and I will stand upon the car to fight;[1] or else withstand thou him, and to the horses will I look.'

To him made answer Lykaon's glorious son: 'Aineias, take thou thyself the reins and thine own horses; better will they draw the curved car for their wonted charioteer, if perchance it hap that we must flee from Tydeus' son; lest they go wild for fear and will not take us from the fight, for lack of thy voice, and so the son of great-hearted Tydeus attack us and slay us both and drive away the whole-hooved horses. So drive thou thyself thy chariot and thy horses, and I will await his onset with my keen spear.' So saying mounted they upon the well-dight chariot, and eagerly drave the fleet horses against Tydeides. And Sthenelos, the glorious son of Kapaneus, saw them, and anon spake to Tydeides winged words: 'Diomedes son of Tydeus, dear to mine heart, I behold two stalwart warriors eager to fight against thee, endued with might beyond measure. The one is well skilled in the bow, even Pandaros, and he moreover boasteth him to be Lykaon's son; and Aineias boasteth himself to be born son of great-hearted Anchises, and his mother is Aphrodite. Come now, let us give place upon the chariot, neither rage thou thus, I pray thee, in the forefront of battle, lest perchance thou lose thy life.'

Then stalwart Diomedes looked sternly at him and said:

'Speak to me no word of flight, for I ween that thou shalt not at all persuade me; not in my blood is it to fight a skulking fight or cower down; my force is steadfast still. I have no mind to mount the chariot, nay, even as I am will I go to face them; Pallas Athene biddeth me not be afraid. And as for these, their fleet horses shall not take both back from us again, even if one or other escape. And this moreover tell I thee, and lay thou it to heart: if Athene rich in counsel grant me this glory, to slay them both, then refrain thou here these my fleet horses, and bind the reins tight to the chariot rim; and be mindful to leap upon Aineias' horses, and drive them forth from the Trojans amid the well-greaved Achaians. For they are of that breed whereof farseeing[2] Zeus gave to Tros recompense for

[1]Reading xxxxxx (grrek writing) with Zenodotos.
[2]Or, 'Zeus of the far-borne voice.'

Ganymede his child, because they were the best of all horses beneath the daylight and the sun. That blood Anchises king of men stole of Laomedon, privily putting mares to them. Thereof a stock was born him in his palace, even six; four kept he himself and reared them at the stall, and the other twain gave he to Aineias deviser of rout.[1] Them could we seize, we should win us great renown.'

In such wise talked they one to the other, and anon those other twain came near, driving their fleet horses. First to him spake Lykaon's glorious son: 'O thou strong-souled and cunning, son of proud Tydeus, verily my swift dart vanquished thee not, the bitter arrow; so now will I make trial with my spear if I can hit thee.'

He spake and poised and hurled his far-shadowing spear, and smote upon Tydeides' shield; right through it sped the point of bronze and reached the breastplate. So over him shouted loudly Lykaon's glorious son: 'Thou art smitten on the belly right through, and I ween thou shalt not long hold up thine head; so thou givest me great renown.'

But mighty Diomedes unaffrighted answered him: 'Thou hast missed, and not hit; but ye twain I deem shall not cease till one or other shall have fallen and glutted with blood Ares the stubborn god of war.'

So spake he and hurled; and Athene guided the dart upon his nose beside the eye, and it pierced through his white teeth. So the hard bronze cut through his tongue at the root and the point issued forth by the base of the chin. He fell from his chariot, and his splendid armour gleaming clanged upon him, and the fleet-footed horses swerved aside; so there his soul and strength were unstrung.

Then Aineias leapt down with shield and long spear, fearing lest perchance the Achaians might take from him the corpse; and strode over him like a lion confident in his strength, and held before him his spear and the circle of his shield, eager to slay whoe'er should come to face him, crying his terrible cry. Then Tydeides grasped in his hand a stone – a mighty deed – such as two men, as men now are, would not avail to lift; yet he with ease wielded it all alone. Therewith he smote Aineias on the hip where the thigh turneth in the hip-joint, and this men call the 'cup-bone.' So he crushed his cup-bone, and brake both sinews withal, and the jagged stone tore apart the skin. Then the hero stayed fallen upon his knees and with stout hand leant upon the earth; and the darkness of night veiled his eyes. And now might Aineias king of men have perished, but that

[1]Reading μήστωρι.

Aphrodite daughter of Zeus was swift to mark, even his mother that conceived him by Anchises as he tended the kine. About her dear son wound she her white arms, and spread before his face a fold of her radiant vesture, to be a covering from the darts, lest any of the fleet-horsed Danaans might hurl the spear into his breast and take away his life.

So was she bearing her dear son away from battle; but the son of Kapaneus forgat not the behest that Diomedes of the loud war-cry had laid upon him; he refrained his own whole-hooved horses away from the tumult, binding the reins tight to the chariot-rim, and leapt on the sleek-coated horses of Aineias, and drave them from the Trojans to the well-greaved Achaians, and gave them to Deïpylos his dear comrade whom he esteemed above all that were his age-fellows, because he was like-minded with himself; and bade him drive them to the hollow ships Then did the hero mount his own chariot and take the shining reins and forthwith drive his strong-hooved horses in quest of Tydeides, eagerly. Now Tydeides had made onslaught with pitiless weapon on Kypris,[1] knowing how she was a coward goddess and none of those that have mastery in battle of the warriors – no Athene she nor Enyo waster of cities. Now when he had pursued her through the dense throng and come on her, then great-hearted Tydeus' son thrust with his keen spear, and leapt on her and wounded the skin of her weak hand; straight through the ambrosial raiment that the Graces themselves had woven her pierced the dart into the flesh, above the springing of the palm. Then flowed the goddess's immortal blood, such ichor as floweth in the blessed gods; for they eat no bread neither drink they gleaming wine, wherefore they are bloodless and are named immortals. And she with a great cry let fall her son: him Phoebus Apollo took into his arms and saved him in a dusky cloud, lest any of the fleet-horsed Danaans might hurl the spear into his breast and take away his life. But over her Diomedes of the loud war-cry shouted afar: 'Refrain thee, thou daughter of Zeus, from war and fighting. Is it not enough that thou beguilest feeble women? But if in battle thou wilt mingle, verily I deem that thou shalt shudder at the name of battle, if thou hear it even afar off.'

So spake he, and she departed in amaze and was sore troubled: and wind-footed Iris took her and led her from the throng tormented with her pain, and her fair skin was stained. There found she impetuous Ares sitting, on the battle's left; and his spear rested

[1] Aphrodite.

upon a cloud, and his fleet steeds. Then she fell on her knees and
with instant prayer besought of her dear brother his golden-
frontleted steeds: 'Dear brother, save me and give me thy steeds,
that I may win to Olympus, where is the habitation of the immortals. Sorely am I afflicted with a wound wherewith a mortal smote
me, even Tydeides, who now would fight even with father Zeus.'

So spake she, and Ares gave her his golden-frontleted steeds: and
she mounted on the chariot sore at heart. By her side mounted Iris,
and in her hands grasped the reins and lashed the horses to start
them; and they flew onward nothing loth. Thus soon they came to
the habitation of the gods, even steep Olympus. There wind-footed
fleet Iris loosed the horses from the chariot and stabled them, and
set ambrosial forage before them; but fair Aphrodite fell upon
Dione's knees that was her mother. She took her daughter in her
arms and stroked her with her hand, and spake and called upon her
name: 'Who now of the sons of heaven, dear child, hath entreated
thee thus wantonly, as though thou wert a wrong-doer in the face of
all?'

Then laughter-loving Aphrodite made answer to her: 'Tydeus'
son wounded me, high-hearted Diomedes, because I was saving
from the battle my dear son Aineias, who to me is dearest far of all
men. For no more is the fierce battle-cry for Trojans and Achaians,
but the Danaans now are fighting even the immortals.'

Then the fair goddess Dione answered her: 'Be of good heart, my
child, and endure for all thy pain; for many of us that inhabit the
mansions of Olympus have suffered through men, in bringing
grievous woes one upon another. So suffered Ares, when Otos and
stalwart Ephialtes, sons of Aloeus, bound him in a strong prison-
house; yea in a vessel of bronze lay he bound thirteen months. Then
might Ares insatiate of battle have perished, but that the stepmother of Aloeus' sons, fair Eëriboia, gave tidings to Hermes, and
he stole away Ares, already pining; for the grievous prison-house
was wearing him out. So suffered Hera when Amphitryon's stalwart
son smote her on the right breast with a three-barbed arrow, so that
pain unassuageable gat hold of her likewise. So suffered awful
Hades a swift arrow like the rest, when this same man, the son of
aegis-bearing Zeus, smote him in Pylos[1] amid the dead and gave
him over to anguish. And he went to the mansion of Zeus and to
high Olympus, grieved at heart, pierced through with anguish; for
the arrow was driven into his stout shoulder, and vexed his soul. But

[1]Or, 'at the gate of hell,' according to Aristarchos.

Paieon spread soothing drugs upon the wound and healed him; seeing that verily he was of no mortal substance. Headstrong man and violent of deed, that recked not of his evil doings, and with his archery vexed the gods that dwell in Olympus! So upon thee was this man sent by the bright-eyed goddess Athene; fond man – for the heart of Tydeus' son knoweth not this, that he of a surety is not long-lived that fighteth with immortals, nor ever do his children prattle upon his knees at his returning from war and terrible fray. Therefore now let Tydeides, though he be very mighty, beware lest one better than thou encounter him; and so Aigialeia, wise daughter of Adrestos, wake from sleep with lamentations all her household, bewailing her wedded lord, the best man of the Achaians, even she that is the brave wife of horse-taming Diomedes.'

So saying with both hands she wiped the ichor from the arm; her arm was comforted, and the grievous pangs assuaged. But Athene and Hera beheld, and with bitter words provoked Zeus the son of Kronos. Of them was the bright-eyed goddess Athene first to speak: 'Father Zeus, wilt thou indeed be wroth with me whate'er I say? Verily I ween that Kypris was urging some woman of Achaia to join her unto the Trojans whom she so marvellously loveth; and stroking such an one of the fair-robed women of Achaia, he tore upon the golden brooch her delicate hand.'

So spake she, and the father of gods and men smiled, and called unto him golden Aphrodite and said: 'Not unto thee, my child, are given the works of war; but follow thou after the loving tasks of wedlock, and to all these things shall fleet Ares and Athene look.'

Now while they thus spake in converse one with the other, Diomedes of the loud war-cry leapt upon Aineias, knowing full well that Apollo himself had spread his arms over him; yet reverenced he not even the great god, but still was eager to slay Aineias and strip from him his glorious armour. So thrice he leapt on him, fain to slay him, and thrice Apollo beat back his glittering shield. And when the fourth time he sprang at him like a god, then Apollo the Far-darter spake to him with terrible shout: 'Think, Tydeides, and shrink, nor desire to match thy spirit with gods; seeing there is no comparison of the race of immortal gods and of men that walk upon the earth.'

So said he, and Tydeides shrank a short space backwards, to avoid the wrath of Apollo the Far-darter. Then Apollo set Aineias away from the throng in holy Pergamos where his temple stood. There Leto and Archer Artemis healed him in the mighty sanctuary, and gave him glory; but Apollo of the silver bow made a wraith like unto

Aineias' self, and in such armour as his; and over the wraith Trojans and goodly Achaians each hewed the others' bucklers on their breasts, their round shields and fluttering targes.

Then to impetuous Ares said Phoebus Apollo: 'Ares, Ares, blood-stained bane of mortals, thou stormer of walls, wilt thou not follow after this man and withdraw him from the battle, this Tydeides, who now would fight even with father Zeus? First in close fight he wounded Kypris in her hand hard by the wrist, and then sprang he upon myself like unto a god.'

So saying he sate himself upon the height of Pergamos, and bale-ful Ares entered among the Trojan ranks and aroused them in the likeness of fleet Akamas, captain of the Thracians. On the heaven-nurtured sons of Priam he called saying: 'O ye sons of Priam, the heaven-nurtured king, how long will ye yet suffer your host to be slain of the Achaians?

Shall it be even until they fight about our well-builded gates? Low lieth the warrior whom we esteemed like unto goodly Hector, even Aineias son of Anchises great of heart. Go to now, let us save from the tumult our valiant comrade.'

So saying he aroused the spirit and soul of every man. Thereat Sarpedon sorely chode noble Hector: 'Hector, where now is the spirit gone that erst thou hadst? Thou saidst forsooth that without armies or allies thou wouldest hold the city, alone with thy sisters' husbands and thy brothers; but now can I not see any of these neither perceive them, but they are cowering like hounds about a lion; and we are fighting that are but allies among you. Yea I being an ally am come from very far; far off is Lykia upon eddying Xanthos, where I left my dear wife and infant son, and left my great wealth that each one cov-eteth that is in need. Yet for all that I urge on my Lykians, and myself am eager to fight my man, though here is naught of mine such as the Achaians might plunder or harry. But thou standest, nay thou dost not even urge all thine hosts to abide and guard their wives. Only beware lest, as though tangled in meshes of all-ensnaring flax, ye be made unto your foemen a prey and a spoil; and they will soon lay waste your well-peopled city. Thee it behoveth to give thought to all these things both by night and day, and to beseech the captains of thy far-famed allies to hold on unflinchingly; and so shalt thou put away their sore rebuking from thee.'

So spake Sarpedon, and his word stung Hector to the heart. Forthwith he leapt from his chariot in his armour to the earth, and brandishing two keen spears went everywhere through the host, urging them to fight, and roused the dread battle-cry. So they were rallied and stood to face the Achaians: and the Argives withstood them in close array and fled not. Even as a wind carrieth the chaff about the sacred threshing-floors when men are winnowing, what time golden-haired Demeter in rush of wind maketh division of grain and chaff, and so the chaff-heaps grow white – so now grew the Achaians white with falling dust which in their midst the horses' hooves beat up into the brazen heaven, as fight was joined again, and the charioteers wheeled round. Thus bare they forward the fury of their hands: and impetuous Ares drew round them a veil of night to aid the Trojans in the battle,[1] ranging everywhere; so fulfilled he the behest of Phoebus Apollo of the golden sword, who bade him rouse the Trojans' spirit when he beheld Pallas Athene departed; for she was helper to the Danaans. And Apollo himself sent forth Aineias from his rich sanctuary and put courage in the heart of him, shepherd of the hosts. So Aineias took his place amid his comrades, and they were glad to see him come among them alive and sound and full of valiant spirit. Yet they questioned him not at all, for all the toil forbade them that the god of the silver bow was stirring and Ares bane of men and Strife raging insatiably.

And on the other side the two Aiantes and Odysseus and Diomedes stirred the Danaans to fight; yet these of themselves feared neither the Trojans' violence nor assaults, but stood like mists that Kronos' son setteth in windless air on the mountain tops, at peace, while the might of the north wind sleepeth and of all the violent winds that blow with keen breath and scatter apart the shadowing clouds. Even so the Danaans withstood the Trojans steadfastly and fled not. And Atreides ranged through the throng exhorting instantly: 'My friends, quit you like men and take heart of courage, and shun dishonour in one another's eyes amid the stress of battle. Of men that shun dishonour more are saved than slain, but for them that flee is neither glory found nor any safety.'

So saying he darted swiftly with his javelin and smote a foremost warrior, even great-hearted Aineias' comrade Deïkoon son of Pergasos, whom the Trojans held in like honour with Priam's sons, because he was swift to do battle amid the foremost. Him lord Agamemnon smote with his dart upon the shield, and it stayed not the spear, but the point passed through, so that he drave it through the belt into his nethermost belly and he fell with a crash and his armour clanged upon him.

Then did Aineias slay two champions of the Danaans, even the

[1] Or, drew round the battle a veil of night to help the Trojans.

sons of Diokles, Krethon and Orsilochos, whose father dwelt in stablished Phere, a man full of substance, whose lineage was of the river Alpheios, that floweth in broad stream through the land of the Pylians; Alpheios begat Orsilochos to be king of many men, and Orsilochos begat great-hearted Diokles, and of Diokles were born twin sons, even Krethon and Orsilochos, well skilled in all the ways of war. Now when these were of full age, they bare the Argives company on their black ships to Ilios home of horses, to win recompense for Atreus' sons, Agamemnon and Menelaos; but now the issue of death shrouded them about. Like them, two lions on the mountain tops are nurtured by their dam in the deep forest thickets; and these harry the kine and goodly sheep and make havoc of the farmsteads of men, till in their turn they too are slain at men's hands with the keen bronze; in such wise were these twain vanquished at Aineias' hands and fell like tall pine-trees.

But Menelaos dear to Ares had pity of them in their fall, and strode through the forefront, harnessed in flashing bronze, brandishing his spear; and Ares stirred his courage, with intent that he might fall beneath Aineias' hand. But Antilochos, great-hearted Nestor's son, beheld him, and strode through the forefront; because he feared exceedingly for the shepherd of the host, lest aught befall him and disappoint them utterly of their labour. So those two were now holding forth their hands and sharp spears each against the other, eager to do battle; when Antilochos came and stood hard by the shepherd of the host. But Aineias faced them not, keen warrior though he was, when he beheld two men abiding side by side; so these haled away the corpses to the Achaians' host, and laid the hapless twain in their comrades' arms, and themselves turned back and fought on amid the foremost.

Then slew they Pylaimenes, peer of Ares, captain of the great-hearted Paphlagonians bearers of the shield. Him as he stood still Atreus' son, spear-famed Menelaos, pierced with his javelin, smiting upon the collar-bone; and Antilochos hurled at Mydon, his squire and charioteer, Atymnios' brave son, even as he was wheeling the whole-hooved horses, and with a stone smote his elbow in the midst; so the reins white with ivory fell from his hands to earth, even into the dust. Then Antilochos sprang on him and drave the sword into his temple, and he fell gasping from the well-wrought chariot headlong in the dust on crown and shoulders. A while he stood there, being lighted on deep sand, until his horses spurned him and cast him to earth, even in the dust; and them Antilochos lashed, and drave them to the Achaians' host.

But Hector marked them across the ranks, and sprang on them

with a shout, and the battalions of the Trojans followed him in their might: and Ares led them on and dread Enyo, she bringing ruthless turmoil of war, the while Ares wielded in his hands his monstrous spear, and ranged now before Hector's face, and now behind.

Then Diomedes of the loud war-cry shuddered to behold him; and even as a shiftless man crossing a great plain cometh on a swift-streaming river flowing on to the sea, and seeing it boil with foam springeth backwards, even so now Tydeides shrank back and spake to the host: 'Friends, how marvel we that noble Hector is a spearman and bold man of war! Yet ever is there beside him some god that wardeth off destruction; even as now Ares is there by him in likeness of a mortal man. But with faces towards the Trojans still give ground backwards, neither be desirous to fight amain with gods.'

So said he, and the Trojans came very close upon them. Then Hector slew two that knew well the battle joy, riding in one chariot, even Menesthes and Anchialos. And the great Telamonian Aias had pity of them in their fall, and came hard by and darted with his bright javelin, and smote Amphios son of Selagos, that dwelt in Paisos, a man rich in substance, rich in meadow land; but fate led him to bring succour to Priam and his sons. Him Telamonian Aias smote upon the belt, and in his nether belly the far-shadowing spear stuck and he fell with a crash. Then glorious Aias ran at him to strip him of his armour, and the Trojans rained on him keen javelins glittering, and his shield caught many thereof. But he set his heel upon the corpse and plucked forth the spear of bronze; only he could not strip from his shoulders all the fair armour therewith, being overwhelmed of spears. Moreover he feared the haughty Trojans' stout defence, they being many and brave that with their spears pressed on him, so that for all he was so great and valiant and proud they thrust him from them; and he was shaken and shrank back.

Thus toiled these in violent battle; and Tlepolemos son of Herakles, valiant and tall, was driven of forceful fate against godlike Sarpedon. Then when the twain were come nigh in onset on each other, even the son and grandson of Zeus the cloud- gatherer, then first to the other spake Tlepolemos: 'Sarpedon, counsellor of the Lykians, why must thou be skulking here, being a man unskilled in battle? Falsely do men say that thou art offspring of aegis-bearing Zeus, seeing thou art found lacking greatly beside those men that in days of old were born of Zeus. Ah, what an one do men say[1] was mighty Herakles, even my father the steadfast lion-heart, who erst

---

[1]Or, 'of other sort, men say,' if we read ἀλλοῖον for ἀλλ' οἷον.

came hither for Laomedon's mares with but six ships and a scantier host, yet sacked the city of Ilios and made her highways desolate. But thine is a base spirit, and thy folk are minishing. I ween that thou art in no wise come from Lykia to be a bulwark unto the Trojans, for all thy great strength, but that thou shalt be vanquished at my hand and pass the gates of Hades.'

Then Sarpedon captain of the Lykians answered him: 'Tlepolemos, he verily overthrew holy Ilios by the folly of the proud man Laomedon, that rewarded his good deed with harsh upbraiding, and paid him not the steeds wherefor he came from afar. And for thee I say that slaughter and black death shall come about here at my hands; vanquished by my spear thou shalt yield to me my glory, and thy life to Hades of the goodly steeds.'

So spake Sarpedon, and Tlepolemos lifted his ashen spear, and both their long javelins sped from their hands together. Sarpedon smote the midst of his neck, and the grievous point past right through, and the darkness of night fell on his eyes and shrouded him: and Tlepolemos with long spear smote the other's left thigh, and the point sped through furiously, grazing the bone; but his father yet warded off destruction.

So his goodly comrades bare away godlike Sarpedon from the battle, but the long spear dragging was heavy upon him, and no man marked it or took thought in their haste to draw the ashen spear out from his thigh that he might stand upright; such labour had they in tending him. And over against them the well-greaved Achaians bare Tlepolemos from the battle. And noble Odysseus of the patient soul marked it, and his heart was stirred within him. Then doubted he in mind and soul whether first to pursue the son of Zeus the loud thunderer, or take the lives of the common sort of the Lykians. But it was not destined to great-hearted Odysseus to slay with his keen blade the mighty son of Zeus; so Athene turned his fury upon the multitude of the Lykians. Then slew he Koiranos and Alastor and Chromios and Alkandros and Halios and Noëmon and Prytanis; and yet more Lykians had noble Odysseus slain but that great Hector of the glancing helm was swift to mark him, and strode through the forefront of battle, harnessed in flashing bronze, and brought terror to the Danaans; but Sarpedon the son of Zeus was glad at his coming, and spake to him a word of pain: 'O son of Priam, let me not now be left a prey unto the Danaans, but bring me succour; howbeit thereafter let my life depart from me in your city, seeing it might not be that I should return home to my dear native land, to make glad my dear wife and infant son.'

So said he, but Hector of the glancing helm spake no word to him, but hastened on, desirous with all speed to thrust back the Argives and take the lives of many. So his goodly comrades made godlike Sarpedon to sit beneath a fair oak-tree of aegis-bearing Zeus, and valiant Pelagon that was his dear comrade thrust forth from his thigh the ashen spear; and his spirit failed him and mist overspread his eyes. Then breathed he again, and the breath of the north wind blew round about him and brought him to life from the grievous swoon of his soul.

Now the Argives before the face of Ares and mail-clad Hector neither turned them round about toward their black ships, nor charged forward in battle, but still fell backward, when they heard of Ares amid the Trojans. And now who first was slaughtered, and who last, by Hector son of Priam and brazen Ares? Even godlike Teuthras, and thereafter Orestes the charioteer, and Trechos spearman of Aitolia, and Oinomaos and Helenos son of Oinops and Oresbios with gleaming taslets, who dwelt in Hyle and had great care of his substance, lying beside the Kephisian mere; and near him dwelt all the Boiotians, inhabiters of a full rich domain.

Now when the white-armed goddess Hera marked them making havoc of the Argives in the press of battle, anon she spake winged words to Athene: 'Out on it, thou daughter of aegis-bearing Zeus, unwearied maiden! Was it for naught we pledged our word to Menelaos, that he should not depart till he had laid waste well-walled Ilios, – if thus we let baleful Ares rage? Go to now, let us twain also take thought of impetuous valour.'

So said she, and the bright-eyed goddess Athene disregarded not. So Hera the goddess queen, daughter of great Kronos, went her way to harness the gold-frontleted steeds; and Hebe quickly put to the car the curved wheels of bronze, eight-spoked, upon their axle-tree of iron. Golden is their felloe, imperishable, and tires of bronze are fitted thereover, a marvel to look upon; and the naves are of silver, to turn about on either side. And the car is plaited tight with gold and silver thongs, and two rails run round about it. And the silver pole stood out therefrom; upon the end bound she the fair golden yoke, and set thereon the fair breaststraps of gold, and Hera led beneath the yoke the horses fleet of foot, and hungered for strife and the battle-cry. And Athene, daughter of aegis-bearing Zeus, cast down at her father's threshold her woven vesture many-coloured, that herself had wrought and her hands had fashioned, and put on her the tunic of Zeus the cloud-gatherer, and arrayed her in her armour for dolorous battle. About her shoulders cast she the tasselled aegis terrible, whereon is Panic as a crown all round about, and Strife is therein and Valour and horrible Onslaught withal, and therein is the dreadful monster's Gorgon head, dreadful and grim, portent of aegis-bearing Zeus. Upon her head set she the two-crested golden helm with fourfold plate, bedecked with men-at-arms of a hundred cities. Upon the flaming chariot set she her foot, and grasped her heavy spear, great and stout, wherewith she vanquisheth the ranks of men, even of heroes with whom she of the awful sire is wroth. Then Hera swiftly smote the horses with the lash; self-moving groaned upon their hinges the gates of heaven whereof the Hours are warders, to whom is committed great heaven and Olympus, whether to throw open the thick cloud or set it to. There through the gates guided they their horses patient of the lash. And they found the son of Kronos sitting apart from all the gods on the topmost peak of many-ridged Olympus. Then the white-armed goddess Hera stayed her horses and questioned the most high Zeus, the son of Kronos, and said: 'Father Zeus, hast thou no indignation with Ares for these violent deeds? How great and goodly a company of Achaians hath he destroyed recklessly and in unruly wise, unto my sorrow. But here in peace Kypris and Apollo of the silver bow take their pleasure, having set on this mad one that knoweth not any law. Father Zeus, wilt thou at all be wroth with me if I smite Ares and chase him from the battle in sorry plight?'

And Zeus the cloud-gatherer answered and said to her: 'Go to now, set upon him Athene driver of the spoil, who most is wont to bring sore pain upon him.'

So spake he, and the white-armed goddess Hera disregarded not, and lashed her horses; they nothing loth flew on between earth and starry heaven. As far as a man seeth with his eyes into the haze of distance as he sitteth on a place of outlook and gazeth over the wine-dark sea, so far leap the loudly neighing horses of the gods. Now when they came to Troy and the two flowing rivers, even to where Simoeis and Skamandros join their streams, there the white-armed goddess Hera stayed her horses and loosed them from the car and poured thick mist round about them, and Simoeis made ambrosia spring up for them to graze. So the goddesses went their way with step like unto turtle-doves, being fain to bring succour to the men of Argos. And when they were now come where the most and most valiant stood, thronging about mighty Diomedes tamer of horses, in the semblance of ravening lions or wild boars whose strength is nowise feeble, then stood the white-armed goddess Hera and shouted in the likeness of great-hearted Stentor with voice of bronze, whose cry was loud as the cry of fifty other men: 'Fie upon you, Argives, base things of shame, so brave in semblance! While yet noble Achilles entered continually into battle, then issued not the Trojans even from the Dardanian gate; for they had dread of his terrible spear. But now fight they far from the city at the hollow ships.'

So saying she aroused the spirit and soul of every man. And to Tydeides' side sprang the bright-eyed goddess Athene. That lord she found beside his horses and chariot, cooling the wound that Pandaros with his dart had pierced, for his sweat vexed it by reason of the broad baldrick of his round shield; therewith was he vexed and his arm grew weary, so he was lifting up the baldrick and wiping away the dusky blood. Then the goddess laid her hand on his horses' yoke, and said: 'Of a truth Tydeus begat a son little after his own likeness. Tydeus was short of stature, but a man of war; yea even when I would not have him fight nor make display – what time he came apart from the Achaians on an embassage to Thebes, to the midst of the multitude of the Kadmeians, I bade him feast in their halls at peace; but he, possessing his valiant soul as of old time, challenged the young men of the Kadmeians and in everything vanquished them [easily; so sure a helper was I unto him]. But for thee, beside thee stand I and guard thee and with all my heart bid thee fight the Trojans; yet either hath weariness of much striving entered into thy limbs, or disheartening terror hath taken hold of thee. If that be so, no offspring art thou of Tydeus, the wise son of Oineus.'

And stalwart Diomedes made answer to her and said: 'I know thee, goddess daughter of aegis-bearing Zeus: therefore with my whole heart will I tell thee my thought and hide it not. Neither hath disheartening terror taken hold upon me, nor any faintness, but I am still mindful of thy behest that thou didst lay upon me. Thou forbadest me to fight face to face with all the blessed gods, save only if Zeus' daughter Aphrodite should enter into battle, then to wound her with the keen bronze. Therefore do I now give ground myself and have bidden all the Argives likewise to gather here together; for I discern Ares lording it in the fray.'

Then the bright-eyed goddess Athene answered him: 'Diomedes son of Tydeus, thou joy of mine heart, fear thou, for that, neither Ares nor any other of the immortals; so great a helper am I to thee. Go to now, at Ares first guide thou thy whole-hooved horses, and smite him hand to hand, nor have any awe of impetuous Ares,

raving here, a curse incarnate, the renegade that of late in converse
with me and Hera pledged him to fight against the Trojans and give
succour to the Argives, but now consorteth with the Trojans and
hath forgotten these.'

So speaking, with her hand she drew back Sthenelos and thrust
him from the chariot to earth, and instantly leapt he down; so the
goddess mounted the car by noble Diomedes' side right eagerly.
The oaken axle creaked loud with its burden, bearing the dread
goddess and the man of might. Then Pallas Athene grasped the
whip and reins; forthwith against Ares first guided she the whole-
hooved horses. Now he was stripping huge Periphas, most valiant
far of the Aitolians, Ochesios' glorious son. Him was blood-stained
Ares stripping; and Athene donned the helm of Hades, that terrible
Ares might not behold her. Now when Ares scourge of mortals
beheld noble Diomedes, he left huge Periphas lying there, where at
the first he had slain him and taken away his life, and made straight
at Diomedes tamer of horses. Now when they were come nigh in
onset on one another, first Ares thrust over the yoke and horses'
reins with spear of bronze, eager to take away his life. But the
bright-eyed goddess Athene with her hand seized the spear and
thrust it up over[1] the car, to spend itself in vain. Next Diomedes of
the loud war cry attacked with spear of bronze; and Pallas Athene
drave it home against Ares' nethermost belly, where his taslets were
girt about him. There smote he him and wounded him, rending
through his fair skin, and plucked forth the spear again. Then
brazen Ares bellowed loud as nine thousand warriors or ten thousand cry in battle as they join in strife and fray. Thereat trembling
gat hold of Achaians and Trojans for fear, so mightily bellowed Ares
insatiate of battle.

Even as gloomy mist appeareth from the clouds when after heat a
stormy wind ariseth, even so to Tydeus' son Diomedes brazen Ares
appeared amid clouds, faring to wide heaven. Swiftly came he to the
gods' dwelling, steep Olympus, and sat beside Zeus son of Kronos
with grief at heart, and shewed the immortal blood flowing from
the wound, and piteously spake to him winged words: 'Father Zeus,
hast thou no indignation to behold these violent deeds? For ever
cruelly suffer we gods by one another's devices, in shewing men
grace. With thee are we all at variance, because thou didst beget
that reckless maiden and baleful, whose thought is ever of iniquitous deeds. For all the other gods that are in Olympus hearken to

[1]Reading ὑπὲρ with the best MS. for ὑπ' ἐκ.

thee, and we are subject every one; only her thou chastenest not, neither in deed nor word, but settest her on, because this pestilent one is thine own offspring. Now hath she urged on Tydeus' son, even overweening Diomedes, to rage furiously against the immortal gods. Kypris first he wounded in close fight, in the wrist of her hand, and then assailed he me, even me, with the might of a god. Howbeit my swift feet bare me away; else had I long endured anguish there amid the grisly heaps of dead, or else had lived strengthless from the smitings of the spear.'

Then Zeus the cloud-gatherer looked sternly at him and said: 'Nay, thou renegade, sit not by me and whine. Most hateful to me art thou of all gods that dwell in Olympus: thou ever lovest strife and wars and battles. Truly thy mother's spirit is intolerable, unyielding, even Hera's; her can I scarce rule with words. Therefore I deem that by her prompting thou art in this plight. Yet will I no longer endure to see thee in anguish; mine offspring art thou, and to me thy mother bare thee. But wert thou born of any other god unto this violence, long ere this hadst thou been lower than the sons of Heaven.'[1]

So spake he and bade Paieon heal him. And Paieon laid assuaging drugs upon the wound [and healed him; seeing he was verily of no mortal substance]. Even as fig juice maketh haste to thicken white milk, that is liquid but curdleth speedily as a man stirreth, even so swiftly healed he impetuous Ares. And Hebe bathed him, and clothed him in gracious raiment, and he sate him down by Zeus son of Kronos, glorying in his might.

Then fared the twain back to the mansion of great Zeus, even Hera of Argos and Alalkomenean Athene, having stayed Ares scourge of mortals from his man-slaying.

---

[1]The Titans, imprisoned in Tartaros. Others explain 'lower than the heavenly gods.' Zenodotos read ἐνέρτατος, 'lowest of the sons of heaven.'

BOOK VI

How Diomedes and Glaukos being about to fight, were known to each other, and parted in friendliness. And how Hector returning to the city bade farewell to Andromache his wife.

So WAS THE DREAD fray of Trojans and Achaians left to itself, and the battle swayed oft this way and that across the plain, as they aimed against each other their bronze-shod javelins, between Simoeis and the streams of Xanthos.

First Aias son of Telamon, bulwark of the Achaians, brake a battalion of the Trojans and brought his comrades salvation, smiting a warrior that was chiefest among the Thracians, Eussoros' son Akamas the goodly and great. Him first he smote upon his thick-crested helmet-ridge and drave into his forehead, so that the point of bronze pierced into the bone; and darkness shrouded his eyes.

Then Diomedes of the loud war-cry slew Axylos Teuthranos' son that dwelt in stablished Arisbe, a man of substance dear to his fellows; for his dwelling was by the roadside and he entertained all men. Howbeit of all these was there then not one to meet the foe before his face and save him from fell destruction; but Diomedes took the life of both of them, even of him and Kalesios his squire that now was the driver of his chariot; so passed both below the earth.

And Euryalos slew Dresos and Opheltios, and followed after Aisepos and Pedasos whom erst the fountain-nymph Abarbarea bare to noble Boukolion. Now Boukolion was son of proud Laomedon, his eldest born, begotten of a mother unwedded; and as he tended his flocks he had converse with the nymph in love, and she conceived and bare twin sons. And lo, the strength of these and their glorious limbs Mekisteus' son unstrung, and stripped the armour from their shoulders. And stubborn Polypoites slew Astyalos, and Odysseus with spear of bronze laid low Pidytes of Perkote, and so did Teukros to goodly Aretaon. Then was Ableros killed by the glistening spear of Antilochos, Nestor's son, and Elatos by Agamemnon king of men; beside the banks of fair-flowing Satnioeis dwelt he in steep Pedasos. And Leïtos the warrior caught Phylakos, as he fled; and Eurypylos slew Melanthios.

Now did Menelaos of the loud war-cry take Adrestos alive; for his horses took flight across the plain, and stumbling in a tamarisk bough brake the curved car at the pole's foot; so they themselves fared towards the city where the rest were fleeing in rout, and their lord rolled from out the car beside the wheel, prone in the dust upon his face. Then came Atreus' son Menelaos to his side bearing his far-shadowing spear. Thereat Adrestos caught him by his knees and besought him: 'Take me captive, thou son of Atreus, and accept a worthy ransom; many a treasure is stored up in my father's rich palace, bronze and gold and smithied iron; thereof would my father yield thee ransom beyond the telling, if he but heard that I am alive at the ships of the Achaians.'

So spake he, and moved the spirit in his breast. And now had he forthwith given him to his squire to lead him to the Achaians' fleet ships, but that Agamemnon came running to meet him, and spake a word of chiding to him: 'Good Menelaos, why art thou so careful of the foemen? Have then such good deeds been wrought thee in thy house by Trojans? Of them let not one escape sheer destruction at our hands, not even the man-child that the mother beareth in her womb; let not even him escape, but all perish together out of Ilios, uncared for and unknown.'

So spake the hero and turned his brother's mind with righteous persuasion; so with his hand he thrust the hero Adrestos from him, and lord Agamemnon smote him in the flank, and he was overthrown, and Atreus' son set his heel upon his chest and plucked forth his ashen spear.

Then Nestor called to the Argives with far-reaching shout: 'My friends, Danaan warriors, men of Ares' company, let no man now take thought of spoils to tarry behind, that he may bring the greatest burden to the ships; but let us slay the foemen. Thereafter shall ye at your ease also strip of their spoil the dead corpses about the plain.'

So spake he and stirred the spirit and soul of every man. Now had the Trojans been chased again by the Achaians, dear to Ares, up into Ilios, in their weakness overcome, but that Priam's son Helenos, far best of augurs, stood by Aineias' side and Hector's, and spake to them: 'Aineias and Hector, seeing that on you lieth the task of war in chief of Trojans and Lykians, because for every issue ye are foremost both for fight and counsel, stand ye your ground, and range the host everywhither to rally them before the gates, ere yet they fall fleeing in their women's arms, and be made a rejoicing to the foe. Then when ye have aroused all our battalions we will abide here and fight the Danaans, though in sore weariness; for necessity presseth us hard: but thou, Hector, go into the city, and speak there to thy mother and mine; let her gather the aged wives to bright-eyed Athene's temple in the upper city, and with her key open the doors of the holy house; and let her lay the robe, that seemeth to her the most gracious and greatest in her hall and far dearest unto herself, upon the knees of beauteous-haired Athene; and vow to her to sacrifice in her temple twelve sleek kine, that have not felt the goad, if she will have mercy on the city and the Trojans' wives and little children. So may she perchance hold back Tydeus' son from holy Ilios, the furious spearman, the mighty deviser of rout, whom in good sooth I deem to have proved himself mightiest of the Achaians. Never in this wise feared we Achilles, prince of men, who they say is born of a goddess; nay, but he that we see is beyond measure furious; none can match him for might.'

So spake he, and Hector disregarded not his brother's word, but leapt forthwith from his chariot in his armour to earth, and brandishing two sharp spears passed every where through the host, rousing them to battle, and stirred the dread war-cry. So they were rallied and stood to face the Achaians, and the Argives gave ground and ceased from slaughter, and deemed that some immortal had descended from starry heaven to bring the Trojans succour, in such wise rallied they. Then Hector called to the Trojans with far-reaching shout: 'O high-souled Trojans and ye far-famed allies, quit you like men, my friends, and take thought of impetuous courage, while I depart to Ilios and bid the elders of the council and our wives pray to the gods and vow them hecatombs.'

So saying Hector of the glancing helm departed, and the black hide beat on either side against his ankles and his neck, even the rim that ran uttermost about his bossed shield.

Now Glaukos son of Hippolochos and Tydeus' son met in the mid-space of the foes, eager to do battle. Thus when the twain were come nigh in onset on each other, to him first spake Diomedes of the loud war-cry: 'Who art thou, noble sir, of mortal men? For never have I beheld thee in glorious battle ere this, yet now hast thou far outstripped all men in thy hardihood, seeing thou abidest my far-shadowing spear. Luckless are the fathers whose children face my might. But if thou art some immortal come down from heaven, then will not I fight with heavenly gods. Nay moreover even Dryas' son mighty Lykurgos was not for long when he strove with heavenly gods, he that erst chased through the goodly land of Nysa the nursing-mothers of frenzied Dionysos; and they all cast

their wands upon the ground, smitten with murderous Lykurgos'
ox-goad. Then Dionysos fled and plunged beneath the salt sea-
wave, and Thetis took him to her bosom, affrighted, for a mighty
trembling had seized him at his foe's rebuke. But with Lykurgos the
gods that live at ease were wroth, and Kronos' son made him blind,
and he was not for long, because he was hated of all the immortal
gods. So would neither I be fain to fight the blessed gods. But if
thou art of men that eat the fruit of the field, come nigh, that anon
thou mayest enter the toils of destruction.'

Then Hippolochos' glorious son made answer to him: 'Great-
hearted Tydeides, why enquirest thou of my generation? Even as
are the generations of leaves such are those likewise of men; the
leaves that be the wind scattereth on the earth, and the forest bud-
deth and putteth forth more again, when the season of spring is at
hand; so of the generations of men one putteth forth and another
ceaseth. Yet if thou wilt, have thine answer, that thou mayest well
know our lineage, whereof many men have knowledge. There is a
city Ephyre in the heart of Argos, pasture land of horses, and there
dwelt Sisyphos that was craftiest of men, Sisyphos son of Aiolos;
and he begat a son, even Glaukos, and Glaukos begat noble
Bellerophon. To him the gods granted beauty and lovely manhood;
but Proitos in his heart devised ill for him, and being mightier far
drave him from the land of the Argives, whom Zeus had made subject to his sceptre[1] Now Proitos' wife, goodly Anteia, lusted after
him, to have converse in secret love, but no whit prevailed she, for
the uprightness of his heart, on wise Bellerophon. Then spake she
lyingly to king Proitos: 'Die, Proitos, or else slay Bellerophon, that
would have converse in love with me against my will.' So spake she,
and anger gat hold upon the king at that he heard. To slay him he
forbare, for his soul had shame of that; but he sent him to Lykia,
and gave him tokens of woe, graving in a folded tablet many deadly
things, and bade him shew these to Anteia's father, that he might be
slain. So fared he to Lykia by the blameless convoy of the gods.
Now when he came to Lykia and the stream of Xanthos, then did
the king of wide Lykia honour him with all his heart; nine days he
entertained him and killed nine oxen. And when on the tenth day
rosy-fingered dawn appeared, then he questioned him and asked to
see what token he bare from his son-in-law, even Proitos. Now
when he had received of him Proitos' evil token, first he bade him
slay Chimaira the unconquerable. Of divine birth was she and not

[1]Or, 'for Zeus had brought him [Bellerophon] under his sceptre's sway.'

of men, in front a lion, and behind a serpent, and in the midst a goat; and she breathed dread fierceness of blazing fire. And her he slew, obedient to the signs of heaven. Next fought he with the famed Solymi; this, said he, was the mightiest battle of warriors wherein he entered. And thirdly he slew the Amazons, women peers of men. And as he turned back therefrom, the king devised another cunning wile; he picked from wide Lykia the bravest men, and set an ambush. But these returned nowise home again; for noble Bellerophon slew them all. So when the king now knew that he was the brave offspring of a god, he kept him there, and plighted him his daughter, and gave him the half of all the honour of his kingdom; moreover the Lykians meted him a domain preeminent above all, fair with vineyards and tilth to possess it.[1] And his wife bare wise Bellerophon three children, Isandros and Hippolochos and Laodameia. With Laodameia lay Zeus the lord of counsel, and she bare godlike Sarpedon, the warrior with arms of bronze. But when even Bellerophon came to be hated of all the gods, then wandered he alone in the Aleian plain, devouring his own soul, and avoiding the paths of men; and Isandros his son was slain by Ares insatiate of battle, as he fought against the famed Solymi, and his daughter was slain in wrath of gold-gleaming[2] Artemis. But Hippolochos begat me, and of him do I declare me to be sprung; he sent me to Troy and bade me very instantly to be ever the best and to excel all other men, nor put to shame the lineage of my fathers that were of noblest blood in Ephyre and in wide Lykia. This is the lineage and blood whereof I avow myself to be.'

So said he, and Diomedes of the loud war-cry was glad. He planted his spear in the bounteous earth and with soft words spake to the shepherd of the host: 'Surely then thou art to me a guest-friend of old times through my father: for goodly Oineus of yore entertained noble Bellerophon in his halls and kept him twenty days. Moreover they gave each the other goodly gifts of friendship; Oineus gave a belt bright with purple, and Bellerophon a gold twy-handled cup, the which when I came I left in my palace. But of Tydeus I remember naught, seeing I was yet little when he left me, what time the Achaian host perished at Thebes. Therefore now am I to thee a dear guest-friend in midmost Argos, and thou in Lykia, whene'er I fare to your land. So let us shun each other's spears, even amid the throng; Trojans are there in multitudes and famous allies

[1] Or, if we read πυροφόροιο, 'tilth of wheat-land.'
[2] Or, 'Artemis of the golden reins.'

for me to slay, whoe'er it be that God vouchsafeth me and my feet overtake; and for thee are there Achaians in multitude, to slay whome'er thou canst. But let us make exchange of arms between us, that these also may know how we avow ourselves to be guest-friends by lineage.'

So spake the twain, and leaping from their cars clasped each the other by his hand, and pledged their faith. But now Zeus son of Kronos took from Glaukos his wits, in that he made exchange with Diomedes Tydeus' son of golden armour for bronze, the price of five score oxen for the price of nine.

Now when Hector came to the Skaian gates and to the oak-tree, there came running round about him the Trojans' wives and daughters, enquiring of sons and brethren and friends and husbands. But he bade them thereat all in turn pray to the gods; but sorrow hung over many.

But when he came to Priam's beautiful palace, adorned with polished colonnades – and in it were fifty chambers of polished stone, builded hard by one another, wherein Priam's sons slept beside their wedded wives; and for his daughters over against them on the other side within the courtyard were twelve roofed chambers of polished stone builded hard by one another, wherein slept Priam's sons-in-law beside their chaste wives – then came there to meet him his bountiful mother, leading with her Laodike, fairest of her daughters to look on; and she clasped her hand in his, and spake, and called upon his name: 'My son, why hast thou left violent battle to come hither? Surely the sons of the Achaians – name of evil! – press thee hard in fight about thy city, and so thy spirit hath brought thee hither, to come and stretch forth thy hands to Zeus from the citadel. But tarry till I bring thee honey-sweet wine, that thou mayest pour libation to Zeus and all the immortals first, and then shalt thou thyself also be refreshed if thou wilt drink. When a man is awearied wine greatly maketh his strength to wax, even as thou art awearied in fighting for thy fellows.'

Then great Hector of the glancing helm answered her: 'Bring me no honey-hearted wine, my lady mother, lest thou cripple me of my courage and I be forgetful of my might[1] Moreover I have awe to make libation of gleaming wine to Zeus with hands unwashen; nor can it be in any wise that one should pray to the son of Kronos, god of the storm-cloud, all defiled with blood and filth. But go thou to

---

[1] Omitting δ' after μένεος, with the best MSS, and probably Aristarchos. So also Plato, Crat. 415 A.

the temple of Athene, driver of the spoil, with offerings, and gather the aged wives together; and the robe that seemeth to thee the most gracious and greatest in thy palace, and dearest unto thyself, that lay thou upon the knees of beauteous-haired Athene, and vow to her to sacrifice in her temple twelve sleek kine, that have not felt the goad, if she will have mercy on the city and the Trojans' wives and little children. So may she perchance hold back Tydeus' son from holy Ilios, the furious spearman, the mighty deviser of rout. So go thou to the temple of Athene, driver of the spoil; and I will go after Paris, to summon him, if perchance he will hearken to my voice. Would that the earth forth-with might swallow him up! The Olympian fostered him to be a sore bane to the Trojans and to great-hearted Priam, and to Priam's sons. If I but saw him going down to the gates of death, then might I deem that my heart had forgotten its sorrow.'[1]

So said he, and she went unto the hall, and called to her handmaidens, and they gathered the aged wives throughout the city. Then she herself went down to her fragrant chamber where were her embroidered robes, the work of Sidonian women, whom godlike Alexandros himself brought from Sidon, when he sailed over the wide sea, that journey wherein he brought home high-born Helen. Of these Hekabe took one to bear for an offering to Athene, the one that was fairest for adornment and greatest, and shone like a star, and lay nethermost of all. Then went she her way and the multitude of aged wives hasted after her.

Now when they came to the temple of Athene in the citadel, faircheeked Theano opened them the doors, even Kisseus' daughter, wife of horse-taming Antenor; for her the Trojans had made priestess of Athene. Then lifted they all their hands to Athene with lamentation: and fair-cheeked Theano took the robe and laid it on the knees of beauteous-haired Athene, and lifted up her voice and prayed to the daughter of great Zeus: 'Lady Athene, saviour of the city fair among goddesses, break now Diomedes' spear, and grant moreover that himself may fall prone before the Skaian gates; that we may sacrifice thee now forthwith in thy temple twelve sleek kine, that have not felt the goad, if thou wilt have mercy on the city and the Trojans' wives and little children.' So spake she praying, but Pallas Athene denied the prayer.

So were these praying to the daughter of great Zeus; and Hector was come to Alexandros' fair palace, that himself had builded with

[1] Reading with Zenodotos φίλον ἦτορ for φρέν' ἀτέρπου.

them that were most excellent carpenters then in deep-soiled Troy-land; these made him his chamber and hall and courtyard hard by to Priam and Hector, in the upper city. There entered in Hector dear to Zeus, and his hand bare his spear, eleven cubits long: before his face glittered the bronze spear-point, and a ring of gold ran round about it. And he found Paris in his chamber busied with his beauteous arms, his shield and breastplate, and handling his curved bow; and Helen of Argos sate among her serving-women and appointed brave handiwork for her handmaidens. Then when Hector saw him he rebuked him with scornful words: 'Good sir, thou dost not well to cherish this rancour in thy heart. The folk are perishing about the city and high wall in battle, and for thy sake the battle-cry is kindled and war around this city; yea thyself wouldest thou fall out with another, didst thou see him shrinking from hateful war. Up then, lest the city soon be scorched with burning fire.'

And godlike Alexandros answered him: 'Hector, since in measure thou chidest me and not beyond measure, therefore will I tell thee; lay thou it to thine heart and hearken to me. Not by reason so much of the Trojans, for wrath and indignation, sate I me in my chamber, but fain would I yield me to my sorrow. Even now my wife hath persuaded me with soft words, and urged me into battle; and I moreover, even I, deem that it will be better so; for victory shifteth from man to man. Go to then, tarry awhile, let me put on my armour of war; or else fare thou forth, and I will follow; and I think to overtake thee.'

So said he, but Hector of the glancing helm answered him not a word. But Helen spake to him with gentle words: 'My brother, even mine that am a dog, mischievous and abominable, would that on the day when my mother bare me at the first, an evil storm-wind had caught me away to a mountain or a billow of the loud-sounding sea, where the billow might have swept me away before all these things came to pass. Howbeit, seeing the gods devised all these ills in this wise, would that then I had been mated with a better man, that felt dishonour and the multitude of men's reproachings. But as for him, neither hath he now sound heart, nor ever will have; thereof deem I moreover that he will reap the fruit. But now come, enter in and sit thee here upon this bench, my brother, since thy heart chiefly trouble hath encompassed, for the sake of me, that am a dog, and for Alexandros' sin; on whom Zeus bringeth evil doom, that even in days to come we may be a song in the ears of men that shall be hereafter.'

Then great Hector of the glancing helm answered her: 'Bid me not sit, Helen, of thy love; thou wilt not persuade me. Already my heart is set to succour the men of Troy, that have great desire for me that am not with them. But rouse thou this fellow, yea let himself make speed, to overtake me yet within the city. For I shall go into mine house to behold my housefolk and my dear wife, and infant boy; for I know not if I shall return home to them again, or if the gods will now overthrow me at the hands of the Achaians.'

So spake Hector of the glancing helm and departed; and anon he came to his well stablished house. Put he found not white-armed Andromache in the halls; she with her boy and fair-robed handmaiden had taken her stand upon the tower, weeping and wailing. And when Hector found not his noble wife within, he came and stood upon the threshold, and spake amid the serving women: 'Come tell me now true, my serving women. Whither went white armed Andromache forth from the hall? Hath she gone out to my sisters or unto my brothers' fair-robed wives, or to Athene's temple, where all the fair-tressed Trojan women propitiate the awful goddess?'

Then a busy housedame spake in answer to him: 'Hector, seeing thou straitly chargest us tell thee true, neither hath she gone out to any of thy sisters or thy brothers' fair-robed wives, neither to Athene's temple, where all the fair-tressed Trojan women are propitiating the awful goddess; but she went to the great tower of Ilios, because she heard the Trojans were hard pressed, and great victory was for the Achaians. So hath she come in haste to the wall, like unto one frenzied; and the nurse with her beareth the child.'

So spake the housedame, and Hector hastened from his house back by the same way down the well-builded streets. When he had passed through the great city and was come to the Skaian gates, whereby he was minded to issue upon the plain, then came his dear-won[1] wife, running to meet him, even Andromache daughter of great-hearted Eëtion, Eëtion that dwelt beneath wooded Plakos, in Thebe under Plakos, and was king of the men of Kilikia; for his daughter was wife to bronze-harnessed Hector. So she met him now, and with her went the handmaid bearing in her bosom the tender boy, the little child, Hector's loved son, like unto a beautiful star. Him Hector called Skamandrios, but all the folk Astyanax; for only Hector guarded Ilios.[2] So now he smiled and gazed at his boy silently, and Andromache stood by his side weeping, and clasped

[1] Or, 'bounteous.'
[2] Astyanax = 'City King.'

her hand in his, and spake and called upon his name. 'Dear my lord, this thy hardihood will undo thee, neither hast thou any pity for thine infant boy, nor for me forlorn that soon shall be thy widow; for soon will the Achaians all set upon thee and slay thee. But it were better for me to go down to the grave if I lose thee; for never more will any comfort be mine, when once thou, even thou, hast met thy fate, but only sorrow. Moreover I have no father nor lady mother: my father was slain of goodly Achilles, for he wasted the populous city of the Kilikians, even high-gated Thebe, and slew Eëtion; yet he despoiled him not, for his soul had shame of that, but he burnt him in his inlaid armour and raised a barrow over him; and all about were elm-trees planted by the mountain nymphs, daughters of aegis-bearing Zeus. And the seven brothers that were mine within our halls, all these on the selfsame day went within the house of Hades; for fleet-footed goodly Achilles slew them all amid their kine of trailing gait and white-fleeced sheep. And my mother, that was queen beneath wooded Plakos, her brought he hither with the other spoils, but afterward took a ransom untold to set her free; but in her father's halls was she smitten by the Archer Artemis. Nay, Hector, thou art to me father and lady mother, yea and brother, even as thou art my goodly husband. Come now, have pity and abide here upon the tower, lest thou make thy child an orphan and thy wife a widow. And stay thy folk beside the fig-tree, where best the city may be scaled and the wall is assailable. Thrice came thither the most valiant that are with the two Aiantes and famed Idomeneus and the sons of Atreus and Tydeus' valiant son, and essayed to enter; whether one skilled in soothsaying revealed it to them, or whether their own spirit urgeth and biddeth them on.'

Then great Hector of the glancing helm answered her: 'Surely I take thought for all these things, my wife; but I have very sore shame of the Trojans and Trojan dames with trailing robes, if like a coward I shrink away from battle. Moreover mine own soul forbiddeth me, seeing I have learnt ever to be valiant and fight in the forefront of the Trojans, winning my father's great glory and mine own. Yea of a surety I know this in heart and soul; the day shall come for holy Ilios to be laid low, and Priam and the folk of Priam of the good ashen spear. Yet doth the anguish of the Trojans hereafter not so much trouble me, neither Hekabe's own, neither king Priam's, neither my brethren's, the many and brave that shall fall in the dust before their foemen, as doth thine anguish in the day when some mail-clad Achaian shall lead thee weeping and rob thee of the light of freedom. So shalt thou abide in Argos and ply the loom at another woman's bidding, and bear water from fount Messeis or Hypereia, being grievously entreated, and sore constraint shall be laid upon thee. And then shall one say that beholdeth thee weep: "This is the wife of Hector, that was foremost in battle of the horse-taming Trojans when men fought about Ilios." Thus shall one say hereafter, and fresh grief will be thine for lack of such an husband as thou hadst to ward off the day of thraldom. But me in death may the heaped-up earth be covering, ere I hear thy crying and thy carrying into captivity.'

So spake glorious Hector, and stretched out his arm to his boy. But the child shrunk crying to the bosom of his fair-girdled nurse, dismayed at his dear father's aspect, and in dread at the bronze and horse-hair crest that he beheld nodding fiercely from the helmet's top. Then his dear father laughed aloud, and his lady mother; forthwith glorious Hector took the helmet from his head, and laid it, all gleaming, upon the earth; then kissed he his dear son and dandled him in his arms, and spake in prayer to Zeus and all the gods, 'O Zeus and all ye gods, vouchsafe ye that this my son may likewise prove even as I, pre-eminent amid the Trojans, and as valiant in might, and be a great king of Ilios. Then may men say of him, "Far greater is he than his father" as he returneth home from battle; and may he bring with him blood-stained spoils from the foeman he hath slain, and may his mother's heart be glad.'

So spake he, and laid his son in his dear wife's arms; and she took him to her fragrant bosom, smiling tearfully. And her husband had pity to see her, and caressed her with his hand, and spake and called upon her name: 'Dear one, I pray thee be not of oversorrowful heart; no man against my fate shall hurl me to Hades; only destiny, I ween, no man hath escaped, be he coward or be he valiant, when once he hath been born. But go thou to thine house and see to thine own tasks, the loom and distaff, and bid thine handmaidens ply their work; but for war shall men provide and I in chief of all men that dwell in Ilios.'

So spake glorious Hector, and took up his horse-hair crested helmet; and his dear wife departed to her home oft looking back, and letting fall big tears. Anon she came to the well-stablished house of man-slaying Hector, and found therein her many hand-maidens, and stirred lamentation in them all. So bewailed they Hector, while yet he lived, within his house: for they deemed that he would no more come back to them from battle, nor escape the fury of the hands of the Achaians.

Neither lingered Paris long in his lofty house, but clothed on him his brave armour, bedight with bronze, and hasted through the city, trusting to his nimble feet. Even as when a stalled horse, full-fed at the manger, breaketh his tether and speedeth at the gallop across the plain, being wont to bathe him in the fair-flowing stream, exultingly; and holdeth his head on high, and his mane floateth about his shoulders, and he trusteth in his glory, and nimbly his limbs bear him to the haunts and pasturage of mares; even so Priam's son Paris, glittering in his armour like the shining sun, strode down from high Pergamos laughingly, and his swift feet bare him. Forthwith he overtook his brother noble Hector, even as he was on the point to turn him away from the spot where he had dallied with his wife. To him first spake godlike Alexandros: 'Sir, in good sooth I have delayed thee in thine haste by my tarrying, and came not rightly as thou badest me.'

And Hector of the glancing helm answered him and said: 'Good brother, no man that is rightminded could make light of thy doings in fight, seeing thou art strong: but thou art wilfully remiss and hast no care; and for this my heart is grieved within me, that I hear shameful words concerning thee in the Trojans' mouths, who for thy sake endure much toil. But let us be going; all this will we make good hereafter, if Zeus ever vouchsafe us to set before the heavenly gods that are for everlasting the cup of deliverance in our halls, when we have chased out of Troy-land the well-greaved Achaians.'

BOOK VII

Of the single combat between Aias and Hector, and of the burying of the dead, and the building of a wall about the Achaian ships.

SO SPAKE GLORIOUS HECTOR and issued from the gates, and with him went his brother Alexandros; and both were eager of soul for fight and battle. Even as God giveth to longing seamen fair wind when they have grown weary of beating the main with polished oars, and their limbs are fordone with toil, even so appeared these to the longing Trojans.

Then the one of them slew king Areïthoös' son, Menesthios dwelling in Arne, whom Areïthoös the Mace-man[1] and ox-eyed Phylomedusa begat; and the other, even Hector, with his sharp spear smote Eïoneus' neck beneath his bronze helmet-rim, and unstrung his limbs. And Glaukos son of Hippolochos, captain of the men of Lykia, cast his spear at Iphinoos through the press of battle, even at the son of Dexios, as he sprang up behind his fleet mares, and smote his shoulder; so fell he from his chariot to earth and his limbs were unstrung.

Now when the goddess bright-eyed Athene marked them making havoc of the Argives in the press of battle, she darted down from the crests of Olympus to holy Ilios. But Apollo rose to meet her, for he beheld her from Pergamos, and would have victory for the Trojans. So the twain met each the other by the oak-tree. To her spake first king Apollo son of Zeus: 'Why now art thou come thus eagerly from Olympus, thou daughter of great Zeus, and why hath thy high heart sent thee? Surely it is to give the Danaans unequal victory in battle! seeing thou hast no mercy on the Trojans, that perish. But if thou wouldest hearken to me – and it were far better so – let us now stay battle and warring for the day; hereafter shall they fight again, till they reach the goal of Ilios, since thus it seemeth good to your hearts, goddesses immortal, to lay waste this city.'

And the goddess bright-eyed Athene made answer to him: 'So be it, Far-darter; in this mind I likewise came from Olympus to the midst of Trojans and Achaians. But come, how thinkest thou to stay the battle of the warriors?'

[1]For this surname see line 138.

And king Apollo, son of Zeus, made answer to her: 'Let us arouse the stalwart spirit of horse-taming Hector, if so be he will challenge some one of the Danaans in single fight man to man to meet him in deadly combat. So shall the bronze-greaved Achaians be jealous and stir up one to fight singly with goodly Hector.'

So spake he and the bright-eyed goddess Athene disregarded not. Now Helenos Priam's dear son understood in spirit their resolve that the gods in counsel had approved; and he went to Hector and stood beside him, and spake a word to him: 'Hector son of Priam, peer of Zeus in counsel, wouldest thou now hearken at all to me? for I am thy brother. Make the other Trojans sit, and all the Achaians, and thyself challenge him that is best of the Achaians to meet thee man to man in deadly combat. It is not yet thy destiny to die and meet thy doom; for thus heard I the voice of the gods that are from everlasting.'

So said he, and Hector rejoiced greatly to hear his saying, and went into the midst and refrained the battalions of the Trojans with his spear grasped by the middle, and they all sate them down: and Agamemnon made the well-greaved Achaians sit. And Athene withal and Apollo of the silver bow, in the likeness of vulture birds, sate them upon a tall oak holy to aegis-bearing father Zeus, rejoicing in their warriors; and the ranks of all of them sate close together, bristling with shields and plumes and spears. Even as there spreadeth across the main the ripple of the west wind newly risen, and the sea grows black beneath it, so sate the ranks of Achaians and Trojans upon the plain. And Hector spake between both hosts: 'Hearken to me, Trojans and well-greaved Achaians, that I may speak what my mind within my breast biddeth me. Our oaths of truce Kronos' son, enthroned on high, accomplished not; but evil is his intent and ordinance for both our hosts, until either ye take fair-towered Troy or yourselves be vanquished beside your seafaring ships. But in the midst of you are the chiefest of all the Achaians; therefore now let the man whose heart biddeth him fight with me come hither from among you all to be your champion against goodly Hector. And this declare I, and be Zeus our witness thereto; if that man slay me with the long edged sword, let him spoil me of my armour and bear it to the hollow ships, but give back my body to my home, that Trojans and Trojans' wives may give me my due of burning in my death. But if I slay him and Apollo vouchsafe me glory, I will spoil him of his armour and bear it to holy Ilios and hang it upon the temple of far-darting Apollo, but his corpse will I render back to the well-decked ships, that the flowing-haired Achaians may entomb him, and build him a barrow beside wide Hellespont. So shall one say even of men that be late born, as he saileth in his benched ship over the wine-dark sea: "This is the barrow of a man that died in days of old a champion whom glorious Hector slew." So shall a man say hereafter, and this my glory shall never die.'

So spake he and they all were silent and held their peace; to deny him they were ashamed, and feared to meet him. But at the last stood up Menelaos and spake amid them and chiding upbraided them, and groaned deep at heart: 'Ah me, vain threateners, ye women of Achaia and no more men, surely all this shall be a shame, evil of evil, if no one of the Danaans now goeth to meet Hector. Nay, turn ye all to earth and water, sitting there each man disheartened, helplessly inglorious; against him will I myself array me; and from on high the threads of victory are guided of the immortal gods.'

So spake he and donned his fair armour. And now, O Menelaos, had the end of life appeared for thee at Hector's hands, seeing he was stronger far, but that the princes of the Achaians started up and caught thee. And Atreus' son himself, wide-ruling Agamemnon, took him by his right hand and spake a word and called upon his name: 'Thou doest madly, Menelaos fosterling of Zeus; yet is it no time for this thy madness. Draw back, though it be with pain, nor think for contention's sake to fight with one better than thou, with Hector Priam's son, whom others beside thee abhor. Yea, this man even Achilles dreadeth to meet in battle, wherein is the warrior's glory; and Achilles is better far than thou. Go therefore now and sit amid the company of thy fellows; against him shall the Achaians put forth another champion. Fearless though he be and insatiate of turmoil, I ween that he shall be fain to rest his knees, if he escape from the fury of war and terrible fray.'

So spake the hero and persuaded his brother's heart with just counsel; and he obeyed. So his squires thereat with gladness took his armour from his shoulders; and Nestor stood up and spake amid the Argives: 'Fie upon it, verily sore lamentation cometh on the land of Achaia. Verily old Peleus driver of chariots would groan sore, that goodly counsellor of the Myrmidons and orator, who erst questioned me in his house, and rejoiced greatly, inquiring of the lineage and birth of all the Argives. If he heard now of those that all were cowering before Hector, then would he lift his hands to the immortals, instantly praying that his soul might depart from his limbs down to the house of Hades. Ah, would to father Zeus and Athene and Apollo I were young as when beside swift-flowing Keladon the Pylians gathered together to battle and the Arkadians that bear the spear, beneath the walls of Pheia, about the streams of

Iardanos. Then stood up for their champion Ereuthalion, a man the peer of gods, bearing upon his shoulders the armour of king Areïthoös, goodly Areïthoös that by men and fair-girdled women was surnamed the Mace-man, because he fought not with bow and long spear, but with an iron mace clave the battalions. Him Lykurgos slew by guile, and not by strength, in a narrow way, where his mace of iron saved him not from destruction: ere that, Lykurgos came on him unawares and pierced him through the midst with his dart, and he was hurled backward upon the earth. Then Lykurgos despoiled him of his arms that brazen Ares had given him; and these himself he bare thereafter into the mellay of war. But when Lykurgos grew old within his halls he gave them to Ereuthalion his dear squire to wear. So with his arms upon him he challenged all our best; but they trembled sore and were afraid, and no man took heart. But me my hardy spirit aroused to meet him in my confidence;[1] yet was I youngest in years of all. So fought I with him and Athene vouchsafed me glory. Tallest was he and strongest of men that I have slain; as one of huge bulk he lay spread this way and that. Would to God I were thus young and my strength were sound; then would Hector of the glancing helm soon find his combat. But of those of you that be chieftains of the host of the Achaians, yet desireth no man of good heart to meet Hector face to face.'

So the old man upbraided them, and there stood up nine in all. Far first arose Agamemnon king of men, and after him rose Tydeus' son stalwart Diomedes, and after them the Aiantes clothed with impetuous might, and after them Idomeneus and Idomeneus' brother-in-arms Meriones, peer of Enyalios slayer of men, and after them Eurypylos Euaimon's glorious son; and up rose Thoas Andraimon's son and goodly Odysseus. So all these were fain to fight with goodly Hector. And among them spake again knightly Nestor of Gerenia: 'Now cast ye the lot from the first unto the last, for him that shall be chosen; for he shall in truth profit the well-greaved Achaians, yea and he shall have profit of his own soul, if he escape from the fury of war and terrible fray.'

So said he, and they marked each man his lot and cast them in the helmet of Agamemnon Atreus' son; and the hosts prayed and lifted up their hands to the gods. And thus would one say, looking up to wide heaven: 'O father Zeus, vouchsafe that the lot fall upon Aias or Tydeus' son, or else on the king of Mykene rich in gold.'

So spake they, and knightly Nestor of Gerenia shook the helmet,

---

[1]Or, 'to meet his might,' according to the usual interpretation ψ.

and there leapt forth the lot that themselves desired, even the lot of Aias. The herald bare it every-whither through the throng, shewing it from right to left to all the princes of the Achaians; but they knew it not, and every man denied it. But when he came, bearing it every-whither through the throng, to him that had marked it and cast it in the helm, even glorious Aias, then he held forth his hand, and the herald stood by him and put it therein. And Aias saw and knew the token upon the lot, and rejoiced in heart. He cast it by his foot upon the earth, and spake: 'My friends, verily the lot is mine, yea and myself am glad at heart, because I deem that I shall vanquish goodly Hector. But come now, while I clothe me in my armour of battle, pray ye the while to Kronos' son king Zeus, in silence to yourselves, that the Trojans hear you not – nay rather, openly if ye will, for we have no fear of any man soever. For none by force shall chase me, he willing me unwilling, neither by skill; seeing I hope that not so skill-less, either, was I born in Salamis nor nurtured.'

So said he, and they prayed to Kronos' son, king Zeus; and thus would one speak, looking up to wide heaven: 'O father Zeus that rulest from Ida, most glorious, most great, vouchsafe to Aias victory and the winning of great glory. But if thou so lovest Hector indeed, and carest for him, grant unto either equal prowess and renown.'

So said they, while Aias arrayed him in flashing bronze. And when he had now clothed upon his flesh all his armour, then marched he as huge Ares coming forth, when he goeth to battle amid heroes whom Kronos' son setteth to fight in fury of heart-consuming strife. So rose up huge Aias, bulwark of the Achaians, with a smile on his grim face: and went with long strides of his feet beneath him, shaking his far-shadowing spear. Then moreover the Argives rejoiced to look upon him, but sore trembling came upon the Trojans, on the limbs of every man, and Hector's own heart beat within his breast. But in no wise could he now flee nor shrink back into the throng of the host, seeing he had challenged him to battle. And Aias came near bearing his tower-like shield of bronze, with sevenfold ox-hide, that Tychios had wrought him cunningly; Tychios far best of curriers, that had his home in Hyle, who made him his glancing shield, of sevenfold hides of stalwart bulls, and overlaid the seven with bronze. This bare Telamonian Aias before his breast, and stood near to Hector, and spake to him threatening: 'Hector, now verily shalt thou well know, man to man, what manner of princes the Danaans likewise have among them, even after Achilles, render of men, the lion-hearted. But he amid his beaked seafaring ships lieth in sore wrath with Agamemnon shepherd of the host; yet are we such as to face thee, yea and many of us, but make thou beginning of war and battle.'

And great Hector of the glancing helm answered him: 'Aias of the seed of Zeus, son of Telamon, chieftain of the host, tempt not thou me like some puny boy or woman that knoweth not deeds of battle. But I well know wars and slaughterings. To right know I, to left know I the wielding of my tough targe; therein I deem is stalwart soldiership. And I know how to charge into the mellay of fleet chariots, and how in close battle to join in furious Ares dance. Howbeit, I have no mind to smite thee, being such an one as thou art, by spying thee unawares; but rather openly, if perchance I may hit thee.'

He spake, and poised his far-shadowing spear, and hurled and smote Aias' dread shield of sevenfold hide upon the uttermost bronze, the eighth layer that was thereon. Through six folds went the stubborn bronze cleaving, but in the seventh hide it stayed. Then heaven-sprung Aias hurled next his far-shadowing spear, and smote upon the circle of the shield of Priam's son. Through the bright shield passed the violent spear, and through the curiously wrought corslet pressed it on; and straight forth beside the flank the spear rent his doublet; but he swerved aside and escaped black death. Then both together with their hands plucked forth their long spears and fell to like ravening lions or wild boars whose might is nowise feeble. Then Priam's son smote the shield's midst with his dart, but the bronze brake not through, for the point turned back; but Aias leapt on him and pierced his buckler, and straight through went the spear and staggered him in his onset, and cleft its way unto his neck, so that the dark blood gushed up. Yet even then did not Hector of the glancing helm cease from fight, but yielded ground and with stout hand seized a stone lying upon the plain, black and rugged and great; therewith hurled he and smote Aias' dread shield of sevenfold ox-hide in the midst upon the boss, and the bronze resounded. Next Aias lifted a far greater stone, and swung and hurled it, putting might immeasurable therein. So smote he the buckler and burst it inwards with the rock like unto a millstone, and beat down his knees; and he was stretched upon his back, pressed into his shield; but Apollo straightway raised him up. And now had they been smiting hand to hand with swords, but that the heralds, messengers of gods and men, came, one from the Trojans, one from the mail-clad Achaians, even Talthybios and Idaios, both men discreet. Between the two held they their staves, and herald Idaios spake a word, being skilled in wise counsel: 'Fight ye no more, dear sons, neither do battle; seeing Zeus the cloud-gatherer loveth you both, and both are men of war; that verily know we all. But night already is upon us: it is well withal to obey the hest of night.'

Then Telamonian Aias answered and said to him: 'Idaios, bid ye Hector to speak those words; of his own self he challenged to combat all our best. Let him be first, and I will surely follow as he saith.'

Then great Hector of the glancing helm said to him: 'Aias, seeing God gave thee stature and might and wisdom, and with the spear thou art excellent above all the Achaians, let us now cease from combat and battle for the day; but hereafter will we fight until God judge between us, giving to one of us the victory. But night already is upon us; it is well withal to obey the hest of night; that so thou mayest rejoice all the Achaians beside their ships, and chiefly the kinsmen and fellows that are thine; and I throughout the great city of king Priam will rejoice the Trojan men and Trojan dames with trailing robes, that with prayer I ween will enter the holy assemblage. But come, let us give each the other famous gifts, that men may thus say, Achaians alike and Trojans: "These, having fought for sake of heart-consuming strife, parted again reconciled in friendship." '

So said he, and gave him his silver-studded sword, with scabbard and well-cut baldrick; and Aias gave his belt bright with purple. So they parted and one went to the Achaian host, and one betook him to the throng of Trojans. And these rejoiced to behold him come to them alive and sound, escaped from the fury of Aias and his hands unapproachable; and they brought him to the city saved beyond their hope. And Aias on their side the well-greaved Achaians brought to noble Agamemnon, exulting in his victory.

So when these were come unto the huts of Atreides, then did Agamemnon king of men slay them an ox, a male of five years old, for the most mighty son of Kronos. This they flayed and made ready, and divided it all, and minced it cunningly, and pierced it through with spits, and roasted it carefully, and drew all off again. Then as soon as they had rest from the task and had made ready the meal, they began the feast, nor was their soul aught stinted of the equal banquet. And the hero son of Atreus, wide-ruling Agamemnon, gave to Aias slices of the chine's full length for his honour. And when they had put from them the desire of meat and drink, then first the old man began to weave the web of counsel, even Nestor whose rede of old time was proved most excellent. He of good intent made harangue among them and said: 'Son of Atreus and ye other princes of the Achaians, seeing that many flowing-haired Achaians are dead, and keen Ares hath spilt their dusky blood about fair-flowing Skamandros, and their souls have gone down to the house of Hades; therefore it behoveth thee to make the battle of the Achaians cease with daybreak; and we will assemble to wheel hither the corpses with oxen and mules; so let us burn them [a little way from the ships, that each man may bear their bones home to their children, whene'er we return again to our native land]; and let us heap one barrow about the pyre, rearing it from the plain for all alike; and thereto build with speed high towers, a bulwark for our ships and for ourselves. In the midst thereof let us make gates well compact, that through them may be a way for chariot-driving. And without let us dig a deep foss hard by, to be about it and to hinder horses and footmen, lest the battle of the lordly Trojans be heavy on us hereafter.'

So spake he and all the chiefs gave assent. But meanwhile there was in the high town of Ilios an assembly of the Trojans, fierce, confused, beside Priam's gate. To them discreet Antenor began to make harangue: 'Hearken to me, Trojans and Dardanians and allies, that I may tell you that my soul within my breast commandeth me. Lo, go to now, let us give Helen of Argos and the wealth with her for the sons of Atreus to take away. Now fight we in guilt against the oaths of faith; therefore is there no profit for us that I hope to see fulfilled, unless we do thus.'

So spake he and sate him down; and there stood up among them noble Alexandros, lord of Helen beautiful-haired; he made him answer and spake winged words: 'Antenor, these words from thee are no longer to my pleasure; yet thou hast it in thee to devise other sayings more excellent than this. But if indeed thou sayest this in earnest, then verily the gods themselves have destroyed thy wit. But I will speak forth amid the horse-taming Trojans, and declare out-right; my wife will I not give back; but the wealth I brought from Argos to our home, all that I have a mind to give, and add more of mine own substance.'

So spake he and sate him down, and there stood up among them Priam of the seed of Dardanos, the peer of gods in counsel; he of good intent made harangue to them, and said: 'Hearken to me, Trojans and Dardanians and allies, that I may tell you that my soul within my breast commandeth me. Now eat your supper through-out the city as of old, and take thought to keep watch, and be wake-ful every man. And at dawn let Idaios fare to the hollow ships to tell to Atreus' sons Agamemnon and Menelaos the saying of Alexandros, for whose sake strife is come about: and likewise to ask them this wise word, whether they are minded to refrain from noisy war till we have burned our dead; afterwards will we fight again, till heaven part us and give one or other victory.'

So spake he, and they hearkened diligently to him and obeyed; [then took they their supper throughout the host by ranks,] and at dawn Idaios fared to the hollow ships. He found the Danaans in assembly, the men of Ares' company, beside the stern of Agamemnon's ship; and so the loud-voiced herald stood in their midst and said unto them: 'Atreides and ye other princes of the Achaians, Priam and all the noble Trojans bade me tell you – if perchance it might find favour and acceptance with you – the saying of Alexandros, for whose sake strife hath come about. The wealth that Alexandros brought in his hollow ships to Troy – would he had perished first! – all that he hath a mind to give, and to add more thereto of his substance. But the wedded wife of glorious Menelaos he saith he will not give; yet verily the Trojans bid him do it. Moreover they bade me ask this thing of you; whether ye are minded to refrain from noisy war until we have burned our dead; afterwards will we fight again, till heaven part us and give one or other victory.'

So said he and they all kept silence and were still. But at the last spake Diomedes of the loud war-cry in their midst: 'Let no man now accept Alexandros' substance, neither Helen's self; known is it, even to him that hath no wit at all, how that the issues of destruction hang already over the Trojans.'

So spake he, and all the sons of the Achaians shouted, applauding the saying of horse-taming Diomedes. And then lord Agamemnon spake to Idaios: 'Idaios, thyself thou hearest the saying of the Achaians, how they answer thee; and the like seemeth good to me. But as concerning the dead, I grudge you not to burn them; for dead corpses is there no stinting, when they once are dead, of the swift propitiation of fire. And for the oaths let Zeus be witness, the loud-thundering lord of Hera.'

So saying he lifted up his sceptre in the sight of all the gods, and Idaios departed back to holy Ilios. Now Trojans and Dardanians sate in assembly, gathered all together to wait till Idaios should come; and he came and stood in their midst and declared his message. Then they made them ready very swiftly for either task, some to bring the dead, and some to seek for wood. And on their part the Argives hasted from their well-decked ships, some to bring the dead and some to seek for wood.

Now the sun was newly beating on the fields as he climbed

heaven from the deep stream of gently-flowing Ocean, when both sides met together. Then was it a hard matter to know each man again; but they washed them with water clean of clotted gore, and with shedding of hot tears lifted them upon the wains. But great Priam bade them not wail aloud; so in silence heaped they the corpses on the pyre, stricken at heart; and when they had burned them with fire departed to holy Ilios. And in like manner on their side the well-greaved Achaians heaped the corpses on the pyre, stricken at heart, and when they had burned them with fire departed to the hollow ships.

And when day was not yet, but still twilight of night, then was the chosen folk of the Achaians gathered together[1] around the pyre, and made one barrow about it, rearing it from the plain for all alike; and thereto built they a wall and lofty towers, a bulwark for their ships and for themselves. In the midst thereof made they gates well-compacted, that through them might be a way for chariot-driving. And without they dug a deep foss beside it, broad and great, and planted a palisade therein.

Thus toiled the flowing-haired Achaians: and the gods sate by Zeus, the lord of lightning, and marvelled at the great work of the mail-clad Achaians. And Poseidon shaker of earth spake first to them: 'O father Zeus, is there any man throughout the boundless earth that will any more declare to the immortals his mind and counsel? Seest thou not how the flowing-haired Achaians have now again built them a wall before their ships, and drawn a foss around it, but gave not excellent hecatombs to the gods? Verily the fame thereof shall reach as far as the dawn spreadeth, and men will forget the wall that I and Phoebus Apollo built with travail for the hero Laomedon.'

And Zeus the cloud-gatherer said to him, sore troubled: 'Out on it, far-swaying Shaker of earth, for this thing thou sayest. Well might some other god fear this device, one that were far feebler than thou in the might of his hands: but thine shall be the fame as far as the dawn spreadeth. Go to now, hereafter when the flowing-haired Achaians be departed upon their ships to their dear native land, then burst thou this wall asunder and scatter it all into the sea, and cover the great sea-beach over with sand again, that the great wall of the Achaians be brought thee to naught.'

Such converse held these one with the other, and the sun went down, and the work of the Achaians was accomplished; and they

[1] Reading ἤγρετο for ἔγρετο.

slaughtered oxen amid the huts, and took supper. And many ships from Lemnos, bearing wine, were at hand, sent of Jason's son Euneos, whom Hypsipyle bare to Jason shepherd of the host. And specially for Atreus' sons, Agamemnon and Menelaos, Jason's son gave a freight of wine, even a thousand measures So the flowing-haired Achaians bought them wine thence, some for bronze and some for gleaming iron, and some with hides and some with whole kine, and some with captives; and they set a rich feast before them. Then all night long feasted the flowing-haired Achaians, and in the city the Trojans and allies; and all night long Zeus the lord of counsel devised them ill with terrible thunderings. Then pale fear gat hold upon them, and they spilt wine from their cups upon the earth, neither durst any drink till he had made libation to most mighty Kronion. Then laid they them to rest and took the boon of sleep.

BOOK VIII

How Zeus bethought him of his promise to avenge Achilles' wrong on
Agamemnon: and therefore bade the gods refrain from war, and gave victory to
the Trojans.

NOW DAWN the saffron-robed was spreading over all the earth, and
Zeus whose joy is in the thunder let call an assembly of the gods
upon the topmost peak of manyridged Olympus, and himself made
harangue to them and all the gods gave ear: 'Hearken to me, all
gods and all ye goddesses, that I may tell you that my heart within
my breast commandeth me. One thing let none essay, be it goddess
or be it god, to wit, to thwart my saying; approve ye it all together,
that with all speed I may accomplish these things. Whomsoever I
shall perceive minded to go, apart from the gods, to succour Trojans or Danaans, chastened m no seemly wise shall he return to
Olympus, or I will take and cast him into misty Tartaros, right far
away, where is the deepest gulf beneath the earth; there are the gate
of iron and threshold of bronze, as far beneath Hades as heaven is
high above the earth: then shall he know how far I am mightiest of
all gods. Go to now, ye gods, make trial that ye all may know.
Fasten ye a rope of gold from heaven, and all ye gods lay hold
thereof and all goddesses; yet could ye not drag from heaven to
earth Zeus, counsellor supreme, not though ye toiled sore. But once
I likewise were minded to draw with all my heart, then should I
draw you up with very earth and sea withal. Thereafter would I bind
the rope about a pinnacle of Olympus, and so should all those
things be hung in air. By so much am I beyond gods and beyond
men.'

[So said he, and they all kept silence and were still, marvelling at
his saying; for he spake very masterfully. But at the last there spake
to them the bright-eyed goddess Athene: 'O our father Kronides,
supreme of lords, well we know, even we, that thy might is unyielding; yet still have we pity for the Danaan spearmen, that now shall
perish and fulfil a grievous fate. Yet will we refrain from battle as
thou biddest us, but counsel will we offer to the Argives for their
profit, that they perish not all at thy wrath.'

Then Zeus the cloud-gatherer smiled at her and said: 'Be of good comfort, dear child, Trito-born; I speak not at all of earnest purpose, but I am minded to be kindly to thee.]'

So saying he let harness to his chariot his bronze-shod horses, fleet of foot, with flowing manes of gold; and himself clad him with gold upon his flesh, and grasped the whip of gold, well-wrought, and môunted upon his car, and lashed the horses to start them; they nothing loth sped on between earth and starry heaven. So fared he to many-fountained lda, mother of wild beasts, even unto Gargaros, where is his demesne and fragrant altar. There did the father of men and gods stay his horses, and unloose them from the car, and cast thick mist about them; and himself sate on the mountain-tops rejoicing in his glory, to behold the city of the Trojans and ships of the Achaians.

Now the flowing-haired Achaians took meat hastily among the huts and thereafter arrayed themselves. Likewise the Trojans on their side armed them throughout the town – a smaller host, yet for all that were they eager to fight in battle, of forceful need, for their children's sake and their wives'. And the gates were opened wide and the host issued forth, footmen and horsemen; and mighty din arose.

So when they were met together and come unto one spot, then clashed they targe and spear and fury of bronzeclad warrior; the bossed shields pressed each on each, and mighty din arose. Then were heard the voice of groaning and the voice of triumph together of the slayers and the slain, and the earth streamed with blood.

Now while it yet was morn and the divine day waxed, so long from either side lighted the darts amain and the people fell. But when the sun bestrode mid-heaven, then did the Father balance his golden scales, and put therein two fates of death that layeth men at their length,[1] one for horse-taming Trojans, one for mail-clad Achaians; and he took the scale-yard by the midst and lifted it, and the Achaians' day of destiny sank down. So lay the Achaians' fates on the bounteous earth, and the Trojans' fates were lifted up towards wide heaven. And the god thundered aloud from Ida, and sent his blazing flash amid the host of the Achaians and they saw and were astonished, and pale fear gat hold upon all.

Then had Idomeneus no heart to stand, neither Agamemnon, neither stood the twain Aiantes, men of Ares' company. Only Nestor of Gerenia stood his ground, he the Warden of the Achaians; neither he of purpose, but his horse was fordone, which noble

[1] Perhaps rather 'death that bringeth long woe.'

Alexandros, beauteous-haired Helens lord, had smitten with an arrow upon the top of the crest where the foremost hairs of horses grow upon the skull; and there is the most deadly spot. So the horse leapt up in anguish and the arrow sank into his brain, and he brought confusion on the steeds as he writhed upon the dart. While the old man leapt forth and with his sword began to hew the traces, came Hector's fleet horses through the tumult, bearing a bold charioteer, even Hector. And now had the old man lost his life, but that Diomedes of the loud war-cry was swift to mark. Terribly shouted he, summoning Odysseus: 'Heaven-born son of Laertes, Odysseus of many wiles, whither fleest thou with thy back turned, like a coward in the throng? Beware lest as thou seest one plant a spear between thy shoulders. Nay, stand thy ground, till we thrust back from the old man his furious foe.'

So spake he, but much-enduring noble Odysseus heard him not, but hastened by to the hollow ships of the Achaians. Yet Tydeides, though but one, mingled amid the fighters in the forefront, and took his stand before the steeds of the old man, Neleus' son, and spake to him winged words, and said: 'Old man, of a truth young warriors beset thee hard; and thy force is abated, and old age is sore upon thee, and thy squire is but a weakling, and thy steeds are slow. Come then, mount upon my car, that thou mayest see of what sort are the steeds of Tros, well skilled for following or fleeing hither or thither very fleetly across the plain, even those that erst I took from Aineias inspirer of fear.[1] Thine let our squires tend, and these let us guide straight against the horse-taming Trojans, that even Hector may know whether my spear also rageth in my hands.'

So said he, and knightly Nestor of Gerenia disregarded not. Then the two squires tended Nestor's horses, even Sthenelos the valiant and kindly Eurymedon: and the other twain both mounted upon Diomedes' car. And Nestor took into his hands the shining reins, and lashed the horses; and soon they drew nigh Hector. Then Tydeus' son hurled at him as he charged straight upon them: him missed he, but his squire that drave his chariot, Eniopeus, high-hearted Thebaios' son, even him as he held the reins, he smote upon the breast beside the nipple. So he fell from out the car, and his fleet-footed horses swerved aside; and there his soul and spirit were unstrung. Then sore grief encompassed Hector's soul for sake of his charioteer. Yet left he him there lying, though he sorrowed for his comrade, and drave in quest of a bold charioteer; and his

[1] Reading μῆστωρα. See Book V. 272.

horses lacked not long a master, for anon he found Iphitos' son, bold Archeptolemos, and him he made mount behind his fleet horses, and gave the reins into his hands.

Then had destruction come and deeds beyond remedy been wrought, and so had they been penned in Ilios like lambs, had not the father of gods and men been swift to mark. So he thundered terribly and darted his white lightning and hurled it before Diomedes' steeds to earth; and there arose a terrible flame of sulphur burning, and the two horses were affrighted and cowered beneath the car. And the shining reins dropped from Nestor's hands, and he was afraid at heart and spake to Diomedes: 'Come now Tydeides, turn back thy whole-hooved horses to flight: seest thou not that victory from Zeus attendeth not on thee? Now doth Kronos' son vouchsafe glory to this Hector, for the day; hereafter shall he grant it us likewise, if he will a man may not at all ward off the will of Zeus, not though one be very valiant; he verily is mightier far.'

Then Diomedes of the loud war-cry answered him: 'Yea verily, old man, all this thou sayest is according unto right. But this is the sore grief that entereth my heart and soul; Hector some day shall say as he maketh harangue amid the Trojans: "Tydeides betook him to the ships in flight before my face." So shall he boast – in that day let the wide earth yawn for me.'

Then knightly Nestor of Gerenia answered him: 'Ah me, thou son of wise Tydeus, that thou shouldest speak on this wise! Even though Hector call thee a base man and coward, yet will not the Trojans hearken to him nor the Dardanians, neither the wives of the great-hearted men of Troy, bearers of the shield, the wives whose lusty bedfellows thou hast laid low in the dust.'

So spake he and turned the whole-hooved horses to flight, back through the tumult; and the Trojans and Hector with wondrous uproar poured upon them their dolorous darts. And over him shouted loudly great Hector of the glancing helm: 'Tydeides, the fleet-horsed Danaans were wont to honour thee with the highest place, and meats, and cups brimful, but now will they disdain thee; thou art after all no better than a woman. Begone, poor puppet; not for my flinching shalt thou climb on our towers, neither carry our wives away upon thy ships; ere that will I deal thee thy fate.'

So said he, and Tydeides was of divided mind, whether to wheel his horses and fight him face to face. Thrice doubted he in heart and soul, and thrice from Ida's mountains thundered Zeus the lord of counsel, and gave to the Trojans a sign, the turning of the course of battle. And Hector with loud shout called to the Trojans: 'Trojans and Lykians and Dardanians that love close fight, be men, my friends, and bethink you of impetuous valour. I perceive that of good will Kronion vouchsafeth me victory and great glory, and to the Danaans destruction. Fools, that devised these walls weak and of none account; they shall not withhold our fury, and lightly shall our steeds overleap the delved foss. But when I be once come amid the hollow ships, then be thought taken of consuming fire, that with fire I may burn the ships and slay the men, [even the Argives amid their ships, in confusion beneath the smoke].'

So spake he and shouted to his steeds, and said: 'Xanthos, and thou Podargos, and Aithon and goodly Lampos, now pay me back your tending, even the abundance that Andromache, great-hearted Eëtion's daughter, set before you of honey-hearted wheat, and mingled wine to drink at the heart's bidding, sooner than for me, that verily allow me to be her lusty spouse. Pursue ye now and haste, that we may seize Nestor's shield the fame whereof now reacheth unto heaven, how that it is of gold throughout, armrods and all; and may seize moreover from horsetaming Diomedes' shoulders his richly dight breastplate that Hephaistos wrought cunningly. Could we but take these, then might I hope this very night to make the Achaians to embark on their fleet ships.'

So spake he boastfully, and queen Hera had indignation, and stirred her upon her throne and made high Olympus quake, and answered and said to the great god Poseidon: 'Out on it, far-swaying Shaker of Earth; not even thine heart within thy breast hath pity on the Danaans perishing. Yet bring they to thee in Helike and Aigai offerings many and gracious: wish thou them victory. Did we but will, we that are confederate with the Danaans, to drive the Trojans back and withhold far-seeing Zeus, then would he vex himself that he should sit there alone in Ida.'

Then was the lord the Shaker of earth sore troubled and made answer: 'Hera headstrong in speech, what is this thing thou sayest? I am not he that would fain see us all at strife with Zeus Kronion, for he verily is mightier far.'

Thus spoke they to each other; and now was all the space that from the ships the moat enclosed, even unto the wall, filled full of horses together and shield-bearing warriors pent: so pent them Hector Priam's son, peer of fleet Ares, now that Zeus vouchsafed him glory. And now had he burned the trim ships with blazing fire, but that queen Hera put it in Agamemnon's heart himself to bestir him and swiftly arouse the Achaians. So he went his way along the huts and ships of the Achaians, holding a great cloak of purple in his stalwart hand, and stood by Odysseus' black ship of mighty burden, that was in the midst, so that a voice could be heard to either end, [whether to the huts of Aias son of Telamon, or of Achilles; for these had drawn their trim ships up at the uttermost ends, trusting to their valour and to the might of their hands.] Then shouted he in a piercing voice, and called to the Danaans aloud: 'Fie upon you, Argives, ye sorry things of shame, so brave in semblance! Whither are gone our boastings when we said that we were bravest, the boasts ye uttered vaingloriously when in Lemnos, as ye ate your fill of flesh of tall-horned oxen and drank goblets crowned with wine, and said that every man should stand in war to face fivescore yea tenscore Trojans? yet now can we not match one, even this Hector that anon will burn our ships with flame of fire. O father Zeus, didst ever thou blind with such a blindness any mighty king, and rob him of great glory? Yet I ween that never in my benched ship passed I by a fair altar of thine on my mad way hither, but upon all I burnt fat and thighs of oxen, being eager to lay waste well-walled Troy. Nay, Zeus, this hope fulfil thou me; suffer that we ourselves at least flee and escape, neither suffer that the Achaians be thus vanquished of the Trojans.'

So spake he, and the Father had pity on him as he wept, and vouchsafed him that his folk should be saved and perish not. Forthwith sent he an eagle – surest sign among winged fowl – holding in his claws a fawn, the young of a fleet hind; beside the beautiful altar of Zeus he let fall the fawn where the Achaians did sacrifice unto Zeus lord of all oracles. So when they saw that the bird was come from Zeus, they sprang the more upon the Trojans and bethought them of the joy of battle.

Now could no man of the Danaans, for all they were very many, boast that he before Tydeus' son had guided his fleet horses forth, and driven them across the trench and fought man to man; first by far was Tydeides to slay a warrior of the Trojans in full array, even Agelaos son of Phradmon. Now he had turned his steeds to flee; but as he wheeled the other plunged the spear into his back between his shoulders, and drave it through his breast. So fell he from his chariot, and his armour clanged upon him.

And after him came Atreus' sons, even Agamemnon and Menelaos, and after them the Aiantes clothed upon with impetuous valour, and after them Idomeneus and Idomeneus' brother in arms Meriones, peer of Enyalios slayer of men and after them Eurypylos, Euaimon's glorious son. And ninth came Teukros, stretching his back-bent bow, and took his stand beneath the shield of Aias son of

Telamon. And so Aias would stealthily withdraw the shield, and Teukros would spy his chance; and when he had shot and smitten one in the throng, then fell such an one and gave up the ghost, and Teukros would return, and as a child beneath his mother, so gat he him to Aias; who hid him with the shining shield

Now who first of the Trojans was slain of noble Teukros? Orsilochos first and Ormenos and Ophelestes and Daitor and Chromios and godlike Lykophontes and Amopaon Polyaimon's son and Melanippos; [all these in turn laid he upon the bounteous earth.] And Agamemnon king of men rejoiced to behold him making havoc with his stalwart bow of the battalions of the Trojans, and he came and stood by his side and spake to him, saying: 'Teukros, dear heart, thou son of Telamon, prince of the host, shoot on in this wise, if perchance thou mayest be found the salvation of the Danaans and glory of thy father Telamon; who nurtured thee when thou wast little, and reared thee, though a bastard, in his house; exalt thou him to honour, though he be afar Moreover I will say to thee that which shall indeed be fulfilled. If aegis-bearing Zeus and Athene vouchsafe me to lay waste the stablished city of Ilios, in thine hand first, after myself, will I bestow the meed of honour, be it a tripod or two steeds with their chariot, or a woman that shall go up into thy bed.'

And noble Teukros made answer and said to him: 'Most noble son of Atreus, why urgest thou me that myself am eager? Verily with such strength as is in me forbear I not, but ever since we drave them towards Ilios I watch with my bow to slay the foemen. Eight long-barbed arrows have I now sped, and all are buried in the flesh of young men swift in battle; only this mad dog can I not smite.'

He said, and shot another arrow from the string right against Hector; and his heart was fain to smite him. Yet him he missed, but noble Gorgythion, Priam's good son, he smote with an arrow in the breast, him born of a mother wedded from Aisyme, even fair Kastianeira, of favour like unto the gods. Even as in a garden a poppy droopeth its head aside, being heavy with fruit and the showers of spring; so bowed he aside his head laden with his helm.

And Teukros shot another arrow from the string, right against Hector, and his heart was fain to smite him. Yet missed he once again, for Apollo turned the dart away; but Archeptolemos, Hector's bold charioteer, he smote on the breast beside the nipple as he hasted into battle: so he fell from his car and his fleet-footed horses swerved aside; and there his soul and spirit were unstrung. Then sore grief encompassed Hector's soul for his charioteer's sake; yet left he him, though he sorrowed for his comrade, and bade

Kebriones his own brother, being hard by, take the chariot reins; and he heard and disregarded not. And himself he leapt to earth from the resplendent car, with a terrible shout; and in his hand he caught a stone, and made right at Teukros, and his heart bade him smite him. Now Teukros had plucked forth from his quiver a keen arrow, and laid it on the string; but even as he drew it back, Hector of the glancing helm smote him with the jagged stone, as he aimed eagerly against him, even beside his shoulder, where the collar-bone fenceth off neck and breast, and where is the most deadly spot; and he brake the bowstring,[1] and his hand from the wrist grew numb, and he stayed fallen upon his knee, and his bow dropped from his hand. But Aias disregarded not his brother's fall, but ran and strode across him and hid him with his shield. Then two trusty comrades bent down to him, even Mekisteus son of Echios and goodly Alastor, and bare him, groaning sorely, to the hollow ships. And once again the Olympian aroused the spirit of the Trojans. So they drove the Achaians straight toward the deep foss, and amid the foremost went Hector exulting in his strength. And even as when a hound behind wild boar or lion, with swift feet pursuing snatcheth at him, at flank or buttock, and watcheth for him as he wheeleth, so Hector pressed hard on the flowing-haired Achaians, slaying ever the hindmost, and they fled on. But when they were passed in flight through palisade and foss, and many were fallen beneath the Trojans' hands, then halted they and tarried beside the ships, calling one upon another, and lifting up their hands to all the gods prayed each one instantly. But Hector wheeled round his beauteous-maned steeds this way and that, and his eyes were as the eyes of Gorgon or Ares bane of mortals.

Now at the sight of them the white-armed goddess Hera had compassion, and anon spake winged words to Athene: 'Out on it, thou child of aegis-bearing Zeus, shall not we twain any more take thought for the Danaans that perish, if only for this last time? Now will they fill up the measure of evil destiny and perish by one man's onslaught; seeing that he is furious now beyond endurance, this Hector son of Priam, and verily hath wrought many a deed of ill.'

And the bright-eyed goddess Athene made answer to her, 'Yea in good sooth, may this fellow yield up strength and life, and perish at the Argives' hands in his native land; only mine own sire is furious, with no good intent, headstrong, ever sinful, the foiler of my purposes. Neither remembereth he at all those many times and oft that

[1] *νευρήν* may mean 'the sinew of his arm.'

I saved his son fordone with Eurystheus' tasks. For he would make lament toward heaven, and me would Zeus speed forth from heaven to succour him. Had I but known all this in my prudent heart, what time Eurystheus sent him forth to the house of Hades the Warder of the Gate, to bring from Erebos the hound of loathed Hades, then had he not escaped the sheer stream of the water of Styx. But now Zeus hateth me, and fulfilleth the purposes of Thetis, that kissed his knees and with her hand touched his beard, beseeching him to do honour to Achilles waster of cities. Merily the day shall come when he shall call me again his bright-eyed darling. But now make thou ready our wholehooved horses, while I enter in to the palace of aegis-bearing Zeus and gird me in my armour for battle, that I may see if Priam's son, Hector of the glancing helm, shall be glad at the appearing of us twain amid the highways of the battle. Surely shall many a Trojan likewise glut dogs and birds with fat and flesh, fallen dead at the ships of the Achaians.'

So said she, and the white-armed goddess Hera disregarded not. So Hera, the goddess queen, daughter of great Kronos, went her way and harnessed the golden-frontleted steeds; and Athene, daughter of aegis-bearing Zeus, cast down at her father's threshold her woven vesture many-coloured, that herself had wrought and her hands had fashioned; and put on her the tunic of Zeus the cloud-gatherer, and arrayed her in her armour for dolorous battle. Upon the flaming chariot set she her foot, and grasped her heavy spear great and stout, wherewith she vanquisheth the ranks of men, even of heroes with whom she of the awful sire is wroth. Then Hera swiftly smote the horses with the lash; self-moving groaned upon their hinges the gates of heaven whereof the Hours are warders, to whom is committed great heaven and Olympus, whether to throw open the thick cloud or set it to. There through the gates guided they their horses patient of the lash.

But when father Zeus beheld from Ida, he was sore wroth, and sped Iris golden-winged to bear a message: 'Go thy way, fleet Iris, turn them back neither suffer them to face me; for in no happy wise shall we join in combat. For thus will I declare, and even so shall the fulfilment be; I will maim their fleet horses in the chariot, and them will I hurl out from the car, and will break in pieces the chariot; neither within the courses of ten years shall they heal them of the wounds the thunderbolt shall tear; that the bright-eyed one may know the end when she striveth against her father. But with Hera have I not so great indignation nor wrath seeing it ever is her wont to thwart me, whate'er I have decreed.'

So said he, and whirlwind-footed Iris arose to bear the message, and departed from the mountains of Ida unto high Olympus. And even at the entrance of the gates of Olympus many-folded she met them and stayed them, and told them the saying of Zeus: 'Whither hasten ye? Why are your hearts furious within your breasts? Kronides forbiddeth you to give the Argives succour. For thus the son of Kronos threateneth, even as he will fulfil; to wit, to main: your fleet horses in the chariot, and you will he hurl out from the car, and break the chariot in pieces; neither within the courses of ten years shall ye heal you of the wounds that the thunderbolt shall tear; that thou, bright-eyed goddess, mayst know the end when thou strivest against thy father. But with Hera hath he not so great indignation nor wrath; seeing it ever is her wont to thwart him, whate'er he have decreed. But most fell art thou, reckless vixen! if thou indeed wilt dare to lift thy huge spear against the face of Zeus.'

So said fleet-footed Iris, and departed; but Hera spake to Athene and said: 'Out on it, thou child of aegis-bearing Zeus, I verily would no more have us war against Zeus for mortals' sake. Of them let one man perish and another live, even as the lot falleth; and for him, let him take counsel for himself in his heart, and give judgment for Trojans and for Danaans, as is meet.'

So saying she turned back her whole-hooved horses. Then the Hours unyoked them their beauteous-maned horses, and tethered them to their ambrosial mangers, and leant the chariots against the shining faces of the gateway; and the goddesses sate them upon their golden thrones amid the throng of all the gods, and were grieved at heart.

And father Zeus drave from Ida his fair-wheeled chariot and horses unto Olympus, and came unto the session of the gods. For him also the noble Shaker of Earth unyoked the steeds, and set the car upon the stand, and spread a cloth thereover; and far-seeing Zeus himself sate upon his golden throne, and beneath his feet great Olympus quaked Only Athene and Hera sate apart from Zeus, and spake no word to him neither questioned him. But he was ware thereof in his heart, and said, 'Why are ye thus vexed, Athene and Hera? Surely ye are not wearied of making havoc in glorious battle of the Trojans, for whom ye cherish bitter hate! Howsoever, seeing that my might is so great and my hands invincible, all the gods that are in Olympus could not turn me: and for you twain, tremblin,, erst gat hold upon your bright limbs ere that ye beheld war and war's fell deeds. For thus will I declare, and even so had the fulfilment been – never had ye, once smitten with the thunderbolt, fared on your chariots back unto Olympus where is the habitation of the immortals.'

So spake he, and Athene and Hera murmured, that were sitting by him and devising ills for the Trojans. Now Athene held her peace, and said not anything, for wrath at father Zeus, and fierce anger gat hold upon her; but Hera's heart contained not her anger, and she spake: 'Most dread son of Kronos, what word is this thou hast said? Well know we, even we, that thy might is no wise puny; yet still have we pity for the Danaan spearmen, that now shall perish and fill up the measure of grievous fate. [Yet will we refrain from battle, if thou biddest us; but counsel will we offer to the Argives, such as shall profit them, that they perish not all at thy wrath.]'

And Zeus the cloud-gatherer answered and said: 'At morn shalt thou behold most mighty Kronion, if thou wilt have it so, O Hera, ox-eyed queen, making yet more havoc of the vast army of Argive spearmen; for headlong Hector shall not refrain from battle till that Peleus' son fleet of foot have arisen beside the ships, that day when these shall fight amid the sterns in most grievous stress, around Patroklos fallen. Such is the doom of heaven. And for thine anger reck I not, not even though thou go to the nethermost bounds of earth and sea, where sit Iapetos and Kronos and have no joy in the beams of Hyperion the Sun-god, neither in any breeze, but deep Tartaros is round about them. Though thou shouldest wander till thou come even thither, yet reck I not of thy vexation, seeing there is no thing more unabashed than thou.'

So said he, but white-armed Hera spake him no word. And the sun's bright light dropped into Ocean, drawing black night across Earth the grain-giver. Against the Trojans' will daylight departed, but welcome, thrice prayed for, to the Achaians came down the murky night.

Now glorious Hector made an assembly of the Trojans, taking them apart from the ships, beside the eddying river, in an open space where was found a spot clear of dead. And they came down from their chariots to the ground to hear the word that Hector, dear unto Zeus, proclaimed He in his hand held his spear eleven cubits long; before his face gleamed the spear-head of bronze, and a ring of gold ran round about it. Thereon he leaned and spake to the Trojans, saying: 'Hearken to me, Trojans and Dardanians and allies. I thought but now to make havoc of the ships and all the Achaians and depart back again to windy Ilios; but dusk came too soon, and that in chief hath now saved the Argives and the ships

beside the beach of the sea. So let us now yield to black night, and
make our supper ready; unyoke ye from the chariots your fair-
maned horses, and set fodder beside them. And from the city bring
kine and goodly sheep with speed; and provide you with honey-
hearted wine, and corn from your houses, and gather much wood
withal, that all night long until early-springing dawn he may burn
many fires, and the gleam may reach to heaven; lest perchance even
by night the flowing-haired Achaians strive to take flight over the
broad back of the sea Verily must they not embark upon their ships
unvexed, at ease: but see ye that many a one of them have a wound
to nurse even at home, being stricken with arrow or keen-pointed
spear as he leapeth upon his ship; that so many another man may
dread to wage dolorous war on the horse-taming men of Troy. And
let the heralds dear to Zeus proclaim throughout the city that
young maidens and old men of hoary heads camp round the city on
the battlements builded of the gods; and let the women folk burn a
great fire each in her hall; and let there be a sure watch set, lest an
ambush enter the city when the host is absent. Thus be it, great-
hearted Trojans, as I proclaim; the counsel that now is sound, let
that stand spoken; further will I proclaim at dawn amid the horse-
taming men of Troy. I pray with good hope to Zeus and all the
gods, to drive from hence these dogs borne onward by the fates,
[them that the fates bear on in the black ships]. Howbeit for the
night will we guard our own selves, and at morn by daybreak,
arrayed in our armour, let us awake keen battle at the hollow ships.
I will know whether Tydeus' son stalwart Diomedes shall thrust me
from the ships back to the wall, or I shall lay him low with my spear
and bear away his gory spoils. Tomorrow shall he prove his valour,
whether he can abide the onslaught of my spear. But he amid the
foremost, I ween, shall lie stricken, and many comrades round about
their lord at the rising of to-morrow's sun. Would that I were
immortal and ageless all my days and honoured like as Athene is
honoured and Apollo, so surely as this day bringeth the Argives ill.'

So Hector made harangue, and the Trojans clamoured applause.
And they loosed their sweating steeds from the yoke, and tethered
them with thongs, each man beside his chariot; and from the city
they brought kine and goodly sheep with speed, and provided them
with honey-healted wine and corn from their houses, and gathered
much wood withal; [and sacrificed to the immortals unblemished
hecatombs]. And from the plain the winds bare into heaven the
sweet savour. [But the blessed gods regaled not themselves nor
would they aught thereof; for sore was holy Ilios hated of them, and

Priam and the folk of Priam of the good ashen spear.] But these
with high hopes sate them all night along the highways of the
battle, and their watchfires burned in multitude. Even as when in
heaven the stars about the bright moon shine clear to see, when the
air is windless, and all the peaks appear and the tall headlands and
glades, and from heaven breaketh open the infinite air, and all stars
are seen, and the shepherd's heart is glad; even in like multitude
between the ships and the streams of Xanthos appeared the watch-
fires that the Trojans kindled in front of Ilios. A thousand fires
burned in the plain and by the side of each sate fifty in the gleam of
blazing fire. And the horses champed white barley and spelt, and
standing by their chariots waited for the throned Dawn.

BOOK IX

How Agamemnon sent an embassage to Achilles, beseeching him to be appeased; and how Achilles denied him.

THUS KEPT THE TROJANS WATCH; but the Achaians were holden of heaven-sent panic, handmaid of palsying fear, and all their best were stricken to the heart with grief intolerable. Like as two winds stir up the main, the home of fishes, even the north wind and the west wind that blow from Thrace, coming suddenly; and the dark billow straightway lifteth up its crest and casteth much tangle out along the sea; even so was the Achaians' spirit troubled in their breast.

But Atreides was stricken to the heart with sore grief, and went about bidding the clear-voiced heralds summon every man by name to the assembly, but not to shout aloud; and himself he toiled amid the foremost. So they sat sorrowful in assembly, and Agamemnon stood up weeping like unto a fountain of dark water that from a beetling cliff poureth down its black stream; even so with deep groaning he spake amid the Argives and said: 'My friends, leaders and captains of the Argives, Zeus son of Kronos hath bound me with might in grievous blindness of soul; hard of heart is he, for that erewhile he promised and gave his pledge that not till I had laid waste well-walled Ilios should I depart, but now hath planned a cruel wile, and biddeth me return in dishonour to Argos with the loss of many of my folk. Such meseemeth is the good pleasure of most mighty Zeus, that hath laid low the heads of many cities, yea and shall lay low; for his is highest power So come, even as I shall bid let us all obey; let us flee with our ships to our dear native land, for now shall we never take wide-wayed Troy.'

So said he, and they all held their peace and kept silence. Long time were the sons of the Achaians voiceless for grief, but at the last Diomedes of the loud war-cry spake amid them and said: 'Atreides, with thee first in thy folly will I contend, where it is just, O king, even in the assembly; be not thou wroth therefor. My valour didst thou blame in chief amid the Danaans, and saidst that I was no man of war but a coward; and all this know the Argives both young and old. But the son of crooked-counselling Kronos hath endowed thee but by halves; he granted thee to have the honour of the sceptre above all men, but valour he gave thee not, wherein is highest power. Sir, deemest thou that the sons of the Achaians are thus indeed cowards and weaklings as thou sayest? But and if thine own heart be set on departing, go thy way; the way is before thee, and thy ships stand beside the sea, even the great multitude that followed thee from Mykene. But all the other flowing-haired Achaians will tarry here until we lay waste Troy. Nay, let them too flee on their ships to their dear native land; yet will we twain, even I and Sthenelos, fight till we attain the goal of Ilios; for in God's name are we come.'

So said he, and all the sons of the Achaians shouted aloud, applauding the saying of horse-taming Diomedes. Then knightly Nestor arose and said amid them: 'Tydeides. in battle art thou passing mighty, and in council art thou best among thine equals in years; none of all the Achaians will make light of thy word nor gainsay it; but thou hast not made a full end of thy words Moreover thou art a young man indeed, and mightest even be my son, my youngest-born; yet thou counsellest prudently the princes of the Achaians, because thou speakest according unto right. But lo, I that avow me to be older than thou will speak forth and expound everything; neither shall any man despise my saying, not even the lord Agamemnon. A tribeless, lawless, homeless man is he that loveth bitter civil strife. Howbeit now let us yield to black night and make ready our meal; and let the sentinels bestow them severally along the deep-delved foss without the wall. This charge give I to the young men; and thou, Atreides, lead then the way, for thou art the most royal. Spread thou a feast for the councillors; that is thy place and seemly for thee. Thy huts are full of wine that the ships of the Achaians bring thee by day from Thrace across the wide sea; all entertainment is for thee, being king over many. In the gathering of many shalt thou listen to him that deviseth the most excellent counsel; sore need have al; the Achaians of such as is good and prudent, because hard by the ships our foemen are burning their watch-fires in multitude; what man can rejoice thereat? This night shall either destroy or save the host.'

So said he, and they gladly hearkened to him and obeyed. Forth sallied the sentinels in their harness, around Thrasymedes Nestor's son, shepherd of the host, and Askalaphos and Ialmenos sons of Ares, and Meriones and Aphareus and Deïpyros and Kreion's son noble Lykomedes. Seven were the captains of the sentinels, and with each went fivescore young men bearing their long spears in their hands; and they took post midway betwixt foss and wall, and kindled a fire and made ready each man his meal.

Then Atreides gathered the councillors of the Achaians, and led them to his hut, and spread before them an abundant feast. So they put forth their hands to the good cheer that lay before them. And when they had put away from them the desire of meat and drink, then the old man first began to weave his counsel, even Nestor, whose rede of old time was approved the best. He of good intent spake to them and said: 'Most noble son of Atreus, Agamemnon king of men, in thy name will I end and with thy name begin, because thou art king over many hosts, and to thy hand Zeus hath entrusted sceptre and law, that thou mayest take counsel for thy folk. Thee therefore more than any it behoveth both to speak and hearken, and to accomplish what another than thou may say, when his heart biddeth him speak for profit: wheresoever thou leadest all shall turn on thee, so I will speak as meseemeth best. No other man shall have a more excellent thought than this that I bear in mind from old time even until now, since the day when thou, O heaven-sprung king, didst go and take the damsel Briseis from angry Achilles' hut by no consent of ours. Nay, I right heartily dissuaded thee; but thou yieldedst to thy proud spirit, and dishonouredst a man of valour whom even the immortals honoured; for thou didst take and keepest from him his meed of valour. Still let us even now take thought how we may appease him and persuade him with gifts of friendship and kindly words.'

And Agamemnon king of men answered and said to him: 'Old sir, in no false wise hast thou accused my folly. Fool was I, I myself deny it not. Worth many hosts is he whom Zeus loveth in his heart, even as now he honoureth this man and destroyeth the host of the Achaians. But seeing I was a fool in that I yielded to my sorry passion, I will make amends and give a recompense beyond telling In the midst of you all I will name the excellent gifts; seven tripods untouched of fire, and ten talents of gold and twenty gleaming caldrons, and twelve stalwart horses, winners in the race, that have taken prizes by their speed. No lackwealth were that man, neither undowered of precious gold, whose substance were as great as the prizes my wholehooved steeds have borne me off. And seven women will I give, skilled in excellent handiwork, Lesbians whom I chose me from the spoils the day that he himself took stablished Lesbos, surpassing womankind in beauty. These will I give him, and with them shall be she whom erst I took from him, even the daughter of Briseus; moreover I will swear a great oath that never I went

up into her bed nor had with her converse as is the wont of
mankind, even of men and women. All these things shall be set
straightway before him; and if hereafter the gods grant us to lay
waste the great city of Priam, then let him enter in when we Achaians be dividing the spoil, and lade his ship full of gold and bronze,
and himself choose twenty Trojan women, the fairest that there be
after Helen of Argos. And if we win to the richest of lands, even
Achaian Argos, he shall be my son and I will hold him in like
honour with Orestes, my stripling boy that is nurtured in all abundance. Three daughters are mine in my well-builded hall,
Chrysothemis and Laodike and Iphianassa; let him take of them
which he will, without gifts of wooing, to Peleus' house; and I will
add a great dower such as no man ever yet gave with his daughter.
And seven well-peopled cities will I give him, Kardamyle and
Enope and grassy Hire and holy Pherai and Antheia deep in meads,
and fair Aipeia and Pedasos land of vines. And all are nigh to the salt
sea, on the uttermost border of sandy Pylos; therein dwell men
abounding in flocks and kine, men that shall worship him like a god
with gifts, and beneath his sway fulfil his prosperous ordinances. All
this will I accomplish so he but cease from wrath. Let him yield;
Hades I ween is not to be softened neither overcome, and therefore
is he hatefullest of all gods to mortals. Yea, let him be ruled by me,
inasmuch as I am more royal and avow me to be the elder in years.'

Then knightly Nestor of Gerenia answered and said: 'Most noble
son of Atreus, Agamemnon king of men, now are these gifts not
lightly to be esteemed that thou offerest king Achilles. Come therefore, let us speed forth picked men to go with all haste to the hut of
Peleus' son Achilles. Lo now, whomsoever I appoint let them consent. First let Phoinix dear to Zeus lead the way, and after him great
Aias and noble Odysseus; and for heralds let Odios and Eurybates
be their companions. And now bring water for our hands, and bid
keep holy silence, that we may pray unto Zeus the son of Kronos, if
perchance he will have mercy upon us.'

So said he, and spake words that were well-pleasing unto all.
Forthwith the heralds poured water on their hands, and the young
men crowned the bowls with drink and gave each man his portion
after they had poured the libation in the cups. And when they had
made libation and drunk as their heart desired, they issued forth
from the hut of Agamemnon son of Atreus. And knightly Nestor of
Gerenia gave them full charge, with many a glance to each, and
chiefest to Odysseus, how they should essay to prevail on Peleus'
noble son.

So the twain went along the shore of the loud-sounding sea, making instant prayer to the earth-embracer, the Shaker of the Earth, that they might with ease prevail on Aiakides' great heart. So they came to the huts and ships of the Myrmidons, and found their king taking his pleasure of a loud lyre, fair, of curious work, with a silver cross-bar upon it; one that he had taken from the spoils when he laid Eëtion's city waste. Therein he was delighting his soul, and singing the glories of heroes. And over against him sate Patroklos alone in silence, watching till Aiakides should cease from singing. So the twain came forward, and noble Odysseus led the way, and they stood before his face; and Achilles sprang up amazed with the lyre in his hand, and left the seat where he was sitting, and in like manner Patroklos when he beheld the men arose. Then Achilles fleet of foot greeted them and said: 'Welcome; verily ye are friends that are come – sore indeed is the need – even ye that are dearest of the Achaians to me even in my wrath.'

So spake noble Achilles and led them forward, and made them sit on settles and carpets of purple; and anon he spake to Patroklos being near: 'Bring forth a greater bowl, thou son of Menoitios; mingle stronger drink, and prepare each man a cup, for dearest of men are these that are under my roof.'

So said he, and Patroklos hearkened to his dear comrade. He cast down a great fleshing-block in the fire-light, and laid thereon a sheep's back and a fat goat's, and a great hog's chine rich with fat. And Automedon held them for him, while Achilles carved. Then he sliced well the meat and pierced it through with spits, and Menoitios' son, that godlike hero, made the fire burn high. Then when the fire was burned down and the flame waned, he scattered the embers and laid the spits thereover, resting them on the spit-racks, when he had sprinkled them with holy salt. Then when he had roasted the meat and apportioned it in the platters, Patroklos took bread and dealt it forth on the table in fair baskets, and Achilles dealt the meat. And he sate him over against godlike Odysseus by the other wall, and bade his comrade Patroklos do sacrifice to the gods; so he cast the first-fruits into the fire. Then put they forth their hands to the good cheer lying before them. And when they had put from them the desire of meat and drink, Aias nodded to Phoinix. But noble Odysseus marked it, and filled a cup with wine and pledged Achilles: 'Hail, O Achilles! The fair feast lack we not either in the hut of Agamemnon son of Atreus neither now in thine; for feasting is there abundance to our heart's desire, but our thought is not for matters of the delicious feast; nay, we behold very sore destruction, thou fosterling of Zeus, and are afraid. Now is it in doubt whether we save the benched ships or behold them perish, if thou put not on thy might. Nigh unto ships and wall have the high-hearted Trojans and famed allies pitched their camp, and kindled many fires throughout their host, and ween that they shall no more be withheld but will fall on our black ships. And Zeus son of Kronos sheweth them signs upon the right by lightning, and Hector greatly exulteth in his might and rageth furiously, trusting in Zeus, and recketh not of god nor man, for mighty madness hath possessed him. He prayeth bright Dawn to shine forth with all speed, for he hath passed his word to smite off from the ships the ensigns' tops, and to fire the hulls with devouring flame, and hard thereby to make havoc of the Achaians confounded by the smoke. Therefore am I sore afraid in my heart lest the gods fulfil his boastings, and it be fated for us to perish here in Troyland, far from Argos pasture-land of horses. Up then! if thou art minded even at the last to save the failing sons of the Achaians from the war-din of the Trojans. Thyself shalt have grief hereafter, and when the ill is done is there no way to find a cure therefor; in good time rather take thou thought to ward the evil day from the Danaans. Friend, surely to thee thy father Peleus gave commandment the day he sent thee to Agamemnon forth from Phthia: My son, strength shall Athene and Hera give thee if they will; but do thou refrain thy proud soul in thy breast, for gentlemindedness is the better part; and withdraw from mischievous strife, that so the Argives may honour thee the more, both young and old. Thus the old man charged thee, but thou forgettest. Yet cease now at the last, and eschew thy grievous wrath; Agamemnon offereth thee worthy gifts, so thou wilt cease from anger. Lo now, hearken thou to me, and I will tell thee all the gifts that in his hut Agamemnon promised thee: seven tripods untouched of fire, and ten talents of gold and twenty gleaming caldrons and twelve stalwart horses, winners in the race, that have taken prizes by their speed. No lackwealth were that man, neither undowered of precious gold, whose substance were as great as the prizes Agamemnon's steeds have borne him off. And seven women will he give, skilled in excellent handiwork, Lesbians whom he chose him from the spoils the day that thou thyself tookest Lesbos, surpassing womankind in beauty. These will he give thee, and with them shall be she whom erst he took from thee, even the daughter of Briseus; moreover he will swear a great oath that never he went up into her bed nor had with her converse as is the wont of mankind, O king, even of men and women. All these things shall be set straightway before thee; and if hereafter the gods grant us to lay waste the great city of Priam, then enter thou in when we Achaians be dividing the spoil, and lade thy ship full of gold and bronze, and thyself choose twenty Trojan women, the fairest that there be after Helen of Argos. And if we win to the richest of lands, even Achaian Argos, thou shalt be his son and he will hold thee in like honour with Orestes, his stripling boy that is nurtured in all abundance. Three daughters are his in his well-builded hall. Chrysothemis and Laodike and Iphianassa; take thou of them which thou wilt, without gifts of wooing, to Peleus' house; and he will add a great dower such as no man ever yet gave with his daughter. And seven well-peopled cities will he give thee, Kardamyle and Enope and grassy Hire and holy Pherai and Antheia deep in meads, and fair Aipeia and Pedasos land of vines. And all are nigh to the sea, on the uttermost border of sandy Pylos; therein dwell men abounding in flocks and kine, men that shall worship thee like a god with gifts, and beneath thy sway fulfil thy prosperous ordinances. All this will he accomplish so thou but cease from wrath But and if Agamemnon be too hateful to thy heart, both he and his gifts, yet have thou pity on all the Achaians that faint throughout the host; these shall honour thee as a god, for verily thou wilt earn exceeding great glory at their hands. Yea now mightest thou slay Hector, for he would come very near thee in his deadly madness, because he deemeth that there is no man like unto him among the Danaans that the ships brought hither.'

And Achilles fleet of foot answered and said unto him: 'Heaven-sprung son of Laertes, Odysseus of many wiles, in openness must I now declare unto you my saying, even as I am minded and as the fulfilment thereof shall be, that ye may not sit before me and coax this way and that. For hateful to me even as the gates of hell is he that hideth one thing in his heart and uttereth another: but I will speak what meseemeth best. Not me, I ween, shall Agamemnon son of Atreus persuade, nor the other Danaans, seeing we were to have no thank for battling with the foemen ever without respite. He that abideth at home hath equal share with him that fighteth his best, and in like honour are held both the coward and the brave; death cometh alike to the untoiling and to him that hath toiled long. Neither have I any profit for that I endured tribulation of soul, ever staking my life in fight. Even as a hen bringeth her unfledged chickens each morsel as she winneth it, and with herself it goeth hard, even so I was wont to watch out many a sleepless night and pass through many bloody days of battle, warring with folk for their women's sake. Twelve cities of men have I laid waste from ship-board, and from land eleven, I do you to wit, throughout deep-soiled Troy-land; out of all these took I many goodly treasures and would bring and give them all to Agamemnon son of Atreus, and he staying behind amid the fleet ships would take them and portion out some few but keep the most. Now some he gave to be meeds of honour to the princes and the kings, and theirs are left untouched; only from me of all the Achaians took he my darling lady and keepeth her – let him sleep beside her and take his joy! But why must the Argives make war on the Trojans? why hath Atreides gathered his host and led them hither? is it not for lovely-haired Helen's sake? Do then the sons of Atreus alone of mortal men love their wives? surely whatsoever man is good and sound of mind loveth his own and cherisheth her, even as I too loved mine with all my heart, though but the captive of my spear. But now that he hath taken my meed of honour from mine arms and hath deceived me, let him not tempt me that know him full well; he shall not prevail. Nay, Odysseus, let him take counsel with thee and all the princes to ward from the ships the consuming fire. Verily without mine aid he hath wrought many things, and built a wall and dug a foss about it wide and deep, and set a palisade therein; yet even so can he not stay murderous Hector's might. But so long as I was fighting amid the Achaians, Hector had no mind to array his battle far from the wall, but scarce came unto the Skaian gates and to the oak-tree; there once he awaited me alone and scarce escaped my onset. But now, seeing I have no mind to fight with noble Hector, I will tomorrow do sacrifice to Zeus and all the gods, and store well my ships when I have launched them on the salt sea – then shalt thou see, if thou wilt and hast any care therefor, my ships sailing at break of day over Hellespont, the fishes' home, and my men right eager at the oar; and if the great Shaker of the Earth grant me good journey, on the third day should I reach deep-soiled Phthia There are my great possessions that I left when I came hither to my hurt; and yet more gold and ruddy bronze shall I bring from hence, and fair-girdled women and grey iron, all at least that were mine by lot; only my meed of honour hath he that gave it me taken back in his despitefulness, even lord Agamemnon son of Atreus. To him declare ye everything even as I charge you, openly, that all the Achaians likewise may have in dignation, if haply he hopeth to beguile yet some other Danaan, for that he is ever clothed in shamelessness. Verily not in my face would he dare to look, though he have the front of a dog. Neither will I devise counsel with him nor any enterprise, for utterly he hath deceived me and done wickedly; but never again shall he beguile me with fair speech – let this suffice him. Let him begone in peace; Zeus the lord of counsel hath taken away his wits. Hateful to me are his gifts, and I hold him at a straw's worth. Not even if he gave me ten times, yea twenty, all that now is his, and all that may come to him otherwhence, even all the revenue of Orchomenos or Egyptian Thebes where the treasure-houses are stored fullest – Thebes of the hundred gates, whence sally forth two hundred warriors through each with horses and chariots – nay, nor gifts in number as sand or dust; not even so shall Agamemnon persuade my soul till he have paid me back all the bitter despite. And the daughter of Agamemnon son of Atreus will I not wed, not were she rival of golden Aphrodite for fairness and for handiwork matched bright-eyed Athene – not even then will I wed her; let him choose him of the Achaians another that is his peer and is more royal than I. For if the gods indeed preserve me and I come unto my home, then will Peleus himself seek me a wife. Many Achaian maidens are there throughout Hellas and Phthia, daughters of princes that ward their cities; whomsoever of these I wish will I make my dear lady. Very often was my high soul moved to take me there a wedded wife, a help meet for me, and have joy of the possessions that the old man Peleus possesseth. For not of like worth with life hold I even all the wealth that men say was possessed of the well-peopled city of Ilios in days of peace gone by, before the sons of the Achaians came; neither all the treasure that the stone threshold of the archer Phoebus Apollo encompasseth in rocky Pytho. For kine and goodly flocks are to be had for the harrying, and tripods and chestnut horses for the purchasing; but to bring back man's life neither harrying nor earning availeth when once it hath passed the barrier of his lips. For thus my goddess mother telleth me, Thetis the silver-footed, that twain fates are bearing me to the issue of death. If I abide here and besiege the Trojans' city, then my returning home is taken from me, but my fame shall be imperishable; but if I go home to my dear native land, my high fame is taken from me, but my life shall endure long while, neither shall the issue of death soon reach me. Moreover I would counsel you all to set sail homeward, seeing ye shall never reach your goal of steep Ilios; of a surety far-seeing Zeus holdeth his hand over her and her folk are of good courage. So go your way and tell my answer to the princes of the Achaians, even as is the office of elders, that they may devise in their hearts some other better counsel, such as shall save them their ships and the host of the Achaians amid the hollow ships: since this counsel availeth them naught that they have now devised, by reason of my fierce wrath. But let Phoinix now abide with us and lay him to rest, that he may follow with me on my ships to our dear native land to-morrow, if he will; for I will not take him perforce.'

So spake he, and they all held their peace and were still, and marvelled at his saying; for he denied them very vehemently. But at the last spake to them the old knight Phoinix, bursting into tears, because he was sore afraid for the ships of the Achaians: 'If indeed thou ponderest departure in thy heart, glorious Achilles, and hast no mind at all to save the fleet ships from consuming fire, because that wrath hath entered into thy heart; how can I be left of thee, dear son, alone thereafter? To thee did the old knight Peleus send me the day he sent thee to Agamemnon forth from Phthia, a stripling yet unskilled in equal war and in debate wherein men wax pre-eminent. Therefore sent he me to teach thee all these things, to be both a speaker of words and a doer of deeds. So would I not be left alone of thee, dear son, not even if god himself should take on him to strip my years from me, and make me fresh and young as in the day when first I left Hellas the home of fair women, fleeing from strife against my father Amyntor son of Ormenos: for he was sore angered with me by reason of his lovely-haired concubine, whom he ever cherished and wronged his wife my mother. So she besought me continually by my knees to go in first unto the concubine, that the old man might be hateful to her. I hearkened to her and did the deed; but my sire was ware thereof forthwith and cursed me mightily, and called the dire Erinyes to look that never should any dear son sprung of my body sit upon my[1] knees: and the gods fulfilled his curse, even Zeus of the under world and dread Persephone. [Then took I counsel to slay him with the keen sword; but some immortal stayed mine anger, bringing to my mind the people's voice and all the reproaches of men, lest I should be called a father-slayer amid the Achaians.] Then would my soul no more be refrained at all within my breast to tarry in the halls of mine angered father. Now my fellows and my kinsmen came about me with many prayers, and refrained me there within the halls, and slaughtered many goodly sheep and shambling kine with crooked horns; and many swine rich with fat were stretched to singe over the flames of Hephaistos, and wine from that old man's jars was drunken without stint. Nine nights long slept they all night around my body; they kept watch in turn, neither were the fires quenched, one beneath the colonnade of the fenced courtyard and another in

---

[1]Or 'his knees,' according to the more usual interpretation of κου.

the porch before the chamber doors. But when the tenth dark night was come upon me, then burst I my cunningly fitted chamber doors, and issued forth and overleapt the courtyard fence lightly, unmarked of watchmen and handmaidens. Then fled I far through Hellas of wide lawns, and came to deep-soiled Phthia, mother of flocks, even unto king Peleus; and he received me kind]y and cherished me as a father cherisheth his only son, his stripling heir of great possessions; and he made me rich and gave much people to me, and I dwelt in the uttermost part of Phthia and was king over the Dolopians. Yea, I reared thee to this greatness, thou godlike Achilles, with my heart's love; for with none other wouldest thou go unto the feast, neither take meat in the hall, till that I had set thee upon my knees and stayed thee with the savoury morsel cut first for thee, and put the wine-cup to thy lips. Oft hast thou stained the doublet on my breast with sputtering of wine in thy sorry helplessness Thus I suffered much with thee and much I toiled, being mindful that the gods in nowise created any issue of my body; but I made thee my son, thou godlike Achilles, that thou mayest yet save me from grievous destruction. Therefore, Achilles, rule thy high spirit; neither beseemeth it thee to have a ruthless heart. Nay, even the very gods can bend, and theirs withal is loftier majesty and honour and might. Their hearts by incense and reverent vows and drink-offering and burnt-offering men turn with prayer, so oft as any transgresseth and doeth sin. Moreover Prayers of penitence are daughters of great Zeus, halting and wrinkled and of eyes askance, that have their task withal to go in the steps of Sin. For Sin is strong and fleet of foot, wherefore she far outrunneth all prayers, and goeth before them over all the earth making men fall, and Prayers follow behind to heal the harm. Now whosoever reverenceth Zeus' daughters when they draw near, him they greatly bless and hear his petitions; but when one denieth them and stiffly refuseth, then depart they and make prayer unto Zeus the son of Kronos that sin may come upon such an one, that he may fall and pay the price. Nay, Achilles, look thou too that there attend upon the daughters of Zeus the reverence that bendeth the heart of all men that be right-minded. For if Atreides brought thee not gifts and foretold thee not more hereafter, but were ever furiously wroth, then I were not he that should bid thee cast aside thine anger and save the Argives, even in their sore need of thee. But now he both offereth thee forthwith many gifts, and promiseth thee more hereafter, and hath sent heroes to beseech thee, the best men chosen throughout the host of the Achaians and that to thyself are dearest of the Argives;

dishonour not thou their petition nor their journey hither; though erst it were no wrong that thou wast wroth Even in like manner have we heard the fame of those heroes that were of old, as oft as furious anger came on any; they might be won by gifts and prevailed upon by speech. This tale have I in mind of old time and not of yesterday, even as it was; and I will tell it among you that all are friends The Kuretes[1] fought and the staunch Aitolians about the city of Kalydon, and slew one another, the Aitolians defending lovely Kalydon, the Kuretes eager to lay it waste in war. For Artemis of the golden throne had brought a plague upon them, in wrath that Oineus offered her not the harvest first-fruits on the fat of his garden land; for all the other gods had their feast of hecatombs, and only to the daughter of great Zeus offered he not, whether he forgat or marked it not; and therein sinned he sore in his heart. So the Archer-goddess was wroth and sent against him a creature of heaven, a fierce wild boar, white-tusked, that wrought sore ill continually on Oineus' garden land; many a tall tree laid he low utterly, even root and apple blossom therewith. But him slew Meleagros the son of Oineus, having gathered together from many cities huntsmen and hounds; for not of few men could the boar be slain, so mighty was he; and many an one brought he to the grievous pyre. But the goddess made much turmoil over him and tumult concerning the boar's head and shaggy hide, between the Kuretes and great-hearted Aitolians. Now so long as Meleagros dear to Ares fought, so long it went ill with the Kuretes, neither dared they face him without their city walls, for all they were very many. But when Meleagros grew full of wrath, such as swelleth the hearts of others likewise in their breasts, though they be wise of mind, then in anger of heart at his dear mother Althaia he tarried beside his wedded wife, fair Kleopatra, daughter of Marpessa fair-ankled daughter of Euenos, and of Ides that was strongest of men that were then upon the earth; he it was that took the bow to face the king Phoebus Apollo for sake of the fair-ankled damsel.[2] And she was called Alkyone of her father and lady mother by surname in their hall, because her mother in the plight of the plaintive halcyon-bird wept when the far-darter Phoebus Apollo snatched her away. By her side lay Meleagros, brooding on his grievous anger, being wroth by reason of his mother's curses: for she, grieved for her brethren's death, prayed instantly to the gods, and with her hands likewise beat

[1]Note 2.
[2]Note 3.

instantly upon the fertile earth, calling on Hades and dread Persephone, while she knelt upon her knees and made her bosom wet
with tears, to bring her son to death; and Erinnys that walketh in
darkness, whose heart knoweth not ruth, heard her from Erebos.
Now was the din of foemen about their gates quickly risen, and a
noise of battering of towers; and the elders of the Aitolians sent the
best of the gods' priests and besought him to come forth and save
them, with promise of a mighty gift; to wit, they bade him, where
the plain of lovely Kalydon was fattest, to choose him out a fair
demesne of fifty plough-gates, the half thereof vine-land and the
half open plough-land, to be cut from out the plain. And old
knightly Oineus prayed him instantly, and stood upon the threshold
of his high-roofed chamber, and shook the morticed doors to
beseech his son; him too his sisters and his lady mother prayed
instantly – but he denied them yet more – instantly too his comrades prayed, that were nearest him and dearest of all men. Yet even
so persuaded they not his heart within his breast, until his chamber
was now hotly battered and the Kuretes were climbing upon the
towers and firing the great city. Then did his fair-girdled wife pray
Meleagros with lamentation, and told him all the woes that come
on men whose city is taken; the warriors are slain, and the city is
wasted of fire, and the children and the deep-girdled women are led
captive of strangers. And his soul was stirred to hear the grievous
tale, and he went his way and donned his glittering armour. So he
saved the Aitolians from the evil day, obeying his own will; but they
paid him not now the gifts many and gracious; yet nevertheless he
drave away destruction. But be not thine heart thus minded, neither
let heaven so guide thee, dear son; that were a hard thing, to save
the ships already burning. Nay, come for the gifts; the Achaians
shall honour thee even as a god. But if without gifts thou enter into
battle the bane of men, thou wilt not be held in like honour, even
though thou avert the fray.'

And Achilles fleet of foot made answer and said to him: 'Phoinix
my father, thou old man fosterling of Zeus, such honour need I in
no wise; for I deem that I have beer honoured by the judgment of
Zeus, which shall abide upon me amid my beaked ships as long as
breath tarrieth in my body and my limbs are strong. Moreover I will
say this thing to thee and lay thou it to thine heart; trouble not my
soul by weeping and lamentation, to do the pleasure of warrior
Atreides; neither beseemeth it thee to cherish him! lest thou be
hated of me that cherish thee. It were good that thou with me
shouldest vex him that vexeth me. Be thou king even as I, and share

my sway by halves, but these shall bear my message. So tarry thou here and lay thee to rest in a soft bed, and with break of day will we consider whether to depart unto our own, or to abide.'

He spake, and nodded his brow in silence unto Patroklos to spread for Phoinix a thick couch, that the others might bethink them to depart from the hut with speed Then spake to them Aias, Telamon's godlike son, and said: 'Heaven-sprung son of Laertes, Odysseus of many wiles, let us go hence; for methinks the purpose of our charge will not by this journey be accomplished; and we must tell the news, though it be no wise good, with all speed unto the Danaans, that now sit awaiting. But Achilles hath wrought his proud soul to fury within him – stubborn man, that recketh naught of his comrades' love, wherein we worshipped him beyond all men amid the ships – unmerciful! Yet doth a man accept recompense of his brother's murderer or for his dead son; and so the man-slayer for a great price abideth in his own land, and the kinsman's heart is appeased, and his proud soul, when he hath taken the recompense. But for thee, the gods have put within thy breast a spirit implacable and evil, by reason of one single damsel. And now we offer thee seven damsels, far best of all, and many other gifts besides; entertain thou then a kindly spirit, and have respect unto thine home; because we are guests of thy roof, sent of the multitude of Danaans, and we would fain be nearest to thee and dearest beyond all other Achaians, as many as there be.'

And Achilles fleet of foot made answer and said to him: 'Aias sprung of Zeus, thou son of Telamon, prince of the folk, thou seemest to speak all this almost after mine own mind; but my heart swelleth with wrath as oft as I bethink me of those things, how Atreides entreated me arrogantly among the Argives, as though I were some worthless sojourner. But go ye and declare my message; I will not take thought of bloody war until that wise Priam's son, noble Hector, come to the Myrmidons' huts and ships, slaying the Argives, and smirch the ships with fire. But about mine hut and black ship I ween that Hector, though he be very eager for battle, shall be refrained.'

So said he, and they took each man a two-handled cup, and made libation and went back along the line of ships; and Odysseus led the way And Patroklos bade his fellows and handmaidens spread with all speed a thick couch for Phoinix; and they obeyed and spread a couch as he ordained, fleeces and rugs and fine flock of linen. Then the old man laid him down and tarried for bright Dawn. And Achilles slept in the corner of the morticed hut, and by his side lay a woman that he brought from Lesbos, even Phorbas' daughter fair-cheeked Diomede. And on the other side Patroklos lay, and by his side likewise fair-girdled Iphis, whom noble Achilles gave him at the taking of steep Skyros, the city of Enyeus.

Now when those were come unto Atreides' huts, the sons of the Achaians stood up on this side and on that, and pledged them in cups of gold, and questioned them; and Agamemnon king of men asked them first: 'Come now, tell me, Odysseus full of praise, thou great glory of the Achaians; will he save the ships from consuming fire, or said he nay, and hath wrath yet hold of his proud spirit?'

And steadfast goodly Odysseus answered him: 'Most noble son of Atreus, Agamemnon king of men, he yonder hath no mind to quench his wrath, but is yet more filled of fury, and spurneth thee and thy gifts. He biddeth thee take counsel for thyself amid the Argives, how to save the ships and folk of the Achaians. And for himself he threateneth that at break of day he will launch upon the sea his trim well-benched ships. Moreover he said that he would counsel all to sail for home, because ye now shall never reach your goal of steep Ilios; surely far-seeing Zeus holdeth his hand over and her folk are of good courage. Even so said he, and here are also these to tell the tale that were my companions, Aias and the two heralds, both men discreet. But the old man Phoinix laid him there to rest, even as Achilles bade him, that he may follow with him on his ships to his dear native land to-morrow, if he will; for he will not take him perforce.'

So said he, and they all held their peace and were still, marvelling at his saying? for he harangued very vehemently. Long were the sons of the Achaians voiceless for grief, but at the last Diomedes of the loud war-cry spake amid them: 'Most noble son of Atreus, Agamemnon king of men, would thou hadst never besought Peleus' glorious son with offer of gifts innumerable; proud is he at any time, but now hast thou yet far more encouraged him in his haughtiness. Howbeit we will let him bide, whether he go or tarry; hereafter he shall fight, whenever his heart within him biddeth and god arouseth him. Come now, even as I shall say let us all obey. Go ye now to rest, full to your hearts' desire of meat and wine, wherein courage is and strength; but when fair rosy-fingered Dawn appeareth, array thou with all speed before the ships thy folk and horsemen, and urge them on; and fight thyself amid the foremost.'

So said he, and all the princes gave assent, applauding the saying of Diomedes tamer of horses. And then they made libation and went every man to his hut, and there laid them to rest and took the boon of sleep.

BOOK X

Diomedes and Odysseus slew Dolon, a spy of the Trojans, and themselves spied on the Trojan camp, and took the horses of Rhesos, the Thracian king.

NOW BESIDE THE SHIPS the other leaders of the whole Achaian host were sleeping all night long, by soft Sleep overcome, but Agamemnon son of Atreus, shepherd of the host, sweet Sleep held not, so many things he debated in his mind. And even as when the lord of fair-tressed Hera lighteneth, fashioning either a mighty rain unspeakable, or hail, or snow, when the flakes sprinkle all the ploughed lands, or fashioning perchance the wide mouth of bitter war, even so oft in his breast groaned Agamemnon, from the very deep of his heart, and his spirits trembled within him. And whensoever he looked toward that Trojan plain, he marvelled at the many fires that blazed in front of Ilios, and at the sound of flutes and pipes, and the noise of men; but whensoever to the ships he glanced and the host of the Achaians, then rent he many a lock clean forth from his head, to Zeus that is above, and greatly groaned his noble heart.

And this in his soul seemed to him the best counsel, to go first of all to Nestor son of Neleus, if perchance he might contrive with him some right device that should be for the warding off of evil from all the Danaans.

Then he rose, and did on his doublet about his breast, and beneath his shining feet he bound on fair sandals, and thereafter clad him in the tawny skin of a lion fiery and great, a skin that reached to the feet, and he grasped his spear.

And even in like wise did trembling fear take hold on Menelaos, (for neither on his eyelids did Sleep settle down,) lest somewhat should befall the Argives, who verily for his sake over wide waters were come to Troy-land, with fierce war in their thoughts.

With a dappled pard's skin first he covered his broad shoulders, and he raised and set on his head a casque of bronze, and took a spear in his strong hand. Then went he on his way to rouse his brother, that mightily ruled over all the Argives, and as a god was honoured by the people. Him found he harnessing his goodly gear about his shoulders, by the stern of the ship, and glad to his brother was his coming. Then Menelaos of the loud war-cry first accosted him: 'Wherefore thus, dear brother, art thou arming? Wilt thou speed forth any of thy comrades to spy on the Trojans? Nay, terribly I fear lest none should undertake for thee this deed, even to go and spy out the foemen alone through the ambrosial night; needs must he be a man right hardy of heart.'

Then the lord Agamemnon answered him and spake: 'Need of good counsel have I and thou, Menelaos fosterling of Zeus, of counsel that will help and save the Argives and the ships, since the heart of Zeus hath turned again. Surely on the sacrifices of Hector hath he set his heart rather than on ours. For never did I see, nor heard any tell, that one man devised so many terrible deeds in one day, as Hector, dear to Zeus, hath wrought on the sons of the Achaians, unaided; though no dear son of a goddess is he, nor of a god He hath done deeds that methinks will be a sorrow to the Argives, lasting and long, such evils hath he devised against the Achaians. But go now, run swiftly by the ships, and surnmon Aias and Idomeneus, but I will betake me to noble Nestor, and bid him arise, if perchance he will be fain to go to the sacred company of the sentinels and lay on them his command. For to him above others would they listen, for his own son is chief among the sentinels, he and the brother in arms of Idomeneus, even Meriones, for to them above all we entrusted this charge.'

Then Menelaos of the loud war cry answered him: 'How meanest thou this word wherewith thou dost command and exhort me? Am I to abide there with them, waiting till thou comest, or run back again to thee when I have well delivered to them thy commandment?'

Then the king of men, Agamemnon, answered him again: 'There do thou abide lest we miss each other as we go, for many are the paths through the camp. But call aloud, wheresoever thou goest, and bid men awake, naming each man by his lineage, and his father's name, and giving all their dues of honour, nor be thou proud of heart. Nay rather let us ourselves be labouring, for even thus did Zeus from our very birth dispense to us the heaviness of toil.'

So he spake, and sent his brother away, having clearly laid on him his commandment. Then went he himself after Nestor, the shepherd of the host, whom he found by his hut and black ship, in his soft bed: beside him lay his fair dight arms, a shield, and two spears, and a shining helmet. Beside him lay his glittering girdle wherewith the old man was wont to gird himself when he harnessed him for war, the bane of men, and led on the host, for he yielded not to grievous old age. Then he raised him on his elbow, lifting his head, and spake to the son of Atreus, inquiring of him with this word: 'Who art thou that farest alone by the ships, through the camp, in the dark night, when other mortals are sleeping? Seekest thou one of thy mules, or of thy comrades? speak, and come not silently upon me. What need hast thou?'

Then the king of men, Agamemnon, answered him: 'O Nestor, son of Neleus, great glory of the Achaians, thou shalt know Agamemnon, son of Atreus, whom above all men Zeus hath planted for ever among labours, while my breath abides within my breast, and my knees move. I wander thus, for that sweet sleep rests not on mine eyes, but war is my care, and the troubles of the Achaians. Yea, greatly I fear for the sake of the Danaans, nor is my heart firm, but I am tossed to and fro, and my heart is leaping from my breast, and my good knees tremble beneath me. But if thou wilt do aught, since neither on thee cometh sleep, let us go thither to the sentinels, that we may see them, lest they be fordone with toil and drowsihead, and so are slumbering, and have quite forgotten to keep watch. And hostile men camp hard by, nor know we at all but that they are keen to do battle in the night.'

Then knightly Nestor of Gerenia answered him: 'Most renowned son of Atreus, Agamemnon king of men, assuredly not all his designs will wise-counselling Zeus fulfil for Hector, even all that now he thinketh; nay methinks he w ill contend with even more troubles if but Achilles turn back his heart from grievous anger. And verily will I follow after thee, but let us also rouse others again, both the son of Tydeus, spearman renowned, and Odysseus, and swift Aias, and the strong son of Phyleus. But well it would be if one were to go and call those also, the godlike Aias, and Idomeneus the prince; for their ships are furthest of all, and nowise close at hand. But Menelaos will I blame, dear as he is and worshipful, yea, even if thou be angry with me, nor will I hide my thought, for that he slumbereth, and to thee alone hath left the toil; now should he be toiling among all the chiefs and beseeching them, for need no longer tolerable is coming upon us.'

And the king of men, Agamemnon, answered him again: 'Old man, another day I even bid thee blame him, for often is he slack, and willeth not to labour, yielding neither to unreadiness nor heedlessness of heart, but looking toward me, and expecting mine instance. But as now he awoke far before me, and came to me, and him I sent forward to call those concerning whom thou inquirest.

But let us be gone, and them shall we find before the gates, among the sentinels, for there I bade them gather.'

Then knightly Nestor of Gerenia answered him: 'So will none of the Argives be wroth with him or disobey him, whensoever he doth urge any one, and give him his commands.'

So spake he and did on his doublet about his breast, and beneath his bright feet he bound goodly shoon, and all around him buckled a purple cloak, with double folds and wide, and thick down all over it.

And he took a strong spear, pointed with sharp bronze, and he went among the ships of the mail-clad Achaians. Then Odysseus first, the peer of Zeus in counsel, did knightly Gerenian Nestor arouse out of sleep, with his voice, and quickly the cry came all about his heart, and he came forth from the hut and spake to them saying: 'Wherefore thus among the ships and through the camp do ye wander alone, in the ambrosial night; what so great need cometh upon you?'

Then knightly Nestor of Gerenia answered him: 'Laertes son, of the seed of Zeus, Odysseus of many a wile, be not wroth, for great trouble besetteth the Achaians. Nay follow, that we may arouse others too, even all that it behoveth to take counsel, whether we should fly, a fight.'

So spake he, and Odysseus of the many counsels came to the hut, and cast a shield bedight about his shoulders, and went after them.

And they went to seek Diomedes, son of Tydeus, and him they found outside his hut, with his arms, and around him his comrades were sleeping with their shields beneath their heads, but their spears were driven into the ground erect on the spikes of the butts, and afar shone the bronze, like the lightning of father Zeus. Now that hero was asleep, and under him was strewn the hide of an ox of the field, but beneath his head was stretched a shining carpet. Beside him went and stood knightly Nestor of Gerenia and stirred him with a touch of his foot, and aroused him, chiding him to his face, saying: 'Wake, son of Tydeus, why all night long dost thou sleep? Knowest thou not that the Trojans on the high place of the plain are camped near the ships, and but a little space holdeth them apart?'

So spake he, and Diomedes sprang swiftly up out of sleep, and spake out to him winged words: 'Hard art thou, old man, and from toil thou never ceasest. Now are there not other younger sons of the Achaians, who might rouse when there is need each of the kings, going all round the host? but thou, old man, art indomitable.'

And him knightly Nestor of Gerenia answered again, 'Nay verily, my son, all this that thou sayest is according unto right. Noble sons have I, and there be many of the host, of whom each man might go and call the others. But a right great need hath assailed the Achaians. For now to all of us it standeth on a razor's edge, either pitiful ruin for the Achaians, or life. But come now, if indeed thou dost pity me, rouse swift Aias, and the son of Phyleus, for thou art younger than I.'

So spake he, and Diomedes cast round his shoulders the skin of a great fiery lion, that reached to his feet, and he grasped his spear, and started on his way, and roused the others from their place and led them on.

Now when they had come among the assembled sentinels, they found not the leaders of the sentinels asleep, but they all sat wide awake with their arms. And even as hounds keep difficult guard round the sheep in a fold, having heard a hardy wild beast that cometh through the wood among the hills, and much clamour riseth round him of hounds and men, and sleep perisheth from them, even so sweet sleep did perish from their eyes, as they watched through the wicked night, for ever were they turning toward the plains, when they heard the Trojans moving.

And that old man was glad when he saw them, and heartened them with his saying, and calling out to them he spake winged words: 'Even so now, dear children, do ye keep watch, nor let sleep take any man, lest we become a cause of rejoicing to them that hate us.'

So saying he sped through the moat, and they followed with him, the kings of the Argives, who had been called to the council. And with them went Meriones, and the glorious son of Nestor, for they called them to share their counsel. So they went clean out of the delved foss, and sat down in the open, where the mid-space was clear of dead men fallen, where fierce Hector had turned again from destroying the Argives, when night covered all. There sat they down, and declared their saying each to the other, and to them knightly Nestor of Gerenia began discourse: 'O friends, is there then no man that would trust to his own daring spirit, to go among the great-hearted Trojans, if perchance he might take some straggler of the enemy, yea, or hear perchance some rumour among the Trojans, and what things they devise among themselves, whether they are fain to abide there by the ships, away from the city, or will retreat again to the city, now that they have conquered the Achaians? All this might such an one learn, and back to us come scathless: great would be his fame under heaven among all men, and a goodly gift will be given him. For all the best men that bear sway by the ships, each and all of them will give him a black ewe, with her lamb at her foot, – no chattel may compare with her, – and ever will he be present at feasts and clan-drinkings.'

So spake he, and thereon were they all silent, holding their peace, but to them spake Diomedes of the loud war-cry: 'Nestor, my heart and manful spirit urge me to enter the camp of the foemen hard by, even of the Trojans: but and if some other man will follow with me, more comfort and more courage will there be. If two go together, one before another perceiveth a matter, how there may be gain therein; but if one alone perceive aught, even so his wit is shorter, and weak his device.'

So spake he, and many were they that wished to follow Diomedes. The two Aiantes were willing, men of Ares' company, and Meriones was willing, and right willing the son of Nestor, and the son of Atreus, Menelaos, spearman renowned, yea and the hardy Odysseus was willing to steal into the throng of Trojans, for always daring was his heart within him. But among them spake the king of men, Agamemnon

'Diomedes son of Tydeus, joy of mine heart, thy comrade verily shalt thou choose, whomsoever thou wilt, the best of them that be here, for many are eager. But do not thou, out of reverent heart, leave the better man behind, and give thyself the worse companion, yielding to regard for any, and looking to their lineage, even if one be more kingly born.'

So spake he, but was in fear for the sake of fair-haired Menelaos. But to them again answered Diomedes of the loud war-cry: 'If indeed ye bid me choose myself a comrade, how then could I be unmindful of godlike Odysseus, whose heart is passing eager, and his spirit so manful in all manner of toils; and Pallas Athene loveth him. But while he cometh with me, even out of burning fire might we both return, for he excelleth in understanding.'

Then him again answered the steadfast noble Odysseus: 'Son of Tydeus, praise me not overmuch, neither blame me aught, for thou speakest thus among the Argives that themselves know all But let us be going, for truly the night is waning, and near is the dawn, and the stars have gone onward, and the night has advanced more than two watches, but the third watch is yet left.'

So spake they and harnessed them in their dread armour. To the son of Tydeus did Thrasymedes steadfast in war give a two-edged sword, (for his own was left by his ship) and a shield, and about his head set a helm of bull's hide, without cone or crest, that is called a skull cap, and keeps the heads of stalwart youths. And Meriones gave Odysseus a bow and a quiver, and a sword, and on his head set a helm made of leather, and with many a thong was it stiffly wrought within, while without the white teeth of a boar of flashing tusks were arrayed thick set on either side, well and cunningly, and in the midst was fixed a cap of felt. This casque Autolykos once stole from Amyntor son of Ormenos, out of Eleon, breaking into his well-builded house; and he gave it to Amphidamas of Kythera to take to Skandeia and Amphidamas gave it for a guest-gift to Molos, who gave it to his own son Meriones to wear, and now it was set to cover the head of Odysseus.

So when these twain had harnessed them in their dread armour, they set forth to go, and left there all the best of the host. And to them did Pallas Athene send forth an omen on the right, a heron hard by the way, and they beheld it not with their eyes, through the dark night, but they heard its shrill cry. And Odysseus was glad in the omen of the bird, and prayed to Athene: 'Listen to me, thou child of aegis-bearing Zeus that ever in all toils dost stand by me, nor doth any motion of mine escape thee: but now again above all be thou friendly to me, Athene, and grant that we come back with renown to the ships, having wrought a great work, that shall be sorrow to the Trojans.'

Next again prayed Diomedes of the loud war-cry: 'Listen now likewise to me, thou child of Zeus, unwearied maiden, and follow with me as when with my father thou didst follow, even noble Tydeus, into Thebes, when he went forth as a messenger from the Achaians. And them he left by the Asopos, the mail-clad Achaians, and a honeyed word he bare to the Kadmeians in that place; but on his backward way he devised right terrible deeds, with thee, fair goddess, for eager didst thou stand by him. Even so now stand thou by me willingly, and protect me. And to thee will I sacrifice a year-ling heifer, broad of brow, unbroken, that never yet hath man led below the yoke. Her will I sacrifice to thee, and gild her horns with gold'

So spake they in their prayer, and Pallas Athene heard them. And when they bad prayed to the daughter of mighty Zeus, they went forth on their way, like two lions, through the dark night, amid the slaughter, amid the slain men, through the arms and the black blood.

Nay, nor the stout-hearted Trojans did Hector suffer to sleep, but he called together all the best of them, all that were chiefs and leaders of the Trojans, them did he call together, and contrived a crafty counsel: 'Who is there that would promise and perform for me this deed, for a great gift? yea his reward shall be sufficient. For I will give him a chariot, and two horses of arching neck, the best that be at the swift ships of the Achaians, to whosoever shall dare the deed, and for himself shall win glory. And the deed is this; to go near the swift-faring ships, and seek out whether the swift ships are guarded, as of old, or whether already, being subdued beneath our hands, the foes are devising of flight among themselves, and have no care to watch through the night, being fordone with dread weariness.'

So spake he, but they were all silent and held their peace. Now there was among the Trojans one Dolon, the son of Eumedes the godlike herald, and he was rich in gold, and rich in bronze: and verily he was ill favoured to look upon, but swift of foot; now he was an only son among five sisters. So he spake then a word to the Trojans and to Hector: 'Hector, my heart and manful spirit urge me to go near the swift-faring ships, and spy out all. But come, I pray thee, hold up the staff, and swear to me, that verily thou wilt give me the horses and the chariots bedight with bronze that bear the noble son of Peleus. But to thee I will prove no vain spy, nor disappoint thy hope. For I will go straight to the camp, until I may come to the ship of Agamemnon, where surely the chiefs are like to hold council, whether to fight or flee.'

So spake he, and Hector took the staff in his hand, and sware to him: 'Now let Zeus himself be witness, the loud-thundering lord of Hera, that no other man of the Trojans shall mount those horses, but thou, I declare, shalt rejoice in them for ever.'

So spake he, and sware a bootless oath thereto, and aroused Dolon to go. And straightway he cast on his shoulders his crooked bow, and did on thereover the skin of a grey wolf, and on his head a helm of ferret-skin, and took a sharp javelin, and went on his way to the ships from the host. But he was not like to come back from the ships and bring word to Hector.

But when he had left the throng of men and horses, he went forth eagerly on the way, and Odysseus of the seed of Zeus was ware of him as he approached, and said unto Diomedes: 'Lo, here is some man, Diomedes, coming from the camp, I know not whether as a spy to our ships, or to strip certain of the dead men fallen. But let us suffer him to pass by us a little way on the plain, and thereafter may we rush on him and take him speedily, and if it chance that he outrun us by speed of foot, ever do thou hem him in towards the ships and away from the camp, rushing on him with thy spear, lest in any wise he escape towards the city.'

So they spake, and turning out of the path they lay down among the bodies of the dead; and swiftly Dolon ran past them in his witlessness. But when he was as far off as is the length of the furrow made by mules, (for better far are they than kine, to drag the jointed plough through the deep fallow,) these twain ran after him, and he stood still when he heard the sound, supposing in his heart that they were friends come from among the Trojans to turn him back, at the countermand of Hector. But when they were about a spear-cast off, or even less, he knew them for foemen, and stirred his swift limbs to fly, and speedily they started in pursuit.

And as when two sharp-toothed hounds, well skilled in the chase, press ever hard on a doe or a hare through a wooded land, and it runs screaming before them, even so Tydeus' son and Odysseus the sacker of cities cut Dolon off from the host, and ever pursued hard after him. But when he was just about to come among the sentinels, in his flight towards the ships, then Athene poured strength into the son of Tydeus, that none of the mail-clad Achaians might boast himself the first to smite, and he come second. And strong Diomedes leaped upon him with the spear, and said: 'Stand, or I shall overtake thee with the spear, and methinks that thou shalt not long avoid sheer destruction at my hand.'

So spake he, and threw his spear, but of his own will he missed the man, and passing over his right shoulder the point of the polished spear stuck fast in the ground: and Dolon stood still, in great dread and trembling, and the teeth chattered in his mouth, and he was green with fear. Then the twain came up with him, panting, and gripped his hands, and weeping he spake: 'Take me alive, and I will ransom myself, for within our house there is bronze, and gold, and smithied iron, wherefrom my father would do you grace with ransom untold, if he should learn that I am alive among the ships of the Achaians.'

Then Odysseus of the many counsels answered him and said: 'Take courage, let not death be in thy mind, but come speak and tell me truly all the tale, why thus from the host dost thou come all alone among the ships, through the black night, when other mortals are sleeping? Comest thou to strip certain of the dead men fallen, or did Hector send thee forth to spy out everything at the hollow ships, or did thine own spirit urge thee on?'

Then Dolon answered him, his limbs trembling beneath him: 'With many a blind hope did Hector lead my wits astray, who vowed to give me the whole-hooved horses of the proud son of Peleus, and his car bedight with bronze: and he bade me fare through the swift black night, and draw nigh the foemen, and seek out whether the swift ships are guarded, as of old. or whether, already, being subdued beneath our hands, they are devising of flight among them selves, and have no care to watch through the night, being fordone with dread weariness.'

And smiling thereat did Odysseus of the many counsels make him answer: 'Verily now thy soul was set on great rewards, even the horses of the wise son of Aiakos, but hard are they for mortal men to master, and hard to drive, for any but Achilles only, whom a deathless mother bare. But come, tell me all this truly, all the tale: where when thou camest hither didst thou leave Hector, shepherd of the host, and where lie his warlike gear, and where his horses? And how are disposed the watches, and the beds of the other Trojans? And what counsel take they among themselves; are they fain to abide there nigh the ships, afar from the city, or will they return to the city again, seeing that they have subdued unto them the Achaians?'

Then Dolon son of Eumedes made him answer again. 'Lo, now all these things will I recount to thee most truly. Hector with them that are counsellors holdeth council by the barrow of godlike Ilos, apart from the din, but as for the guards whereof thou askest, oh hero, no chosen watch nor guard keepeth the host. As for all the watch fires of the Trojans – on them is necessity, so that they watch and encourage each other to keep guard; but, for the allies called from many lands, they are sleeping and to the Trojans they leave it to keep watch, for no wise near dwell the children and wives of the allies.'

Then Odysseus of the many counsels answered him and said: 'How stands it now, do they sleep amidst the horsetaming Trojans, or apart? tell me clearly, that I may know.'

Then answered him Dolon son of Eumedes: 'Verily all this likewise will I recount to thee truly. Towards the sea lie the Karians, and Paionians of the bended bow, and the Leleges and Kaukones, and noble Pelasgoi. And towards Thymbre the Lykians have their place, and the haughty Mysians, and the Phrygians that fight from chariots, and Maionians lords of chariots. But wherefore do ye inquire of me throughly concerning all these things? for if ye desire to steal into the throng of Trojans, lo, there be those Thracians, new comers, at the furthest point apart from the rest, and among them their king Rhesos, son of Eïoneus. His be the fairest horses that ever I beheld, and the greatest, whiter than snow, and for speed like the winds. And his chariot is fashioned well with gold and silver, and golden is his armour that he brought with him, marvellous, a wonder to behold; such as it is in no wise fit for mortal men to bear, but for the deathless gods. But bring me now to the swift ships, or leave me here, when ye have bound me with a ruthless bond, that ye may go and make trial of me whether I have spoken to you truth, or lies.'

Then strong Diomedes, looking grimly on him, said: 'Put no thought of escape, Dolon, in thy heart, for all the good tidings thou hast brought, since once thou hast come into our hands. For if now we release thee or let thee go, on some later day wilt thou come to the swift ships of the Achaians, either to play the spy, or to fight in open war, but if subdued beneath my hands thou lose thy life, never again wilt thou prove a bane to the Argives.'

He spake, and that other with strong hand was about to touch his chin, and implore his mercy, but Diomedes smote him on the midst of the neck, rushing on him with the sword, and cut through both the sinews, and the head of him still speaking was mingled with the dust. And they stripped him of the casque of ferret's skin from off his head, and of his wolf-skin, and his bended bow, and his long spear, and these to Athene the Giver of Spoil did noble Odysseus hold aloft in his hand, and he prayed and spake a word: 'Rejoice, O goddess, in these, for to thee first of all the Immortals in Olympus will we call for aid; nay, but yet again send us on against the horses and the sleeping places of the Thracian men.'

So spake he aloud, and lifted from him the spoils on high, and set them on a tamarisk bush, and raised thereon a mark right plain to see, gathering together reeds, and luxuriant shoots of tamarisk, lest they should miss the place as they returned again through the swift dark night.

So the twain went forward through the arms, and the black blood, and quickly they came to the company of Thracian men. Now they were slumbering, fordone with toil, but their goodly weapons lay by them on the ground, all orderly, in three rows, and by each man his pair of steeds. And Rhesos slept in the midst, and beside him his swift horses were bound with thongs to the topmost rim of the chariot. Him Odysseus spied from afar, and showed him unto Diomedes: 'Lo, Diomedes, this is the man, and these are the horses whereof Dolon that we slew did give us tidings. But come now, put forth thy great strength; it doth not behove thee to stand idle with thy weapons: nay, loose the horses; or do thou slay the men, and of the horses will I take heed.'

So spake he, and into that other bright-eyed Athene breathed might, and he began slaying on this side and on that, and hideously went up their groaning, as they were smitten with the sword, and the earth was reddened with blood. And like as a lion cometh on flocks without a herdsman, on goats or sheep, and leaps upon them with evil will, so set the son of Tydeus on the men of Thrace, till he had slain twelve. But whomsoever the son of Tydeus drew near and smote with the sword, him did Odysseus of the many counsels seize by the foot from behind, and drag him out of the way, with this design in his heart, that the fairmaned horses might lightly issue forth, and not tremble in spirit, when they trod over the dead; for they were not yet used to dead men. But when the son of Tydeus came upon the king, he was the thirteenth from whom he took sweet life away, as he was breathing hard, for an evil dream stood above his head that night, even the seed of Oineus, through the device of Athene. Meanwhile the hardy Odysseus loosed the whole-hooved horses, and bound them together with thongs, and drave them out of the press, smiting them with his bow, since he had not taken thought to lift the shining whip with his hands from the well-dight chariot: then he whistled for a sign to noble Diomedes.

But Diomedes stood and pondered what most daring deed he might do, whether he should take the chariot, where lay the fair-dight armour, and drag it out by the pole, or lift it upon high, and so bear it forth, or whether he should take the life away from yet more of the Thracians. And while he was pondering this in his heart, then Athene drew near, and stood, and spake to noble Diomedes: 'Bethink thee of returning, O son of great-hearted Tydeus, to the hollow ships, lest perchance thou come thither in flight, and perchance another god rouse up the Trojans likewise.'

So spake she, and he observed the voice of the utterance of the goddess, and swiftly he sprang upon the steeds, and Odysseus smote them with his bow, and they sped to the swift ships of the Achaians.

Nay, nor a vain watch kept Apollo of the silver bow, when he beheld Athene caring for the son of Tydeus; in wrath against her he stole among the crowded press of Trojans, and aroused a counsellor of the Thracians, Hippokoon, the noble kinsman of Rhesos. And he started out of sleep, when he beheld the place desolate where the swift horses had stood, and beheld the men gasping in the death struggle; then he groaned aloud, and called out by name to his com-rade dear. And a clamour arose and din unspeakable of the Trojans hasting together, and they marvelled at the terrible deeds, even all that the heroes had wrought, and had gone thereafter to the hollow ships.

But when those others came to the place where they had slain the spy of Hector, there Odysseus, dear to Zeus, checked the swift horses, and Tydeus' son, leaping to the ground, set the bloody spoil in the hands of Odysseus, and again mounted, and lashed the horses, and they sped onward nothing loth [to the hollow ships, for there they fain would be]. But Nestor first heard the sound, and said: 'O friends, leaders and counsellors of the Argives, shall I be wrong or speak sooth? For my heart bids me speak. The sound of swift-footed horses strikes upon mine ears. Would to god that Odysseus and that strong Diomedes may even instantly be driving the whole-hooved horses from among the Trojans; but terribly I fear in mine heart lest the bravest of the Argives suffer aught through the Trojans' battle-din.'

Not yet was his whole word spoken, when they came themselves, and leaped down to earth, but gladly the others welcomed them with hand-clasping, and with honeyed words. And first did knightly Nestor of Gerenia make question: 'Come, tell me now, renowned Odysseus, great glory of the Achaians, how ye twain took those horses? Was it by stealing into the press of Trojans? Or did some god meet you, and give you them? Wondrous like are they to rays of the sun. Ever with the Trojans do I mix in fight, nor methinks do I tarry by the ships, old warrior as I am. But never yet saw I such horses, nor deemed of such Nay, methinks some god must have encountered you and given you these. For both of you doth Zeus the cloud-gatherer love, and the maiden of aegis-bearing Zeus, bright-eyed Athene.'

And him answered Odysseus of the many counsels: 'O Nestor, son of Neleus, great glory of the Achaians, lightly could a god, if so he would, give even better steeds than these, for the gods are far stronger than we. But as for these new come horses, whereof, old man, thou askest me, they are Thracian, but their lord did brave Diomedes slay, and beside him all the twelve best men of his company. The thirteenth man was a spy we took near the ships, one that Hector and the other haughty Trojans sent forth to pry upon our camp.'

So spake he, and drave the whole-hooved horses through the fosse, laughing; and the other Achaians went with him joyfully. But when they had come to the well-built hut of the son of Tydeus, they bound the horses with well-cut thongs, at the mangers where the swift horses of Diomedes stood eating honey-sweet barley.

And Odysseus placed the bloody spoils of Dolon in the stern of the ship, that they might make ready a sacred offering to Athene.

But for themselves, they went into the sea, and washed off the thick sweat from shins, and neck, and thighs. But when the wave of the sea had washed the thick sweat from their skin, and their hearts revived again, they went into polished baths, and were cleansed.

And when they had washed, and anointed them with olive oil, they sat down at supper, and from the full mixing bowl they drew off the honey-sweet wine, and poured it forth to Athene.

BOOK XI

Despite the glorious deeds of Agamemnon, the Trojans press hard on the Achaians, and the beginning of evil comes on Patroklos.

Now Dawn arose from her couch beside proud Tithonos, to bring light to the Immortals and to mortal men. But Zeus sent forth fierce Discord unto the fleet ships of the Achaians, and in her hands she held the signal of war. And she stood upon the huge black ship of Odysseus, that was in the midst, to make her voice heard on either side, both to the huts of Aias, son of Telamon, and to the huts of Achilles, for these twain, trusting in their valour and the might of their hands, had drawn up their trim ships at the two ends of the line. There stood the goddess and cried shrilly in a great voice and terrible, and mighty strength she set in the heart of each of the Achaians, to war and fight unceasingly. And straightway to them war grew sweeter than to depart in the hollow ships to their dear native land.

Then the son of Atreus cried aloud, and bade the Argives arm them, and himself amid them did on the flashing bronze. First he fastened fair greaves about his legs, fitted with ankle-clasps of silver; next again he did his breastplate about his breast, the breastplate that in time past Kinyras gave him for a guest-gift. For afar in Cyprus did Kinyras hear the mighty rumour how that the Achaians were about to sail forth to Troy in their ships, wherefore did Kinyras give him the breastplate, to do pleasure to the king. Now therein were ten courses of black cyanus, and twelve of gold, and twenty of tin, and dark blue snakes writhed up towards the neck, three on either side, like rainbows that the son of Kronos hath set in the clouds, a marvel of the mortal tribes of men. And round his shoulders he cast his sword, wherein shone studs of gold, but the scabbard about it was silver, fitted with golden chains. And he took the richly-dight shield of his valour that covereth all the body of a man, a fair shield, and round about it were ten circles of bronze, and thereon were twenty white bosses of tin, and one in the midst of black cyanus. And thereon was embossed the Gorgon fell of aspect glaring terribly, and about her were Dread and Terror. And from the shield was hung a baldric of silver, and thereon was curled a snake of cyanus; three heads interlaced had he, growing out of one neck. And on his head Agamemnon set a two-crested helm with fourfold plate, and plume of horse-hair, and terribly the crest nodded from above. And he grasped two strong spears, shod with bronze and keen, and far forth from him into the heaven shone the bronze; and thereat Hera and Athene thundered honouring the king of Mykene rich in gold.

Then each man gave in charge his horses to his charioteer, to hold them in by the fosse, well and orderly, and themselves as heavy men at arms were hasting about, being harnessed in their gear, and unquenchable the cry arose into the Dawn. And long before the charioteers were they arrayed at the fosse, but after them a little way came up the drivers. And among them the son of Kronos aroused an evil din, and from above rained down dew dank with blood out of the upper air, for that he was about to send many strong men down to Hades.

But the Trojans on the other side, on the high ground of the plain, gathered them around great Hector, and noble Polydamas, and Aineias that as a god was honoured by the people of the Trojans, and the three sons of Antenor, Polybos, and noble Agenor, and young Akamas like unto the Immortals. And Hector in the foremost rank bare the circle of his shield. And as from amid the clouds appeareth glittering a baneful star, and then again sinketh within the shadowy clouds, even so Hector would now appear among the foremost ranks, and again would be giving command in the rear, and all in bronze he shone, like the lightning of aegis-bearing father Zeus.

And even as when reapers over against each other drive their swaths through a rich man's field of wheat or barley, and thick fall the handfuls, even so the Trojans and Achaians leaped upon each other, destroying, and neither side took thought of ruinous flight; and equal heads had the battle, and they rushed on like wolves. And woful Discord was glad at the sight, for she alone of the gods was with them in the war; for the other gods were not beside them, but in peace they sat within their halls, where the goodly mansion of each was builded in the folds of Olympus. And they all were blaming the son of Kronos, lord of the storm-cloud, for that he willed to give glory to the Trojans. But of them took the father no heed, but aloof from the others he sat apart, glad in his glory, looking toward the city of the Trojans, and the ships of the Achaians, and the glitter of bronze, and the slayers and the slain.

So long as morning was, and the sacred day still waxed, so long did the shafts of both hosts strike, and the folk fell, but about the hour when a woodman maketh ready his meal, in the dells of a mountain, when he hath tired his hands with felling tall trees, and weariness cometh on his soul, and desire of sweet food taketh his heart, even then the Danaans by their valour brake the battalions, and called on their comrades through the lines. And in rushed Agamemnon first of all, and slew a man, even Bienor, shepherd of the hosts, first himself, and next his comrade Oïleus, the charioteer. He verily leaped from the chariot and stood and faced Agamemnon, but the king smote the brow of him with the sharp spear as he came eagerly on, and his vizor heavy with bronze held not off the spear, but through vizor and bone it sped, and the brain within was all scattered, and so was Oïleus overcome despite his eagerness.

And them did Agamenmon king of men leave in that place, with their breasts gleaming, when he had stripped them of their corslets, and he went on to destroy Isos and Antiphos, two sons of Priam, one born in wedlock, the other a bastard, and both were in one chariot: the bastard held the reins, but renowned Antiphos was fighting by him. These twain did Achilles on the spurs of Ida once bind with fresh withes, taking them as they herded the sheep, and he ransomed them for a price. But now Agamemnon, son of Atreus, of the wide domain, smote Isos on the breast, above the nipple, with his spear, but Antiphos he struck hard by the ear, with the sword, and dashed him from the chariot. Then made he haste, and stripped from them their goodly harness, well knowing who they were, for he had seen them before beside the fleet ships when swift-footed Achilles led them from Ida. And as a lion easily crusheth the young fawns of a swift hind, when that he hath seized them in his strong teeth, and hath come to their lair, and taketh their tender life away, – and the hind, even if she chance to be near at hand, cannot help them, for on herself too cometh dread terror, and swiftly she speedeth through the thick coppice and the woodland, hasting and sweating before the onslaught of the mighty beast, – even so not one of the Trojans did avail to save them from their bane, but themselves were fleeing in fear before the Argives.

Next took he Peisandros and Hippolochos, steadfast in fight. These were sons of wise-hearted Antimachos, who chiefly had taken the gold of Alexandros, goodly gifts, and therefore never would consent to give Helen to fair-haired Menelaos. His two sons then lord Agamemnon took, both being in one car, and together they were driving the swift steeds; for the shining reins had fallen from their hands, and the horses were all distraught with dread, and he

set on against them, like a lion, – even the son of Atreus, – but from
their chariot the twain did supplicate him: 'Take us alive, O son of
Atreus, and receive worthy ransom, for in the halls of Antimachos
lie many possessions, bronze, and gold, and smithied iron; out of
these could our father do thee grace with ransom past telling, if he
heard that we twain were alive by the ships of the Achaians.'

So did the twain weeping beseech the king with soft words, but
they heard a voice wherein was no softness at all: 'If indeed ye be
the sons of wise Antimachos, who once in the assembly of the Trojans bade slay Menelaos there, when he came on an embassy with
godlike Odysseus, nor ever let him return to the Achaians, now
verily shall ye pay the price of your father's foul shame.'

He spake and dashed Peisandros from his chariot to the earth,
smiting him with the spear upon the breast, and he lay supine on
the ground. But Hippolochos rushed away, and him too he smote to
earth, and cut off his arms and his neck with the sword, then tossed
him like a ball of stone to roll through the throng. Then left he
them, and where thickest clashed the battalions, there he set on, and
with him all the well-greaved Achaians. Footmen kept slaying footmen as they were driven in flight, and horsemen slaying horsemen
with the sword, and from beneath them rose up the dust from the
plain, stirred by the thundering hooves of horses. And the lord
Agamemnon, ever slaying, followed after, calling on the Argives.
And as when ruinous fire falleth on dense woodland, and the
whirling wind beareth it everywhere, and the thickets fall utterly
before it, being smitten by the onset of the fire, even so beneath
Agamemnon son of Atreus fell the heads of the Trojans as they fled;
and many strong-necked horses rattled empty cars along the highways of the battle, lacking their noble charioteers; but they on the
earth were lying, far more dear to the vultures than to their wives.

But Hector did Zeus draw forth from the darts and the dust, from
the man-slaying, and the blood, and the din, and the son of Atreus
followed on, crying eagerly to the Danaans. And past the tomb of
ancient Ilos, son of Dardanos, across the mid plain, past the place of
the wild fig-tree they sped, making for the city and ever the son of
Atreus followed shouting, and his invincible hands were defiled with
gore. But when they were come to the Skaian gates, and the oak-
tree, there then they halted, and awaited each other. But some were
still in full flight through the mid plain, like kine that a lion hath
scattered, coming on them in the dead of night; all hath he scattered, but to one sheer death appeareth instantly, and he breaketh
her neck first, seizing her with strong teeth, and thereafter swal-

loweth greedily the blood and all the guts; even so lord Aga
memnon son of Atreus followed hard on the Trojans, ever slaying
the hindmost man, and they were scattered in flight, and on face or
back many of them fell from their chariots beneath the hands of
Agamemnon, for mightily he raged with the spear. But when he was
now about coming below the city, and the steep wall, then did the
father of men and gods sit him down on the crests of many-fountained Ida, from heaven descending, with the thunderbolt in his
hands.

Then sent he forth Iris of the golden wings, to bear his word: 'Up
and go, swift Iris, and tell this word unto Hector: So long as he sees
Agamemnon, shepherd of the host, raging among the foremost
fighters, and ruining the ranks of men, so long let him hold back,
but bid the rest of the host war with the foe in strong battle. But
when, or smitten with the spear or wounded with arrow shot,
Agamemnon leapeth into his chariot, then will I give Hector
strength to slay till he come even to the well-timbered ships, and
the sun go down, and sacred darkness draw on.'

So spake he, and wind-footed swift Iris disobeyed him not, but
she went down from the hills of Ida to sacred Ilios, and she found
the son of wise-hearted Priam, noble Hector, standing among the
horses, and firm-bound chariots, and swift-footed Iris drew near
and spake to him: 'Hector, son of Priam, peer of Zeus in counsel;
lo, Zeus the father hath sent me forth, to bear thee this command:
So long as thou seest Agamemnon, the shepherd of the host, raging
among the foremost fighters, and mining the ranks of men, so long
hold back from the fight, but bid the rest of the host war with the
foe in strong battle. But when, or smitten with the spear or
wounded with arrow shot, Agamemnon leapeth into his chariot,
then will Zeus give thee strength to slay till thou come even to the
well-timbered ships, and the sun go down and sacred darkness draw
on.'

So spake swift-footed Iris and departed, but Hector with his harness leaped from the chariot to the ground, and, shaking his sharp
spears went through all the host, stirring up his men to fight, and he
roused the dread din of battle. And they wheeled round, and stood
and faced the Achaians, while the Argives on the other side
strengthened their battalions. And battle was made ready, and they
stood over against each other, and Agamemnon first rushed in,
being eager to fight far in front of all.

Tell me now, ye Muses that inhabit mansions in Olympus, who
was he that first encountered Agamemnon, whether of the Trojans

themselves, or of their allies renowned? It was Iphidamas, son of Antenor, great and mighty. who was nurtured in Thrace rich of soil, the mother of sheep, and Kisses his mother's father reared him in the halls, while he was but a little child, even the father of Theano fair of face Then when he came to the measure of glorious youth, he tried to keep him there, and offered him his own daughter; but a bridegroom new wed, he went from his bridal chamber after the tidings of the coming of the Achaians, with twelve beaked ships that followed after him. These trim ships he left in Perkote, but himself came by land to Ilios; he it was that then encountered Agamemnon son of Atreus. And when they were come near in onset against each other, Atreus' son missed, and his spear was turned aside, but Iphidamas smote him on the girdle, below the corslet, and himself pressed on, trusting to his heavy hand, but pierced not the gleaming girdle, for long ere that the point struck on the silver, and was bent like lead. Then wide-ruling Agamemnon caught the spear with his hand and drew it toward him furiously, like a lion, and snatched it out of the hand of Iphidamas, and smote his neck with the sword, and unstrung his limbs. So even there he fell, and slept a sleep of bronze most piteously, far from his wedded wife, helping the folk of the city, – far from his bride, of whom he had known no joy, and much had he given for her: first a hundred kine he gave, and thereafter promised a thousand, goats and sheep together, whereof he had herds unspeakable. Then did Agamemnon son of Atreus strip him, and went bearing his goodly harness into the throng of the Achaians.

Now when Koön beheld him, Koön Antenor's eldest son, illustrious among men, strong sorrow came on him, covering his eyes, for his brother's fall: and he stood on one side with his spear, and unmarked of noble Agamemnon smote him on the mid-arm, beneath the elbow, and clean through went the point of the shining spear. Then Agamemnon king of men shuddered, yet not even so did he cease from battle and war, but rushed against Koön, grasping his kind-nurtured spear. Verily then Koön seized right lustily by the foot Iphidamas, his brother, and his father's son, and called to all the best of his men; but him, as he dragged the dead through the press, beneath his bossy shield Agamemnon wounded with a bronze-shod spear, and unstrung his limbs, and drew near and cut off his head over Iphidamas. There the sons of Antenor, at the hands of Agamemnon the king, filled up the measure of their fate, and went down within the house of Hades.

But Agamemnon ranged among the ranks of men, with spear, and sword, and great stones for throwing, while yet the blood welled warm from his wound. But when the wound waxed dry, and the blood ceased to flow, then keen pangs came on the might of the son of Atreus. And even as when the keen shaft cometh upon a woman in her travail, the piercing shaft that the goddesses of the birth-pangs send, even the Eilithyiai, the daughters of Hera that have bitter pangs in their gift, even so keen pains sank into the might of the son of Atreus. Then leaped he into his chariot, and bade his charioteer drive to the hollow ships, for he was sore vexed at heart. And he called in a piercing voice, and shouted to the Danaans: 'O friends, leaders and counsellors of the Argives, do ye now ward from the seafaring ships the harsh din of battle, for Zeus the counsellor suffers me not all day to war with the Trojans.'

So spake he, and his charioteer lashed the fair-maned steeds toward the hollow ships, and they flew onward nothing loth, and their breasts were covered with foam, and their bellies were stained with dust, as they bore the wounded king away from the war.

But Hector, when he beheld Agamemnon departed, cried to the Trojans and Lykians with a loud shout: 'Ye Trojans and Lykians, and Dardanians that war in close fight, be men, my friends, and be mindful of your impetuous valour. The best man of them hath departed and to me hath Zeus, the son of Kronos, given great renown. But straightway drive ye the whole-hooved horses against the mighty Danaans, that ye may he the masters and bear away the higher glory.'

So spake he, and aroused the might and spirit of every man. And even as when some hunter tars on his white-toothed hounds against a boar of the wild, or a lion, even so did Hector, son of Priam, like unto Ares the bane of men, tar on the great-hearted Trojans against the Achaians. Himself with high thoughts he fared among the foremost, and fell upon the fight, like a roaring blast, that leapeth down and stirreth the violet-coloured deep. There whom first, whom last did he slay, even Hector, son of Priam, when Zeus vouchsafed him renown?

Asaios first, and Autonoos, and Opites, and Dolops, son, of Klytios, and Opheltios, and Agelaos, and Aisymnos, and Oros, and Hipponoos steadfast in the fight; these leaders of the Danaans he slew, and thereafter smote the multitude, even as when the West Wind driveth the clouds of the white South Wind, smiting with deep storm, and the wave swelleth huge, rolling onward, and the spray is scattered on high beneath the rush of the wandering wind; even so many heads of the host were smitten by Hector.

There had ruin begun, and deeds remedeless been wrought, and now would all the Achaians have fled and fallen among the ships, if Odysseus had not called to Diomedes, son of Tydeus: 'Tydeus' son, what ails us that we forget our impetuous valour? Nay, come hither, friend, and take thy stand by me, for verily it will be shame if Hector of the glancing helm take the ships.'

And to him strong Diomedes spake in answer: 'Verily will I abide and endure, but short will be all our profit, for Zeus, the cloud-gatherer, clearly desireth to give victory to the Trojans rather than to us.'

He spake, and drave Thymbraios from his chariot to the ground, smiting him with the spear in the left breast, and Odysseus smote Molion the god-like squire of that prince. These then they let be, when they had made them cease from war, and then the twain fared through the crowd with a din, as when two boars full of valour fall on the hunting hounds; so rushed they on again, and slew the Trojans, while gladly the Achaians took breath again in their flight from noble Hector.

There took they a chariot and two of the best men of the people, two sons of Merops of Perkote, who above all men was skilled in soothsaying, nor would he suffer his children to go to ruinous war; but in nowise did the twain obey him, for the Fates of black death led them on. Them did the son of Tydeus, Diomedes, spearman renowned, deprive of life and spirit, and took away their glorious harness. And Odysseus stripped Hippodamos and Hypeirochos. Then Kronion stretched for them the line of battle level, as he looked down from Ida, and they kept slaying each other. Then Tydeus' son smote the hero Agastrophos, son of Paion, on the hipjoint, with his spear; nor were his horses near, for him to flee, and great blindness was on his spirit; for the squire held them aloof, but on foot he was charging through the foremost fighters, till he lost his life. But Hector quickly spied them among the ranks, and rushed upon them shouting, and with him followed the battalions of the Trojans. And beholding him, Diomedes of the loud war-cry shuddered, and straightway spake to Odysseus that was hard by: 'Lo, on us this ruin, even mighty Hector, is rolling: let us stand, and await him, and ward off his onset.'

So spake he, and swayed and sent forth his far-shadowing spear, and smote him nor missed, for he aimed at the head, on the summit of the crest, and bronze by bronze was turned, nor reached his fair flesh, for it was stopped by the threefold helm with its socket, that Phoebus Apollo to Hector gave. But Hector sprang back a wondrous way, and mingled with the throng, and he rested, fallen on his knee, and leaned on the ground with his stout hand, and dark night veiled his eyes.

But while Tydeus' son was following after his spear-cast, far through the foremost fighters, where he saw it sink into the earth, Hector gat breath again, and leaping back into his chariot drave out into the throng, and avoided black Fate. Then rushing on with his spear mighty Diomedes spake to him: 'Dog, thou art now again escaped from death; yet came ill very nigh thee: but now hath Phoebes Apollo saved thee, to whom thou must surely pray when thou goest amid the clash of spears. Verily I will slay thee yet when I meet thee hereafter, if any god is helper of me too. Now will I make after the rest, whomsoever I may seize.'

So spake he, and stripped the son of Paeon, spearman renowned. But Alexandros, the lord of fair-tressed Helen, aimed with his arrows at Tydeides, shepherd of the host; leaning as he aimed against a pillar on the barrow, by men fashioned, of Ilos, son of Dardanos, an elder of the people in time gone by. Now Diomedes was stripping the shining corslet of strong Agastrophos from about his breast, and the shield from his shoulders, and his strong helmet, when Paris drew the centre of his bow; nor vainly did the shaft fly from his hand, for he smote the flat of the right foot of Diomedes, and the arrow went clean through, and stood fixed in the earth; and right sweetly laughing Paris leaped up from his lair, and boasted, and said: 'Thou art smitten, nor vainly hath the dart flown forth; would that I had smitten thee in the nether belly, and taken thy life away. So should the Trojans have breathed again from their trouble, they that shudder at thee, as bleating goats at a lion.'

But him answered strong Diomedes, no wise dismayed: 'Bowman, reviler, proud in thy bow of horn,[1] thou gaper after girls, verily if thou madest trial in full harness, man to man, thy bow and showers of shafts would nothing avail thee, but now thou boastest vainly, for that thou hast grazed the sole of my foot. I care not, more than if a woman had struck me or a senseless boy, for feeble is the dart of a craven man and a worthless. In other wise from my hand, yea, if it do but touch, the sharp shaft flieth, and straightway layeth low its man, and torn are the cheeks of his wife, and fatherless his children, and he, reddening the earth with his blood, doth rot away, more birds than women round him.'

So spake he, and Odysseus, spearman renowned, drew near, and stood in front of him, and Diomedes sat down behind him, and

[1]Or, rather, 'resplendent with thy lovelock.'

drew the sharp arrow from his foot, and a sore pang passed through his flesh. Then sprang he into his car, and bade his charioteer drive back to the hollow ships, for he was hurt at heart. Then Odysseus, spearman renowned, was left alone, nor did one of the Argives abide by him, for fear had fallen on them all. Then in heaviness he spoke to his own great-hearted spirit: 'Ah me, what thing shall befall me! A great evil it is that I flee, in dread of the throng; yet worse is this, if I be taken all alone, for the other Danaans hath Kronion scattered in flight. But wherefore doth my heart thus converse with herself? for I know that they are cowards, who flee the fight, but whosoever is a hero in war, him it mainly behoves to stand stubbornly, whether he be smitten, or whether he smite another.'

While he pondered thus in heart and spirit, the ranks came on of the Trojans under shield, and hemmed him in the midst, setting among them their own bane. And even as when hounds and young men in their bloom press round a boar, and he cometh forth from his deep lair, whetting his white tusk between crooked jaws, and round him they rush, and the sound of the gnashing of tusks ariseth, and straightway they await his assault, so dread as he is, even so then round Odysseus, dear to Zeus, rushed the Trojans. And first he wounded noble Deïopites, from above, in the shoulder, leaping on him with sharp spear, and next he slew Thoon and Ennomos, and next Chersidamas, being leapt down from his chariot, he smote with the spear on the navel beneath the bossy shield, and he fell in the dust and clutched the ground with the hollow of his hand. These left he, and wounded Charops, son of Hippasos, with the spear, the brother of high-born Sokos. And to help him came Sokos, a godlike man, and stood hard by him, and spake saying: 'O renowned Odysseus, insatiable of craft and toil, to-day shalt thou either boast over two sons of Hippasos, as having slain two such men of might, and stripped their harness, or smitten by my spear shalt lose thy life'

So spake he, and smote him on the circle of his shield, through the shining shield passed the strong spear, and through the fair-dight corslet it was thrust, and tore clean off the flesh of the flanks, but Pallas Athene did not suffer it to mingle with the bowels of the hero, and Odysseus knew that the dart had in nowise lighted on a deadly spot, and drawing backward, he spake unto Sokos: 'Ah, wretched one, verily sheer destruction is come upon thee. Surely thou hast made me to cease from warring among the Trojans, but here to thee I declare that slaying and black Fate will be upon thee this day, and beneath my spear overthrown shalt thou give glory to me, and thy soul to Hades of the noble steeds."

He spake, and the other turned, and started to flee, and in his back as he turned he fixed the spear, between the shoulders, and drave it through the breast. Then he fell with a crash, and noble Odysseus boasted over him: 'Ah, Sokos, son of wise-hearted Hippasos the tamer of horses, the end of death hath come upon and caught thee, nor hast thou avoided. Ah, wretch, thy father and lady mother shall not close thine eyes in death, but birds that eat flesh raw shall tear thee, shrouding thee in the multitude of their wings. But to me, if I die, the noble Achaians will yet give due burial.'

So spake he, and drew the mighty spear of wise-hearted Sokos forth from his flesh, and from his bossy shield, and his blood flowed forth when the spear was drawn away, and afflicted his spirit. And the great-hearted Trojans when they beheld the blood of Odysseus, with clamour through the throng carne all together against him. But he gave ground, and shouted unto his comrades: thrice he shouted then, as loud as man's mouth might cry, and thrice did Menelaos dear to Zeus hear his call, and quickly he spake to Aias that was hard by him: 'Aias, of the seed of Zeus, child of Telamon, lord of the hosts, the shout of Odysseus of the hardy heart rings round me, like as though the Trojans were oppressing him alone among them, and had cut him off in the strong battle. Nay, let us speed into the throng, for better it is to rescue him. I fear lest he suffer some evil, being alone among the Trojans, so brave as he is, and lest great sorrow for his loss come upon the Danaans.'

So spake he, and led the way, and the other followed him, a godlike man. Then found they Odysseus dear to Zeus, and the Trojans beset him like tawny jackals from the hills round a wounded horned stag, that a man hath smitten with an arrow from the bow-string, and the stag hath fled from him by speed of foot, as long as the blood is warm and his limbs are strong, but when the swift arrow hath overcome him, then do the ravening jackals rend him in the hills, in a dark wood, and then god leadeth a murderous lion thither, and the jackals flee before him, but he rendeth them, so then, round wise-hearted Odysseus of the crafty counsels, did the Trojans gather, many and mighty, but that hero thrusting on with the spear held off the pitiless day. Then Aias drew near, bearing his shield like a tower, and stood thereby, and the Trojans fled from him, where each man might. Then warlike Menelaos led Odysseus out of the press, holding him by the hand, till the squire drave up the horses.

Then Aias leaped on the Trojans, and slew Doryklos. bastard son of Priam, and thereafter wounded he Pandokos, and he wounded

Lysandros, and Pyrasos, and Pylartes. And as when a brimming river cometh down upon the plain, in winter flood from the hills, swollen by the rain of Zeus, and many dry oaks and many pines it sucketh in, and much soil it casteth into the sea, even so renowned Aias charged them, pursuing through the plain, slaying horses and men. Nor wist Hector thereof at all, for he was fighting on the left of all the battle, by the banks of the river Skamandros, whereby chiefly fell the heads of men, and an unquenchable cry arose, around great Nestor and warlike Idomeneus. And Hector with them was warring, and terrible things did he, with the spear and in horsemanship, and he ravaged the battalions of the young men. Nor would the noble Achaians have yet given ground from the path, if Alexandros, the lord of fair-tressed Helen, had not stayed Machaon shepherd of the host in his valorous deeds, and smitten him on the right shoulder with a three-barbed arrow. Therefore were the Achaians, breathing valour, in great fear, lest men should seize Machaon in the turning of the fight.

Then Idomeneus spake to noble Nestor: 'O Nestor, son of Neleus, great glory of the Achaians, arise, get thee up into thy chariot, and with thee let Machaon go, and swiftly drive to the ships the whole-hooved horses. For a leech is worth many other men, to cut out arrows, and spread soothing medicaments.'

So spake he, nor did knightly Nestor of Gerenia disobey him, but straightway gat up into his chariot, and with him went Machaon, son of Asklepios the good leech, and he lashed the horses, and willingly flew they forward to the hollow ships, where they desired to be.

But Kebriones, the charioteer of Hector, beheld the Trojans driven in flight, and spake to him, and said: 'Hector, here do we contend with the Danaans, at the limit of the wailful war, but, lo, the other Trojans are driven in flight confusedly, men and horses. And Aias son of Telamon is driving them; well I know him, for wide is the shield round his shoulders. Nay, let us too urge thither the horses and chariot, there where horsemen and footmen thickest in the forefront of evil strife are slaying each other, and the cry goes up unquenchable.'

So spake he, and smote the fair-maned horses with the shrill sounding whip, and they felt the lash, and fleetly bore the swift chariot among the Trojans and Achaians, treading on the dead, and the shields, and with blood was sprinkled all the axle-tree beneath, and the rims round the car with the drops from the hooves of the horses, and with drops from the tires about the wheels. And Hector was eager to enter the press of men, and to leap in and break through, and evil din of battle he brought among the Danaans, and brief space rested he from smiting with the spear. Nay, but he ranged among the ranks of other men, with spear, and sword, and with great stones, but he avoided the battle of Aias son of Telamon, [for Zeus would have been wroth with him, if he fought with a better man than himself].

Now father Zeus, throned in the highest, roused dread in Aias, and he stood in amaze, and cast behind him his sevenfold shield of bull's hide, and gazed round in fear upon the throng, like a wild beast, turning this way and that, and slowly retreating step by step. And as when hounds and country folk drive a tawny lion from the mid-fold of the kine, and suffer him not to carry away the fattest of the herd all night they watch, and he in great desire for the flesh maketh his onset, but takes nothing thereby, for thick the darts fly from strong hands against him, and the burning brands, and these he dreads for all his fury, and in the dawn he departeth with vexed heart; even so at that time departed Aias, vexed at heart, from among the Trojans, right unwillingly, for he feared sore for the ships of the Achaians. And as when a lazy ass going past a field hath the better of the boys with him, an ass that hath had many a cudgel broken about his sides, and he fareth into the deep crop, and wasteth it, while the boys smite him with cudgels, and feeble is the force of them, but yet with might and main they drive him forth, when he hath had his fill of fodder, even so did the high-hearted Trojans and allies, called from many lands, smite great Aias, son of Telamon, with darts on the centre of his shield, and ever followed after him. And Aias would now be mindful of his impetuous valour, and turn again, and hold at bay the battalions of the horse-taming Trojans, and once more he would turn him again to flee. Yet he hindered them all from making their way to the fleet ships, and himself stood and smote between the Trojans and the Achaians, and the spears from strong hands stuck some of them in his great shield, fain to win further, and many or ever they reached his white body stood fast halfway in the earth, right eager to sate themselves with his flesh.

But when Eurypylos, the glorious son of Euaimon, beheld him oppressed by showers of darts, he went and took his stand by him, and cast with his shining spear, and smote Apisaon, son of Phausios, shepherd of the host, in the liver, below the midriff, and straightway loosened his knees; and Eurypylos sprang on him, and stripped the harness from his shoulders.

But when godlike Alexandros beheld him stripping the harness

from Apisaon, straightway he drew his bow against Eurypylos, and
smote him with a shaft on the right thigh, and the reed of the shaft
brake, and weighed down the thigh. Then Eurypylos withdrew back
into the host of his comrades, avoiding fate, and with a piercing
voice he shouted to the Danaans: 'O friends, leaders and counsellors
of the Argives, turn and stand and ward off the pitiless day from
Aias, that is oppressed with darts, nor methinks will he escape out of
the evil din of battle. Nay, stand ye the rather at bay round great
Aias, son of Telamon.'

So spake Eurypylos being wounded, and they stood close
together beside him, sloping the shields on their shoulders, and
holding up their spears, and Aias came to meet them, and turned
and stood when he reached the host of his comrades.

So they fought like unto burning fire.

But the mares of Neleus all sweating bare Nestor out of the
battle, and also carried they Machaon, shepherd of the host. Then
the noble Achilles, swift of foot, beheld and was ware of him, for
Achilles was standing by the stern of his great ship, watching the
dire toil, and the woful rout of battle. And straightway he spake to
his own comrade, Patroklos, calling to him from beside the ship,
and he heard, and from the hut he came, like unto Ares; and this to
him was the beginning of evil. Then the strong son of Menoitios
spake first to Achilles: 'Why dost thou call me, Achilles, what need
hast thou of me?'

Then swift-footed Achilles answered him and spake: 'Noble son
of Menoitios, dear to my heart, now methinks that the Achaians will
stand in prayer about my knees, for need no longer tolerable
cometh upon them. But go now, Patroklos dear to Zeus, and ask
Nestor who is this that he bringeth wounded from the war. Verily
from behind he is most like Machaon, that child of Asklepios, but I
beheld not the eyes of the man, for the horses sped past me, straining forward eagerly.'

So spake he, and Patroklos obeyed his dear comrade, and started
and ran past the ships, and the huts of the Achaians.

Now when they came to the hut of the son of Neleus, they
lighted down on the bounteous earth, and the squire, Eury medon,
loosed the horses of that old man from the car, and they dried the
sweat from their doublets, standing before the breeze, by the shore
of the sea, and thereafter came they to the hut, and sat them down
on chairs. And fair-tressed Hekamede mixed for them a mess,
Hekamede that the old man won from Tenedos, when Achilles
sacked it, and she was the daughter of great-hearted Arsinoos, and

her the Achaians chose out for him, because always in counsel he excelled them all. First she drew before them a fair table, polished well, with feet of cyanus, and thereon a vessel of bronze, with onion, for relish to the drink, and pale honey, and the grain of sacred barley, and beside it a right goodly cup, that the old man brought from home, embossed with studs of gold, and four handles there were to it, and round each two golden doves were feeding, and to the cup were two feet below. Another man could scarce have lifted the cup from the table, when it was full, but Nestor the Old raised it easily. In this cup the woman, like unto the goddesses, mixed a mess for them, with Pramnian wine, and therein grated cheese of goats' milk, with a grater of bronze, and scattered white barley thereover, and bade them drink, whenas she had made ready the mess.

So when the twain had drunk, and driven away parching thirst, they took their pleasure in discourse, speaking each to the other. Now Patroklos stood at the doors, a godlike man, and when the old man beheld him, he arose from his shining chair, and took him by the hand, and led him in, and bade him be seated. But Patroklos, from over against him, was for refusing, and spake and said: 'No time to sit have I, old man, fosterling of Zeus, nor wilt thou persuade me. Revered and dreaded is he that sent me forth to ask thee who this man is that thou bringest home wounded. Nay, but I know myself, for I see Machaon, shepherd of the host. And now will I go back again, a messenger, to speak a word to Achilles. And well dost thou know, old man, fosterling of Zeus, how terrible a man he is; lightly would he blame even one that is blameless.'

Then knightly Nestor of Gerenia answered him again

'Wherefore is Achilles thus sorry for the sons of the Achaians, for as many as are wounded with darts? He knoweth not at all what grief hath arisen in the camp: for the best men lie in the ships, wounded by shaft or smitten by spear. Wounded with the shaft is strong Diomedes, son of Tydeus, and smitten is Odysseus, spearman renowned, and Agamemnon, [and Eurypylos hath been shot with an arrow in the thigh], and this other have I but newly carried out of battle? wounded with an arrow from the bowstring. But Achilles, for all his valiance, careth not for the Danaans, nor pities them at all. Doth he wait till the fleet ships hard by the shore shall burn, maugre the Argives, in the consuming fire, and till we be slain one upon another? For my strength is no longer what it was before in my supple limbs. Would that I were in such youth, and my might as steadfast, as when a strife was set between the Eleians and ourselves, about a raid on the kine; what time I slew Itymoneus, the brave son of Hypeirochos, a dweller in Elis, when I was driving the spoil. And in fighting for his kine was he smitten in the foremost rank by a spear from my hand, and he fell, and about him were the country folk in great fear. And a prey exceeding abundant did we drive together out of the plain, fifty herds of kine, and as many flocks of sheep, and as many droves of swine, and as many wide flocks of goats, and chestnut horses a hundred and fifty, all mares, and many with their foals at their feet. And these by night we drave within Neleian Pylos to the citadel, and Neleus was glad at heart, for that so much wealth came to me, the first time I went to war. And the heralds cried aloud, with the coming of the dawn, that all men should meet that had a debt owing to them in goodly Elis. And the men that were leaders of the Pylians gathered together and divided all, for to many did the Epeians owe a debt, for few we were, and oppressed, that dwelt in Pylos. For the mighty Herakles had come and oppressed us, in the former years, and all our best men were slain. For twelve sons were we of noble Neleus, whereof I alone was left, and all the others, perished. And being lifted up with pride because of these things, the mail-clad Epeians did us despite, and devised deeds of violence. And out of the spoil that old man, even Neleus, took him a herd of kine, and a great flock of sheep, choosing three hundred, and the shepherds with them. For to him was a grezt debt owing in goodly Elis: four horses, winners of prizes, with their chariot had gone to the games, and were to run for a tripod; but these did Augeias, king of men, hold in bond in that place, but sent away the driver sorrowing for the horses. By which words and deeds was the old man angered, so he chose out much booty, uncountable. and the rest he gave to the people to divide, lest any man should depart deprived by him of his equal share. So we ordered each thing, and offered victims to the gods about the city; and on the third day all the Eleians came together, many men and whole-hooved horses in full array, and with them the two Moliones in their harness, being still but lads, nor yet well skilled in impetuous valour. Now there is a certain city, Thryoessa, a steep burg, far off on Alpheios, the uttermost city of sandy Pylos, round this they pitched their camp, being eager to raze it utterly. But when they had passed through all the plain, to us came Athene by night rushing down from Olympus, with the message that we should arm us. Nor w ere the folk unwilling that she gathered in Pylos, but right eager for war Now Neleus would not suffer me to arm myself, but hid my horses away, for he deemed that I knew naught as yet of the deeds of war. Yet even so did I shine among our horsemen, on foot though I was, for so Athene led the fight. There is a river Minyeïos, that falleth into the sea near Arene, where the horsemen of us Pylians waited the fair dawn, and thither those ranks of footmen flowed onward. Thence in full array, and harnessed in our gear, we came at midday to the sacred stream of Alpheios. There to Zeus pre-eminent in might we sacrificed goodly victims, and a bull to Alpheios, and a bull to Poseidon, but to bright-eyed Athene a heifer of the herd, and thereafter took we supper in ranks throughout the camp, and lay down to sleep each man in his arms, about the streams of the rivel. Now the great-hearted Epeians were gathered round the citadel, being eager to sack it utterly. But ere that might be, there appeared unto them a great deed of war. For when the bright sun came up above the earth, we joined battle, with prayer to Zeus, and Athene. But when the strife of the Pylians and Epeians began, I was the first that slew a mans and got me his whole-hooved steeds, – the warrior Mulios was he, who had to wife fair-haired Agamede, the eldest daughter of Augeias, and she knew all drugs that the wide earth nourisheth. Him as he came on I smote with a bronze-shod spear, and he fell in the dust and I leaped into the car, and stood among the foremost fighter, But the great-hearted Epeians fled this way and that when they saw the man fall, even the leader of the horsemen, who excelled in battle. But I sprang upon them, like a black tempest, and fifty chariots I took, and beside each chariot two men bit the earth with their teeth, subdued beneath my spear. And now should I have overthrown the twin Moliones, sons of Aktor, if their sire, the Earthshaker of wide sway, had not saved them out of the battle, and covered them with a thick mist.[1] There Zeus gave great might to the Pylians, for we followed through the wide plain, slaying the foe and gathering their goodly arms, even till we brought our horses to Bouprasion, rich in wheat, and the rock Olenian, and where is the hill called the hill of Alision, whence Athene turned the people again. There slew I the last man and left him there, but the Achaians drave back their swift horses from Bouprasion to Pylos, and all gave praise, among the gods to Zeus, and among men to Nestor. Such was I, if ever among men I was such an one. But Achilles is for reaping alone the reward of his valour; surely methinks that he will repent, and lament sore when the host perisheth. O friend, surely Menoitios thus gave thee command, on that day when he sent thee out ol Phthia to Agamemnon. And we twain were within the house,

---

[1]Aktor was the putative, Poseidon the real father of the Moliones.

I and goodly Odysseus, and in the halls heard we all things even as he commanded thee. For we had come to the fair-set halls of Peleus, gathering the host throughout Achaia of the fair dames. There then we found the hero Menoitios within, and thee, and with thee Achilles. And Peleus the Old, the lord of horses, was burning the fat thighs of kine to Zeus, whose joy is in the thunder, in the precinct of his court, and held in his hand a chalice of gold, pouring forth the bright wine upon the burning offerings. And ye were busy about the flesh of the ox, and then stood we in the doorway, and Achilles leaped up in amazement, and took us by the hand, and led us in, and bade us be seated, and set before us well the entertainment of strangers, all that is their due. But when we had taken delight in eating and drinking, I began the discourse, and bade you follow with us, and ye were right eager, and those twain laid on you many commands Peleus the Old bade his son Achilles be ever the boldest in fight, and pre-eminent over others, but to thee did Menoitios thus give command, the son of Aktor: "My child, of lineage is Achilles higher than thou, and thou art elder, but in might he is better far. But do thou speak to him well a word of wisdom, and put it to him gently, and show him what things he should do, and he will obey thee to his profit." So did the old man give thee command, but thou art forgetful. Nay, but even now speak thou thus and thus to wise-hearted Achilles, if perchance he will obey thee. Who knows but that, God helping, thou mightst stir him spirit with thy persuading? and good is the persuasion of a friend. But if in his heart he be shunning some oracle of God, and his lady mother hath told him somewhat from Zeus, natheless let him send forth thee, and let the rest of the host of the Myrmidons follow with thee, if perchance any light shall arise from thee to the Danaans; and let him give thee his fair harness, to bear into the war, if perchance the Trojans may take thee for him, and withhold them from the strife. and the warlike sons of the Achaians might take breath, being wearied; for brief is the breathing time in battle. And lightly might ye, being unwearied, drive men wearied in the war unto the city, away from the ships and the huts.'

So spake he, and roused his heart within his breast, and he started and ran by the ships to Achilles of the seed of Aiakos. But when Patroklos came in his running to the ships of godlike Odysseus, where was their assembly and place of law, and whereby also were their altars of the gods established, there did Eurypylos meet him, Euaimon's son, of the seed of Zeus, wounded in the thigh with an arrow, and limping out of the battle. And sweat ran down streaming from his head and shoulders, and from his cruel wound the black blood was welling, but his mind was unshaken. And the strong son of Menoitios had pity on him when he beheld him, and lamenting he spake winged words: 'Ah, wretched men, ye leaders and counsellors of the Danaans. How are ye now doomed, far from your friends and your own country, to feed full with your white fat the swift hounds in Troia! But come, tell me this, Eurypylos, hero and fosterling of Zeus, will the Achaians yet in any wise restrain mighty Hector, or will they perish even now, subdued beneath his spear?'

And to him again did the wounded Eurypylos make answer: 'No more, Patroklos of the seed of Zeus, will there be any defence of the Achaians, but they will fall among the black ships. For verily all of them, that afore were bravest, are lying in the ships wounded and smitten by the hands of the Trojans, whose strength is waxing always. But me do thou succour, and lead me to the black ship, and cut the arrow out of my thigh, and wash away the black blood from it with warm water, and smear soft healing drugs thereover, these good herbs whereof they say that thou hast learned from Achilles, whom Cheiron taught, the most righteous of the Centaurs. For of the leeches, Podaleirios and Machaon, one methinks, is wounded in the huts, and himself hath need of a good leech, and the other on the plain abideth the keen battle of the Trojans.'

Then the strong son of Menoitios answered him again: 'How should these things be? what shall we do, hero Eurypylos? I am on my way to carry a saying to wise-hearted Achilles, even the command of Nestor of Gerenia, warden of the Achaians; nay, but not even so will I be heedless of thee that art wounded.'

So spake he, and clasped the shepherd of the host below the breast, and led him to the hut; and the squire when he beheld them cast on the ground the skins of oxen. There he stretched him at length, and cut with a knife the sharp arrow from his thigh, and washed from it the black blood with warm water. And thereon he cast a bitter root rubbing it between his hands, a root that took pain away, and ended all his anguish, and the wound began to dry, and the blood ceased.

BOOK XII

How the Trojans and allies broke within the wall of the Achaians.

SO IN THE HUTS the strong son of Menoitios was tending the wounded Eurypylos, but still they fought confusedly, the Argives and Trojans. Nor were the fosse of the Danaans and their wide wall above, long to protect them, the wall they had builded for defence of the ships, and the fosse they had drawn round about; for neither had they given goodly hecatombs to the gods, that it might guard with its bounds their swift ships, and rich spoil. Nay, maugre the deathless gods was it builded, wherefore it abode steadfast for no long time. While Hector yet lived, and yet Achilles kept his wrath, and unsacked was the city of Priam the king, so long the great wall of the Achaians likewise abode steadfast. But when all the bravest of the Trojans died, and many of the Argives, – some were taken, and some were left, – and the city of Priam was sacked in the tenth year, and the Argives had gone back in their ships to their own dear country, then verily did Poseidon and Apollo take counsel to wash away the wall, bringing in the might of the rivers, of all that flow from the hills of Ida to the sea. Rhesos there was, and Heptaporos, and Karesos, and Rhodios, Grenikos, and Aisepos, and goodly Ska-mandros, and Simoeis, whereby many shields and helms fell in the dust, and the generation of men half divine; the mouths of all these waters did Phoebus Apollo turn together, and for nine days he drave their stream against the wall; and still Zeus rained unceas-ingly, that the quicker he might mingle the wall with the salt sea. And the Shaker of the earth, with his trident in his hands, was him-self the leader, and sent forth into the waves all the foundations of beams and stones that the Achaians had laid with toil, and made all smooth by the strong current of Hellespont, and covered again the great beach with sand, when he had swept away the wall, and turned the rivers back to flow in their channel, where of old they poured down their fair flow of water.

So were Poseidon and Apollo to do in the aftertime; but then war and the din of war sounded about the well-builded wall, and the beams of the towers rang beneath the strokes; while the Argives, subdued by the scourge of Zeus, were penned and driven in by the hollow ships, in dread of Hector, the mighty maker of flight, but he, as afore-time, fought like a whirlwind. And as when, among hounds and hunting men, a boar or lion wheeleth him about, raging in his strength, and these array themselves in fashion like a tower, and stand up against him, casting many javelins from their hands; but never is his stout heart confused nor afraid, and his courage is his bane, and often he wheeleth him about, and maketh trial of the ranks of men, and wheresoever he maketh onset there the ranks of men give way, even so Hector went and besought his comrades through the press, and spurred them on to cross the dyke. But his swift-footed horses dared not, but loud they neighed, standing by the sheer edge, for the wide fosse affrighted them, neither easy to leap from hard by, nor to cross, for overhanging banks stood round about it all on either hand, and above it was furnished with sharp stakes that the sons of the Achaians had planted there, thick set and great, a bulwark against hostile men. Thereby not lightly might a horse enter, drawing a well-wheeled chariot; but the footmen were eager, if they might accomplish it. Then Polydamas drew near valiant Hector, and spake to him: 'Hector and ye other leaders of the Trojans and allies, foolishly do we drive our fleet horses through the dyke; nay right hard it is to cross, for sharp stakes stand in it, and over against them the wall of the Achaians. Thereby none may go down and fight in chariots, for strait is the place wherein, methinks, we might come by a mischief. For if Zeus that thunders on high is utterly to destroy them in his evil will, and is minded to help the Trojans, verily then I too would desire that even instantly this might be, that the Achaians should perish here nameless far from Argos: but and if they turn again, and we flee back from among the ships, and rush into the delved ditch, then methinks that not even one from among us to bear the tidings will win back to the city before the force of the Achaians when they rally. But come as I declare, let us all obey. Let our squires hold the horses by the dyke, while we being harnessed in our gear as foot soldiers follow all together with Hector, and the Achaians will not withstand us, if indeed the bands of death be made fast upon them.'

So spake Polydamas, and his wise word pleased Hector well, and straightway in his harness he leaped from his chariot to the ground. Nor were the other Trojans gathered upon the chariots, but they all leaped forth, when they beheld goodly Hector. There each gave it into the charge of his own charioteer, to keep the horses orderly there by the fosse. And they divided, and arrayed themselves, and ordered in five companies they followed with the leaders.

Now they that went with Hector and noble Polydamas, these were most, and bravest, and most were eager to break the wall, and fight by the hollow ships; and with them followed Kebriones for the third, for Hector had left another man with his chariot, a weaker warrior than Kebriones. The second company Paris led, and Alkathoos, and Agenor: and the third company Helenos led, and godlike Deiphobos, – two sons of Priam, – the third was the warrior Asios, Asios Hyrtakos' son, whom his tall sorrel steeds brought out of Arisbe, from the river Selleeïs. And of the fourth company was the brave son of Anchises leader, even Aineias; and with him were two sons of Antenor, Archelochos and Akamas, both well skilled in all warfare.

And Sarpedon led the glorious allies, and to be with him he chose Glaukos and warlike Asteropaios, for they seemed to him to be manifestly the bravest of all after himself, but he was excellent, yea, above all the host. And these when they had arrayed one another with well-fashioned shields of bulls' hide, went straight and eager against the Danaans, nor deemed that they could longer resist them, but that themselves should fall on the black ships.

Then the rest of the Trojans and the far-famed allies obeyed the counsel of blameless Polydamas, but Asios, son of Hyrtakos, leader of men, willed not to leave his horses there, and his squire the chari- oteer, but with them he drew near the swift ships, fond man! for never was he, avoiding evil Fates, to return, rejoicing in his horses and chariot, back from the ships to windy Ilios. Nay, ere that the Fate of ill name overshadowed him, by the spear of Idomeneus, the haughty son of Deukalion. For Asios went against the left flank of the ships, whereby the Achaians returned out of the plain with char- iots and horses: there he drave through his horses and his car, nor found he the doors shut on the gates, and the long bar, but men were holding them open if perchance they might save any of their comrades fleeing out of the battle towards the ships. Straight thereby held he his horses with unswerving aim, and his men fol- lowed him, crying shrilly, for they deemed that the Achaians could no longer hold them off, but that themselves would fall on the black ships: fools, for in the gates they found two men of the bravest, the high-hearted sons of the warrior Lapithae, one the son of Peirithoos, strong Polypoites, and one Leonteus, peer of Ares the bane of men. These twain stood in front of the lofty gates, like high-crested oak trees in the hills, that for ever abide the wind and rain, firm fixed with roots great and long; even so these twain, trust- ing to the mightiness of their hands, abode the coming of great

Asios, and fled not. But straight came the Trojans against the well-built wall, holding their shields of dry bulls' hide on high, with mighty clamour, round the prince Asios, and Iamenos, and Orestes, and Adamas, son of Asios, and Thoon, and Oinomaos. But the other twain for a while, being within the wall, urged the well-greaved Achaians to fight for the ships; but when they saw the Trojans assailing the wall, while the Danaans cried and turned in flight, then forth rushed the twain, and fought in front of the gates like wild boars that in the mountains abide the assailing crew of men and dogs, and charging on either flank they crush the wood around them, cutting it at the root, and the clatter of their tusks waxes loud, till one smite them and take their life away: so clattered the bright bronze on the breasts of the twain, as they were smitten in close fight, for right hardily they fought, trusting to the host above them, and to their own strength.

For the men above were casting with stones from the well-built towers in defence of themselves and of the huts, and of the swift-faring ships. And like snowflakes the stones fell earthward, flakes that a tempestuous wind, as it driveth the dark clouds, rains thickly down on the bounteous earth: so thick fell the missiles from the hands of Achaians and Trojans alike, and their helms rang harsh and their bossy shields, being smitten with mighty stones. Verily then Asios, son of Hyrtakos, gloaned and smote both his thighs, and indignantly he spake: 'Father Zeus, verily thou too dost greatly love a lie, for I deemed not that the Achaian heroes could withstand our might and our hands invincible. But they like wasps of nimble body, or bees that have made their dwellings in a rugged path, and leave not their hollow hold, but abide and keep the hunters at bay for the sake of their little ones, even so these men have no will to give ground from the gates, though they are but two, ere they lay or be slain.'

So spake he, nor with his speech did he persuade the mind of Zeus, for his will was to give renown to Hector.

[But the others were fighting about the other gates, and hard it were for me like a god to tell all these things, for everywhere around the wall of stone rose the fire divine; the Argives, for all their sorrow, defending the ships of necessity; and all the gods were grieved at heart, as many as were defenders of the Danaans in battle. And together the Lapithae waged war and strife.]

There the son of Peirithoos, mighty Polypoites, smote Damasos with the spear, through the helmet with cheek-pieces of bronze; nor did the bronze helm stay the spear, but the point of bronze brake clean through the bone, and all the brain within was scattered, and the spear overcame him in his eagerness. Thereafter he slew Pylon and Ormenos. And Leonteus of the stock of Ares smote Hippomachos, son of Antimachos, with the spear, striking him on the girdle. Then again he drew his sharp sword from the sheath, and smote Antiphates first in close fight, rushing on him through the throng, that he fell on his back on the ground; and thereafter be brought down Menon, and Iamenos, and Orestes one after the other, to the bounteous earth.

While they were stripping from these the shining arms, the young men who followed with Polydamas and Hector, they that were most in number and bravest, and most were eager to break the wall and set the ships on fire, these still stood doubtful by the fosse, for as they were eager to pass over a bird had appeared to them, an eagle of lofty flight, skirting the host on the left hand. In its talons it bore a blood-red monstrous snake, alive, and struggling still; yea, not yet had it forgotten the joy of battle, but writhed backward and smote the bird that held it on the breast, beside the neck, and the bird cast it from him down to the earth, in sore pain, and dropped it in the midst of the throng; then with a cry sped away down the gusts of the wind. And the Trojans shuddered when they saw the gleaming snake lying in the midst of them; an omen of aegis-bearing Zeus.

Then verily Polydamas stood by brave Hector, and spake: 'Hector, ever dost thou rebuke me in the assemblies, though I counsel wisely; since it by no means beseemeth one of the people to speak contrary to thee, in council or in war, but always to increase thy power; but now again will I say all that seemeth to me to be best. Let us not advance and fight with the Danaans for the ships. For even thus, methinks, the end will be, if indeed this bird hath come for the Trojans when they were eager to cross the dyke, this eagle of lofty flight, skirting the host on the left hand, bearing in his talons a blood-red monstrous snake, yet living; then straightway left he hold of him, before he reached his own nest, nor brought him home in the end to give to his nestlings. Even so shall we, though we burst with mighty force the gates and wall of the Achaians, and the Achaians give ground, even so we shall return in disarray from the ships by the way we came; for many of the Trojans shall we leave behind, whom the Achaians will slay with the sword, in defence of the ships. Even so would a soothsayer interpret that in his heart had clear knowledge of omens, and whom the people obeyed.'

Then Hector of the glancing helm lowered on him and said: 'Polydamas, that thou speakest is no longer pleasing to me; yea, thou knowest how to conceive another counsel better than this. But if thou verily speakest thus in earnest, then the gods themselves have utterly destroyed thy wits; thou that bidst us forget the counsels of loud-thundering Zeus, that himself promised me, and confirmed with a nod of his head! But thou bidst us be obedient to birds long of wing, whereto I give no heed, nor take any care thereof, whether they fare to the right, to the dawn and to the sun, or to the left, to mist and darkness. Nay, for us, let us trust to the counsel of mighty Zeus, who is king over all mortals and immortals. One omen is best, to fight for our own country. And wherefore dost thou fear war and battler for if all the rest of us be slain by the ships of the Argives, yet needst thou not fear to perish, for thy heart is not warlike, nor enduring in battle. But if thou dost hold aloof from the fight, or winnest any other with thy words to turn him from war, straightway by my spear shalt thou be smitten, and lose thy life.'

So spake he, and led on, and they followed with a wondrous din; and Zeus that joyeth in the thunder roused from the hills of Ida a blast of wind, which bare the dust straight against the ships; and he made weak the heart of the Achaians, but gave renown to the Trojans and to Hector. Trusting then in his omens, and their might, they strove to break the great wall of the Achaians. They dragged down the machicolations of the towers, and overthrew the battlements, and heaved up the projecting buttresses, that the Achaians set first in the earth, to be the props of the towers. These they overthrew, and hoped to break the wall of the Achaians. Nor even now did the Danaans give ground from the path, but closed up the battlements with shields of bulls' hides, and cast from them at the foemen as they went below the walls.

Now the two Aiantes went everywhere on the towers, ever urging, and arousing the courage of the Achaians. One they would accost with honeyed words, another with hard words they would rebuke, whomsoever they saw utterly giving ground from the fight: 'O friends, whosoever is eminent, or whosoever is of middle station among the Argives, ay, or lower yet, for in no wise are all men equal in war, now is there work for all, and this yourselves well know. Let none turn back to the ships, for that he hath heard one threatening aloud; nay, get ye forward, and cheer another on, if perchance Olympian Zeus, the lord of lightning, will grant us to drive back the assault, and push the foe to the city.'

So these twain shouted in the front, and aroused the battle of the Achaians. But as flakes of snow fall thick on a winter day, when Zeus the Counsellor hath begun to snow, showing forth these arrows of his to men, and he hath lulled the winds, and he snoweth continually, till he hath covered the crests of the high hills, and the uttermost headlands, and the grassy plains, and rich tillage of men; and the snow is scattered over the havens and shores of the grey sea, and only the wave as it rolleth in keeps off the snow, but all other things are swathed over, when the shower of Zeus cometh heavily, so from both sides their stones flew thick, some towards the Trojans, and some from the Trojans against the Achaians, while both sides were smitten, and over all the wall the din arose.

Yet never would the Trojans, then, and renowned Hector have broken the gates of the wall, and the long bar, if Zeus the Counsellor had not roused his son Sarpedon against the Argives, like a lion against the kine of crooked horn. Straightway he held forth his fair round shield of hammered bronze, that the bronze-smith had hammered out, and within had stitched many bulls' hides with rivets of gold, all round the circle, this held he forth, and shook two spears; and sped on his way, like a mountain-nurtured lion, that long lacketh meat, and his brave spirit urgeth him to make assail on the sheep, and come even against a well-builded hornestead. Nay, even if he find herdsmen thereby, guarding the sheep with hounds and spears, yet hath he no mind to be driven without an effort from the steading, but he either leapeth on a sheep, and seizeth it, or himself is smitten in the foremost place with a dart from a strong hand. So did his heart then urge on the godlike Sarpedon to rush against the wall, and break through the battlements. And instantly he spake to Glaukos, son of Hippolochos: 'Glaukos, wherefore have we twain the chiefest honour, – seats of honour, and messes, and full cups in Lykia, and all men look on us as gods? And wherefore hold we a great demesne by the banks of Xanthos, a fair demesne of orchard-land, and wheat-bearing tilth? Therefore now it behoveth us to take our stand in the first rank of the Lykians, and encounter fiery battle, that certain of the well-corsleted Lykians may say, "Verily our kings that rule Lykia be no inglorious men, they that eat fat sheep, and drink the choice wine honey-sweet: nay, but they are also of excellent might, for they war in the foremost ranks of the Lykians. Ah, friend, if once escaped from this battle we were for ever to be ageless and immortal, neither would I fight myself in the foremost ranks, nor would I send thee into the war that giveth men renown, but now – for assuredly ten thousand fates of death do every way beset us, and these no mortal may escape nor avoid – now let us go forward, whether we shall give glory to other men, or others to us.'

So spake he, and Glaukos turned not apart, nor disobeyed him, and they twain went straight forward, leading the great host of the Lykians.

Then Menestheus son of Peteos shuddered when he beheld there for against his tower they went, bringing with them ruin; and he looked along the tower of the Achaians if perchance he might see any of the leaders, that would ward off destruction from his comrades, and he beheld the two Aiantes, insatiate of war, standing there, and Teukros hard by, newly come from his hut; but he could not cry to be heard of them, so great was the din, and the noise went up unto heaven of smitten shields and helms with horse-hair crests, and of the gates, for they had all been shut, and the Trojans stood beside them, and strove by force to break them, and enter in. Swiftly then to Aias he sent the herald Thoötes: 'Go, noble Thoötes, and run, and call Aias: or rather the twain, for that will be far the best of all, since quickly here will there be wrought utter ruin. For hereby press the leaders of the Lykians, who of old are fierce in strong battle. But if beside them too war and toil arise, yet at least let the strong Telamonian Aias come alone. and let Teukros the skilled bowman follow with him.'

So spake he, and the herald listened and disobeyed him not, but started and ran by the wall of the mail-clad Achaians, and came, and stood by the Aiantes, and straight way spake: 'Ye twain Aiantes, leaders of the mail-clad Achaians, the dear son of Peteos, fosterling of Zeus, biddeth you go thither, that, if it be but for a little while, ye may take your part in battle: both of you he more desireth, for that will be for the best of all, since quickly there will there be wrought utter ruin for thereby press the leaders of the Lykians, who of old are fierce in strong battle. But if beside you too war and toil arise, yet at least let the strong Telamonian Aias come alone, and let Teukros the skilled bowman follow with him.'

So spake he, nor did the strong Telamonian Aias disobey, but instantly spake winged words to the son of Oileus: "Aias, do ye twain stand here, thyself and strong Lykomedes, and urge the Danaans to war with all their might; but I go thither, to take my part in battle, and quickly will I come again, when I have well aided them.'

So spake Telamonian Aias and departed, and Teuklos went with him, his brother by the same father, and with them Pandion bare the bended bow of Teukros.

Now when they came to the tower of great-hearted Menestheus, passing within the wall; – and to men sore pressed they came, – the foe were climbing upon the battlements, like a dark whirlwind, even the strong leaders and counsellors of the Lykians, and they hurled together into the war and the battle cry arose. Now first did Aias Telamon's son slay a man, Epikles great of heart, the comrade of Sarpedon. With a jagged stone he smote him, a great stone that lay uppermost within the wall, by the battlements. Not lightly could a man hold it in both hands, however strong in his youth, of such mortals as now are, but Aias lifted it, and cast it from above, and shattered the helm of fourfold crest, and all to bráke the bones of the head, and he fell like a diver from the lofty tower, and his life left his bones. And Teukros smote Glaukos, the strong son of Hippolochos, as he came on, with an arrow from the loft; wall; even where he saw his shoulder bare he smote him, and made him cease from delight in battle. Back from the wall he leapt secretly, lest any of the Achaians should see him smitten, and speak boastfully. But sorrow came on Sarpedon when Glaukos departed, so soon as he was aware thereof, but he forgot not the joy of battle. He aimed at Alkmaon, son of Thestor, with the spear, and smote him, and drew out the spear. And Alkmaon following the spear fell prone, and his bronze-dight arms rang round him. Then Sarpedon seized with strong hands the battlement, and dragged, and it all gave way together, while above the wall was stripped bare, and made a path for many.

Then Aias and Teukros did encounter him: Teukros smote him with an arrow, on the bright baldric of his covering shield, about the breast, but Zeus warded off the Fates from his son, that he should not be overcome beside the ships' sterns. Then Aias leaped on and smote his shield, nor did the spear pass clean through, yet shook he Sarpedon in his eagerness. He gave ground a little way from the battlement, yet retreated not wholly, since his heart hoped to win renown. Then he turned and cried to the godlike Lykians: 'O Lykians, wherefore thus are ye slack in impetuous valour. Hard it is for me, stalwart as I am, alone to break through, and make a path to the ships, nay, follow hard after me, for the more men, the better work.'

So spake he, and they, dreading the rebuke of their king, pressed on the harder around the counsellor and king. And the Argives on the other side made strong their battalions within the wall, and mighty toil began for them. For neither could the strong Lykians burst through the wall of the Danaans, and make a way to the ships, nor could the warlike Danaans drive back the Lykians from the wall, when once they had drawn near thereto. But as two men contend about the marches of their land, with measuring rods in their hands, in a common field, when in narrow space they strive for equal shares, even so the battlements divided them, and over those they smote the round shields of ox hide about the breasts of either side, and the fluttering bucklers. And many were wounded in the flesh with the ruthless bronze, whensoever the back of any of the warriors was laid bare as he turned, ay, and many clean through the very shield. Yea, everywhere the towers and battlements swam with the blood of men shed on either side, by Trojans and Achaians. But even so they could not put the Argives to rout, but they held their ground, as an honest woman that laboureth with her hands holds the balance, and raises the weight and the wool together, balancing them, that she may win scant wages for her children; so evenly was strained their war and battle, till the moment when Zeus have the greater renown to Hector, son of Priam, who was the first to leap within the wall of the Achaians. In a piercing voice he cried aloud to the Trojans: 'Rise, ye horse-taming Trojans, break the wall of the Argives, and cast among the ships fierce blazing fire.'

So spake he, spurring them on, and they all heard him with their ears, and in one mass rushed straight against the wall, and with sharp spears in their hands climbed upon the machicolations of the towers. And Hector seized and carried a stone that lay in front of the gates, thick in the hinder part, but sharp at point: a stone that not the two best men of the people, such as mortals now are, could Lightly lift from the ground on to a wain, but easily he wielded it alone, for the son of crooked-counselling Kronos made it light for him. And as when a shepherd lightly beareth the fleece of a ram, taking it in one hand, and little doth it burden him, so Hector lifted the stone, and bare it straight against the doors that closely guarded the stubborn-set portals, double gates and tall, and two cross bars held them within, and one bolt fastened them. And he came, and stood hard by, and firmly planted himself, and smote them in the midst, setting his legs well apart, that his cast might lack no strength. And he brake both the hinges, and the stone fell within by reason of its weight, and the gates rang loud around, and the bars held not, and the doors burst this way and that beneath the rush of the stone. Then glorious Hector leaped in, with face like the sudden night, shining in wondrous mail that was clad about his body, and with two spears in his hands. No man that met him could have held him back when once he leaped within the gates: none but the gods, and his eyes shone with fire. Turning towards the throng he cried to the Trojans to overleap the wall, and they obeyed his summons, and speedily some overleaped the wall, and some poured into the fair-wrought gateways, and the Danaans fled in fear among the hollow ships, and a ceaseless clamour arose.

BOOK XIII

Poseidon stirreth up the Achaians to defend the ships.
The valour of Idomeneus.

NOW ZEUS, after that he had brought the Trojans and Hector to the ships, left them to their toil and endless labour there, but otherwhere again he turned his shining eyes, and looked upon the land of the Thracian horsebreeders, and the Mysians, fierce fighters hand to hand, and the proud Hippemolgoi that drink mare's milk, and the Abioi, the most righteous of men. To Troy no more at all he turned his shining eyes, for he deemed in his heart that not one of the Immortals would draw near, to help either Trojans or Danaans.

But the mighty Earthshaker held no blind watch, who sat and marvelled on the war and strife, high on the topmost crest of wooded Samothrace, for thence all Ida was plain to see; and plain to see were the city of Priam, and the ships of the Achaians. Thither did he go from the sea and sate him down, and he had pity on the Achaians, that they were subdued to the Trojans, and strong was his anger against Zeus.

Then forthwith he went down from the rugged hill, faring with swift steps, and the high hills trembled, and the woodland, beneath the immortal footsteps of Poseidon as he moved. Three strides he made, and with the fourth he reached his goal, even Aigae, and there was his famous palace in the deeps of the mere, his glistering golden mansions builded, imperishable for ever. Thither went he, and let harness to the car his bronze-hooved horses, swift of flight, clothed with their golden manes. He girt his own golden array about his body, and seized the well-wrought lash of gold, and mounted his chariot, and forth he drove across the waves. And the sea beasts frolicked beneath him, on all sides out of the deeps, for well they knew their lord, and with gladness the sea stood asunder, and swiftly they sped, and the axle of bronze was not wetted beneath, and the bounding steeds bare him on to the ships of the Achaians.

Now there is a spacious cave in the depths of the deep mere, between Tenedos and rugged Imbros; there did Poseidon, the Shaker of the earth, stay his horses, and loosed them out of the chariot, and cast before them ambrosial food to graze withal, and golden tethers he bound about their hooves, tethers neither to be broken nor loosed, that there the horses might continually await their lord's return. And he went to the host of the Achaians.

Now the Trojans like flame or storm-wind were following in close array, with fierce intent, after Hector, son of Priam. With shouts and cries they came, and thought to take the ships of the Achaians, and to slay thereby all the bravest of the host. But Poseidon, that girdleth the world, the Shaker of the earth, was urging on the Argives, and worth he came from the deep salt sea, in form and untiring voice like unto Kalchas. First he spake to the two Aiantes, that themselves were eager for battle: 'Ye Aiantes twain, ye shall save the people of the Achaians, if ye are mindful of your might, and reckless of chill fear. For verily I do not otherwhere dread the invincible hands of the Trojans, that have climbed the great wall in their multitude, nay, the well greaved Achaians will hold them all at bay; but hereby verily do I greatly dread lest some evil befall us, even here where that furious one is leading like a flame of fire, Hector, who boasts him to be son of mighty Zeus. Nay, but here may some god put it into the hearts of you twain, to stand sturdily yourselves, and urge others to do the like; thereby might ye drive him from the fleet-faring ships, despite his eagerness, yea, even if the Olympian himself is rousing him to war.'

Therewith the Shaker of the world, the girdler of the earth, struck the twain with his staff, and filled them with strong courage, and their limbs he made light, and their feet, and their hands withal. Then, even as a swift-winged hawk speeds forth to fly, poised high above a tall sheer rock, and swoops to chase some other bird across the plain, even so Poseidon sped from them, the Shaker of the world. And of the twain Oileus' son, the swift-footed Aias, was the first to know the god, and instantly he spake to Aias, son of Telamon: 'Aias, since it is one of the gods who hold Olympus, that in the semblance of a seer commands us now to fight beside the ships – not Kalchas is he, the prophet and soothsayer, for easily I knew the tokens of his feet and knees as he turned away, and the gods are easy to discern – lo, then mine own heart within my breast is more eagerly set on war and battle, and my feet beneath and my hands above are lusting for the fight.'

Then Aias, son of Telamon, answered him saying: 'Even so, too, my hands invincible now rage about the spear-shaft, and wrath has risen within me, and both my feet are swift beneath me; yea, I am keen to meet, even in single fight, the ceaseless rage of Hector son of Priam.'

So they spake to each other, rejoicing in the delight of battle, which the god put in their heart. Then the girdler of the earth stirred up the Achaians that were in the rear and were renewing their strength beside the swift ships. Their limbs were loosened by their grievous toil, yea, and their souls filled with sorrow at the sight of the Trojans, that had climbed over the great wall in their multitude. And they looked on them, and shed tears beneath their brows, thinking that never would they escape destruction. But the Shaker of the earth right easily came among them, and urged on the strong battalions of warriors. Teukros first he came and summoned, and Leitos, and the hero Peneleos, and Thoas, and Deïpyros, and Meriones, and Antilochos, lords of the war cry, all these he spurred on with winged words: 'Shame on you, Argives, shame, ye striplings, in your battle had I trusted for the salvation of our ships. But if you are to withdraw from grievous war, now indeed the day doth shine that shall see us conquered by the Trojans. Out on it, for verily a great marvel is this that mine eyes behold, a terrible thing that methought should never come to pass, the Trojans advancing against our ships! Of yore they were like fleeting hinds, that in the wild wood are the prey of jackals, and pards, and wolves, and wander helpless, strengthless, empty of the joy of battle. Even so the Trojans of old cared never to wait and face the wrath and the hands of the Achaians, not for a moment. But now they are fighting far from the town, by the hollow ships, all through the baseness of our leader and the remissness of the people, who, being at strife with the chief, have no heart to defend the swift-faring ships, nay, thereby they are slain. But if indeed and in truth the hero Agamemnon, the wide-ruling son of Atreus, is the very cause of all, for that he did dishonour the swift-footed son of Peleus, not even so may we refrain in any wise from war. Nay, let us right our fault with speed, for easily righted are the hearts of the brave. No longer do ye well to refrain from impetuous might, all ye that are the best men of the host. I myself would not quarrel with one that, being a weakling, abstained from war, but with you I am heartily wroth. Ah, friends, soon shall ye make the mischief more through this remissness, – but let each man conceive shame in his heart, and indignation, for verily great is the strife that hath arisen. Lo, the mighty Hector of the loud war-cry is fighting at the ships, and the gates and the long bar he hath burst in sunder.'

On this wise did the Earth-enfolder call to and spur on the Achaians. And straightway they made a stand around the two Aiantes, strong bands that Ares himself could not enter and make light of, nor Athene that marshals the host. Yea, they were the chosen best that abode the Trojans and goodly Hector, and spear on spear made close-set fence, and shield on serried shield, buckler pressed on buckler, and helm on helm, and man on man. The horse-hair crests on the bright helmet-ridges touched each other as they nodded, so close they stood each by other, and spears brandished in bold hands were interlaced; and their hearts were steadfast and lusted for battle.

Then the Trojans drave forward in close array, and Hector led them, pressing straight onwards, like a rolling rock from a cliff, that the winter-swollen water thrusteth from the crest of a hill, having broken the foundations of the stubborn rock with its wondrous flood; leaping aloft it flies, and the wood echoes under it, and unstayed it runs its course, till it reaches the level plain, and then it rolls no more for all its eagerness, – even so Hector for a while threatened lightly to win to the sea through the huts and the ships of the Achaians, slaying as he came, but when he encountered the serried battalions, he was stayed when he drew near against them. But they of the other part, the sons of the Achaians, thrust with their swords and doublepointed spears, and drave him forth from them, that he gave ground and reeled backward. Then he cried with a piercing voice, calling on the Trojans: 'Trojans, and Lykians, and close-fighting Dardanians, hold your ground, for the Achaians will not long ward me off, nay, though they have arrayed themselves in fashion like a tower. Rather, methinks, they will flee back before the spear, if verily the chief of gods has set me on, the loud-thundering lord of Hera.'

Therewith he spurred on the heart and spirit of each man; and Deiphobos, the son of Priam, strode among them with high thoughts, and held in front of him the circle of his shield, and lightly he stepped with his feet, advancing beneath the cover of his shield Then Meriones aimed at him with a shining spear, and struck, and missed not, but smote the circle of the bulls'-hide shield, yet no whit did he pierce it; nay, well ere that might be, the long spear-shaft snapped in the socket. Now Deiphobos was holding off from him the bulls'-hide shield, and his heart feared the lance of wise Meriones, but that hero shrunk back among the throng of his comrades, greatly in wrath both for the loss of victory, and of his spear, that he had shivered. So he set forth to go to the huts and the ships of the Achaians, to bring a long spear, that he had left in his hut.

Meanwhile the others were fighting on, and there arose an inextinguishable cry. First Teukros, son of Telamon, slew a man, the spearman Imbrios, the son of Mentor rich in horses. In Pedaion he dwelt, before the coming of the sons of the Achaians, and he had for wife a daughter of Priam, born out of wedlock, Medesikaste; but when the curved ships of the Danaans came, he returned again to Ilios, and was pre-eminent among the Trojans, and dwelt with Priam, who honoured him like his own children. Him the son of Telamon pierced below the ear with his long lance, and plucked back the spear. Then he fell like an ash that on the crest of a far-seen hill is smitten with the axe of bronze, and brings its delicate foliage to the ground; even so he fell, and round him rang his armour bedight with bronze. Then Teukros rushed forth, most eager to strip his armour, and Hector cast at him as he came with his shining spear. But Teukros, steadily regarding him, avoided by a little the spear of bronze; so Hector struck Amphimachos, son of Kteatos, son of Aktor, in the breast with the spear, as he was returning to the battle. With a crash he fell, and his armour rang upon him.

Then Hector sped forth to tear from the head of great-hearted Amphimachos the helmet closely fitted to his temples, but Aias aimed at Hector as he came, with a shining spear, yet in no wise touched his body, for he was all clad in dread armour of bronze; but he smote the boss of his shield, and drave him back by main force, and he gave place from behind the two dead men, and the Achaians drew them out of the battle. So Stichios and goodly Menestheus, leaders of the Athenians, conveyed Amphimachos back among the host of the Achaians, but Imbrios the two Aiantes carried, with hearts full of impetuous might. And as when two lions have snatched away a goat from sharp-toothed hounds, and carry it through the deep thicket, holding the body on high above the ground in their jaws, so the two warrior Aiantes held Imbrios aloft and spoiled his arms. Then the son of Oileus cut his head from his delicate neck, in wrath for the sake of Amphimachos, and sent it rolling like a ball through the throng, and it dropped in the dust before the feet of Hector.

Then verily was Poseidon wroth at heart, when his son's son fell in the terrible fray.[1] So he set forth to go by the huts and the ships of the Achaians, to spur on the Danaans, and sorrows he was contriving for the Trojans. Then Idomeneus, spearman renowned, met him on his way from his comrade that had but newly returned to him out of the battle, wounded on the knee with the sharp bronze.

[1] Kteatos, father of Amphimachos, was Poseidon's son: see p. 226.

Him his comrades carried forth, and Idomeneus gave charge to the leeches, and so went on to his hut, for he still was eager to face the war. Then the mighty Shaker of the earth addressed him, in the voice of Thoas, son of Andraimon, that ruled over the Aitolians in all Pleuron, and mountainous Kalydon, and was honoured like a god by the people: 'Idomeneus, thou counsellor of the Cretans, says whither have thy threats fared, wherewith the sons of the Achaians threatened the Trojans?'

Then Idomeneus, leader of the Cretans, answered him again: 'O Thoas, now is there no man to blame, that I wot of, for we all are skilled in war. Neither is there any man that spiritless fear holds aloof, nor any that gives place to cowardice, and shuns the cruel war, nay, but even thus, methinks, must it have seemed good to almighty Kronion, even that the Achaians should perish nameless here, far away from Argos. But Thoas, seeing that of old thou wert staunch, and dost spur on some other man, wheresoever thou mayst see any give ground, therefore slacken not now, but call aloud to every warrior.'

Then Poseidon, the Shaker of the earth, answered him again: 'Idomeneus, never may that man go forth out of Troy-land, but here may he be the sport of dogs, who this day wilfully is slack in battle. Nay, come, take thy weapons and away: herein we must play the man together, if any avail there may be, though we are no more than two. Ay, and very cowards get courage from company, but we twain know well how to battle even with the brave.'

Therewith the god went back again into the strife of men, but Idomeneus, so soon as he came to his well-builded hut, did on his fair armour about his body, and grasped two spears, and set forth like the lightning that Kronion seizes in his hand and brandishes from radiant Olympus, showing forth a sign to mortal men, and far seen are the flames thereof. Even so shone the bronze about the breast of Idomeneus as he ran, and Meriones, his good squire, met him, while he was still near his hut, – he was going to bring his spear of bronze, – and mighty Idomeneus spake to him: 'Meriones son of Molos, fleet of foot, dearest of my company, wherefore hast thou come hither and left the war and strife? Art thou wounded at all, and vexed by a dart's point, or dost thou come with a message for me concerning aught? Verily I myself have no desire to sit in the huts, but to fight.'

Then wise Meriones answered him again, saying: '[I do meneus, thou counsellor of the mail-clad Cretans,] I have come to fetch a spear, if perchance thou hast one left in the huts, for that which before I carried I have shivered in casting at the shield of proud Deiphobos.'

Then Idomeneus, leader of the Cretans, answered him again: 'Spears, if thou wilt, thou shalt find, one, ay, and twenty, standing in the hut, against the shining side walls, spears of the Trojans whereof I have spoiled their slain. Yea, it is not my mood to stand and fight with foemen from afar, wherefore I have spears, and bossy shields, and helms, and corslets of splendid sheen.'

Then wise Meriones answered him again: 'Yea, and in mine own hut and my black ship are many spoils of the Trojans, but not ready to my hand. Nay, for methinks that neither am I forgetful of valour; but stand forth among the foremost to face the glorious war, whensoever ariseth the strife of battle. Any other, methinks, of the mail-clad Achaians should sooner forget my prowess, but thou art he that knoweth it.'

Then Idomeneus, leader of the Cretans, answered him again: 'I know what a man of valour thou art, wherefore shouldst thou tell me thereof? Nay, if now beside the ships all the best of us were being chosen for an ambush – wherein the valour of men is best discerned; there the coward, and the brave man most plainly declare themselves: for the colour of the coward changes often, and his spirit cannot abide firm within him, but now he kneels on one knee, now on the other, and rests on either foot, and his heart beats noisily in his breast, as he thinks of doom, and his teeth chatter loudly. But the colour of the brave man does not change, nor is he greatly afraid, from the moment that he enters the ambush of heroes, but his prayer is to mingle instantly in woful war. Were we being chosen for such ambush, I say, not even then would any man reckon lightly of thy courage and thy strength. Nay, and even if thou wert stricken in battle from afar, or smitten in close fight, the dart would not strike thee in the hinder part of the neck, nor in the back, but would encounter thy breast or belly, as thou dost press on, towards the gathering of the foremost fighters. But come, no more let us talk thus, like children, loitering here, lest any man be vehemently wroth, but go thou to the hut, and bring the strong spear.'

Thus he spake, and Meriones, the peer of swift Ares, quickly bare the spear of bronze from the hut, and went after Idomeneus, with high thoughts of battle. And even as Ares, the bane of men, goes forth into the war, and with him follows his dear son Panic, stark and fearless, that terrifies even the hardy warrior; and these twain leave Thrace, and harness them for fight with the Ephyri, or the great-hearted Phlegyans, yet hearken not to both peoples, but give honour to one only; like these gods did Meriones and Idomeneus, leaders of men, set forth into the fight, harnessed in gleaming bronze. And Meriones spake first to Idomeneus saying: 'Child of Deukalion, whither art thou eager to enter into the throng: on the right of all the host, or in the centre, or on the left? Ay, and no other where, methinks, are the flowing-haired Achaians so like to fail in fight.'

Then Idomeneus, the leader of the Cretans, answered him again: 'In the centre of the ships there are others to bear the brunt, the two Aiantes, and Teukros, the best bowman of the Achaians, ay, and a good man in close fight; these will give Hector Priam's son toil enough, howsoever keen he be for battle; yea, though he be exceeding stalwart. Hard will he find it, with all his lust for war, to overcome their strength and their hands invincible, and to fire the ships, unless Kronion himself send down on the swift ships a burning brand. But not to a man would he yield, the great Telamonian Aias, to a man that is mortal and eateth Demeter's grain, and may be cloven with the sword of bronze, and with hurling of great stones. Nay, not even to Achilles the breaker of the ranks of men would he give way, not in close fight; but for speed of foot none may in any wise strive with Achilles. But guide us twain, as thou sayest, to the left hand of the host, that speedily we may learn whether we are to win glory from others, or other men from us.'

So he spake, and Meriones, the peer of swift Ares, led the way, till they came to the host, in that place whither he bade him go.

And when the Trojans saw Idomeneus, strong as flame, and his squire with him, and their glorious armour, they all shouted and made for him through the press. Then their mellay began, by the sterns of the ships. And as the gusts speed on, when shrill winds blow, on a day when dust lies thickest on the roads, and the winds raise together a great cloud of dust, even so their battle clashed together, and all were fain of heart to slay each other in the press with the keen bronze. And the battle, the bane of men, bristled with the long spears, the piercing spears they grasped? and the glitter of bronze from gleaming helmets dazzled the eyes, and the sheen of new-burnished corslets, and shining shields, as the men thronged all together. Right hardy of heart would he have been that joyed and sorrowed not at the sight of this Labour of battle.

Thus the two mighty sons of Kronos, with contending will, were contriving sorrow and anguish for the heroes. Zeus desired victory for the Trojans and Hector, giving glory to swift-footed Achilles; yet he did not wish the Achaian host to perish utterly before Ilios, but only to give renown to Thetis and her strong-hearted son. But Poseidon went among the Argives and stirred them to war, stealing secretly forth from the grey salt sea: for he was sore vexed that they were overcome by the Trojans, and was greatly in wrath against Zeus. Verily both were of the same lineage and the same place of birth? but Zeus was the elder and the wiser. Therefore also Poseidon avoided to give open aid, but secretly ever he spurred them on? throughout the host, in the likeness of a man. These twain had strained the ends of the cords of strong strife and equal war, and had stretched them over both Trojans and Achaians, a knot that none might break nor undo, for the loosening of the knees of many.

Even then Idomeneus, though his hair w as flecked with grey, called on the Danaans, and leaping among the Trojans, roused their terror. For he slew Othryoneus of Kabesos, a sojourner there, who but lately had followed after the rumour of war, and asked in marriage the fairest of the daughters of Priam, Kassandra, without gifts of wooing, but with promise of a mighty deed, namely that he would drive perforce out of Troy-land the sons of the Achaians. To him the old man Priam promised and appointed that he would give her, so he fought trusting in his promises. And Idomeneus aimed at him with a bright spear, and cast and smote him as he came proudly striding on, and the corslet of bronze that he wore availed not, but the lance stuck in the midst of his belly. And he fell with a crash, and Idomeneus boasted over him, and lifted up his voice, saying: 'Othryoneus, verily I praise thee above all mortal men, if indeed thou shalt accomplish all that thou hast promised to Priam, son of Dardanos, that promised thee again his own daughter. Yea, and we likewise would promise as much to thee, and fulfil it, and would give thee the fairest daughter of the son of Atreus, and bring her from Argos, and wed her to thee, if only thou wilt aid us to take the fair-set citadel of Ilios. Nay, follow us that we may make a covenant of marriage by the seafaring ships, for we are no hard exacters of gifts of wooing.'

Therewith the hero Idomeneus dragged him by the foot across the fierce mellay. But Asios came to his aid, on foot before his horses that the charioteer guided so that still their breath touched the shoulders of Asios. And the desire of his heart was to cast at Idomeneus, who was beforehand with him, and smote him with the spear in the throat, below the chin, and drove the point straight through And he fell as an oak falls, or a poplar, or he pine tree, that craftsmen have felled on the hills with new whetted axes, to be a ship's timber, even so he lay stretched out before the horses and the

chariot, groaning, and clutching the bloody dust. And the charioteer was amazed, and kept not his wits, as of old, and dared not turn
his horses and avoid out of the hands of foemen; and Antilochos the
steadfast in war smote him, and pierced the middle of his body with
a spear. Nothing availed the corslet of bronze he was wont to wear,
but he planted the spear fast in the midst of his belly. Therewith he
fell gasping from the well-wrought chariot, and Antilochos, the son
of great-hearted Nestor, drave the horses out from the Trojans,
among the well greaved Achaians. Then Deiphobos, in sorrow for
Asios, drew very nigh Idomeneus, and cast at him with his shining
spear. But Idomeneus steadily watching him, avoided the spear of
bronze, being hidden beneath the circle of his shield, the shield covered about with ox-hide and gleaming bronze, that he always bore,
fitted with two arm-rods: under this he crouched together, and the
spear of bronze flew over. And his shield rang sharply, as the spear
grazed thereon. Yet it flew not vainly from the heavy hand of Deiphobos, but smote Hypsenor, son of Hippasos, the shepherd of the
hosts, in the liver, beneath the midriff, and instantly unstrung his
knees. And Deiphobos boasted over him terribly, crying aloud: 'Ah,
verily, not unavenged lies Asios, nay, methinks, that even on his
road to Hades, strong Warden of the gate, he will rejoice at heart,
since, lo, I have sent him escort for the way!'

So spake he, but grief came on the Argives by reason of his boast,
and stirred above all the soul of the wisehearted Antilochos, yet,
despite his sorrow, he was not heedless of his dear comrade, but ran
and stood over him, and covered him with his buckler. Then two
trusty companions, Mekisteus, son of Echios, and goodly Alastor,
stooped down and lifted him, and with heavy groaning bare him to
the hollow ships.

And Idomeneus relaxed not his mighty force, but ever was striving, either to cover some one of the Trojans with black night, or
himself to fall in warding off death from the Achaians. There the
dear son of Aisyetes, fosterling of Zeus, even the hero Alkathoos,
was slain, who was son-in-law of Anchises, and had married the
eldest of his daughters, Hippodameia, whom her father and her lady
mother dearly loved in the halls, for she excelled all the maidens of
her age in beauty, and skill, and in wisdom, wherefore the best man
in wide Troy took her to wife. This Alkathoos did Poseidon subdue
to Idomeneus, throwing a spell over his shining eyes, and snaring
his glorious limbs; so that he might neither flee backwards, nor
avoid the stroke, but stood steady as a pillar, or a tree with lofty
crown of leaves, when the hero Idomeneus smote him in the midst

of the breast with the spear, and rent the coat of bronze about him, that aforetime warded death from his body, but now rang harsh as it was rent by the spear. And he fell with a crash, and the lance fixed in his heart, that, still beating, shook the butt-end of the spear. Then at length mighty Ares spent its fury there; but Idomeneus boasted terribly, and cried aloud: 'Deiphobos, are we to deem it fair acquittal that we have slain three men for one, since thou boastest thus? Nay, sir, but stand thou up also thyself against me, that thou mayst know what manner of son of Zeus am I that have come hither! For Zeus first begat Minos, the warden of Crete, and Minos got him a son, the noble Deukalion, and Deukalion begat me, a prince over many men in wide Crete, and now have the ships brought me hither, a bane to thee and thy father, and all the Trojans.'

Thus he spake, but the thoughts of Deiphobos were divided, whether he should retreat, and call to his aid some one of the great-hearted Trojans, or should try the adventure alone. And on this wise to his mind it seemed the better, to go after Aineias, whom he found standing the last in the press, for Aineias was ever wroth against goodly Priam, for that Priam gave him no honour, despite his valour among men. So Deiphobos stood by him, and spake winged words to him: 'Aineias, thou counsellor of the Trojans, now verily there is great need that thou shouldst succour thy sister's husband, if any care for kin doth touch thee. Nay follow, let us succour Alkathoos, thy sister's husband, who of old did cherish thee in his hall, while thou wert but a little one, and now, lo, spear-famed Idomeneus hath stripped him of his arms!'

So he spake, and roused the spirit in the breast of Aineias, who went to seek Idomeneus, with high thoughts of war. But fear took not hold upon Idomeneus, as though he had been some tender boy, but he stood at bay, like a boar on the hills that trusteth to his strength, and abides the great assailing throng of men in a lonely place, and he bristles up his back, and his eyes shine with fire, while he whets his tusks, and is right eager to keep at bay both men and hounds. Even so stood spear-famed Idomeneus at bay against Aineias, that came to the rescue, and gave ground no whit, but called on his comrades, glancing to Askalaphos, and Aphareus, and Deipyros, and Meriones, and Antilochos, all masters of the war-cry; them he spurred up to battle, and spake winged words: 'Hither, friends, and rescue me, all alone as I am, and terribly I dread the onslaught of swiftfooted Aineias, that is assailing me; for he is right strong to destroy men in battle, and he hath the flower of youth, the greatest avail that may be. Yea, if he and I were of like age, and in this spirit whereof now we are, speedily should he or I achieve high victory.'

So he spake, and they all being of one spirit in their hearts, stood hard by each other, with buckler laid on shoulder. But Aineias, on the other side, cried to his comrades, glancing to Deiphobos, and Paris, and noble Agenor, that with him were leaders of the Trojans; and then the hosts followed them, as sheep follow their leader to the water from the pasture, and the shepherd is glad at heart; even so the heart of Aineias was glad in his breast, when he saw the hosts of the people following to aid him.

Then they rushed in close fight around Alkathoos with their long spears, and round their breasts the bronze rang terribly, as they aimed at each other in the press, while two men of war beyond the rest, Aineias and Idomeneus, the peers of Ares, were each striving to hew the flesh of the other with the pitiless bronze. Now Aineias first cast at Idomeneus, who steadily watching him avoided the spear of bronze, and the point of Aineias went quivering in the earth, since vainly it had flown from his stalwart hand. But Idomeneus smote Oinomaos in the midst of the belly, and brake the plate of his corslet, and the bronze let forth the bowels through the corslet, and he fell in the dust and clutched the earth in his palms. And Idomeneus drew forth the far-shadowing spear from the dead, but could not avail to strip the rest of the fair armour from his shoulders. for the darts pressed hard on him Nay, and his feet no longer served him firmly in a charge, nor could he rush after his own spear, nor avoid the foe. Wherefore in close fight he still held off the pitiless day of destiny, but in retreat his feet no longer bore him swiftly from the battle. And as he was slowly departing, Deiphobos aimed at him with his shining spear, for, verily he ever cherished a steadfast hatred against Idomeneus. But this time, too, he missed him, and smote Askalaphos, the son of Enyalios, with his dart, and the strong spear passed through his shoulder, and he fell in the dust, and clutched the earth in his outstretched hand. But loud-voiced awful Ares was not yet aware at all that his son had fallen in strong battle, but he was reclining on the peak of Olympus, beneath the golden clouds, being held there by the design of Zeus, where also were the other deathless gods, restrained from the war.

Now the people rushed in close fight around Askalaphos, and Deiphobos tore from Askalaphos his shining helm, but Meriones, the peer of swift Ares, leaped forward and smote the arm of Deiphobos with his spear, and from his hand the vizored casque fell clanging to the ground. And Meriones sprang forth instantly, like a vulture, and drew the strong spear from the shoulder of Deiphobos, and fell back among the throng of his comrades. But the own brother of Deiphobos, Polites, stretched his hands round his waist, and led him forth from the evil din of war, even till he came to the swift horses, that waited for him behind the battle and the fight, with their charioteer, and well-dight chariot. These bore him heavily groaning to the city, worn with his hurt, and the blood ran down from his newly wounded arm.

But the rest still were fighting, and the war-cry rose unquenched. There Aineias rushed on Aphareus, son of Kaletor, and struck his throat, that chanced to be turned to him, with the keen spear, and his head dropped down and his shield and helm fell with him, and death that slays the spirit overwhelmed him. And Antilochos watched Thoon as he turned the other way, and leaped on him, and wounded him, severing all the vein that runs up the back till it reaches the neck; this he severed clean, and Thoon fell on his back in the dust, stretching out both his hands to his comrades dear. Then Antilochos rushed on, and stripped the armour from his shoulders, glancing around while the Trojans gathered from here and there, and smote his wide shining shield, yet did not avail to graze, behind the shield, the delicate flesh of Antilochos with the pitiless bronze. For verily Poseidon, the Shaker of the earth, did guard on every side the son of Nestor, even in the midst of the javelins. And never did Antilochos get free of the foe, but turned him about among them, nor ever was his spear at rest, but always brandished and shaken, and the aim of his heart was to smite a foeman from afar, or to set on him at close quarters. But as he was aiming through the crowd, he escaped not the ken of Adamas, son of Asios, who smote the midst of his shield with the sharp bronze, setting on nigh at hand; but Poseidon of the dark locks made his shaft of no avail, grudging him the life of Antilochos. And part of the spear abode there, like a burned stake, in the shield of Antilochos, and half lay on the earth, and back retreated Adamas to the ranks of his comrades, avoiding Fate. But Meriones following after him as he departed, smote him with a spear between the privy parts and the navel, where a wound is most baneful to wretched mortals. Even there he fixed the spear in him and he fell, and writhed about the spear, even as a bull that herdsmen on the hills drag along perforce when they have bound him with withes, so he when he was smitten writhed for a moment, not for long, till the hero Meriones came near, and drew the spear out of his body. And darkness covered his eyes.

And Helenos in close fight smote Deipyros on the temple, with a great Thracian sword, and tore away the helm, and the helm, being dislodged, fell on the ground, and one of the Achaians in the fight picked it up as it rolled between his feet. But dark night covered the eyes of Deipyros.

Then grief took hold of the son of Atreus, Menelaos of the loud war-cry, and he went with a threat against the warrior Helenos, the prince, shaking his sharp spear, while the other drew the centre-piece of his bow. And both at once were making ready to let fly, one with his sharp spear, the other with the arrow from the string. Then the son of Priam smote Menelaos on the breast with his arrow, on the plate of the corslet, and off flew the bitter arrow. Even as from a broad shovel in a great threshing floor, fly the black-skinned beans and pulse, before the whistling wind, and the stress of the win-nower's shovel, even so from the corslet of renowned Menelaos flew glancing far aside the bitter arrow. But the son of Atreus, Menelaos of the loud war-cry, smote the hand of Helenos wherein he held the polished bow, and into the bow, clean through the hand, was driven the spear of bronze. Back he withdrew to the ranks of his comrades, avoiding Fate, with his hand hanging down at his side, for the ashen spear dragged after him. And the great-hearted Agenor drew the spear from his hand, and himself bound up the hand with a band of twisted sheep's-wool, a sling that a squire carried for him, the shep-herd of the host.

Then Peisandros made straight for renowned Menelaos, but an evil Fate was leading him to the end of Death; by thee, Menelaos, to be overcome in the dread strife of battle. Now when the twain had come nigh in onset upon each other, the son of Atreus missed, and his spear was turned aside, but Peisandros smote the shield of renowned Menelaos, yet availed not to drive the bronze clean through, for the wide shield caught it, and the spear brake in the socket, yet Peisandros rejoiced in his heart, and hoped for the vic-tory. But the son of Atreus drew his silver-studded sword, and leaped upon Peisandros. And Peisandros, under his shield, clutched his goodly axe of fine bronze, with long and polished haft of olive-wood, and the twain set upon each other. Then Peisandros smote the crest of the helmet shaded with horse hair, close below the very plume, but Menelaos struck the other, as he came forward, on the brow, above the base of the nose, and the bones cracked, and the eyes, all bloody, fell at his feet in the dust. Then he bowed and fell, and Menelaos set his foot on his breast, and stripped him of his arms, and triumphed, saying: 'Even thus then surely, ye will leave

the ships of the Danaans of the swift steeds, ye Trojans overweening, insatiate of the dread din l)f war. Yea, and ye shall not lack all
other reproof and shame, wherewith ye made me ashamed, ye
hounds of evil, having no fear in your hearts of the strong wrath of
loud-thundering Zeus, the god of guest and host, who one day will
destroy your steep citadel. O ye that wantonly carried away my
wedded wife and many of my possessions, when ye were entertained
by her, now again ye are fain to throw ruinous fire on the seafaring
ships, and to slay the Achaian heroes. Nay, but ye will yet refrain
you from battle, for as eager as ye be. O father Zeus, verily they say
that thou dost excel in wisdom all others, both gods and men, and
all these things are from thee. How wondrously art thou favouring
men of violence, even the Trojans, whose might is ever iniquitous,
nor can they have their fill of the din of equal war. Of all things
there is satiety, yea, even of love and sleep, and of sweet song, and
dance delectable, whereof a man would sooner have his fill than of
war, but the Trojans are insatiable of battle.'

Thus noble Menelaos spake, and stripped the bloody arms from
the body, and gave them to his comrades, and instantly himself
went forth again, and mingled in the forefront of the battle. Then
Harpalion, the son of king Pylaimenes, leaped out against him,
Harpalion that followed his dear father to Troy, to the war, nor
ever came again to his own country. He then smote the middle of
the shield of Atreus' son with his spear, in close fight, yet availed
not to drive the bronze clean through, but fell back into the host of
his comrades, avoiding Fate, glancing round every way, lest one
should wound his flesh with the bronze. But Meriones shot at him
as he retreated with a bronze-shod arrow, and smote him in the
right buttock, and the arrow went right through the bladder and
came out under the bone. And sitting down, even there, in the arms
of his dear comrades, he breathed away his soul, lying stretched like
a worm on the earth, and out flowed the black blood, and wetted
the ground. And the Paphlagonians great of heart, tended him
busily, and set him in a chariot, and drove him to sacred Ilios sorrowing, and with them went his father, shedding tears, and there
was no atonement for his dead son.

Now Paris was very wroth at heart by reason of his slaying, for he
had been his host among the many Paphlagonians, wherefore, in
wrath for his sake, he let fly a bronze-shod arrow. Now there was a
certain Euchenor, the son of Polyidos the seer, a rich man and a
good, whose dwelling was in Corinth. And well he knew his own
ruinous fate, when he went on ship-board, for often would the old

man, the good Polyidos, tell him, that he must either perish of a sore disease in his halls, or go with the ships of the Achaians, and be overcome by the Trojans. Wherefore he avoided at once the heavy war-fine of the Achaians, and the hateful disease, that so he might not know any anguish. This man did Paris smite beneath the jaw and under the ear, and swiftly his spirit departed from his limbs, and, lo, dread darkness overshadowed him.

So they fought like flaming fire, but Hector, beloved of Zeus, had not heard nor knew at all that, on the left of the ships, his host was being subdued by the Argives, and soon would the Achaians have won renown, so mighty was the Holder and Shaker of the earth that urged on the Argives; yea, and himself mightily defended them. But Hector kept where at first he had leaped within the walls and the gate, and broken the serried ranks of shield-bearing Danaans, even where were the ships of Aias and Protesilaos, drawn up on the beach of the hoary sea, while above the wall was builded lowest, and thereby chiefly the heroes and their horses were raging in battle.

There the Boiotians, and Ionians with trailing tunics, and Lokrians and Phthians and illustrious Epeians scarcely availed to stay his onslaught on the ships, nor yet could they drive back from them noble Hector, like a flame of fire. And there were the picked men of the Athenians; among them Menestheus son of Peteos was the leader; and there followed with him Pheidas and Stichios, and brave Bias, while the Epeians were led by Meges, son of Phyleus, and Amphion and Drakios, and in front of the Phthians were Medon, and Podarkes resolute in war. Now the one, Medon, was the bastard son of noble Oileus! and brother of Aias, and he dwelt in Phylake, far from his own country, for that he had slain a man, the brother of his stepmother Eriopis, wife of Oileus. But the other, Podarkes, was the son of Iphiklos son of Phylakos, and they in their armour, in the van of the great-hearted Phthians, were defending the ships, and fighting among the Boiotians.

Now never at all did Aias, the swift son of Oileus, depart from the side of Aias, son of Telamon, nay, not for an instant, but even as in fallow land two wine-dark oxen with equal heart strain at the shapen plough, and round the roots of their horns springeth up abundant sweat, and nought sunders them but the polished yoke, as they labour through the furrow, till the end of the furrow brings them up, so stood the two Aiantes close by each other. Now verily did many and noble hosts of his comrades follow with the son of Telamon, and bore his shield when labour and sweat came upon his limbs. But the Lokrians followed not with the high-hearted son of

Oileus, for their hearts were not steadfast in close brunt of battle, seeing that they had no helmets of bronze, shadowy with horse-hair plumes, nor round shields, nor ashen spears, but trusting in bows and well twisted slings of sheep's wool they followed with him to Ilios. Therewith, in the war, they shot thick and fast, and brake the ranks of the Trojans. So the one party in front, with their well-dight arms contended with the Trojans, and with Hector arrayed in bronze, while the others from behind kept shooting from their ambush, and the Trojans lost all memory of the joy of battle, for the arrows confounded them.

There then right ruefully from the ships and the huts would the Trojans have withdrawn to windy Ilios, had not Polydamas come near valiant Hector and said: 'Hector, thou art hard to be persuaded by them that would counsel thee; for that god has given thee excellence in the works of war, therefore in council also thou art fain to excel other men in knowledge. But in nowise wilt thou be able lo take everything on thyself For to one man has god given for his portion the works of war, [to another the dance, to another the lute and song,] but in the heart of yet another hath far-seeing Zeus placed an excellent understanding, whereof many men get gain, yea he saveth many an one, and himself best knoweth it. But, lo, I will speak even as it seemeth best to me. Behold all about thee the circle of war is blazing, but the great-hearted Trojans, now that they have got down the wall, are some with their arms standing aloof and some are fighting, few men against a host, being scattered among the ships. Nay, withdraw thee, and call hither all the best of the warriors. Thereafter shall we take all counsel carefully, whether we should fall on the ships of many benches, if indeed god willeth to give us victory, or after counsel held, should return unharmed from the ships. For verily I fear lest the Achaians repay their debt of yesterday, since by the ships there tarrieth a man insatiate of war, and never, methinks, will he wholly stand aloof from battle.'

So spake Polydamas, and his safe counsel pleased Hector well, who [straightway sprang to earth from the chariot with his arms, and] spake to him winged words and said: 'Polydamas, do thou stay here all the best of the host, but I will go thither to face the war, and swiftly will return again, when have straitly laid on them my commands.'

So he spake, and set forth, in semblance like a snowy mountain, and shouting aloud he flew through the Trojans and allies. And they all sped to Polydamas, the kindly son of Panthoos, when they heard the voice of Hector. But he went seeking Deiphobos, and the strong

prince Helenos, and Adamas son of Asios, and Asios son of Hyrtakos, among the warriors in the foremost line, if anywhere he
might find them. But them he found not at all unharmed, nor free
of bane, but, lo, some among the sterns of the ships of the Achaians
lay lifeless, slain by the hands of the Argives, and some w ere within
the wall wounded by thrust or cast. But one he readily found, on the
left of the dolorous battle, goodly Alexandros, the lord of fair-
tressed Helen, heartening his comrades and speeding them to war
And he drew near to him, and addressed him with words of shame:
'Thou evil Paris, fairest of face, thou that lustest for women, thou
seducer, where, prithee, are Deiphobos, and the strong prince
Helenos, and Adamas son of Asios, and Asios son of Hyrtakos, and
where is Othryoneus? Now hath all high Ilios perished utterly.
Now, too, thou seest, is sheer destruction sure.'

Then godlike Alexandros answered him again saying: 'Hector,
since thy mind is to blame one that is blameless, some other day
might I rather withdraw me from the war, since my mother bare
not even me wholly a coward. For from the time that thou didst
gather the battle of thy comrades about the ships, from that hour do
we abide here, and war with the Danaans ceaselessly; and our comrades concerning whom thou inquirest are slain. Only Deiphobos
and the strong prince Helenos have both withdrawn, both of them
being wounded in the hand with long spears, for Kronion kept
death away from them. But now lead on, wheresoever thy heart and
spirit bid thee, and we will follow with thee eagerly, nor methinks
shall we lack for valour, as far as we have strength; but beyond his
strength may no man fight, howsoever eager he be.'

So spake the hero, and persuaded his brother's heart, and they
went forth where the war and din were thickest, round Kebriones,
and noble Polydamas, and Phalkes, and Orthaios, and godlike
Polyphetes, and Palmys, and Askanios, and Morys, son of Hippotion, who had come in their turn, out of deep-soiled Askanie, on the
morn before, and now Zeus urged them to fight. And these set forth
like the blast of violent winds, that rushes earthward beneath the
thunder of father Zeus, and with marvellous din doth mingle with
the salt sea, and therein are many swelling waves of the loud roaring
sea, arched over and white with foam, some vanward, others in the
rear; even so the Trojans arrayed in van and rear and shining with
bronze, followed after their leaders. And Hector son of Priam was
leading them, the peer of Ares, the bane of men. In front he held
the circle of his shield, thick with hides, and plates of beaten bronze,
and on his temples swayed his shining helm. And everywhere he

went in advance and made trial of the ranks, if perchance they would yield to him as he charged under cover of his shield. But he could not confound the heart within the breast of the Achaians. And Aias, stalking with long strides, challenged him first: 'Sir, draw nigh, wherefore dost thou vainly try to dismay the Argives? We are in no wise ignorant of war, but by the cruel scourge of Zeus are we Achaians vanquished. Surely now thy heart hopes utterly to spoil the ships, but we too have hands presently to hold our own. Verily your peopled city will long ere that beneath our hands be taken and sacked. But for thee, I tell thee that the time is at hand, when thou shalt pray in thy flight to father Zeus, and the other immortal gods, that thy fair-maned steeds may be fleeter than falcons: thy steeds that are to bear thee to the city, as they storm in dust across the plain.'

And even as he spake, a bird flew forth on the right hand, an eagle of lofty flight, and the host of the Achaians shouted thereat, encouraged by the omen, but renowned Hector answered: 'Aias, thou blundering boaster, what sayest thou! Would that indeed I were for ever as surely the son of aegis-bearing Zeus, and that my mother were lady Hera, and that I were held in such honour as Apollo and Athene, as verily this day is to bring utter evil on all the Argives! And thou among them shalt be slain, if thou hast the heart to await my long spear, which shall rend thy lily skin, and thou shalt glut with thy fat and flesh the birds and dogs of the Trojans, falling among the ships of the Achaians.'

So he spake and led the way, and they followed with wondrous din, and the whole host shouted behind. And the Argives on the other side answered with a shout, and forgot not their valiance, but abode the onslaught of the bravest of the Trojans. And the cry of the two hosts went up through the higher air, to the splendour of Zeus.

BOOK XIV

How Sleep and Hera beguiled Zeus to slumber on the heights of Ida, and Poseidon spurred on the Achaians to resist Hector, and how Hector was wounded.

YET THE CRY OF BATTLE escaped not Nestor, albeit at his wine, but he spake winged words to the son of Asklepios: 'Bethink thee, noble Machaon, what had best be done; lo, louder waxes the cry of the strong warriors by the ships. Nay, now sit where thou art, and drink the bright wine, till Hekamede of the fair tresses shall heat warm water for the bath, and wash away the clotted blood, but I will speedily go forth and come to a place of outlook.'

Therewith he took the well-wrought shield of his son, horsetaming Thrasymedes, which was lying in the hut, all glistering with bronze, for the son had the shield of his father. And he seized a strong spear, with a point of keen bronze, and stood outside the hut, and straightway beheld a deed of shame, the Achaians fleeing in rout, and the high-hearted Trojans driving them, and the wall of the Achaians was overthrown. And as when the great sea is troubled with a dumb wave, and dimly bodes the sudden paths of the shrill winds, but is still unmoved nor yet rolled forward or to either side, until some steady gale comes down from Zeus, even so the old man pondered, – his mind divided this way and that, – whether he should fare into the press of the Danaans of the swift steeds, or go after Agamemnon, son of Atreus, shepherd of the host. And thus as he pondered, it seemed to him the better counsel to go to the son of Atreus. Meanwhile they were warring and slaying each other, and the stout bronze rang about their bodies as they were thrust with swords and double-pointed spears.

Now the kings, the fosterlings of Zeus, encountered Nestor, as they went up from the ships, even they that were wounded with the bronze, Tydeus' son, and Odysseus, and Agamemnon, son of Atreus. For far apart from the battle were their ships drawn up, on the shore of the grey sea, for these were the first they had drawn up to the plain, but had builded the wall in front of the hindmost. For in no wise might the beach, for as wide as it was, hold all the ships, and the host was straitened. Wherefore they drew up the ships row within row, and filled up the wide mouth of all the shore that the headlands held between them. Therefore the kings were going together, leaning on their spears, to look on the war and fray, and the heart of each was sore within his breast. And the old man met them, even Nestor, and caused the spirit to fail within the breasts of the Achaians.

And mighty Agamemnon spake and accosted him: 'O Nestor, son of Neleus, great glory of the Achaians, wherefore dost thou come hither and hast deserted the war, the bane of men? Lo, I fear the accomplishment of the word that dread Hector spake, and the threat wherewith he threatened us, speaking in the assembly of the Trojans, namely, that never would he return to Ilios from the ships, till he had burned the ships with fire, and slain the men. Even so he spake, and, lo, now all these things are being fulfilled. Alas, surely even the other well-greaved Achaians store wrath against me in their hearts, like Achilles, and have no desire to fight by the rear-most ships.'

Then Nestor of Gerenia the knight answered him saying: 'Verily these things are now at hand, and being accomplished, nor other-wise could Zeus himself contrive them, he that thundereth on high. For, lo, the wall is overthrown, wherein we trusted that it should be an unbroken bulwark of the ships and of our own bodies. And these men by the swift ships have endless battle without sparing, and no more couldst thou tell, howsoever closely thou mightst spy, from what side the Achaians are driven in rout, so confusedly are they slain, and the cry of battle goeth up to heaven. But let us take coun-sel, how these things may best be done, if wit may do aught: but into the war I counsel not that we should go down, for in no wise may a wounded man do battle.'

Then Agamemnon king of men answered him again: 'Nestor, for that they are warring by the rearmost ships, and the well-built wall hath availed not, nor the trench, whereat the Achaians endured so much labour, hoping in their hearts that it should be the unbro-ken bulwark of the ships, and of their own bodies – such it seemeth must be the will of Zeus supreme, [that the Achaians should perish here nameless far from Argos]. For I knew it when he was forward to aid the Danaans, and now I know that he is giving to the Trojans glory like that of the blessed gods, and hath bound our hands and our strength. But come, as I declare, let us all obey. Let us drag down the ships that are drawn up in the first line near to the sea, and speed them all forth to the salt sea divine, and moor them far out with stones, till the divine night comes, if even at night the Tro-jans will refrain from war, and then might we drag down all the ships. For there is no shame in fleeing from ruin, yea, even in the night. Better doth he fare who flees from trouble, than he that is overtaken.'

Then, looking on him sternly, spake Odysseus of many counsels: 'Atreus' son, what word hath passed the door of thy lips? Man of mischief, sure thou shouldst lead some other inglorious army, not be king among us, to whom Zeus hath given it, from youth even unto age, to wind the skein of grievous wars, till every man of us perish. Art thou indeed so eager to leave the wide-wayed city of the Trojans, the city for which we endure with sorrow so many evils? Be silent, lest some other of the Achaians hear this word, that no man should so much as suffer to pass through his mouth, none that understandeth in his heart how to speak fit counsel, none that is a sceptred king, and hath hosts obeying him so many as the Argives over whom thou reignest. And now I wholly scorn thy thoughts, such a word as thou hast uttered, thou that, in the midst of war and battle, dost bid us draw down the well-timbered ships to the sea, that even more than ever the Trojans may possess their desire, albeit they win the mastery even now, and sheer destruction fall upon us. For the Achaians will not make good the war, when the ships are drawn down to the salt sea, but will look round about to flee, and withdraw from battle. There will thy counsel work a mischief, O marshal of the host!'

Then the king of men, Agamemnon, answered him: 'Odysseus, right sharply hast thou touched my heart with thy stern reproof: nay, I do not bid the sons of the Achaians to drag, against their will, the well-timbered ships to the salt sea. Now perchance there may be one who will utter a wiser counsel than this of mine, – a young man or an old, – welcome would it be to me.'

Then Diomedes of the loud war-cry spake also among them: 'The man is near, – not long shall we seek him, if ye be willing to be persuaded of me, and each of you be not resentful at all, because in years I am the youngest among you. Nay, but I too boast me to come by lineage of a noble sire, Tydeus, whom in Thebes the piled-up earth doth cover. For Portheus had three well-born children, and they dwelt in Pleuron, and steep Kalydon, even Agrios and Melas, and the third was Oineus the knight, the father of my father and in valour he excelled the others. And there he abode, but my father dwelt at Argos, whither he had wandered, for so Zeus and the other gods willed that it should be. And he wedded one of the daughters of Adrastos, and dwelt in a house full of livelihood, and had wheat-bearing fields enow, and many orchards of trees apart, and many sheep were his, and in skill with the spear he excelled all the Achaians: these things ye must have heard, if I speak sooth. Therefore ye could not say that I am weak and a coward by lineage, and so dishonour my spoken counsel, that well I may speak. Let us go down to the battle, wounded as we are, since we needs must; and then might we hold ourselves aloof from the battle, beyond the range of darts, lest any take wound upon wound; but the others will we spur on, even them that aforetime gave place to their passion, and stand apart, and fight not.'

So he spake, and they all heard him readily, and obeyed him. And they set forth, led by Agamemnon the king of men.

Now the renowned Earth-shaker held no vain watch, but went with them in the guise of an ancient man, and he seized the right hand of Agamemnon, Atreus' son, and uttering winged words he spake to him, saying: 'Atreides. now methinks the ruinous heart of Achilles rejoices in his breast, as he beholds the slaughter and flight of the Achaians, since he hath no wisdom, not a grain. Nay, even so may he perish likewise, and god mar him. But with thee the blessed gods are not utterly wroth, nay, even yet methinks the leaders and rulers of the Trojans will cover the wide plain with dust, and thyself shalt see them fleeing to the city from the ships and the huts.'

So spake he, and shouted mightily, as he sped over the plain. And loud as nine thousand men, or ten thousand cry in battle, when they join the strife of war, so mighty was the cry that the strong Shaker of the earth sent forth from his breast, and great strength he put into the heart of each of the Achaians, to strive and war unceasingly.

Now Hera of the golden throne stood on the peak of Olympus, and saw with her eyes, and anon knew him that was her brother and her lord's going to and fro through the glorious fight, and she rejoiced in her heart. And she beheld Zeus sitting on the topmost crest of many-fountained Ida, and to her heart he was hateful. Then she took thought, the ox-eyed lady Hera, how she might beguile the mind of aegis-bearing Zeus. And this seemed to her in her heart to be the best counsel, namely to fare to Ida, when she had well adorned herself, if perchance he would desire to sleep beside her and embrace her body in love, and a sweet sleep and a kindly she could pour on his eyelids and his crafty wits. And she set forth to her bower, that her dear son Hephaistos had fashioned, and therein had made first strong doors on the pillars, with a secret bolt, that no other god might open. There did she enter in and closed the shining doors. With ambrosia first did she cleanse every stain from her winsome body, and anointed her with olive oil, ambrosial, soft, and of a sweet savour; if it were but shaken, in the bronze-floored mansion of Zeus, the savour thereof went right forth to earth and heaven. Therewith she anointed her fair body, and combed her hair, and with her hands plaited her shining tresses, fair and ambrosial, flowing from her immortal head. Then she clad her in her fragrant robe that Athene wrought delicately for her, and therein set many things beautifully made, and fastened it over her breast with clasps of gold. And she girdled it with a girdle arrayed with a hundred tassels, and she set earrings in her pierced ears, earrings of three drops, and glistering, therefrom shone grace abundantly. And with a veil over all the peerless goddess veiled herself, a fair new veil, bright as the sun, and beneath her shining feet she bound goodly sandals. But when she had adorned her body with all her array, she went forth from her bower, and called Aphrodite apart from the other gods, and spake to her saying: 'Wilt thou obey me, dear child, in that which I shall tell thee? or wilt thou refuse, with a grudge in thy heart, because I succour the Danaans, and thou the Trojans?'

Then Aphrodite the daughter of Zeus answered her: 'Hera, goddess queen, daughter of mighty Kronos, say the thing that is in thy mind, my heart bids me fulfil it, if fulfil it I may, and if it may be accomplished.'

Then with crafty purpose the lady Hera answered her: 'Give me now Love and Desire wherewith thou dost overcome all the Immortals, and mortal men. For I am going to visit the limits of the bountiful Earth, and Okeanos, father of the gods, and mother Tethys, who reared me well and nourished me in their halls, having taken me from Rhea, when far-seeing Zeus imprisoned Kronos beneath the earth and the unvintaged sea. Them am I going to visit, and their endless strife will I loose, for already this long time they hold apart from each other, apart from love and the marriage bed, since wrath hath settled in their hearts. If with words I might persuade their hearts, and bring them back to love and the marriage bed, ever should I be called dear to them and worshipful.'

Then laughter-loving Aphrodite answered her again:

'It may not be, nor seemly were it to deny that thou askest, for thou sleepest in the arms of Zeus, the chief of gods.'

Therewith from her breast she loosed the broidered girdle, fair-wrought, wherein are all her enchantments; therein are love, and desire, and loving converse, that steals the wits even of the wise. This girdle she laid in her hands, and spake, and said: 'Lo now, take this girdle and lay it up in thy bosom, this fair-wrought girdle, wherein all things are fashioned; methinks thou wilt not return with that unaccomplished, which in thy heart thou desirest.'

So spake she, and the ox-eyed lady Hera smiled, and smiling laid up the zone within her breast.

Then the daughter of Zeus, Aphrodite, went to her house, and Hera, rushing down, left the peak of Olympus, and touched on Pieria and pleasant Emathia, and sped over the snowy hills of the Thracian horsemen, even over the topmost crests, nor grazed the ground with her feet, and from Athos she fared across the foaming sea, and came to Lemnos, the city of godlike Thoas. There she met Sleep, the brother of Death, and clasped her hand in his, and spake and called him by name: 'Sleep, lord of all gods and of all men, if ever thou didst hear my word, obey me again even now, and I will be grateful to thee always. Lull me, I pray thee, the shining eyes of Zeus beneath his brows, so soon as I have laid me down by him in love. And gifts I will give to thee, even a fair throne, imperishable for ever, a golden throne, that Hephaistos the Lame, mine own child, shall fashion skilfully, and will set beneath it a footstool for the feet, for thee to set thy shining feet upon, when thou art at a festival.'

Then sweet Sleep answered her and said: 'Hera, goddess and queen, daughter of mighty Kronos, another of the eternal gods might I lightly lull to slumber, yea, were it the streams of Okeanos himself, that is the father of them all. But to Zeus the son of Kronos might I not draw near, nor lull him to slumber, unless himself commanded it. For ere now did a behest of thine teach me a lesson, on the day when that famed high-hearted son of Zeus sailed from Ilios, when he had sacked the city of the Trojans. Then verily I lulled the soul of aegis-bearing Zeus, with my sweet influence poured about him, and thou didst contrive evil against him in thy heart, and didst rouse over the sea the blasts of violent winds, and Herakles thou then didst bear to well-peopled Kos, far from all his friends. But Zeus, when he wakened, was wrathful, and dashed the gods about his mansion, and me above all he sought, and he would have cast me from the upper air to perish in the deep, if Night had not saved me, Night, that subdues both gods and men. To her I came as a suppliant in my flight, and he ceased from pursuing, wrathful as he was, for he was in awe of doing aught displeasing to swift Night. And now again thou biddest me accomplish this other task that may not be accomplished.'

Then the ox-eyed lady Hera answered him again: 'Sleep, wherefore dost thou consider these things in thy heart? dost thou deem that Zeus of the far-borne voice will succour the Trojans even as he was wroth for the sake of Herakles, his own child? Nay come, and I will give thee one of the younger of the Graces, to wed and to be called thy wife [even Pasithea, that ever thou longest for all thy days].'

So she spake, and Sleep was glad, and answered and said: 'Come now, swear to me by the inviolable water of Styx, and with one of thy hands grasp the bounteous earth, and with the other the shining sea, that all may be witnesses to us, even all the gods below that are with Kronos, that verily thou wilt give me one of the younger of the Graces, even Pasithea, that myself do long for all my days.'

So spake he, nor did she disobey, the white-armed goddess Hera; she sware as he bade her, and called all the gods by name, even those below Tartaros that are called Titans. But when she had sworn and ended that oath, the twain left the citadel of Lemnos, and of Imbros, clothed on in mist, and swiftly they accomplished the way. To many-fountained Ida they came, the mother of wild beasts, to Lekton, where first they left the sea, and they twain fared above the dry land, and the topmost forest waved beneath their feet. There Sleep halted, ere the eyes of Zeus beheld him, and alighted on a tall pine tree, the loftiest pine that then in all Ida rose through the nether to the upper air. Therein sat he, hidden by the branches of the pine, in the likeness of the shrill bird that on the mountains the gods call *chalkis*, but men *kymindis*.[1] But Hera swiftly drew nigh to topmost Gargaros, the highest crest of Ida, and Zeus the cloud-gatherer beheld her. And as he saw her, so love came over his deep heart, even as when first they mingled with each other in delight, and went together to the couch, their dear parents knowing it not. And he stood before her, and spoke, and said: 'Hera, with what desire comest thou thus hither from Olympus, and thy horses and chariot are not here, whereon thou mightst ascend?'

Then with crafty purpose lady Hera answered him: 'I am going to visit the limits of the bountiful earth, and Okeanos, father of the gods, and mother Tethys, who reared me well and cherished me in their halls. Them am I going to visit, and their endless strife will I loose, for already this long time they hold apart from each other, from love and the marriage bed, since wrath hath settled in their hearts.

But my horses are standing at the foot of many-fountained Ida,

[1]The names of Night-jar, Goat-sucker, Doehawk, and Fern-owl are given in Bewick for this bird, which is really a kind of swift. – R. W. R.

my horses that shall bear me over wet and dry. And now it is because of thee that I am thus come hither, down from Olympus, lest perchance thou mightest be wroth with me hereafter, if silently I were gone to the mansion of deep-flowing Okeanos.'

Then Zeus, the gatherer of the clouds, answered her and said: 'Hera, thither mayst thou go on a later day. But come let us twain take pleasure in the bed of love. For never once as thus did the love of goddess or woman so mightily overflow and conquer the heart within my breast. Not when I loved the wife of Ixion, who bore Pirithoos, the peer of gods in counsel, nor when I loved Danae of the fair ankles, daughter of Akrisios, who bore Perseus, most renowned of all men, nor when I loved the famed daughter of Phoinix, who bore me Minos, and godlike Rhadamanthys, nay, nor even when I loved Semele, nor Alkmene in Thebes, and she bore Herakles, a child hardy of heart, but Semele bore Dionysos, a delight to mortals, nay, nor when I loved the fair-tressed queen, Demeter, nor renowned Leto, nay, nor thy very self, as now I love thee, and sweet desire possesses me.'

And him the lady Hera answered with crafty purpose: 'Most dread son of Kronos, what a word thou hast spoken! If now thou dost long to be couched in love on the crests of Ida, and all stands plain to view, how would it be if some one of the eternal gods should see us slumbering, and go and tell it to all the gods? It is not I that could arise from the couch and go again to thy house, nay, it would be a thing for righteous anger. But if thou wilt, and it is dear to thy heart, thou hast a chamber that thine own son Hephaistos builded, and fastened strong doors to the pillars, thither let us go and lie down, if the couch be thy desire.'

Then Zeus the cloud gatherer answered her and said

'Hera, fear not lest any god, or any man should spy the thing, so great a golden cloud will I cast all over thee. Nay, methinks not even the sun might see through it, the sun, whose light is keenest of all to behold.'

So spake he, and the son of Kronos clasped his consort in his arms. And beneath them the divine earth sent forth fresh new grass, and dewy lotus, and crocus, and hyacinth, thick and soft, that raised them aloft from the ground. Therein they lay, and were clad on with a fair golden cloud, whence fell drops of glittering dew.

Thus slept the Father in quiet on the crest of Gargaros, by Sleep and love overcome, with his bedfellow in his arms. But sweet Sleep started and ran to the ships of the Achaians, to tell his tidings to the god that holdeth and shaketh the earth. And he stood near him, and spake winged words: 'Eagerly now, Poseidon, do thou aid the Danaans, and give them glory for a little space, while yet Zeus sleepeth, for over him have I shed soft slumber, and Hera hath beguiled him to couch in love.'

So he spake, and passed to the renowned tribes of men, and still the more did he set on Poseidon to aid the Danaans, who straightway sprang far afront of the foremost, and called to them: 'Argives, are we again to yield the victory to Hector, son of Priam, that he may take our ships and win renown? Nay, even so he saith and declareth that he will do, for that Achilles by the hollow ships abides angered at heart. But for him there will be no such extreme regret, if we spur us on to aid each the other. Nay come, as I command, let us all obey. Let us harness us in the best shields that are in the host, and the greatest, and cover our heads with shining helms, and take the longest spears in our hands, and so go forth. Yea. and I will lead the way, and methinks that Hector, son of Priam, will not long await us, for all his eagerness. And whatsoever man is steadfast in battle, and hath a small buckler on his shoulder, let him give it to a worse man, and harness him in a larger shield.'

So spake he, and they heard him eagerly and obeyed him And them the kings themselves arrayed, wounded as they were, Tydeus' son, and Odysseus, and Agamemnon, son of Atreus. They went through all the host; and made exchange of weapons of war. The good arms did the good warrior harness him in, the worse he gave to the worse. But when they had done on the shining bronze about their bodies, they started on the march, and Poseidon led them, the Shaker of the earth, with a dread sword of fine edge in his strong hand, like unto lightning; wherewith it is not permitted that any should mingle in woful war, but fear holds men afar therefrom. But the Trojans on the other side was renowned Hector arraying. Then did they now strain the fiercest strife of war, even dark-haired Poseidon and glorious Hector, one succouring the Trojans, the other with the Argives. And the sea washed up to the huts and ships of the Argives, and they gathered together with a mighty cry. Not so loudly bellows the wave of the sea against the land, stirred up from the deep by the harsh breath of the north wind, nor so loud is the roar of burning fire in the glades of a mountain, when it springs to burn up the forest, nor calls the wind so loudly in the high leafy tresses of the trees, when it rages and roars its loudest, as then was the cry of the Trojans and Achaians, shouting dreadfully as they rushed upon each other.

First glorious Hector cast with his spear at Aias, who was facing

him full, and did not miss, striking him where two belts were
stretched across his breast, the belt of his shield, and of his silver-
studded sword; these guarded his tender flesh And Hector was
enraged because his swift spear had flown vainly from his hand, and
he retreated into the throng of his fellows, avoiding Fate.

Then as he was departing the great Telamonian Aias smote him
with a huge stone; for many stones, the props of swift ships, were
rolled among the feet of the fighters; one of these he lifted, and
smote Hector on the breast, over the shield-rim, near the neck, and
made him spin like a top with the blow, that he reeled round and
round. And even as when an oak falls uprooted beneath the stroke
of father Zeus, and a dread savour of brimstone arises therefrom,
and whoso stands near and beholds it has no more courage, for
dread is the bolt of great Zeus, even so fell mighty Hector straightway in the dust. And the spear fell from his hand, but his shield and
helm were made fast to him, and round him rang his arms adorned
with bronze.

Then with a loud cry they ran up, the sons of the Achaians,
hoping to drag him away, and they cast showers of darts. But not
one availed to wound or smite the shepherd of the host; before that
might be the bravest gathered about him, Polydamas, and Aineias,
and goodly Agenor, and Sarpedon, leader of the Lykians, and noble
Glaukos, and of the rest not one was heedless of him, but they held
their round shields in front of him, and his comrades lifted him in
their arms, and bare him out of the battle, till he reached his swift
horses that were standing waiting for him, with the charioteer and
the fair-dight chariot at the rear of the combat and the war. These
toward the city bore him heavily moaning. Now when they came to
the ford of the fair-flowing river, of eddying Xanthos, that immortal
Zeus begat, there they lifted him from the chariot to the ground,
and poured water over him, and he gat back his breath, and looked
up with his eyes, and sitting on his heels kneeling, he vomited black
blood. Then again he sank back on the ground, and black night covered his eyes, the stroke still conquering his spirit.

Now the Argives when they saw Hector departed rushed yet the
more upon the Trojans, and were mindful of the delight of battle.
There far the foremost did swift Aias, son of Oileus, leap on Satnios, son of Enops, and wounded him with his sharp spear; Satnios
whom the fair Naiad-nymph bore to Enops as he herded his flocks
by the banks of Satnioeis. Him did the spear-famed son of Oileus
draw nigh, and wounded him on the flank, and he fell, and round
him did Trojans and Danaans join in strong battle. Then to his aid

came Polydamas, the wielder of the spear, son of Panthoos, and smote Prothoenor on the right shoulder, Prothoenor, son of Areï-lykos, and through his shoulder went the mighty spear, and he fell in the dust, and clutched the earth with his palm. And Polydamas boasted over him terribly, crying aloud: 'Verily methinks that again from the strong hand of the high-hearted son of Panthoos, the spear hath not leaped in vain. Nay, one of the Argives hath caught it in his flesh, and leaning thereon for a staff, methinks that he will go down within the house of Hades.'

So spake he, and sorrow came on the Argives by reason of his boasting. And chiefly he roused the wrath of the wise son of Tela-mon, Aias, for the man fell close by him. Swiftly he cast at the other, as he departed, with his shining spear. And Polydamas him-self avoided black Fate, starting to one side, but Archelochos, son of Antenor, received the spear, for the gods had willed his death. Him the spear struck at the meeting of the head and neck, on the last joint of the spine, and cut in twain both the tendons. And his head, and mouth, and nose, as he fell, reached the earth long before his legs and knees, and Aias again shouted to noble Polydamas: 'Con-sider, Polydamas, and tell me truly, whether thou sayst not that this man is worth slaying in place of Prothoenor: he seems to me no coward, nor born of cowards, but a brother of horse-taming Antenor, or a child, for he most closely favoureth his house.'

So he spake, knowing the truth right well, and sorrow seized the hearts of the Trojans. Then Akamas wounded Promachos the Boi-otian with his spear, from where he stood above his brother, that Promachos was dragging away by the feet. Over him Akamas boasted terribly, shouting aloud: 'Ye Argive bowmen, insatiate of threats, verily not for us alone shall there be struggle and toil, nay, but even as we shall ye likewise perish. Consider how your Proma-chos sleepeth, vanquished by my spear, that my brother's blood-price may not be long unpaid. Even for this it is that a man may well pray to leave some kinsman in his halls, that will avenge his fall.'

So he spake, and sorrow came on the Argives at his boast. And chiefly he stirred the heart of the wise Peneleos, who made for Akamas, and Akamas abode not the onset of the prince Peneleos. But Peneleos wounded Ilioneus, the son of Phorbas, rich in herds, that Hermes loved most dearly of all the Trojans, and gave him wealth. Now his mother bare Ilioneus, an only child, to Phorbas. Him did Peneleos wound beneath the brows, at the bases of the eye, and drave out the eyeball, and the spear went clean through the eye and through the nape of the neck, and he fell back, stretching out both his hands. And Peneleos, drawing forth his sharp sword, smote him on the middle of the neck, and smote off even to the ground the head with the helmet, and still the strong spear stood in the eye, and lifting it up like a poppy head, he showed it to the Trojans, and spoke his boastful words: 'Ye Trojans, I pray you bid the dear father and the mother of proud Ilioneus to wail in their halls, for neither will the wife of Promachos, son of Alegenor, rejoice in her dear husband's coming, in that hour when we youths of the Achaians return with our ships out of Troyland.'

So he spake, and fear fell on the limbs of all of them; and each man looked about to see where he might flee sheer destruction.

Tell me now, ye Muses, that dwell in the mansions of Olympus, who was the first of the Achaians to lift the bloody spoils, when once the renowned Shaker of the earth turned the battle.

Verily it was Aias, son of Telamon, that first wounded Hyrtios, the son of Gyrtias, the leader of the Mysians strong of heart, and Antilochos stripped the spoils from Phalkes and Mermeros, and Meriones slew Morys and Hippotion, and Teukros slew Prothoon and Periphetes, and next Atreus' son wounded in the flank Hyperenor, the shepherd of the host, and the bronze point tore through and let out the entrails, and the soul through the stricken wound fled hastily, and darkness covered his eyes. But most men did Aias slay, the swift-footed son of Oileus, for there was none so speedy of foot as he, to follow when men fled, when Zeus sent terror among them.

BOOK XV

Zeus awakening, biddeth Apollo revive Hector, and restore the fortunes of the Trojans. Fire is thrown on the ship of Protesilaos.

NOW WHEN THEY HAD SPED IN FLIGHT across the palisade and trench, and many were overcome at the hands of the Danaans, the rest were stayed, and abode beside the chariots in confusion, and pale with terror, and Zeus awoke, on the peaks of Ida, beside Hera of the golden throne. Then he leaped up, and stood, and beheld the Trojans and Achaians, those in flight, and these driving them on from the rear, even the Argives, and among them the prince Poseidon. And Hector he saw lying on the plain, and around him sat his comrades, and he was gasping with difficult breath, and his mind wandering, and was vomiting blood, for it was not the weakest of the Achaians that had smitten him. Beholding him, the father of men and gods had pity on him, and terribly he spoke to Hera, with fierce look: 'O thou ill to deal with, Hera, verily it is thy crafty wile that has made noble Hector cease from the fight, and has terrified the host. Nay, but yet I know not whether thou mayst not be the first to reap the fruits of thy cruel treason, and I beat thee with stripes. Dost thou not remember, when thou wert hung from on high, and from thy feet I suspended two anvils,[1] and round thy hands fastened a golden bond that might not be broken? And thou didst hang in the clear air and the clouds, and the gods were wroth in high Olympus, but they could not come round and unloose thee. Nay, whomsoever I might take, I would clutch, and throw from the threshold, to come fainting to the earth, yet verily not even so did the ceaseless sorrow leave my soul free: sorrow for godlike Herakles. Him didst thou drive, when thou hadst suborned the tempest, with the help of the North Wind, over the unvintaged deep, out of thine evil counsel, and then didst carry him away to well-peopled Kos. Him did I rescue thence, and lead again to Argos, the pastureland of horses, after his much labour. Of these things will I mind thee again, that thou mayst cease from thy wiles, that thou mayst know if it profit thee at all, the dalliance and the love, wherein thou

[1] Or, 'thunderbolts'; i.e. meteoric stones.

didst lie with me, when thou hadst come from among the gods, and didst beguile me.'

So spake he, and the ox-eyed lady Hera shuddered, and spake unto him winged words, saying: 'Let earth now be witness hereto, and wide heaven above, and that falling water of Styx, the greatest oath and the most terrible to the blessed gods, and thine own sacred head, and our own bridal bed, whereby never would I forswear myself, that not by my will does earth-shaking Poseidon trouble the Trojans and Hector, and succour them of the other part. Nay, it is his own soul that urgeth and commandeth him, and he had pity on the Achaians, when he beheld them hard pressed beside the ships. I would even counsel him also to go even where thou, lord of the storm-cloud, mayst lead him.'

So spake she, and the father of gods and men smiled, and answering her he spake winged words: 'If thou, of a truth, O ox-eyed lady Hera, wouldst hereafter abide of one mind with me among the immortal gods, thereon would Poseidon, howsoever much his wish be contrariwise, quickly turn his mind otherwhere, after thy heart and mine. But if indeed thou speakest the truth and soothly, go thou now among the tribes of the gods, and call Iris to come hither, and Apollo, the renowned archer, that Iris may go among the host of mail-clad Achaians and tell Poseidon the prince to cease from the war, and get him unto his own house. But let Phoebus Apollo spur Hector on to the war, and breathe strength into him again, and make him forget his anguish, that now wears down his heart, and drive the Achaians back again, when he hath stirred in them craven fear. Let them flee and fall among the many-benched ships of Achilles son of Peleus, and he shall rouse his own comrade, Patroklos; and him shall renowned Hector slay with the spear, in front of Ilios, after that he has slain many other youths, and among them my son, noble Sarpedon. In wrath therefor shall goodly Achilles slay Hector. From that hour verily will I cause a new pursuit from the ships, that shall endure continually, even until the Achaians take steep Ilios, through the counsels of Athene. But before that hour neither do I cease in my wrath, nor will I suffer any other of the Immortals to help the Danaans there, before I accomplish that desire of the son of Peleus, as I promised him at the first, and confirmed the same with a nod of my head, on that day when the goddess Thetis clasped my knees, imploring me to honour Achilles, the sacker of cities.'

So spake he, nor did the white-armed goddess Hera disobey him, and she sped down from the hills of Ida to high Olympus. And even as when the mind of a man darts speedily, of one that hath travelled over far lands, and considers in his wise heart, 'Would that I were here or there," and he thinketh him of many things, so swiftly fled she in her eagerness, the lady Hera, and came to steep Olympus, and went among the gathering of the immortal gods in the house of Zeus, and when they beheld her they all rose up together, and held out their cups to her in welcome. The others she left alone, but took the cup of Themis of the fair cheeks, for she was the first that came running to meet her, and speaking winged words accosted her: 'Hera, wherefore hast thou come? thou seemest like one confounded; verily the son of Kronos hath made thee adread, thine own husband.'

Then the white-armed goddess Hera answered her, saying: 'Ask me not concerning this, O goddess Themis; thyself knowest it, how overweening is his heart, and unyielding. But do thou begin the equal banquet of the gods in the halls, and thus shalt thou hear among all the Immortals, even what evil deeds Zeus declareth. Nay, methinks, not equally will it delight the minds of all, neither of gods nor mortals, if even now any still sit with pleasure at the feast.'

So spake the lady Hera, and sat her down, while the gods were heavy at heart in the hall of Zeus. And she laughed with her lips, but her forehead above her dark brows was not gladdened, and indignantly she spake among them all: 'Witless that we are to be wroth in our folly against Zeus! Even still we are eager to draw nigh to him, and let him from his will, by word or deed, but he sits apart and careth not, nor takes any thought thereof, for he deems that among the immortal gods he is manifestly pre-eminent in force and might. Wherefore do ye content yourselves with whatsoever sorrow he sends on each of you. Already, methinks, has sorrow been wrought for Ares, for his son has fallen in the fight, ever the dearest of men, Askalaphos, that dread Ares deemeth to be verily his own.'

So spake she, but Ares smote his strong thighs with his hands flatlings, and sorrowing he spake: 'Hold me not now to blame, ye that keep the mansions of Olympus, if I avenge the slaying of my son, and go to the ships of the Achaians, even if it be my doom to be smitten with the bolt of Zeus, and lie among the dead, in the dust and blood.'

So spake he, and bade yoke his horses, Fear and Dread, and himself did on his shining harness. Thereby would yet a greater and more implacable wrath and anger have been caused between Zeus and the Immortals, had not Athene, in terror for the sake of all the gods, leaped out through the doorway, and left the throne wherein she sat, and taken from Ares' head the helmet, and the shield from his shoulders, and drawn the spear of bronze from his stalwart hand, and set it apart, and then with words she rebuked the impetuous Ares: 'Mad that thou art, and distraught of wit – this is thy bane! Verily thou hast ears and hearest not, and perished have thine understanding and thine awe. Hearest thou not what she saith, the white-armed goddess Hera, that even now is come from Olympian Zeus? Dost thou wish both thyself to fill up the measure of mischief and so return to Olympus ruefully, of necessity, and for all the other gods to sow the seed of a great wrong? For straightway will he leave the high-hearted Trojans and the Achaians, and to us will he come to make tumult in Olympus: and he will clutch us each in turn, the blameless with the guilty. Wherefore now again I bid thee to abate thine anger for thy son, for already many a man stronger than he, and more hardy of his hands, has fallen, or yet will fall; and a hard thing it is to save the lineage and offspring *of* all men.'

So spake she, and made impetuous Ares sit down on his throne. But Hera called Apollo without the hall, and Iris, that is the messenger of the immortal gods, and she spake winged words, and addressed them, saying: 'Zeus bids you go to Ida as swiftly as may be, and when ye have gone, and looked on the face of Zeus, do ye whatsoever he shall order and command.'

So spake she, and returned again, the lady Hera, and sat down on her throne, and they flew forward speedily, and came to many-fountained Ida, mother of wild beasts, and found far-seeing Zeus seated on topmost Gargaros, and round him a fragrant cloud was circled like a crown. And these twain came before the face of Zeus the cloud-gatherer, and stood there, and he was no wise displeased at heart when he beheld them, for that speedily they had obeyed the words of his dear wife. And to Iris first he spake winged words: 'Go, get thee, swift Iris, to the prince Poseidon, and tell him all these things, nor be a false messenger. Command him to cease from war and battle, and to go among the tribes of the gods, or into the bright sea. But if he will not obey my words, but will hold me in no regard, then let him consider in his heart and mind, lest he dare not for all his strength to abide me when I come against him, since I deem me to be for mightier than he, and elder born. But this his heart feareth not, – to call himself the peer of me whom even the other gods do hold in dread.'

So spake he, nor did the wind-footed fleet Iris disobey him, but went down the hills of Ida to sacred Ilios. And as when snow or chill hail fleets from the clouds beneath the stress of the North Wind born in the clear air, so fleetly she fled in her eagerness, swift Iris, and drew near the renowned Earth-shaker and spake to him, saying: 'A certain message to thee, O dark-haired embracer of the earth, have I come hither to bring from aegis-bearing Zeus. He biddeth thee cease from the battle and war, and go among the tribes of the gods, or into the bright sea. And if thou wilt not obey his word, but wilt hold him in no regard, he threatens that even himself will come hither against thee in battle, and he biddeth thee avoid thee out of his hands, since he deemeth him far mightier than thou, and elder born, but thy heart feareth not to call thyself the peer of him whom even the other gods do hold in dread.'

Then, in great displeasure the renowned Shaker of the earth answered her: 'Out on it, verily now, for as strong as he is, he hath spoken over-haughtily, if indeed he will subdue by force, against my will, me that am his equal in honour. For three brethren are we, and sons of Kronos, whom Rhea bare, Zeus, and myself, and Hades is the third, the ruler of the folk in the under-world. And in three lots are all things divided, and each drew a domain of his own, and to me fell the hoary sea, to be my habitation for ever, when we shook the lots: and Hades drew the murky darkness, and Zeus the wide heaven, in clear air and clouds, but the earth and high Olympus are yet common to all. Wherefore no whit will I walk after the will of Zeus, but quietly let him abide, for all his strength, in his third portion. And with the might of his hands let him not strive to terrify me withal, as if I were a coward. Better for him were it to threaten with terrible words his daughters and his sons, that himself begat, who will perforce listen to whatso he enjoins.'

Then the fleet wind-footed Iris answered him: 'Is it indeed thy will O dark-haired embracer of the earth, that even thus I shall carry to Zeus this message, hard and froward, of wilt thou turn thee at all, for the hearts of the good may be turned? Thou knowest how the Erinyes do always follow to aid the elder-born.'

Then he answered her again, Poseidon, the Shaker of the earth: 'Goddess Iris, most duly hast thou spoken this word. Yea, an excellent thing is this, when the bearer of a message has a prudent wit. Yet this is a terrible grief that cometh on heart and spirit, whenso any desireth to upbraid with angry words his peer to whom fate hath assigned an equal share with himself. But verily now will I yield, for all mine anger; but another thing will I tell thee, and make this threat in my heart, that if against my will, and the will of Athene, the driver of the prey, and of Hera and Hermes, and prince Hephaistos, Zeus shall spare steep Ilios, nor choose utterly to destroy it, and give great might to the Argives, let him know this, that our wrath will be inappeasable.'

So spake the Shaker of the earth, and left the host of the Achaians, and passed to the sea, and sank, and sorely they missed him, the heroes of the Achaians.

Then Zeus, the gatherer of the clouds, spake to Apollo, saying: 'Go now, dear Phoebus, to Hector of the helm of bronze, for, lo, already the embracer of the world, the Earthshaker, is gone to the bright sea, shunning our utter wrath, ay, and had he not done so, even the others would have heard of our strife, even the gods of the nether world, that are with Kronos. But better far is this, both for me, and for him, that, despite his wrath, he should yield to my hands, for not without sweat would this strife have been accomplished. But do thou take in thy hands the tasselled aegis, and shake it fiercely and affright the Achaian heroes. But, thou Archer-God, let glorious Hector be thy care, and rouse in him great wrath even till the Achaians come in their flight to the ships, and the Hellespont. And from that moment will I devise word and deed wherewithal the Achaians may take breath again from their toil.'

So spake he, nor was Apollo deaf to the word of the Father, but he went down the hills of Ida like a fleet falcon, the bane of doves, that is the swiftest of flying things. And he found the son of wisehearted Priam, noble Hector, sitting up, no longer lying, for he had but late got back his life, and knew the comrades around him, and his gasping and his sweat had ceased, from the moment when the will of aegisbearing Zeus began to revive him. Then far-darting Apollo stood near him, and spake to him: 'Hector, son of Priam, why dost thou sit fainting apart from the others? Is it perchance that some trouble cometh upon thee?'

Then, with faint breath answered him Hector of the glancing helm: 'Nay, but who art thou, best of the gods, who enquirest of me face to face? Dost thou not know that by the hindmost row of the ships of the Achaians, Aias of the loud war-cry smote me on the breast with a stone, as I was slaying his comrades, and made me cease from mine impetuous might? And verily I deemed that this very day I should pass to the dead, and the house of Hades, when I had gasped my life away.'

Then prince Apollo the Far-darter answered him again: 'Take courage now, so great an ally hath the son of Kronos sent thee out of Ida, to stand by thee and defend thee, even Phoebus Apollo of the golden sword, me who of old defend thee, thyself and the steep citadel. But come now bid thy many charioteers drive their swift steeds against the hollow ships, and I will go before and make smooth all the may for the chariots, and will put to flight the Achaian heroes.'

So he spake, and breathed great might into the shepherd of the host, and even as when a stalled horse, full fed at the manger, breaks his tether and speedeth at the gallop over the plain exultingly, being wont to bathe in the fair-flowing stream, and holds his head on high, and the mane floweth about his shoulders, and he trusteth in his glory, and nimbly his knees bear him to the haunts and pasture of the mares, even so Hector lightly moved his feet and knees, urging on his horsemen, when he heard the voice of the god. But as when hounds and country folk pursue a horned stag, or a wild goat, that steep rock and shady wood save from them, nor is it their lot to find him, but at their clamour a bearded lion hath shown himself on the way, and lightly turned them all despite their eagerness, even so the Danaans for a while followed on always in their companies, smiting with swords and double-pointed spears, but when they saw Hector going up and down the ranks of men, then were they afraid, and the hearts of all fell to their feet.

Then to them spake Thoas, son of Andraimon, far the best of the Aitolians, skilled in throwing the dart, and good in close fight, and in council did few of the Achaians surpass him, when the young men were striving in debate; with good intent he made harangue and spake among them: 'Alas, and verily a great marvel is this I behold with mine eyes, how he hath again arisen, and hath avoided the Fates, even Hector. Surely each of us hoped in his heart, that he had died beneath the hand of Aias, son of Telamon. But some one of the gods again hath delivered and saved Hector, who verily hath loosened the knees of many of the Danaans, as methinks will befall even now, for not without the will of loud-thundering Zeus doth he rise in the front ranks, thus eager for battle. But come, as I declare let us all obey. Let us bid the throng turn back to the ships, but let us as many as avow us to be the best in the host, take our stand, if perchance first we may meet him, and hold him off with outstretched spears, and he, methinks, for all his eagerness, will fear at heart to enter into the press of the Danaans.'

So spake he, and they heard him eagerly, and obeyed him. They that were with Aias and the prince Idomeneus, and Teukros, and Meriones, and Meges the peer of Ares, called to all the best of the warriors and sustained the fight with Hector and the Trojans, but behind them the multitude returned to the ships of the Achaians.

Now the Trojans drave forward in close ranks, and with long

strides Hector led them, while in front of him went Phoebus Apollo, his shoulders wrapped in cloud, and still he held the fell aegis, dread, circled with a shaggy fringe, and gleaming, that Hephaistos the smith gave to Zeus, to bear for the terror of men; with this in his hands did he lead the host.

Now the Argives abode them in close ranks, and shrill the cry arose on both sides, and the arrows leaped from the bow-strings, and many spears from stalwart hands, whereof some stood fast in the flesh of young men swift in fight, but many halfway, ere ever they reached the white flesh, stuck in the ground, longing to glut themselves with flesh. Now so long as Phoebus Apollo held the aegis unmoved in his hands, so long the darts smote either side amain, and the folk fell. But when he looked face to face on the Danaans of the swift steeds, and shook the aegis, and himself shouted mightily, he quelled their heart in their breast, and they forgot their impetuous valour. And as when two wild beasts drive in confusion a herd of kine, or a great flock of sheep, in the dark hour of black night, coming swiftly on them when the herdsman is not by, even so were the Achaians terror-stricken and strengthless, for Apollo sent a panic among them, but still gave renown to the Trojans and Hector.

Then man fell upon man, when the close fight was scattered. Hector slew Stichios, and Arkesilaos, one a leader of the mail-clad Boiotians, the other the true comrade of great-hearted Menestheus. And Aineias slew Medon and Iasos, whereof one was the bastard son of divine Oileus, even Medon, brother of Aias, but he dwelt in Phylake, far from his own country, for that he had slain a man the brother of his stepmother Eriopis, the wife of Oileus. But Iasos was a leader of the Athenians, and was called the son of Sphelos, the son of Boukolos. And Polydamas slew Mekisteus, and Polites Echios in the forefront of the battle, and noble Agenor overcame Klonios. And Deïochos as he was flying among the fighters in the foremost rank Paris smote behind the lower part of the shoulder, and drave the bronze clean through.

Now while they were stripping the spoil from these, even then the Achaians were dashing into the delved fosse, and against the palisade, fleeing hither and thither in their terror, and were driven perforce within the wall, but Hector called with a loud shout to the Trojans: 'Make ye against the ships, and leave the bloody spoils. Whomsoever I shall see apart from the ships on the other side, his death will I there devise, nor forthwith shall his kinsmen and kinswomen lay him dead on the funeral fire, but dogs shall tear him in front of our citadel.'

So speaking he smote his horses on the shoulder with the lash, and called aloud on the Trojans along the ranks. And they all cried out, and level with his held the steeds that drew their chariots, with a marvellous din, and in front of them Phoebus Apollo lightly dashed down with his feet the banks of the deep ditch, and cast them into the midst thereof, making a bridgeway long and wide as is a spearcast, when a man throws to make trial of his strength. Thereby the Trojans poured forward in their battalions, while in their van Apollo held the splendid aegis. And most easily did he cast down the wall of the Achaians, as when a boy scatters the sand beside the sea, first making sand buildings for sport in his childishness, and then again, in his sport, confounding them with his feet and hands; even so didst thou, archer Apollo, confound the long toil and labour of the Argives, and among them rouse a panic fear.

So they were halting, and abiding by the ships, calling each to other; and lifting their hands to all the gods did each man pray vehemently, and chiefly prayed Gerenian Nestor, the Warden of the Achaians, stretching his hand towards the starry heaven: 'O father Zeus, if ever any one of us in wheat-bearing Argos did burn to thee fat thighs of bull or sheep, and prayed that he might return, and thou didst promise and assent thereto, of these things be thou mindful, and avert, Olympian, the pitiless day, nor suffer the Trojans thus to overcome the Achaians.'

So spake he in his prayer, and Zeus, the Lord of counsel, thundered loudly, hearing the prayers of the ancient son of Neleus.

But the Trojans, when they heard the thunder of aegisbearing Zeus, rushed yet the more eagerly upon the Argives, and were mindful of the joy of battle. And as when a great wave of the wide sea sweeps over the bulwarks of a ship, the might of the wind constraining it, which chiefly swells the waves, even so did the Trojans with a great cry bound over the wall, and drave their horses on, and at the hindmost row of the ships were fighting hand to hand with double-pointed spears, the Trojans from the chariots, but the Achaians climbing up aloft, from the black ships with long pikes that they had lying in the ships for battle at sea, jointed pikes shod at the head with bronze.

Now Patroklos, as long as the Achaians and Trojans were fighting about the wall, without the swift ships, sat in the hut of kindly Eurypylos, and was making him glad with talk, and on his cruel wound was laying herbs, to medicine his dark pain. But when he perceived the Trojans rushing over the wall, and the din and flight of the Danaans began, then did he groan, and smote his two thighs with his hands flatlings, and sorrowing he spake: 'Eurypylos, no longer at all may I abide with thee here, though great thy need, for verily a great strife has arisen. But thee let thy squire comfort, while I hasten to Achilles, that I may urge him to join the battle. who knows but with god's help I may arouse his spirit with my persuasion? And a good thing is the persuasion of a friend.'

Even as he spake, his feet were bearing him away, but the Achaians abode the onset of the Trojans steadfastly, yet availed not to drive them, though fewer they were, from the ships: neither at all could the Trojans break the ranks of the Danaans and pour among the huts and the ships. But even as the carpenter's line doth straighten the timber of a ship, in the hands of a cunning shipwright that is well skilled in all craft, by the inspiration of Athene, so equally was strained their war and battle, and divers of them were fighting about divers ships. Now Hector made for renowned Aias, and they twain were warring about the same ship, nor could the one drive back the other and set fire to the ship, nor could the other thrust him away, since the god urged him on. There did glorious Aias smite Kaletor son of Klytios in the breast with a spear, as he was carrying fire against the ship, and he fell with a crash, and the torch dropped from his hand. But Hector, when he beheld with his eyes his cousin fallen in the dust, in front of the black ship, called with a loud cry to the Trojans and Lykians: 'Ye Trojans, and Lykians, and Dardanians that fight hand to hand, slacken not at all from the battle in this strait, but save the son of Klytios; lest the Achaians spoil him of his harness, now that he hath fallen in the precinct of the ships.'

So spake he, and hurled at Aias with a shining spear: and Aias he missed, but Lykophron, the son of Mastor, the Kytherian squire of Aias, who dwelt with him, having slain a man in divine Kythera, him Hector smote on the head above the ear with the sharp bronze, even as he stood near Aias; and backward in the dust he fell to earth from the stern of the ship, and his limbs were loosened. And Aias shuddered, and spake to his brother: 'Dear Teukros, lo our true comrade hath been slain, even the son of Mastor out of Kythera whom we honoured at home in the halls like our own parents. Him hath great-hearted Hector slain. Where now are thy swift shafts of doom, and the bow that Phoebus Apollo gave thee?'

So spake he, and the other marked him, and ran, and came and stood close by him, with the bended bow in his hand, and the quiver with the arrows, and right swiftly he showered his shafts upon the

Trojans. And he smote Kleitos, the splendid son of Peisenor, the comrade of Poly damas, the haughty son of Panthoos, with the reins in his hand, as he was busy with the horses, for thither was he driving them where far the most of the companies were broken in confusion, and he was showing a favour to Hector and the Trojans. But swiftly on himself came his bane, that not one of them could ward off from him, despite their desire. For the woful arrow lighted on the back of his neck, and he fell from the chariot, and back started his horses, shaking the empty car. But straight- ay the prince Polydamas beheld it, and was the first to come over against the horses. Them he gave to Astynoos, the son of Protiaon, and enjoined him straitly to hold the horses close at hand, and look on, and himself went back, and mingled with the foremost fighters. Then Teukros aimed another shaft against Hector of the helm of bronze, and would have made cease the battle by the ships of the Achaians, if he had smitten him in his prowess and taken his life away. But he escaped not the wise mind of Zeus, who guarded Hector, but took away the praise from Teukros son of Telamon, for he brake the well twisted string on the goodly bow, even as Teukros was aiming at Hector, and his arrow weighted with bronze wandered otherwhere, and the bow fell from his hands. But Teukros shuddered, and spake to his brother saying: 'Alas, now verily the god breaks altogether the purpose of our battle, in that he hath cast the bow from my hand, and hath broken the newly twisted cord, which I bound on but this morning, that it might sustain the many shafts that should leap from the bow.'

Then the great Aias son of Telamon answered him saying: 'Yea, friend, but let the bow and the many arrows lie, even so, since the god has confounded them, being jealous of the Danaans, but take in thy hands a long spear, and a shield on thy shoulder, and war with the Trojans, and arouse the rest of the host. Verily not without labour, for all their victory, let them take the well-timbered ships; nay, let us be mindful of the delight of battle.'

So spake he, and Teukros set the bow within the huts again, but round his shoulder he set a fourfold shield, and on his mighty head a well-wrought helmet, [with a horse-hair plume, and terribly the crest nodded above.] And he seized a strong spear, shod with sharp bronze, and started on his way, and started and running right speedily stood beside Aias.

But when Hector saw the artillery of Teukros harmed, he cried, with a mighty shout, to the Trojans and Lykians: 'Trojans, and Lykians, and Dardanians that love close fight, play the man, my friends, and be mindful of impetuous valour, here by the hollow ships, for I have seen with mine eyes, how the artillery of the bravest warrior was harmed by Zeus. And most easily discerned is the aid of Zeus to men, both to whomso he gives the meed of the greater honour, and whom he would minish and hath no will to aid, as even now he minisheth the strength of the Argives, but us he aideth. But fight in your firm companies at the ships, and whosoever of you be smitten by dart or blow and meeteth death and fate, so let him die. Lo, it is no dishonourable thing for him to fall fighting for his country, but his wife and his children after him are safe, and his house unharmed, and his lot of land, if but the Achaians fare with their ships to their dear native land.'

So spake he and aroused the might and the spirit of every man.

But Aias again, on the other side, called unto his comrades:

'Shame on you, Argives: now is one thing sure, either that we must perish utterly, or be saved and drive the peril from the ships. Think ye that if Hector of the glancing helm take the ships, ye will come by dry land each to his own country? Hear ye not Hector exhorting all the host, so eager, verily, is he to burn the ships? Truly he bids not men to the dance but to battle. And for us there is no better counsel nor device, but to put forth our hands and all our might in close combat. Better it were to risk life or death, once for all, than long to be straitened in the dread stress of battle, thus vainly by the ships, at the hands of worse men than we be.'

So spake he, and aroused the might and the spirit of every man.

Then Hector slew Schedios, the son of Perimedes, a leader of the Phokians, while Aias slew Laodamas, the leader of the foot-men, the noble son of Antenor, and Polydamas slew Otos, of Kyllene, comrade of Phyleides, a chief of the high-hearted Epeians. And Meges, when he beheld it rushed on him, but Polydamas stooped downwards, and him Meges missed, – for Apollo suffered not the son of Panthoos to be smitten among the foremost fighters, – but he wounded Kroismos in the midst of the breast with his spear. And he fell with a crash, and the other set to stripping the harness from his shoulders. Then Dolops rose against him, a warrior skilled, Dolops son of Lampos, whom Lampos Laomedon's son begat, his bravest son, well skilled in impetuous valour; who then smote the midst of the shield of Phyleus' son, setting on him at close quarters. But his well-wrought corslet guarded him., the corslet that he wore, fashioned of plates of mail. This corslet did Phyleus once bear out of Ephyre, from the river Selleëis. Now a guest friend of his had given him the same, even Euphetes, king of men, that he might bear

it in war, a defence against foemen; and now from his son's flesh too
it warded off his bane. Now Meges smote with sharpened spear at
the topmost crest of his helmet of bronze with horse-hair plume,
and brake off his plume *of* horse-hair, and it all fell earthward in the
dust, shining with its new scarlet dye. Now while he abode, and
fought, and yet hoped for victory, there came against him to the
rescue warlike Menelaos, and stood unmarked on his flank with his
spear, and smote him on the shoulder from behind, and the eager
spear rushed through his breast, in forward flight, and then fell he
forward. Then the twain made for him to strip from his shoulders
his harness of bronze. But Hector called to all his kinsmen, and first
he chid the son of Hiketaon, the strong Melanippos. Now till then
was Melanippos wont to feed his kine of trailing gait in Perkote, far
off from hostile men, but when the curved ships of the Danaans
came, he returned to Ilios, and excelled among the Trojans, and
dwelt hard by Priam, who honoured him equally with his own children. Him did Hector chide, and spake out, and called him by
name: 'Melanippos, are we to be thus slack? Is thy heart not moved
at all, at sight of thy kinsman slain!" Seest thou not how they are
busied about the harness of Dolops? nay, follow on, for no longer
may we fight with the Argives from afar, till either we slay them or
they utterly take steep Ilios, and slay her people.'

So spake he, and led on, while the other followed him, a godlike
man. Put the great Aias, son of Telamon, exhorted the Argives,
saying: 'O friends, play the man, and take shame in your hearts; yea,
have sharme each of the other's contempt, in the strong battle. For
of men thus shamefast more escape than fall, but of men that flee
cometh neither glory, nor any avail.'

So spake he, and they likewise themselves were eager to drive off
the others, and laid up his word in their hearts, and begirt the ships
with a ring of bronze, while Zeus urged on the Trojans. Then
Menelaos of the loud war-cry exhorted Antilochos, 'Antilochos, not
one of the Achaians is younger than thou, nor swifter of foot, nor
strong as art thou in fight; see now if thou canst leap out, and smite
some man of the Trojans.'

So spake he, and hasted back again, having heartened the other,
and forth Antilochos leaped from the foremost ranks, and cast his
shining spear, glancing all around him, and the Trojans gave
ground before him when he threw. And no vain dart threw he, but
smote Melanippos, the proud son of Hiketaon, as he was returning
to the combat; on the breast hard by the nipple he smote him. And
he fell with a crash, and darkness covered his eyes. And Antilochos

set on like a hound that rushes upon a wounded fawn, that the hunter hath aimed at and smitten as it leaped from its lair, and hath loosened all its limbs. Even so upon thee, Melanippos, leaped Antilochos steadfast in battle, to spoil thy harness. But noble Hector marked him, and came running against him through the battle. But Antilochos abode not his onset, swift warrior though he was, but he fled, like a wild beast that hath done some evil thing, having slain a dog, or a herdsman by the kine, and flees, before the press of men can gather; even so fled the son of Nestor. Now the Trojans and Hector, with wonderful clamour, showered upon him their dolorous darts, but he turned, and stood, when he had reached the host of his comrades.

Now the Trojans, like ravening lions, rushed upon the ships, fulfilling the behests of Zeus, that ever was rousing their great wrath, but softened the temper of the Argives, and took away their glory, while he spurred on the others. For the heart of Zeus was set on giving glory to Hector, the son of Priam, that withal he might cast fierce-blazing fire, unwearied, upon the beaked ships, and so fulfil all the presumptuous prayer of Thetis; wherefore wise-counselling Zeus awaited, till his eyes should see the glare of a burning ship. For even from that hour was he to ordain the backward chase of the Trojans from the ships, and to give glory to the Danaans. With this design was he rousing Hector, Priam's son, that himself was right eager, against the hollow ships. And he was raging, like Ares, the brandisher of the spear, or as when ruinous fire rages on the hills, in the folds of a deep woodland; and foam grew about his mouth, and his eyes shone beneath his dreadful brows, and around the temples of Hector as he fought his helm shook terribly. For Zeus out of heaven was his ally, and gave him honour and renown, he being but one man against so many. For short of life was he to be, yea, and already Pallas Athene was urging against him the day of destiny, at the hand of the son of Peleus. And fain he was to break the ranks of men, trying them wheresoever he saw the thickest press, and the goodliest harness. Yet not even so might he break them for all his eagerness. Nay, they stood firm, and embattled like a steep rock and a great, hard by the hoary sea, a rock that abides the swift paths of the shrill winds, and the swelling waves that roar against it. Even so the Danaans steadfastly abode the Trojans, and fled not away. But Hector shining with fire on all sides leaped on the throng, and fell upon them, as when beneath the stormclouds a fleet wave reared of the winds falls on a swift ship, and she is all hidden with foam, and the dread blast of the wind roars against the sail and the sailors fear, and tremble in their hearts, for by but a little way are they borne forth from death, even so the spirit was torn in the breasts of the Achaians. But he came on like a ravening lion making against the kine, that are feeding innumerable in the low-lying land of a great marsh, and among them is a herdsman that as yet knoweth not well how to fight with a wild beast concerning the slaughter of the kine of crooked horn, and ever he paces abreast with the rear or the van of the cattle, but the lion leaps into the midst, and devours a cow, and they all tremble for fear, even so the Achaians all were made terribly adread by Hector and father Zeus. But Hector slew Periphetes of Mykene only, the dear son of Kopreus, that was wont to go on the errands of Eurystheus, to the mighty Herakles. From him, a far baser father, was born a better son, in all manner of excellence, in fleetness of foot, and in war, and of mind he was wise among the first of the Mykenaeans. He thus then yielded Hector the greater glory. For as he turned back, he tripped against the rim of his shield which he was wont to bear, a shield that reached to the feet, a fence against javelins – thereon he stumbled, and fell back, and his helm rang wondrously around his temples as he fell. And Hector quickly spied it, and ran up swiftly and stood by him, and fixed a spear in his breast, and slew him hard by his dear comrades that could not aid him, despite all their sorrow for their friend, for themselves greatly dreaded noble Hector,

Now were they come between the ships, and the prows protected them, the prows of the ships drawn up in the first line, but the Trojans rushed in after them. And the Argives were compelled even of necessity to give back from the foremost ships, yet there they abode in close rank beside the huts, and did not scatter throughout the camp. For shame and fear restrained them and ceaselessly they kept shouting each to other. Now Gerenian Nestor above all, the Warden of the Achaians, implored each man by the memory of them that begat him, and spake beseechingly: 'O friends, play the man, and set shame of other men's contempt in your hearts. Let each also be mindful of children and wives, and of his possessions, and of them that begat him, whether any have parents yet alive or they be already dead. For their sake do I here beseech you, for the sake of them that are not with us, to stand stoutly, nor turn to flight.'

So spake he, and roused each man's courage and might, and from their eyes Athene lifted the wondrous cloud of mist, and light came mightily upon them from either side, both from the side of the ships, and from the quarter of even-balanced war. And they beheld

Hector of the loud war-cry, and his comrades, both them that stood in the rear and were not fighting, and all them that fought in the battle by the swift ships.

Nor yet did it please the spirit of high-hearted Aias, to stand in the place whereto the other sons of the Achaians had withdrawn, but he kept faring with long strides, up and down the decks of the ships, and he wielded in his hands a great pike for sea-battles, jointed with rings, two and twenty cubits in length. And even as a man right well skilled in horsemanship that couples four horses out of many, and hurrying them from the plain towards a great city, drives along the public way, many men and women manelling on him, and firmly ever he leaps, and changes his stand from horse to horse, while they fly along, even so Aias went with long strides, over many a deck of the swift ships, and his voice went up unto heaven. And always with terrible cries he summoned the Danaans to defend the ships and the huts. Nor did Hector abide in the throng of well-armed Trojans, but even as a tawny eagle rushes on a flock of winged fowl, that are feeding by a riverside, a flock of geese, or cranes, or long-necked swans, even so Hector made straight for a black-beaked ship, rushing right on it, and mightily Zeus urged him on from behind with his strong hand, and roused on the host along with him.

So again keen battle was set by the ships. Thou wouldst deem that unwearied and unworn they met each other in war, so eagerly they fought. And in their striving they were minded thus; the Achaians verily deemed that never would they flee from the danger, but perish there, but the heart of each Trojan hoped in his breast, that they should fire the ships, and slay the heroes of the Achaians. With these imaginations they stood to each other, and Hector seized the stern of a seafaring ship, a fair ship, swift on the brine, that had borne Protesilaos to Troia, but brought him not back again to his own country. Now round his ship the Achaians and Trojans warred on each other hand to hand, nor far apart did they endure the flights of arrows, nor of darts, but standing hard each by other, with one heart, with sharp axes and hatchets they fought, and with great swords, and double-pointed spears. And many fair brands, dark-scabbarded and hilted, fell to the ground, some from the hands, some from off the shoulders of warring men, and the black earth ran with blood. But Hector, after that once he had seized the ship's stern, left not his hold, keeping the ensign in his hands, and he called to the Trojans: 'Bring fire, and all with one voice do ye raise the war-cry; now hath Zeus given us the dearest day of all, – to take

the ships that came hither against the will of the gods, and brought
many woes upon us, by the cowardice of the elders, who withheld
me when I was eager to fight at the sterns of the ships, and kept
back the host. But if even then far-seeing Zeus did harm our wits,
now he himself doth urge and command us onwards.'

So spake he, and they set yet the fiercer on the Argives. And Aias
no longer abode their onset, for he was driven back by the darts, but
he withdrew a little, – thinking that now he should die, – onto the
oarsmen's bench of seven feet long, and he left the decks of the trim
ship. There then he stood on the watch, and with his spear he ever
drave the Trojans from the ships, whosoever brought unwearied
fire, and ever he shouted terribly, calling to the Danaans: 'O
friends, Danaan heroes, men of Ares' company, play the man, my
friends, and be mindful of impetuous valour. Do we deem that there
be allies at our backs, or some wall stronger than this to ward off
death from men? Verily there is not hard by any city arrayed with
towers, whereby we might defend ourselves, having a host that
could turn the balance of battle. Nay, but we are set down in the
plain of the mailed men of Troy, with our backs against the sea, and
far off from our own land. Therefore is safety in battle, and not in
slackening from the fight.'

So spake he, and rushed on ravening for battle, with his keen
spear. And whosoever of the Trojans was coming against the ship
with blazing fire, to pleasure Hector at his urging, him would Aias
wound, awaiting him with his long spear, and twelve men in front of
the ships at close quarters did he wound.

BOOK XVI

How Patroklos fought in the armour of Achilles, and drove the Trojans from the ships, but was slain at last by Hector.

SO THEY WERE WARRING round the well-timbered ship, but Patroklos drew near Achilles, shepherd of the host, and he shed warm tears, even as a fountain of dark water that down a steep cliff pours its cloudy stream. And noble swift-footed Achilles when he beheld him was grieved for his sake, and accosted him, and spake winged words, saying: 'Wherefore weepest thou, Patroklos, like a fond little maid, that runs by her mother's side, and bids her mother take her up, snatching at her gown, and hinders her in her going, and tearfully looks at her, till the mother takes her up? Like her, Patroklos, dost thou let fall soft tears. Hast thou aught to tell to the Myrmidons, or to me myself, or is it some tidings out of Phthia that thou alone hast heard? They say that Menoitios son of Aktor still lives: and Peleus son of Aiakos lives yet among the Myrmidons, for which twain, were they dead, right sore would we sorrow. Or dost thou lament for the sake of the Argives, – how they perish by the hollow ships through their own transgression? Speak out, and hide it not within thy spirit, that we may both know all.'

But with a heavy groan didst thou speak unto him, O knight Patroklos: 'O Achilles, son of Peleus, far the bravest of the Achaians, be not wroth, seeing that so great calamity has beset the Achaians. For verily all of them that aforetime were the best are lying among the ships, smitten and wounded. Smitten is the son of Tydeus, strong Diomedes, and wounded is Odysseus, spearman renowned, and Agamemnon; and smitten is Eurypylos on the thigh with an arrow. And about them the leeches skilled in medicines are busy, healing their wounds, but thou art hard to reconcile, Achilles. Never then may such wrath take hold of me as that thou nursest; thou brave to the hurting of others. What other man later born shall have profit of thee, if thou dost not ward off base ruin from the Argives? Pitiless that thou art, the knight Peleus was not then thy father, nor Thetis thy mother, but the grey sea bare thee, and the sheer cliffs, so untoward is thy spirit. But if in thy heart thou art shunning some oracle, and thy lady mother hath told thee somewhat from Zeus, yet me do thou send forth quickly, and make the rest of the host of the Myrmidons follow me, if yet any light may arise from me to the Danaans. And give me thy harness to buckle about my shoulders, if perchance the Trojans may take me for thee, and so abstain from battle, and the warlike sons of the Achaians may take breath, wearied as they be, for brief is the breathing in war. And lightly might we that are fresh drive men wearied with the battle back to the citadel, away from the ships and the huts.'

So he spake and besought him, in his unwittingness, for truly it was to be his own evil death and fate that he prayed for. Then to him in great heaviness spake swift-footed Achilles: 'Ah me, Patroklos of the seed of Zeus, what word hast thou spoken? Neither take I heed of any oracle that I wot of, nor yet has my lady mother told me somewhat from Zeus, but this dread sorrow comes upon my heart and spirit, from the hour that a man wishes to rob me who am his equal, and to take away my prize, for that he excels me in power. A dread sorrow to me is this, after all the toils that my heart hath endured. The maiden that the sons of the Achaians chose out for me as my prize, and that I won with my spear when I sacked a well-walled city, her has mighty Agamemnon the son of Atreus taken back out of my hands, as though I were but some sojourner dishonourable. But we will let bygones be bygones. No man may be angry of heart for ever, yet verily I said that I would not cease from my wrath, until that time when to mine own ships should come the war-cry and the battle. But do thou on thy shoulders my famous harness, and lead the war-loving Myrmidons to the fight, if indeed the dark cloud of the Trojans hath mightily surrounded the ships, and if the Argives are driven back to the shore of the sea, holding but a narrow space of land, and the whole town of Troy hath come boldly against them. Yea, for they behold not the vizor of my helm shining hard at hand; swiftly would they flee, and fill the water-courses with dead, if mighty Agamemnon had been but kindly to me. – but now are they warring round the camp. For not in the hands of Diomedes, the son of Tydeus, rageth the spear, to ward off destruction from the Danaans. Neither as yet have I heard the voice of the son of Atreus, shouting out of his hated mouth, but of Hector the slayer of men doth the voice burst around me, as he calls on the Trojans, and they with their cries fill all the plain, overcoming the Achaians in the battle. But even so, Patroklos, to ward off destruction from the ships, do thou fall on mightily, lest they even burn the ships with blazing fire, and take away our desired return. But do thou obey, even as I shall put into thy mind the end of my commandment, that in my sight thou mayst win great honour and fame of all the Danaans and they may give me back again the fairest maiden, and thereto add splendid gifts. When thou hast driven them from the ships, return, and even if the loud-thundering lord of Hera grant thee to win glory, yet long not thou apart from me to fight with the war-loving Trojans; thereby wilt thou minish mine honour. Neither do thou, exulting in war and strife. and slaying the Trojans, lead on toward Ilios, lest one of the eternal gods from Olympus come against thee; right dearly loth Apollo the Far-darter love them. Nay, return back when thou hast brought safety to the ships, and suffer the rest to fight along the plain. For would, O father Zeus, and Athene, and Apollo, would that not one of all the Trojans might escape death, nor one of the Argives, but that we twain might avoid destruction, that alone we might undo the sacred coronal of Troy.'

So spake they each to other, but Aias no longer abode the onset, for he was overpowered by darts; the counsel of Zeus was subduing him, and the shafts of the proud Trojans; and his bright helmet, being smitten, kept ringing terribly about his temples: for always it was smitten upon the fair-wrought cheek-pieces. Moreover his left shoulder was wearied, as steadfastly he held up his glittering shield, nor yet could they make him give ground, as they pressed on with their darts around him. And ever he was worn out with difficult breath, and much sweat kept running from all his limbs, nor had he a moment to draw breath, so on all sides was evil heaped on evil.

Tell me now, ye Muses that have mansions in Olympus, how first fire fell on the ships of the Achaians. Hector drew near, and the ashen spear of Aias he smote with his great sword, hard by the socket, behind the point, and shore it clean away, and the son of Telamon brandished in his hand no more than a pointless spear, and far from him the head of bronze fell ringing on the ground.

And Aias knew in his noble heart, and shuddered at the deeds of the gods, even how Zeus that thundereth on high did utterly cut off from him avail in war, and desired victory for the Trojans. Then Aias gave back out of the darts. But the Trojans cast on the swift ship unwearying fire, and instantly the inextinguishable flame streamed over her: so the fire begirt the stern, whereon Achilles smote his thighs, and spake to Patroklos: 'Arise, Patroklos of the seed of Zeus, commander of the horsemen, for truly I see by the ships the rush of the consuming fire. Up then, lest they take the ships, and there be no more retreat; do on thy harness speedily, and I will summon the host.'

So spake he, while Patroklos was harnessing him in shining bronze. His goodly greaves, fitted with silver clasps, he first girt round his legs, and next did on around his breast the well-dight starry corslet of the swift-footed son of Aiakos. And round his shoulders he cast a sword of bronze, with studs of silver, and next took the great and mighty shield, and on his proud head set a well-wrought helm with a horse-hair crest, and terribly nodded the crest from above. Then seized he two strong lances that fitted his grasp, only he took not the spear of the noble son of Aiakos, heavy, and huge, and stalwart, that none other of the Achaians could wield, but Achilles alone availed to wield it: even the ashen Pelian spear that Cheiron gave to his father dear, from a peak of Pelion, to be the death of warriors. And Patroklos bade Automedon to yoke the horses speedily, even Automedon whom most he honoured after Achilles, the breaker of the ranks of men, and whom he held trusti-est in battle to abide his call. And for him Automedon led beneath the yoke the swift horses, Xanthos and Balios, that fly as swift as the winds, the horses that the harpy Podarge bare to the West Wind, as she grazed on the meadow by the stream of Okeanos. And in the side-traces he put the goodly Pedasos, that Achilles carried away, when he took the city of Eetion; and being but a mortal steed, he followed with the immortal horses.

Meanwhile Achilles went and harnessed all the Myrmidons in the huts with armour, and they gathered like ravening wolves with strength in their hearts unspeakable, that have slain a great horned stag in the hills and rend him piecemeal; and all their jaws are red with blood, and in a herd they go, to lap with their thin tongues the surface of the dark water in a dusky well, belching out the blood of the slaughter, their heart steadfast within their breasts, and their bellies swollen, even so hastened the leaders and chiefs of the Myrmidons around the good squire of swift-footed Achilles. And among them all stood warlike Achilles. urging on the horses and the targeteers.

Fifty were the swift ships which Achilles, beloved of Zeus, led to Troia, and in each ship on the benches sat fifty men his comrades, and five leaders he made, wherein he trusted to give command, and himself with great lordship was chief of them all. One rank led Men-esthios of the shining corslet, the son of Spercheios, the River that falleth from Zeus. Him did the daughter of Peleus bear, beautiful Polydora, to tireless Spercheios, a woman couched with a god. But by name was he the son of Boros, Perieres' son, who openly wedded her, giving countless gifts of wooing. And the next company did war-

like Eudoros lead, the son of an unwedded girl, and him bare Polymele, fair in the dance, the daughter of Phylas. Her did the strong
slayer of Argus love, when he had beheld her with his eyes among
the singing maidens, in the choir of Artemis, the swift-rushing goddess of the golden arrows. Then straightway he went up into her
upper chamber, and lay with her secretly, even Hermes the bearer of
all things good, and gat by her a glorious son, Eudoros, swift of foot
and a man of war. But when Eilithyia, goddess of the pains of travail,
had brought him to the light, and he saw the rays of the sun, then
the strong Echekles, son of Aktor, led Polymele to his halls, after he
had given countless gifts of wooing, but Eudoros did the old Phylas
rear well and nourish tenderly, loving him dearly as he had been his
own son.

And the third company led warlike Peisandros, the son of
Maimalos, most excellent among the Myrmidons in fighting with
the spear, after the comrade of the son of Peleus. And the ancient
knight Phoinix led the fourth company, and the fifth Alkimedon the
noble son of Laerkes led. But when Achilles had stationed them all,
and arrayed them well with their leaders, he laid on them a strong
command: 'Myrmidons, let me find none of you forgetful of the
threats wherewith by the swift ships ye threatened the Trojans,
through all the time of my wrath, and ye did each accuse me, saying,
"Hard-hearted son of Peleus, surely on gall thy mother reared thee,
thou pitiless one that restrainest thy comrades at the ships, against
their will. Nay, homewards let us return again with our seafaring
ships, since such an evil wrath has sunk into thy heart." Even thus
did ye often clamour against me in your gatherings, but now hath
appeared the mighty work of war, wherewith in time past ye were in
love. Therefore let each man keep a stout heart in the battle with
the Trojans.'

So spake he, and aroused the heart and valour of each of them,
and the ranks were yet the closer serried when they heard the
prince. And as when a man builds the wall of a high house with
close-set stones, to avoid the might of the winds, even so close were
arrayed the helmets and bossy shields, and shield pressed on shield,
helm on helm, and man on man, and the horse-hair crests on the
bright helmet-ridges touched each other when they nodded, so
close they stood by each other.

But in front of them all were two men harnessed, Patroklos and
Automedon, both of one heart, to war in the van of the Myrmidons.
But Achilles went into his hut, and opened the lid of a fair and well-
wrought coffer, that silver-footed Thetis placed on board his ship to

carry with him, and filled it well with doublets, and cloaks to keep the wind away, and thick carpets. Therein had he a fair-fashioned cup, and neither was any other man wont to drink therefrom the bright wine, nor to any other god was he wont to do libation therewith, save to Zeus the Father only. This cup he took from the coffer, and first purified it with brimstone, and then washed it in fair streams of water, and himself washed his hands, and drew bright wine. Then prayed he, standing in the mid-court, and poured forth the wine, looking up to heaven, and Zeus that hath joy of the thunder was ware of him: 'King Zeus, Dodonaean, Pelasgian, thou that dwellest afar, ruling over wintry Dodona – and around thee dwell the Selloi, thy prophets, with unwashen feet, and couching on the ground, – even as once thou didst hear my voice in prayer, and didst honour me, and mightily afflict the host of the Achaians, even now too fulfil for me this my desire. For I myself will abide in the gathering of the ships, but my comrade I send with many Myrmidons to war: to him do thou speed the victory, O far-seeing Zeus, and strengthen his heart within him, that Hector too may know whether my squire hath skill to war even alone, – or whether his hands invincible rage only when I enter the moil of war. But when he has driven from the ships the war and din of battle, scatheless then let him return to me at the swift ships with all his arms, and his comrades that fight hand to hand.'

So spake he in his prayer, and wise-counselling Zeus heard him, and the Father granted part to him, and part he denied. He granted him that Patroklos should drive the war and the fight from the ships, but denied him to return safe out of the fight. Then Achilles, having made libation and prayer to father Zeus, went back into his hut, and placed the cup in the coffer again, and came forth and stood in front of his hut, for still his heart desired to see the dread strife of the Trojans and Achaians.

But they that were armed about the high-hearted Patroklos marched forward till they rushed in their pride on the Trojans. And straightway they poured forth like wasps that have their dwelling by the wayside, and that boys are ever wont to vex, always tormenting them in their nests beside the way in childish sport, and a common evil they make for many. And they, if ever some wayfaring man passing by stir them unwittingly, fly forth every one of them, with a heart of valour, and each defends his children; with heart and spirit like theirs the Myrmidons poured out now from the ships, and a cry arose unquenchable, and Patroklos called on his comrades, shouting aloud: 'Myrmidons, ye comrades of Achilles son of Peleus, be men, my friends, and be mindful of your impetuous valour, that so we may win honour for the son of Peleus, that is far the bravest of the Argives by the ships, and whose close- fighting squires are the best. And let wide-ruling Agamemnon the son of Atreus learn his own blindness of heart, in that he nothing honoured the best of the Achaians.'

So spake he, and aroused each man's heart and courage, and all in a mass they fell on the Trojans, and the ships around echoed wondrously to the cry of the Achaians. But when the Trojans beheld the strong son of Menoitios, himself and his squire, shining in their armour, the heart was stirred in all of them, and the companies wavered, for they deemed that by the ships the swift-footed son of Peleus had cast away his wrath, and chosen reconcilement: then each man glanced round, to see where he might flee sheer destruction.

But Patroklos first with a shining spear cast straight into the press, where most men were thronging, even by the stern of the ship of great-hearted Protesilaos, and he smote Pyraichmes, who led his Paionian horsemen out of Amydon, from the wide water of Axios; him he smote on the right shoulder, and he fell on his back in the dust with a groan, and his comrades around him, the Paeonians, were afraid, for Patroklos sent fear among them all, when he slew their leader that was ever the best in fight. Then he drove them out from the ships, and quenched the burning fire. And the half-burnt ship was left there, and the Trojans fled, with a marvellous din, and the Danaans poured in among the hollow ships, and ceaseless was the shouting. And as when from the high crest of a great hill Zeus, the gatherer of the lightning, hath stirred a dense cloud, and forth shine al] the peaks, and sharp promontories, and glades, and from heaven the infinite air breaks open, even so the Danaans, having driven the blazing fire from the ships, for a little while took breath, but there was no pause in the battle. For not yet were the Trojans driven in utter rout by the Achaians, dear to Ares, from the black ships, but they still stood up against them, and only perforce gave ground from the ships. Then man slew man of the chieftains, in the scattered fight. First the strong son of Menoitios smote the thigh of Areïlykos, at the moment when he turned, with a sharp spear, and drave the bronze clean through, and the spear brake the bone, and he fell on his face, on the ground. Meanwhile warlike Menelaos wounded Thoas on his breast where it was left uncovered, by the edge of the shield, and loosened his limbs. And Phyleides watched Amphiklos as he set on, and was beforehand with him, stretching forward at the thigh, where a man's muscle is thickest, and the sinews were rent with the point of the spear, and darkness covered his eyes. And as for the sons of Nestor, one of them, Antilochos, smote Atymnios with the sharp spear, and drave the spear of bronze through his flank, and he fell forward. But hard at hand Maris rushed on Antilochos with the spear, in wrath for his brother's sake, and stood in front of the dead; but godlike Thrasymedes was beforehand with him, and smote forward instantly at his shoulder ere he could deal a wound, and missed not, for the point of the spear rent the root of the arm from the muscles, and tore it to the bone. Then fell he with a crash, and darkness covered his eyes. So these twain, subdued by the two brothers, went to Erebos, even the noble comrades of Sarpedon, the warrior sons of Amisodaros, that reared the invincible Chimaira, the bane of many a man. But Aias son of Oileus rushed on Cleoboulos, and took him alive, entangled in the press; so even there he loosened his might, and smote him on the neck with the hilted sword. And all the blade was warm with his blood, and dark death closed his eyes, and mighty Fate.

Then Peneleos and Lykon ran together, for with their spears they missed each other, yea, both had cast in vain, and instantly they ran together with their swords. There Lykon smote the socket of the horse-hair crest, and his sword brake at the hilt, but Peneleos smote his neck be hind the ear, and all the blade sank in, and naught but the skin held, and the head hung slack, and loosened were his limbs.

Now Meriones overtook Akamas with swift strides, and smote him on the right shoulder, as he went up into his chariot, and he slipped out of his chariot, and mist was poured over his eyes. And Idomeneus wounded Erymas on the mouth with the pitiless bronze, and the spear of bronze went clean through below, beneath the brain, and shattered his white bones, and his teeth were shaken out, and both his eyes were filled with blood, and he blew blood up through mouth and nostrils as he gaped, and the black cloud of death covered him about.

Thus those leaders of the Danaans slew each his man. But even as robber wolves fall on the lambs or kids, choosing them out of the herds, when they are scattered on hills by the witlessness of the shepherd, and the wolves behold it, and speedily harry the younglings that have no heart of courage, – even so the Danaans fell on the Trojans, and they were mindful of ill-sounding flight, and forgot their impetuous valour.

But that great Aias ever was fain to cast his spear at Hector of the helm of bronze, but he, in his cunning of war, covered his broad shoulders with his shield of bulls' hide, and watched the hurtling of the arrows, and the noise of spears. And verily well he knew the change in the mastery of war, but even so he abode, and was striving to rescue his trusty comrades.

And as when from Olympus a cloud fares into heaven from the sacred air, when Zeus spreadeth forth the tempest, even so from the ships came the war-cry and the rout, nor in order due did they cross the ditch again. But his swift-footed horses bare Hector forth with his arms, and he left the host of Troy, whom the delved trench restrained against their will. And in the trench did many swift steeds that draw the car break the fore-part of the pole, and leave the chariots of their masters.

But Patroklos followed after, crying fiercely to the Danaans, and full of evil will against the Trojans, while they with cries and flight filled all the ways, for they were scattered, and on high the storm of dust was scattered below the clouds, and the whole-hooved horses strained back towards the city, away from the ships and the huts.

But even where Patroklos saw the folk thickest in the rout, thither did he guide his horses with a cry, and under his axle-trees men fell prone from their chariots, and the cars were overturned with a din of shattering. But straight over the ditch, in forward flight, leaped the swift [immortal] horses [that the gods gave for glorious gifts to Peleus]. And the heart of Patroklos urged him against Hector, for he was eager to smite him, but his swift steeds bore Hector forth and away. And even as beneath a tempest the whole black earth is oppressed, on an autumn day, when Zeus pours forth rain most vehemently, being in wrath and anger against men, who judge crooked judgments forcefully in the assembly, and drive justice out, and reck not of the vengeance of the gods, and all their rivers run full, and many a scaur the torrents tear away, and down to the dark sea they rush headlong from the hills, roaring mightily, and minished are the works of men, even so mighty was the roar of the Trojan horses as they ran.

Now Patroklos when he had cloven the nearest companies, drave them backward again to the ships, nor suffered them to approach the city, despite their desire, but between the ships, and the river, and the lofty wall, he rushed on them, and slew them, and avenged many a comrade slain. There first he smote Pronoos with a shining spear, where the shield left bare the breast, and loosened his limbs, and he fell with a crash. Then Thestor the son of Enops he next assailed, as he sat crouching in the polished chariot, for he was struck distraught, and the reins flew from his hands. Him he drew near, and smote with the lance on the right jaw, and clean pierced through his teeth. And Patroklos caught hold of the spear and dragged him over the rim of the car, as when a man sits on a jutting rock, and drags a sacred fish forth from the sea, with line and glittering hook of bronze: so on the bright spear dragged he Thestor gaping from the chariot, and cast him down on his face, and life left him as he fell. Next, as Euryalos came on, he smote him on the midst of the head with a stone, and all his head was shattered within the strong helmet, and prone on the earth he fell, and death that slayeth the spirit overwhelmed him. Next Erymas, and Amphoteros, and Epaltes and Tlepolemos son of Damastor, and Echios and Pyris, and Ipheus and Euippos, and Polymelos son of Argeas, all these in turn he brought low to the bounteous earth. But when Sarpedon beheld his comrades with ungirdled doublets, subdued beneath the hands of Patroklos son of Menoitios, he cried aloud, upbraiding the godlike Lykians: 'Shame, ye Lykians, whither do ye flee? Now be ye strong, for I will encounter this man that I may know who he is that conquers here, and verily many evils hath he wrought the Trojans, in that he hath loosened the knees of many men and noble.'

So spake he, and leaped with his arms from the chariot to the ground. But Patroklos, on the other side, when he beheld him leaped from his chariot. And they, like vultures of crooked talons and curved beaks, that war with loud yells on some high cliff, even so they rushed with cries against each other. And beholding then the son of Kronos of the crooked counsels took pity on them, and he spake to Hera, his sister and wife: 'Ah woe is me for that it is fated that Sarpedon, the best-beloved of men to me, shall be subdued under Patroklos son of Menoitios. And in two ways my heart within my breast is divided, as I ponder whether I should catch him up alive out of the tearful war, and set him down in the rich land of Lykia, or whether I should now subdue him beneath the hands of the son of Menoitios.'

Then the ox-eyed lady Hera made answer to him: 'Most dread son of Kronos, what word is this thou hast spoken? A mortal man long doomed to fate dost thou desire to deliver again from death of evil name? Work thy will, but all we other gods will in nowise praise thee. And another thing I will tell thee, and do thou lay it up in thy heart; if thou dost send Sarpedon living to his own house, consider lest thereon some other god likewise desire to send his own dear son away out of the strong battle. For round the great citadel of Priam war many sons of the Immortals, and among the

Immortals wilt thou send terrible wrath. But if he be deal to thee, and thy heart mourns for him, truly then suffer him to be subdued in the strong battle beneath the hands of Patroklos son of Menoitios, but when his soul and life leave that warrior, send Death and sweet Sleep to bear him, even till they come to the land of wide Lykia, there will his kindred and friends bury him, with a barrow and a pillar, for this is the due of the dead.'

So spake she, nor did the father of gods and men disregard her. But he shed bloody raindrops on the earth, honouring his dear son, that Patroklos was about to slay in the deep-soiled land of Troia, far off from his own country. Now when they were come near each other in onset, there verily did Patroklos smite the renowned Thrasymelos, the good squire of the prince Sarpedon, on the lower part of the belly, and loosened his limbs. But Sarpedon missed him with his shining javelin, as he in turn rushed on, but wounded the horse Pedasos on the right shoulder with the spear, and he shrieked as he breathed his life away, and fell crying in the dust, and his spirit fled from him. Put the other twain reared this way and that, and the yoke creaked, and the reins were confused on them, when their trace-horse lay in the dust. But thereof did Automedon, the spearman renowned, find a remedy, and drawing his long-edged sword from his stout thigh, he leaped forth, and cut adrift the horse, with no delay, and the pair righted themselves, and strained in the reins, and they met again in life-devouring war.

Then again Sarpedon missed with his shining dart, and the point of the spear flew over the left shoulder of Patroklos and smote him not, but he in turn arose with the bronze, and his javelin flew not vainly from his hand, but struck Sarpedon even where the midriff clasps the beating heart. And he fell as falls an oak, or a silver poplar, or a slim pine tree, that on the hills the shipwrights fell with whetted axes, to be timber for shipbuilding; even so before the horses and chariot he lay at length, moaning aloud, and clutching at the bloody dust. And as when a lion hath fallen on a herd, and slain a bull, tawny and high of heart, among the kine of trailing gait, and he perishes groaning beneath the claws of the lion, even so under Patroklos did the leader of the Lykian shieldmen rage, even in death, and he called to his dear comrade: 'Dear Glaukos, warrior among warlike men, now most doth it behove thee to be a spearman, and a hardy fighter: now let baneful war be dear to thee, if indeed thou art a man of might. First fare all about and urge on the heroes that be leaders of the Lykians, to fight for Sarpedon, and thereafter thyself do battle for me with the sword. For to thee even in time to come shall I be shame and disgrace for ever, all thy days, if the Achaians strip me of mine armour, fallen in the gathering of the ships. Nay, hold out manfully, and spur on all the host.'

Even as he spake thus, the end of death veiled over his eyes and his nostrils, but Patroklos, setting foot on his breast, drew the spear out of his flesh, and the midriff followed with the spear, so that he drew forth together the spear point, and the soul of Sarpedon; and the Myrmidons held there his panting steeds, eager to fly afar, since the chariot was reft of its lords.

Then dread sorrow came on Glaukos, when he heard the voice of Sarpedon, and his heart was stirred, that he availed not to succour him. And with his hand he caught and held his arm, for the wound galled him, the wound of the arrow wherewith, as he pressed on towards the lofty wall, Teukros had smitten him, warding off destruction from his fellows. Then in prayer spake Glaukos to far-darting Apollo: 'Hear, O Prince that art somewhere in the rich land of Lykia, or in Troia, for thou canst listen everywhere to the man that is in need as even now need cometh upon me. For I have this stark wound, and mine arm is throughly pierced with sharp pains, nor can my blood be stanched, and by the wound is my shoulder burdened, and I cannot hold my spear firm, nor go and fight against the enemy. And the best of men has perished, Sarpedon, the son of Zeus, and he succours not even his own child. But do thou, O Prince, heal me this stark wound, and lull my pains, and give me strength, that I may call on my Lykian kinsmen, and spur them to the war, and myself may fight about the dead man fallen.'

So spake he in his prayer, and Phoebus Apollo heard him. Straightway he made his pains to cease, and in the grievous wound stanched the black blood, and put courage into his heart. And Glaukos knew it within him, and was glad, for that the great god speedily heard his prayer. First went he all about and urged on them that were leaders of the Lykians to fight around Sarpedon, and thereafter he went with long strides among the Trojans, to Poly-damas son of Panthoos and noble Agenor, and he went after Aineias, and Hector of the helm of bronze, and standing by them spake winged words: 'Hector, now surely art thou utterly forgetful of the allies, that for thy sake far from their friends and their own country, breathe their lives away! But thou carest not to aid them! Sarpedon lies low, the leader of the Lykian shieldmen, he that defended Lykia by his dooms and his might, yea him hath mailed Ares subdued beneath the spear of Patroklos. But, friends, stand by him, and be angry in your hearts lest the Myrmidons strip him of his harness, and dishonour the dead, in wrath for the sake of the Danaans, even them that perished, whom we slew with spears by the swift ships.'

So spake he, and sorrow seized the Trojans utterly, ungovernable and not to be borne; for Sarpedon was ever the stay of their city, all a stranger as he was, for many people followed with him, and himself the best warrior of them all. Then they made straight for the Danaaus eagerly, and Hector led them, being wroth for Sarpedon's sake. But the fierce heart of Patroklos son of Menoitios urged on the Achaians. And he spake first to the twain Aiantes that themselves were right eager: 'Aiantes, now let defence be your desire, and be such as afore ye were among men, or even braver yet. That man lies low who first leaped on to the wall of the Achaians, even Sarpedon. Nay, let us strive to take him, and work his body shame, and strip the harness from his shoulders, and many a one of his comrades fighting for his sake let us subdue with the pitiless bronze.'

So spake he, and they themselves were eager in defence. So on both sides they strengthened the companies, Trojans and Lykians, Myrmidons and Achaians, and they joined battle to fight around the dead man fallen; terribly they shouted and loud rang the harness of men. But Zeus drew baneful night above the strong battle, that round his dear son might be the woful toil of war. Now first the Trojans drove back the bright-eyed Achaians, for a man in no wise the worst among the Myrmidons was smitten, the son of great-hearted Agakles, goodly Epeigeus, who ruled fair-set Boudeion of old, but when he had slain a good man of his kin, to Peleus he came as a suppliant, and to silver-footed Thetis. And they sent him to follow with Achilles, the breaker of the ranks of men, to Ilios of the goodly steeds, to war with the Trojans. Then him, as he was laying hold of the dead man, did renowned Hector smite on the head with a stone, and all his head was broken in twain within the strong helm, and prone on the dead he fell, and round him was poured death that slayeth the spirit. Then grief came on Patroklos for his comrade slain, and he rushed through the foremost fighters, like to a falcon swift of flight, that scareth daws and starlings, even so against the Lykians, O Patroklos, warrior-charioteer, and against the Trojans didst thou rush, being wroth at heart for thy comrade's sake. And he smote Sthenelaos, the dear son of Ithaimenes, on the neck, with a stone, and brake away his sinews. Then back drew the foremost fighters, and renowned Hector. And as far as is the flight of a long javelin, that a man casts, making trial of his skill, either in a contest for a prize, or in war, being pressed by deadly foemen, so far did the Trojans draw back, and the Achaians drave them. And Glaukos first, the leader of the Lykian shieldmen, turned him about, and slew Bathykles great of heart, the dear son of Chalkon, that dwelt in his home in Hellas, and for wealth and riches was preeminent among the Myrmidons. Him did Glaukos wound in the mid-breast with a spear, turning suddenly about, when Bathykles was about to seize him as he followed hard after him. With a crash he fell, and great woe came on the Achaians, that a good man was down, but mightily did the Trojans rejoice. And they all thronged around him and stood firm, nor did the Achaians forget their valour, but bare their might straight down on them. There likewise Meriones slew a mailed warrior of the Trojans, Laogonos, the bold son of Onetor, that was priest of Idaean Zeus, and as a god was honoured by the people, – him he smote beneath the jaw and the ear, and swiftly his spirit departed from his limbs, and so loathly darkness gat hold on him. And Aineias cast against Meriones his spear of bronze, for he hoped to smite him as he came on beneath the shield. But he kept a forward watch, and avoided the spear of bronze, stooping forward, and behind him the long dart stood fast in the ground, but the butt of the spear quivered, and there then strong Ares took its strength away. [And the spear of Aineias sunk quivering into the earth, since vainly it had sped from his strong hand]. But Aineias was wroth at heart, and spake aloud: 'Meriones, swiftly should my spear have stopped thy dancing for ever, good dancer as thou art, if I had but struck thee.'

But to him again Meriones, spearman renowned, replied: 'Aineias, it is hard for thee, strong as thou art, to quench the might of every man that cometh against thee in battle. Yea, thou too art a mortal. And if ever I should cast at thee and strike thee in the midst with the sharp bronze, quickly shouldst thou for all thy valour and trust in thy hands give glory to me, and thy soul to Hades of the famous steeds.'

So spake he, but him did the strong son of Menoitios rebuke: 'Meriones, why speakest thou thus, thou that art a man of valour? O my friend, not for railing words will the Trojans draw back from the dead, the earth must hold some fast ere that may be. For in the hands of men is the end of war, but of words the end is in council, wherefore in no wise should we multiply words, but do battle.'

So speaking, he began, and the other followed him, a godlike man. And as the din ariseth of woodcutters in the glades of a mountain, and the sound thereof is heard far away, so rose the din of them from the wide-wayed earth, the noise of bronze and of well-tanned bulls' hides smitten with swords and double-pointed spears. And now not even a clear-sighted man could any longer have known noble Sarpedon, for with darts and blood and dust was he covered wholly from head to foot. And ever men thronged about the dead, as in a steading flies buzz around the full milk-pails, in the season of spring, when the milk drenches the bowls, even so thronged they about the dead. Nor ever did Zeus turn from the strong fight his shining eyes, but ever looked down on them, and much in his heart he debated of the slaying of Patroklos, whether there and then above divine Sarpedon glorious Hector should slay him likewise in strong battle with the sword, and strip his harness from his shoulders, or whether to more men yet he should deal sheer labour of war. And thus to him as he pondered it seemed the better way, that the gallant squire of Achilles, Peleus' son, should straightway drive the Trojans and Hector of the helm of bronze towards the city, and should rob many of their life. And in Hector first he put a weakling heart, and leaping into his car Hector turned in flight, and cried on the rest of the Trojans to flee, for he knew the turning of the sacred scales of Zeus. Thereon neither did the strong Lykians abide, but fled all in fear, when they beheld their king stricken to the heart, lying in the company of the dead, for many had fallen above him, when Kronion made fierce the fight. Then the others stripped from the shoulders of Sarpedon his shining arms of bronze, and these the strong son of Menoitios gave to his comrades to bear to the hollow ships. Then Zeus that gathereth the clouds spake to Apollo: 'Prithee, dear Phoebus, go take Sarpedon out of range of darts, and cleanse the black blood from him, and thereafter bear him far away, and bathe him in the streams of the river, and anoint him with ambrosia, and clothe him in garments that wax not old, and send him to be wafted by fleet convoy, by the twin brethren Sleep and Death, that quickly will set him in the rich land of wide Lykia. There will his kinsmen and clansmen give him burial, with barrow and pillar, for such is the due of the dead.'

So spake he, nor was Apollo disobedient to his father. He went down the hills of Ida to the dread battle-din, and straightway bore goodly Sarpedon out of the darts, and carried him far away, and bathed him in the streams of the river, and anointed him with ambrosia, and clad him in garments that wax not old, and sent him to be wafted by fleet convoy, the twin brethren Sleep and Death, that swiftly set him down in the rich land of wide Lykia. But

Patrokios cried to his horses and Autornedon, and after the Trojans and Lykians went he, and so was blindly forgetful, in his witlessness, for if he had kept the saying of the son of Peleus, verily he should have escaped the evil fate of black death. But ever is title wit of Zeus stronger than the wit of men, [for he driveth the valiant man in flight, and easily taketh away the victory, and then again himself rouseth men to fight],so now he roused the spirit of Patroklos in his breast. There whom first, whom last didst thou slay, Patroklos, when the gods called thee deathward? Adrestos first, and Autonoos, and Echeklos, and Perimos, son of Megas, and Epistor, and Mela-nippos, and thereafter Elasos, and Moulios, and Pylartes these he slew, but the others were each man of them fain of flight. Then would the sons of the Achaians have taken high-gated Troy, by the hands of Patroklos, for around and before him he raged with the spear, but that Phoebus Apollo stood on the well-builded wall, with baneful thoughts towards Patroklos, and succouring the Trojans. Thrice clomb Patroklos on the corner of the lofty wall, and thrice did Apollo force him back and smote the shining shield with his immortal hands. But when for the fourth time he came on like a god, then cried far-darting Apollo terribly, and spake winged words: 'Give back, Patroklos of the seed of Zeus! Not beneath thy spear is it fated that the city of the valiant Trojans shall fall, nay nor beneath Achilles, a man far better than thou.'

So spake he, and Patroklos retreated far back, avoiding the wrath of far-darting Apollo. But Hector within the Skaian gates was restraining his whole-hooved horses, pondering whether he should drive again into the din and fight, or should call unto the host to gather to the wall. While thus he was thinking, Phoebus Apollo stood by him in the guise of a young man and a strong, Asios, who was the mother's brother of horse-taming Hector, being own brother of Hekabe, and son of Dymas, who dwelt in Phrygia, on the streams of Sangarios. In his guise spake Apollo, son of Zeus, to Hector: 'Hector, wherefore dost thou cease from fight? It doth not behove thee. Would that I were as much stronger than thou as I am weaker, thereon quickly shouldst thou stand aloof from war to thy hurt. But come, turn against Patroklos thy strong-hooved horses, if perchance thou mayst slay him, and Apollo give thee glory.'

So spake the god, and went back again into the moil of men. But renowned Hector bade wise-hearted Kebriones to lash his horses into the war. Then Apollo went and passed into the press, and sent a dread panic among the Argives, but to the Trojans and Hector gave he renown. And Hector let the other Argives be, and slew none of them, but against Patroklos he turned his strong-hooved horses, and Patroklos on the other side leaped from his chariot to the ground, with a spear in his left hand, and in his other hand grasped a shining jagged stone, that his hand covered. Firmly he planted himself and hurled it, nor long did he shrink from his foe, nor was his cast in vain, but he struck Kebriones the charioteer of Hector, the bastard son of renowned Priam, on the brow with the sharp stone, as he held the reins of the horses. Both his brows the stone drave together, and his bone held not, but his eyes fell to the ground in the dust, there, in front of his feet. Then he, like a diver, fell from the well-wrought car, and his spirit left his bones. Then taunting him didst thou address him, knightly Patroklos: 'Out on it, how nimble a man, how lightly he diveth! Yea, if perchance he were on the teeming deep, this man would satisfy many by seeking for oysters, leaping from the ship, even if it were stormy weather, so lightly now he diveth from the chariot into the plain. Verily among the Trojans too there be diving men.'

So speaking he set on the hero Kebriones with the rush of a lion, that while wasting the cattle-pens is smitten in the breast, and his own valour is his bane, even so against Kebriones, Patroklos, didst thou leap furiously. But Hector, on the other side, leaped from his chariot to the ground. And these twain strove for Kebriones like lions, that on the mountain peaks fight, both hungering, both high of heart, for a slain hind. Even so for Kebriones' sake these two masters of the war-cry, Patroklos son of Menoitios, and renowned Hector, were eager each to hew the other's flesh with the ruthless bronze.

Hector then seized him by the head, and slackened not hold, while Patroklos on the other side grasped him by the foot, and thereon the others, Trojans and Danaans, joined strong battle. And as the East wind and the South contend with one another in shaking a deep wood in the dells of a mountain, shaking beech, and ash, and smooth-barked cornel tree, that clash against each other their long boughs with marvellous din, and a noise of branches broken, so the Trojans and Achaians were leaping on each other and slaying nor had either side any thought of ruinous flight. And many sharp darts were fixed around Kebriones, and winged arrows leaping from the bow-string, and many mighty stones smote the shields of them that fought around him. But he in the whirl of dust lay mighty and mightily fallen, forgetful of his chivalry.

Now while the sun was going about mid-heaven, so long the darts smote either side, and the host fell, but when the sun turned to the time of the loosing of oxen, lo, then beyond their doom the Achaians proved the better. The hero Kebriones drew they forth from the darts, out of the tumult of the Trojans, and stripped the harness from his shoulders, and with ill design against the Trojans, Patroklos rushed upon them. Three times then rushed he or, peel of swift Ares, shouting terribly, and thrice he slew nine men. But when the fourth time he sped on like a god, thereon to thee, Patroklos, did the end of life appear, for Phoebus met thee in the strong battle, in dreadful wise. And Patroklos was not ware of him coming through the press, for hidden in thick mist did he meet him, and stood behind him, and smote his back and broad shoulders with a down-stroke of his hand, and his eyes were dazed. And from his head Phoebus Apollo smote the helmet that rolled rattling away with a din beneath the hooves of the horses, the helm with upright socket, and the crests were defiled with blood and dust. Not of old was it suffered that the helm with horse-hair crest should be defiled with dust, nay, but it kept the head and beautiful face of a man divine, even of Achilles. But as then Zeus gave it to Hector, to bear on his head, yet was destruction near him. And all the long-shadowed spear was shattered in the hands of Patroklos, the spear great and heavy and strong, and sharp, while from his shoulders the tasselled shield with the baldric fell to the ground.

And the prince Apollo, son of Zeus, loosed his corslet, and blindness seized his heart and his shining limbs were unstrung, and he stood in amaze, and at close quarters from behind a Dardanian smote him on the back, between the shoulders, with a sharp spear, even Euphorbos, son of Panthoös, who excelled them of his age in casting the spear, and in horsemanship, and in speed of foot. Even thus, verily, had he cast down twenty men from their chariots, though then first had he come with his car to learn the lesson of war. He it w as that first smote a dart into thee, knightly Patroklos, nor overcame thee, but ran back again and mingled with the throng, first drawing forth from the flesh his ashen spear, nor did he abide the onset of Patroklos, unarmed as he was, in the strife. But Patroklos, being overcome by the stroke of the god, and by the spear, gave ground, and retreated to the host of his comrades, avoiding Fate. But Hector, when he beheld great-hearted Patroklos give ground being smitten with the keen bronze, came nigh unto him through the ranks, and wounded him with a spear, in the lowermost part of the belly, and drave the bronze clean through. And he fell with a crash, and sorely grieved the host of Achaians. And as when a lion hath overcome in battle an untiring boar, they twain fighting with high heart on the crests of a hill, about a little well, and both are desirous to drink, and the lion hath by force overcome the boar that draweth difficult breath; so after that he had slain many did Hector son of Priam take the life away from the strong son of Menoitios, smiting him at close quarters with the spear; and boasting over him he spake winged words: 'Patroklos, surely thou saidst that thou wouldst sack my town, and from Trojan women take away the day of freedom, and bring them in ships to thine own dear country fool! Nay, in front of these were the swift horses of Hector straining their speed for the fight; and myself in wielding the spear excel among the warloving Trojans, even I who ward from them the day of destiny: but thee shall vultures here devour. Ah, wretch, surely Achilles for all his valour, availed thee not, who straitly charged thee as thou camest, he abiding there, saying, "Come not to me, Patroklos lord of steeds, to the hollow ships, till thou hast torn the gory doublet of man-slaying Hector about his breast –" so, surely, he spake to thee, and persuaded the wits of thee in thy witlessness.'

Then faintly didst thou answer him, knightly Patroklos: 'Boast greatly, as now, Hector, for to thee have Zeus, son of Kronos, and Apollo given the victory, who lightly have subdued me; for themselves stripped my harness from mg shoulders. Put if twenty such as thou had encountered me, here had they all perished, subdued beneath my spear. But me have ruinous Fate and the son of Leto slain, and of men Euphorbos, but thou art the third in my slaying. But another thing will I tell thee, and do thou lay it up in thy heart; verily thou thyself art not long to live, but already doth Death stand hard by thee, and strong Fate, that thou art to be subdued by the hands of noble Achilles, of the seed of Aiakos.'

Even as so he spake the end of death overshadowed him, And his soul, fleeting from his limbs, went down to the house of I lades, wailing its own doom, leaving manhood and youth.

Then renowned Hector spake to him even in his death: 'Patroklos, wherefore to me dost thou prophesy sheer destruction? Who knows but that Achilles, the child of fairtressed Thetis, will first be smitten by n y spear, and lose his life?'

So spake he, and drew the spear of bronze from the wound, setting his foot on the dead, and cast him off on his back from the spear. And straightway with the spear he went after Automedon, the godlike squire of the swift-footed Aiakides, for he was eager to smite him; but his swift-footed immortal horses bare him out of the battle, horses that the gods gave to Peleus a splendid gift.

BOOK XVII

Of the battle around the body of Patroklos

BUT ATREUS' SON, Menelaos dear to Ares, was not unaware of the slaying of Patroklos by the Trojans in the fray. He went up through the front of the fight harnessed in flashing bronze, and strode over the body as above a first-born calf standeth lowing its mother, ere then unused to motherhood. Thus above Patroklos strode fair-haired Menelaos, and before him held his spear and the circle of his shield, eager to slay whoever should encounter him. Then was Panthoos' son of the stout ashen spear not heedless of noble Patroklos as he lay, and he stood anigh him and spake to Menelaos dear to Ares: 'Atreus' son Menelaos, Zeus-fostered, captain of the host, give back and leave the body and yield the bloody spoils; for before me was there none of the Trojans and their famed allies who smote Patroklos with the spear in the stress of fight; wherefore yield me this fair glory to win among the Trojans, lest I hurl and smite thee, and bereave thee of sweet life.'

Then sorely wroth spake unto him fair-haired Menelaos: 'O father Zeus, no seemly thing is it to boast above measure. Verily neither is spirit of pard or of lion or of cruel wild boar, in the strength of whose breast rageth fury fiercest of all, so high as those proud spirits of Panthoos' sons of the good ashen spear. Yet had the mighty Hyperenor, tamer of horses, no profit of his youth when he reviled me and abode my onset and deemed that I was the meanest warrior among the Danaans; not on his own feet, I ween, did he fare home to gladden his dear wife and his good parents. Thus, methinketh, will I quench thy spirit also, if thou stand up against me; rather I bid thee get thee back into the throng nor stand to encounter me, or ever some ill thing befall thee; by the event is even a fool made wise.'

Thus he said, but persuaded not the other, but he spake to him in answer: 'Now therefore, Zeus-fostered Menelaos, thou shalt in very deed pay for my brother whom thou slewest and boastest over, and therewithal didst leave his wife a widow in her new bridal-chamber afar, and to his parents broughtest lamentation unspeakable[1] and woe. Verily to those hapless twain shall I be for a withstaying of

[1] Reading ἄρρητον.

their lamentation, if I shall carry back thy head and armour and lay them in the hands of Panthoos and noble Phrontis. But now no longer shall the struggle be untried or unfought, whether for victory or for rout.'

Thus saying he smote on the circle of the shield of Menelaos, but the bronze spear brake it not, but the point was bent back in the stubborn shield. And Menelaos Atreus' son in his turn made at him with his bronze spear, having prayed unto father Zeus, and as he gave back pierced the nether part of his throat, and threw his weight into the stroke, following his heavy hand; and sheer through the tender neck went the point of the spear. And he fell with a crash, and his armour rang upon him. In blood was his hair drenched that was like unto the hair of the Graces, and his tresses closely knit with bands of silver and gold. As wherl a man reareth some lusty sapling of an olive in a clear space where water springeth plenteously, a goodly shoot fair-growing; and blasts of all winds shake it, yet it bursteth into white blossom; then suddenly cometh the wind of a great hurricane and wresteth it out of its abiding place and stretcheth it out upon the earth: even so lay Panthoos' son Euphorbos of the good ashen spear when Menelaos Atreus' son had slain him, and despoiled him of his arms.

Now as when some mountain-bred lion, trusting in his might, hath seized the best heifer out of a feeding herd, and first taketh her neck in his strong teeth and breaketh it, and then devoureth fiercely the blood and all the inward parts, while around him hounds and herdsmen clamour loudly afar off yet will not come up against him, for pale fear taketh hold on them, – even so dared not the heart in the breast of any Trojan to come up against glorious Menelaos. Then easily would the son of Atreus have borne off the noble spoils of Panthoos' son, had not Phoebus Apollo, grudged it him, and aroused against him Hector peer of swift Ares, putting on the semblance of a man, of Mentes chief of the Kikones. And he spake aloud to him winged words: 'Hector, now art thou hasting after things unattainable, even the horses of wise Aiakides; for hard are they to be tamed or driven by mortal man, save only Achilles whom an immortal mother bare. Meanwhile hath warlike Menelaos Atreus' son stridden over Patroklos and slain the best of the Trojans there, even Panthoos' son Euphorbos, and hath stayed him in his impetuous might.'

Thus saying the god went back into the strife of men, but dire grief darkened Hector's inmost soul, and then he gazed searchingly along the lines, and straightway was aware of the one man stripping off the noble arms, and the other lying on the earth; and blood was flowing about the gaping wound. Then he went through the front of the fight harnessed in flashing bronze, crying a shrill cry, like unto Hephaistos' flame unquenchable. Not deaf to his shrill cry was Atreus' son, and sore troubled he spake to his great heart: 'Ay me, if I shall leave behind me these goodly arms, and Patroklos who here lieth for my vengeance" sake, I fear lest some Danaan beholding it be wroth against me. But if for honour's sake I do battle alone with Hector and the Trojans, I fear lest they come about me many against one; for all the Trojans is bright-helmed Hector leading hither. Put wherefore thus debateth my heart? When a man against the power of heaven is fain to fight with another whom God exalteth, then swiftly rolleth on him mighty woe. Therefore shall none of the Danaans be wroth with me though he behold me giving place to Hector, since he warreth with gods upon his side. But if I might somewhere find Aias of the loud war-cry, then both together would we go and be mindful of battle even were it against the power of heaven, if haply we might save his dead for Achilles Peleus' son: that were best among these ills.'

While thus he communed with his mind and heart, therewithal the Trojan ranks came onward, and Hector at their head. Then Menelaos gave backward, and left the dead man, turning himself ever about like a deep-maned lion which men and dogs chase from a fold with spears and cries; and his strong heart within him groweth chill, and loth goeth he from the steading; so from Patroklos went fair-haired Menelaos, and turned and stood, when he came to the host of his comrades, searching for mighty Aias Telamon's son. Him very speedily he espied on the left of the whole battle, cheering his comrades and rousing them to fight, for great terror had Phoebus Apollo sent on them; and he hasted him to run, and straightway stood by him and said: 'This way, beloved Aias; let us bestir us for the dead Patroklos, if haply his naked corpse at least we may carry to Achilles, though his armour is held by Hector of the glancing helm.'

Thus spake he, and aroused the heart of wise Aias. And he went up through the front of the fight, and with him fair-haired Menelaos. Now Hector, when he had stripped from Patroklos his noble armour, was dragging him thence that he might cut off the head from the shoulders with the keen bronze and carry his body to give to the dogs of Troy. But Aias came anigh, and the shield that he bare was as a tower; then Hector gave back into the company of his comrades, and sprang into his chariot; and the goodly armour he gave to the Trojans to carry to the city, to be great glory unto him. But Aias spread his broad shield over the son of Menoitios and stood as it were a lion before his whelps when huntsmen in a forest encounter him as he leadeth his young – then waxeth he in his strength, and draweth down all his brows to cover his eyes: so over the hero Patroklos Aias strode. And by his side stood Atreus' son, Menelaos dear to Ares, nursing great sorrow in his breast.

Then Glaukos, Hippolochos' son, chief of the men of Lykia, looked toward Hector with a frown and chode him with rough words: 'Hector, in semblance bravest, lo, in battle sorely art thou lacking. Verily in vain doth fair glory rest on thee since thou turnest runagate. Bethink thee now how thou shalt save thy city and home, thou only with the host who were born in Ilios; for of the Lykians at least shall none go up to fight against the Danaans for the city's sake, since no boon, it seemeth, is it to fight unsparingly ever against men of war. How art thou like to bring back safe into thy host any lesser man, thou hard of heart, when Sarpedon that was both guest and friend thou leftest to the Argives to be their prey and spoil, though in his life he aided oftentimes both thy city and thyself? Yet now thou hast not dared to save him from the dogs. Therefore now if any of the men of Lykia will hearken unto me we will go home, and to Troy shall be revealed sheer doom. For if now a spirit of good courage were in the Trojans, a fearless spirit such as entereth into men who for their native land array toil and strife against men that are their enemies, speedily should we drag Patroklos within Ilios' wall. And if this dead man were brought into the great city of king Priam, and we drew him forth from the battle, then speedily would the Argives give back the goodly armour of Sarpedon, and we should bring his body into Ilios; so great is he whose squire is slain, even the man who is far best of the Argives beside the ships – he and his close-fighting squires. But thou enduredst not to stand up against great-hearted Aias and to look in his face amid the cry of the men of war, nor to do fair battle with him, since he is a better man than thou.'

Then, with a frown, spake unto him Hector of the glancing helm: 'Glaukos, wherefore hath such an one as thou spoken thus over measure? Out on it, I verily thought hat thou in wisdom wert above all others that dwell in deep-soiled Lykia; but now think I altogether scorn of thy wisdom, since thou speakest thus, and sayest that I dared not to meet the mighty Aias. No terror have I of battle or din of chariots, but the intent of aegis-bearing Zeus is ever strongest, and even a brave man he overaweth and lightly snatcheth from him victory, and yet anon himself arouseth him to fight. Come hither, friend, stand beside me and see my handiwork, whether all this day I shall play the coward, according to thy words, or shall yet stay certain of the Danaans, how fierce soever be their valour, from doing battle for Patroklos' corpse.'

Thus saying he called on the Trojans with a mighty shout: 'Trojans and Lykians and Dardanians that fight hand to hand, be men, my friends, and bethink you of impetuous valour, until I do on me the goodly arms of noble Achilles that I stripped from brave Patroklos when I slew him.'

Thus having spoken went Hector of the glancing helm forth out of the strife of war, and ran and speedily with fleet feet following overtook his comrades, not yet far off, who were bearing to the city Peleides' glorious arms. And standing apart from the dolorous battle he changed his armour; his own he gave the warlike Trojans to carry to sacred Ilios, and he put on the divine arms of Achilles, Peleus' son, which to his dear father the gods who inhabit heaven gave, and Peleus committed them unto his child when old himself; but never in his father's armour did that son grow old.

But when Zeus that gathereth the clouds beheld from afar off Hector arming him in the armour of Peleus' godlike son, he shook his head and spake thus unto his soul: 'Ah, hapless man, no thought is in thy heart of death that yet draweth nigh unto thee; thou doest on thee the divine armour of a peerless man before whom the rest have terror. His comrade, gentle and brave, thou hast slain, and unmeetly hast stripped the armour from his head and shoulders; yet now for a while at least I will give into thy hands great might, in recompense for this, even that no wise shalt thou come home out of the battle, for Andromache to receive from thee Peleides' glorious arms.'

Thus spake the son of Kronos and bowed his dark brows therewithal.

But the armour fitted itself unto Hector's body, and Ares the dread war-god entered into him, and his limbs were filled within with valour and strength. Then he sped among the noble allies with a mighty cry, and in the flashing of his armour he seemed to all of them like unto Peleus' great-hearted son. And he came to each and encouraged him with his words – Mesthles and Glaukos and Medon and Thersilochos and Asteropaios and Deisenor and Hippothoos and Phorkys and Chromios and the augur Ennomos – these encouraged he and spake to them winged words: 'Listen, ye countless tribes of allies that dwell round about. It was not for mere numbers that I sought or longed when I gathered each of you from your cities, but that ye might zealously guard the Trojans' wives and infant little ones from the war-loving Achaians. For this end am I wearying my people by taking gifts and food from them, and nursing thereby the courage of each of you. Now therefore let all turn straight against the foe and live or die, for such is the dalliance of war. And whoso shall drag Patroklos, dead though he be, among the horse-taming men of Troy, and make Aias yield, to him will I award half the spoils and keep half myself; so shall his glory be great as mine.'

Thus spake he, and they against the Danaans charged with all their weight, levelling their spears, and their hearts were high of hope to drag the corpse from under Aias, Telamon's son. Fond men! from full many reft he life over that corpse. And then spake Aias to Menelaos of the loud war-cry: 'Dear Menelaos, fosterling of Zeus, no longer count I that we two of ourselves shall return home out of the war. Nor have I so much dread for the corpse of Patroklos, that shall soon glut the dogs and birds of the men of Troy, as for thy head and mine lest some evil fall thereon, for all is shrouded by a storm-cloud of war, even by Hector, and sheer doom stareth in our face. But come, call thou to the best men of the Danaans, if haply any hear.'

Thus spake be, and Menelaos of the loud war-cry disregarded him not, but shouted unto the Danaans, crying a far-heard cry: 'O friends, ye leaders and counsellors of the Argives, who by the side of the sons of Atreus, Agamemnon and Menelaos, drink at the common cost and are all commanders of the host, on whom wait glory and honour from Zeus, hard is it for me to distinguish each chief amid the press – such blaze is there of the strife of war. But let each go forward of himself and be wroth at heart that Patroklos should become a sport among the dogs of Troy.'

Thus spake he, and Oïleus' son fleet Aias heard him clearly, and was first to run along the mellay to meet him, and after him Idomeneus, and Idomeneus' brother-in-arms, Meriones, peer of the man-slaying war-god. And who shall of his own thought tell the names of the rest, even of all that after these aroused the battle of the Achaians?

Now the Trojans charged forward in close array, and Hector led them. And as when at the mouth of some heaven-born river a mighty wave roareth against the stream, and arouseth the high cliffs' echo as the salt sea belloweth on the beach, so loud was the cry wherewith the Trojans came. But the Achaians stood firm around Menoitios' son with one soul all, walled in with shields of bronze. And over their bright helmets the son of Kronos shed thick darkness, for in the former time was Menoitios' son not unloved of him, while he was yet alive and squire of Aiakides. So was Zeus loth that he should become a prey of the dogs of his enemies at Troy, and stirred his comrades to do battle for him.

Now first the Trojans thrust back the glancing-eyed Achaians, who shrank before them and left the dead, yet the proud Trojans slew not any of them with spears, though they were fain, but set to hale the corpse. But little while would the Achaians hold back therefrom, for very swiftly Aias rallied them, Aias the first in presence and in deeds of all the Danaans after the noble son of Peleus. Right through the fighters in the forefront rushed he like a wild boar in his might that in the mountains when he turneth at bay scattereth lightly dogs and lusty young men through the glades Thus did proud Telamon's son the glorious Aias press on the Trojan battalions and lightly scatter them, as they had bestrode Patroklos and were full fain to drag him to their city and win renown.

Then Hippothoos, glorious son of Pelasgian Lethos, set to drag him by the foot through the violent fray, binding him by the ankle with a strap around the sinews, to do pleasure to Hector and the Trojans. But an ill thing came swiftly upon him wherefrom none of his comrades, albeit full fain, might help him. For the son of Telamon set on him through the press and smote him hard at hand through the bronze-cheeked helm. And the horse-hair-plumed headpiece brake about the spear point, smitten by the great spear and stalwart arm, and brain and blood spouted from the wound through the vizor. And Hippothoos' strength was unstrung, and from his hands he let great-hearted Patroklos' foot fall to earth, and close thereon fell he prone upon the corpse, far from deep-soiled Larissa, nor repaid his dear parents for his nurture, for short was his span of life as he fell beneath great-hearted Aias' spear. And Hector in his turn hurled at Aias with his bright spear, but the other saw the bronze dart as it came and hardly avoided it; yet Schedios, son of great-hearted Iphitos, the best man of the Phokians who in famous Panopeus had his dwelling and was king over many men – this man Hector smote beneath the midst of his collar-bone, and right through went the point of the bronze spear and stood out beside the nether part of his shoulder. And he fell with a crash, and his armour rang upon him. And Aias in his turn smote Phorkys in the midst of the belly, the wise son of Phainops, as he bestrode Hippothoös, and brake the plate of his corslet, and the bronze let forth his bowels, and he fell in the dust and grasped the earth with his hand. And the front fighters and glorious Hector gave back, and the Argives shouted aloud and haled the dead men, Phorkys and Hippothoos, and did off the armour from their shoulders.

Then would the Trojans in their turn in their weakness overcome have been driven back into Ilios by the Achaians dear to Ares, and the Argives would have won glory even against the appointment of Zeus by their power and might. But Apollo himself aroused Aineias, putting on the semblance of Periphas the herald, the son of Epytos, who grew old with his old father in his heraldship, of friendly thought toward Aineias. In his similitude spake Apollo, son of Zeus: 'Aineias, how could ye ever guard high Ilios if it were against the will of God? Other men have I seen that trust in their own might and power and valour, and in their host, even though they have scant[1] folk to lead. But here, albeit Zeus is fainer far to give victory to us than to the Danaans, yet ye are dismayed exceedingly and fight not.'

Thus spake he, and Aineias knew far-darting Apollo when he looked upon his face, and spake unto Hector, shouting loud: 'Hector and ye other leaders of the Trojans and their allies, shame were this if in our weakness overcome we were driven back into Ilios by the Achaians dear to Ares. Nay, thus saith a god, who standeth by my side: Zeus, highest Orderer, is our helper in this fight. Therefore let us go right onward against the Danaans. Not easily at least let them take the dead Patroklos to the ships.'

Thus spake he, and leapt forth far before the fighters in the front. And the Trojans rallied and stood up against the Achaians. Then Aineias wounded with his spear Leokritos son of Arisbas, Lykomedes' valiant comrade. And as he fell Lykomedes dear to Ares was grieved for him and came hard by him and halted and hurled his bright spear and smote Hippasos' son Apisaon, shepherd of the host, in the liver beneath the midriff and straightway unstrung his knees, Apisaon who had come out of deep-soiled Paionia and after Asteropaios was their best man in fight. And as he fell warlike Asteropaios was grieved for him and made onward full fain to do battle against the Danaans; but that could he no wise any more, for they were fenced on every side with shields as they stood around Patroklos, and held their spears in front of them. For Aias ranged through them all and called on them now and again, and

---

[1] Reading with all MSS. ὑπερδέα. But Brocks plausibly suggests ὑπὲρ ῥΔία, and would translate 'even against favour of Zeus protecting their own folk.'

bade that none of the Achaians should give back behind the corpse
nor fight in front of the rest but keep close beside the dead and do
battle hand to hand. Thus mighty Aias commanded, and the earth
was wet with dark blood, and the dead fell thickly both of the Trojans and their brave allies, and likewise of the Danaans, for these too
fought no bloodless fight, yet far fewer perished of them, for they
were ever mindful to ward sheer death from one another in the
press.

Thus strove they as it had been fire, nor wouldst thou have
thought there was still sun or moon, for over all the battle where
the chiefs stood around the slain son of Menoitios they were
shrouded in darkness, while the other Trojans and well-greaved
Achaians fought at ease in the clear air, and piercing sunlight was
spread over them, and on all the earth and hills there was no cloud
seen; and they ceased fighting now and again, avoiding each other's
dolorous darts and standing far apart. But they who were in the
midst endured affliction of the darkness and the battle, and all the
best men of them were wearied by the pitiless weight of their
bronze arms. Yet two men, famous warriors, Thrasymedes and
Antilochos, knew not yet that noble Patroklos was dead, but
deemed that he was yet alive and fighting against the Trojans in the
forefront of the press. So they twain in watch against the death or
flight of their comrades were doing battle apart from the rest, since
thus had Nestor charged when he roused them forth to the battle
from the black ships.

Thus all day long waxed the mighty fray of their sore strife, and
unabatingly ever with the sweat of toil were the knees and legs and
feet of each man and arms and eyes bedewed as the two hosts did
battle around the brave squire of fleet Aiakides. And as when a man
giveth the hide of a great bull to his folk to stretch, all soaked in fat,
and they take and stretch it standing in a circle, and straightway the
moisture thereof departeth and the fat entereth in under the haling
of many hands, and it is all stretched throughout, – thus they on
both sides haled the dead man this way and that in narrow space, for
their hearts were high of hope, the Trojans that they should drag
him to Ilios and the Achaians to the hollow ships; and around him
the fray waxed wild, nor might Ares rouser of hosts nor Athene
despise the sight thereof, albeit their anger were exceeding great.

Such was the grievous travail of men and horses over Patroklos
that Zeus on that day wrought. But not as yet knew noble Achilles
aught of Patroklos' death, for far away from the swift ships they
were fighting beneath the wall of the men of Troy. Therefore never

deemed he in his heart that he was dead, but that he should come
back alive, after that he had touched the gates; for neither that other
thought had he anywise, that Patroklos should sack the stronghold
without his aid, nay, nor yet therewithal, for thus had he oft heard
from his mother, hearkening to her apart as she brought tidings
unto him of the purposes of mighty Zeus. Yet verily then his
mother told him not how great an ill was come to pass, that his far
dearest comrade was no more.

Now the rest continually around the dead man with their keen
spears made onset relentlessly and slew each the other. And thus
would one speak among the mail-clad Achaians: 'Friends, it were
verily not glorious for us to go back to the hollow ships; rather let
the black earth yawn for us all beneath our feet. Far better were that
straightway for us if we suffer the horse-taming Trojans to hale this
man to their city and win renown.'

And thus on the other side would one of the great-hearted Trojans say: 'Friends, though it were our fate that all together we be
slain beside this man, let none yet give backward from the fray.'

Thus would one speak, and rouse the spirit of each. So they
fought on, and the iron din went up through the high desert air
unto the brazen heaven. But the horses of Aiakides that were apart
from the battle were weeping, since first they were aware that their
charioteer was fallen in the dust beneath the hand of man-slaying
Hector. Verily Automedon, Diores' valiant son, plied them oft with
blows of the swift lash, and oft with gentle words he spake to them
and oft with chiding, yet would they neither go back to the ships at
the broad Hellespont nor yet to the battle after the Achaians, but as
a pillar abideth firm that standeth on the tomb of a man or woman
dead, so abode they immovably with the beautiful chariot, abasing
their heads unto the earth. And hot tears flowed from their eyes to
the ground as they mourned in sorrow for their charioteer, and
their rich manes were soiled as they drooped from beneath the
yoke-cushion on both sides beside the yoke. And when the son of
Kronos beheld them mourning he had compassion on them, and
shook his head and spake to his own heart: 'Ah, hapless pair, why
gave we you to king Peleus, a mortal man, while ye are deathless
and ever young? Was it that ye should suffer sorrows among ill-
fated men? For methinketh there is nothing more piteous than a
man among all things that breathe and creep upon the earth. But
verily Hector Priam's son shall not drive you and your deftly-
wrought car; that will I not suffer. Is it a small thing that he holdeth
the armour and vaunteth himself vainly thereupon? Nay, I will put

courage into your knees and heart that ye may bring Automedon
also safe out of the war to the hollow ships. For yet further will I
increase victory to the men of Troy, so that they slay until they
come unto the well-timbered ships, and the sun set and divine night
come down.'

Thus saying he breathed good courage into the horses. And they
shook to earth the dust from their manes, and lightly bare the swift
car amid Trojans and Achaians. And behind them fought Automedon, albeit in grief for his comrade, swooping with his chariot as a
vulture on wild geese; for lightly he would flee out of the onset of
the Trojans and lightly charge, pursuing them through the thick
mellay. Yet could he not slay any man as he hasted to pursue them,
for it was impossible that being alone in his sacred car he should at
once assail them with the spear and hold his fleet horses. Then at
last espied him a comrade, even Alkimedon son of Laerkes, son of
Haimon, and he halted behind the car and spake unto Automedon:
'Automedon, what god hath put into thy breast unprofitable counsel
and taken from thee wisdom, that thus alone thou art fighting
against the Trojans in the forefront of the press? Thy comrade even
now was slain, and Hector goeth proudly, wearing on his own
shoulders the armour of Aiakides.'

And Automedon son of Diores answered him, saying: 'Alkimedon, what other Achaian hath like skill to guide the spirit of immortal steeds, save only Patroklos, peer of gods in counsel, while he yet
lived? but now have death and fate overtaken him. But take thou the
lash and shining reins, and I will get me down from my horses, that
I may fight.'

Thus spake he, and Alkimedon leapt on the fleet war-chariot and
swiftly took the lash and reins in his hands, and Automedon leapt
down. And noble Hector espied them, and straightway spake unto
Aineias as he stood near: 'Aineias, counsellor of mail-clad Trojans, I
espy here the two horses of fleet Aiakides come forth to battle with
feeble charioteers. Therefore might I hope to take them if thou in
thy heart art willing, since they would not abide our onset and stand
to do battle against us.'

Thus spake he, and the brave son of Anchises disregarded him
not. And they twain went right onward, their shoulders shielded by
ox-hides dried and tough, and bronze thick overlaid. And with them
went both Chromios and godlike Aretos, and their hearts were of
high hope to slay the men and drive off the strong-necked horses –
fond hope, for not without blood lost were they to get them back
from Automedon. He praying to father Zeus was filled in his inmost

heart with valour and strength. And straightway he spake to Alkimedon, his faithful comrade: 'Alkimedon, hold the horses not far from me, but with their very breath upon my back; for I deem that Hector the son of Priam will not refrain him from his fury until he mount behind Achilles' horses of goodly manes after slaying us twain, and dismay the ranks of Argive men, or else himself fall among the foremost.'

Thus said he, and called upon the Aiantes and Menelaos: 'Aiantes, leaders of the Argives, and Menelaos, lo now, commit ye the corpse unto whoso may best avail to bestride it and resist the ranks of men, and come ye to ward the day of doom from us who are yet alive, for here in the dolorous war are Hector and Aineias, the best men of the Trojans, pressing hard. Yet verily these issues lie in the lap of the gods: I too will cast my spear, and the rest shall Zeus decide.'

He said, and poised his far-shadowing spear and hurled it, and smote on the circle of the shield of Aretos, and the shield sustained not the spear, but right through went the bronze, and he forced it into his belly low down through his belt. And as when a strong man with a sharp axe smiting behind the horns of an ox of the homestead cleaveth the sinew asunder, and the ox leapeth forward and falleth, so leapt Aretos forward and fell on his back; and the spear in his entrails very piercingly quivering unstrung his limbs. And Hector hurled at Automedon with his bright spear, but he looked steadfastly on the bronze javelin as it came at him and avoided it, for he stooped forward, and the long spear fixed itself in the ground behind, and the javelin-butt quivered, and there dread Ares took away its force. And then had they lashed at each other with their swords hand to hand, had not the Aiantes parted them in their fury, when they were come through the mellay at their comrade's call. Before them Hector and Aineias and godlike Chromios shrank backward and gave ground and left Aretos wounded to the death as he lay. And Automedon, peer of swift Ares, stripped off the armour of the dead, and spake exultingly: 'Verily, I have a little eased my heart of grief for the death of Menoitios' son, albeit a worse man than him have I slain.'

Thus saying he took up the gory spoils and set them in his car, and gat him thereon, with feet and hands all bloody, as a lion that hath devoured a bull.

So again above Patroklos was waged the violent fray, cruel and woful, and Athene roused their strife, from heaven descended, for far-seeing Zeus sent her to urge on the Danaans, for his mind was changed. As Zeus stretcheth forth a gleaming rainbow from heaven to be a sign to mortals whether of war or of chill storm that maketh men to cease from their works upon the face of the earth, and afflicteth flocks, thus Athene clothing her in a gleaming cloud entered the Achaians' host, and roused each man thereof First to urge Atreus' son, strong Menelaos, for he was nigh to her, she spake to him, making herself like unto Phoinix in shape and unwearying voice: 'To thee verily, Menelaos, will be it shame and reproach if beneath the wall of the men of Troy fleet dogs tear the faithful comrade of proud Achilles. Nay, bear thee stoutly up, and urge on all the host.'

Then answered her Menelaos of the loud war-cry, saying: 'O Phoinix, ancient father of the elder time, would that Athene may give me strength and keep off the assault of darts. So would I well be fain to stand by Patroklos and to shield him, for his death touched me very close at heart. But Hector hath the terrible fury of fire, neither ceaseth in making havoc with his spear, for to him Zeus giveth glory.'

Thus spake he, and the bright-eyed goddess Athene was glad, for that to her first of all gods whatsoever he prayed. And she put force into his shoulders and his knees, and in his breast the boldness of the fly that albeit driven away once and again from the skin of men still is eager to bite, and sweet to it is the blood of mankind – even with such boldness the goddess filled his inmost heart, and he bestrode Patroklos, and hurled with his bright spear. Now among the Trojans was one Podes, son of Eëtion, a rich man and a brave, and Hector honoured him especially among the people for that he was his dear comrade and boon companion. Him smote fair-haired Menelaos in the belt as he started to flee, and drove his spearhead right through, and he fell with a crash, and Menelaos, Atreus' son, haled his body from amid the Trojans among his comrades' company.

But Apollo came and stood near Hector and aroused him, in the semblance of Asios' son Phainops, who of all guest friends was dearest to him, and had his home in Abydos. [In his likeness spake far-darting Apollo unto Hector]: 'Hector, what other of the Achaians will fear thee any more, if now thou hast shrunk from Menelaos who formerly was an unhardy warrior? Now is he gone and alone hath seized a dead Trojan from among our ranks, and hath slain thy faithful comrade, a good man among the fighters in the front, even Podes, son of Eëtion.'

Thus spake he, and a black cloud of grief fell on Hector, and he went through the forefront of the battle, harnessed in flashing bronze. Then also the son of Kronos took up his tasselled aegis glittering, and shrouded Ida in clouds, and lightened and thundered mightily, and shook the earth;[1] and he gave victory to the Trojans, and the Achaians he dismayed.

First to set dismay on foot was Peneleos the Boiotian. For he was smitten in the shoulder by a javelin grazingly on the surface, as he kept ever his face to the foe; the spear point of Polydamas scratched the bone, for he cast it from nigh at hand. Then again Hector in close fight wounded Leïtos on the wrist, the son of great-hearted Alektryon, and stayed him from the joy of battle: and he shrank back as he gazed around him, for that he might no longer hope to hold spear in hand to do battle against the men of Troy. Then Idomeneus smote Hector as he pursued after Leitos on the corslet of his breast beside the nipple, but the long spear brake at the socket and the Trojans shouted. And Hector hurled at Idomeneus son of Deukalion as he had mounted his car, and missed him by a little, but smote Koiranos, Meriones' brother-in-arms and charioteer who from stablished Lyktos followed him – (for on foot came Idomeneus first from the curved ships and would have yielded great triumph to the Trojans had not Koiranos quickly driven up his fleet horses, and thus come as succour to Idomeneus and guarded him from the day of death, but himself lost his life at the hands of man-slaying Hector) – him Hector smote beneath the jaw and ear, and the spear-end dashed out his teeth and clave his tongue asunder in the midst. And he fell forth from the chariot and let fall the reins to the ground. Then Meriones stooped and gathered them in his own hands from the earth and spake unto Idomeneus: 'Now lay on, till thou come to the swift ships: thyself too knowest that triumph is no longer with the Achaians.'

Thus spake he, and Idomeneus lashed the horses of goodly manes back to the hollow ships; for fear had fallen upon his soul.

Now great-hearted Aias and Menelaos were aware of Zeus how he gave the Trojans their turn of victory. First of these to speak was great Aias son of Telamon: 'Ay me, now may any man, even though he be a very fool, know that father Zeus himself is helping the Trojans. For the darts of all of them strike, whosoever hurleth them, be he good man or bad – Zeus guideth them notwithstanding home: but all our darts only fall idly to the earth. Nay come, let us ourselves devise some excellent means, that we may both hale she

[1]Reading γῆν with Zenodotos.

corpse away and ourselves return home to the joy of our friends, who grieve as they look hitherward and deem that no longer shall the fury of man-slaying Hector's unapproachable hand refrain itself, but fall upon the black ships. And would there were some comrade to carry tidings with all speed unto the son of Peleus, since I deem that he hath not even heard the grievous tidings, how his dear comrade is slain. But nowhere can I behold such an one among the Achaians, for themselves and their horses likewise are wrapped in darkness. O father Zeus, deliver thou the sons of the Achaians from the darkness, and make clear sky and vouchsafe sight unto our eyes. In the light be it that thou slayest us, since it is thy good pleasure that we die.'

Thus spake he, and the Father grieved to see him weep, and straightway scattered the darkness and drave away the mist, and the sun shone out on them, and all the battle was manifest. Then spake Aias to Menelaos of the loud war-cry: 'Look forth now, Menelaos fosterling of Zeus, if haply thou mayest see Antilochos yet alive, great-hearted Nestor's son, and rouse him to go with speed to wise Achilles to tell him that his far dearest comrade is slain.'

Thus spake he, and Menelaos of the loud war-cry disregarded him not, but went forth as a lion from a steading when he is tired of vexing men and dogs that suffer him not to devour fat oxen and all night keep their watch; but he in hunger for flesh presseth onward yet availeth nought, for thickly fly the javelins against him from hardy hands, with blazing firebrands, wherefrom he shrinketh for all his fury, and in the morning departeth afar with grief at heart: – thus from Patroklos went Menelaos of the loud war-cry, sore loth; for exceedingly he feared lest the Achaians in cruel rout should leave him a prey to the enemy. And straitly charged he Meriones and the Aiantes, saying: 'Aiantes, leaders of the Argives, and Meriones, now let each remember the loving-kindness of hapless Patroklos, for he would be gentle unto all while he was yet alive: now death and fate have overtaken him.'

Thus saying fair-haired Menelaos departed glancing everywhither, as an eagle which men say hath keenest sight of all birds under heaven, and though he be far aloft the fleet-footed hare eludeth him not by crouching beneath a leafy bush, but the eagle swoopeth thereon and swiftly seizeth her and taketh her life. Thus in that hour, Menelaos fosterling of Zeus, ranged thy shining eyes everywhither through the multitude of the host of thy comrades, if haply they might behold Nestor's son yet alive. Him quickly he perceived at the left of the whole battle, heartening his comrades and rousing them to fight. And fair-haired Menelaos came and stood nigh and said unto him: 'Antilochos, fosterling of Zeus, come hither that thou mayest learn woful tidings – would it had never been. Ere now, I ween, thou too hast known by thy beholding that God rolleth mischief upon the Danaans, and with the Trojans is victory. And slain is the best man of the Achaians Patroklos, and great sorrow is wrought for the Danaans. But run thou to the ships of the Achaians and quickly tell this to Achilles, if haply he may straightway rescue to his ship the naked corpse: but his armour is held by Hector of the glancing helmet.'

Thus spake he, and Antilochos had horror of the word he heard. And long time speechlessness possessed him and his eyes were filled with tears, and his full voice choked. Yet for all this disregarded he not the bidding of Menelaos, but set him to run, when he had given his armour to a noble comrade, Laodokos, who close anigh him was wheeling his whole-hooved horses.

So him his feet bare out of the battle weeping, to Achilles son of Peleus carrying an evil tale. But thy heart, Menelaos fosterling of Zeus, chose not to stay to aid the wearied comrades from whom Antilochos departed, and great sorrow was among the Pylians. But to them Menelaos sent noble Thrasymedes, and himself went again to bestride the hero Patroklos. And he hasted and stood beside the Aiantes and straightway spake to them: 'So have I sent that man to the swift ships to go to fleet-footed Achilles. Yet deem I not that he will now come, for all his wrath against noble Hector, for he could not fight unarmed against the men of Troy. But let us ourselves devise some excellent means, both how we may hale the dead away, and how we ourselves may escape death and fate amid the Trojans' battle cry.'

Then answered him great Aias Telamon's son, saying: 'All this hast thou said well, most noble Menelaos. But do thou and Meriones put your shoulders beneath the dead and lift him and bear him swiftly out of the fray, while we twain behind you shall do battle with the Trojans and noble Hector, one in heart as we are in name, for from of old time we are wont to await fierce battle side by side.'

Thus spake he, and the others took the dead man in their arms and lifted him mightily on high. But the Trojan host behind cried aloud when they saw the Achaians lifting the corpse, and charged like hounds that spring in front of hunter-youths upon a wounded wild boar, and for a while run in in haste to rend him, but when he wheeleth round among them, trusting in his might, then they give ground and shrink back here and there. Thus for a while the Trojans pressed on with all their power, striking with swords and double-headed spears, but when the Aiantes turned about and halted over against them, then they changed colour, and none dared farther onset to do battle around the dead.

Thus were those twain struggling to bear the corpse out of the battle toward the hollow ships, but the stress of war waxed fierce upon them as fire that leapeth on a city of men and bursteth into sudden blaze, and houses perish amid the mighty glare, and it roareth beneath the strength of the wind. Thus roared the unceasing din of horses and of fighting men against the bearers as they went. As mules that throw their great strength into the draught and drag out of the mountain down a rugged track some beam or huge ship-timber, and their hearts as they strive are spent with toil and sweat, thus were those twain struggling to bear the corpse And behind them the two Aiantes held their ground, as a woody ridge that chanceth to stretch all its length across the plain holdeth back a flood and stayeth even the wasting streams of mighty rivers, and turneth all their current wandering into the plain, neither doth the violence of their stream break through it. Thus ever the Aiantes kept back the Trojans' battle, but they pressed hard anigh, and among them twain the first, even Aineias, Anchises' son, and glorious Hector. As flieth a flock of starlings or of daws with confused cries when they see a hawk coming, to small birds bearer of death, thus before Aineias and Hector the Achaian youth confusedly crying fell back, and forgat the joy of battle. And thickly fell the goodly arms about and around the trench, as the Danaans fled, and there was never a pause of fight.

BOOK XVIII

How Achilles grieved for Patroklos, and how Thetis asked for him new armour of Hephaistos; and of the making of the armour.

THUS FOUGHT THE REST in the likeness of blazing fire, while to Achilles came Antilochos, a messenger fleet of foot. Him found he in front of his ships of upright horns, boding in his soul the things which even now were accomplished. And sore troubled he spake to his great heart: 'Ay me, wherefore again are the flowing-haired Achaians flocking to the ships and firing in rout over the plain? May the gods not have wrought against me the grievous fears at my heart, even as my mother revealed and told me that while I am yet alive the best man of the Myrmidons must by deed of the men of Troy forsake the light of the sun. Surely now must Menoitios' valiant son be dead – foolhardy! surely I bade him when he should have beaten off the fire of the foe to come back to the ships nor with Hector fight amain.'

While thus he held debate in his heart and soul, there drew nigh unto him noble Nestor's son, shedding hot tears, and spake his grievous tidings: 'Ay me, wise Peleus' son, very bitter tidings must thou hear, such as I would had never been. Fallen is Patroklos, and they are fighting around his body, naked, for his armour is held by Hector of the glancing helm.'

Thus spake he, and a black cloud of grief enwapped Achilles, and with both hands he took dark dust and poured it over his head and defiled his comely face, and on his fragrant doublet black ashes fell. And himself in the dust lay mighty and mightly fallen, and with his own hands tore and marred his hair. And the handmaidens, whom Achilles and Patroklos took captive, cried aloud in the grief of their hearts, and ran forth around valiant Achilles, and all beat on their breasts with their hands, and the knees of each of them were unstrung. And Antilochos on the other side wailed and shed tears, holding Achilles' hands while he groaned in his noble heart, for he feared lest he should cleave his throat with the sword. Then terribly moaned Achilles; and his lady mother heard him as she sate in the depths of the sea beside her ancient sire. And thereon she uttered a cry, and the goddesses flocked around her, all the daughters of

Nereus that were in the deep of the sea There were Glauke, and
Thaleia, and Kymodoke, Nesaia and Speio and Thoë and ox-eyed
Halië and Kymothoë and Aktaie and Limnoreia and Melite and
Iaira and Amphithoë and Agauë and Doto and Proto and Pherusa
and Dynamene and Dexamene and Amphinome and Kallianeira,
Doris and Panope and noble Galateia, and Nemertes, and Apseudes
and Kallianassa and there were Klymene and Ianeira and Ianassa
and Maira, and Oreithuia, and fair-tressed Amathyia, and other
Nereïds that were in the deep of the sea With these the bright cave
was filled, and they all beat together on their breasts, and Thetis led
the lament: 'Listen, sister Nereids, that ye all hear and know well
what sorrows are in my heart. Ay me unhappy, ay me that bare to
my sorrow the first of men! For after I had born a son noble and
strong, the chief of heroes, and he shot up like a young branch, then
when I had reared him as a plant in a very fruitful field I sent him in
beaked ships to Ilios to fight against the men of Troy; but never
again shall I welcome him back to his home, to the house of Peleus.
And while he yet liveth in my sight and beholdeth the light of the
sun, he sorroweth, neither can I help him any whit though I go unto
him. But I will go, that I may look upon my dear child, and learn
what sorrow hath come to him though he abide aloof from the war.'

Thus spake she and left the cave; and the nymphs went with her
weeping, and around them the surge of the sea was sundered. And
when they came to deep-soiled Troy-land they went up upon the
shore in order, where the ships of the Myrmidons were drawn up
thickly around fleet Achilles. And as he groaned heavily his lady
mother stood beside him, and with a shrill cry clasped the head of
her child, and spake unto him winged words of lamentation: 'My
child, why weepest thou? what sorrow hath come to thy heart? Tell
it forth, hide it not. One thing at least hath been accomplished of
Zeus according to the prayer thou madest, holding up to him thy
hands, that the sons of the Achaians should all be pent in at the
ships, through lack of thee, and should suffer hateful things.'

Then groaning heavily spake unto her Achilles fleet of foot: 'My
mother, that prayer truly hath the Olympian accomplished for me.
But what delight have I therein, since my dear comrade is dead,
Patroklos, whom I honoured above all my comrades as it were my
very self? Him have I lost, and Hector that slew him hath stripped
from him the armour great and fair, a wonder to behold, that the
gods gave to Peleus a splendid gift, on the day when they Laid thee
in the bed of a mortal man. Would thou hadst abode among the
deathless daughters of the sea, and Peleus had wedded a mortal

bride! But now, that thou mayest have sorrow a thousandfold in thy
heart for a dead son, never shalt thou welcome him back home,
since my soul biddeth me also live no longer nor abide among men,
if Hector be not first smitten by my spear and yield his life, and pay
for his slaughter of Patroklos, Menoitios' son.'

Then answered unto him Thetis shedding tears: 'Shortlived, I
ween, must thou be then, my child, by what thou sayest, for
straightway after Hector is death appointed unto thee.'

Then mightily moved spake unto her Achilles fleet of foot:
'Straightway may I die, since I might not succour my comrade at his
slaying. He hath fallen afar from his country and lacked my help in
his sore need. Now therefore, since I go not back to my dear native
land, neither have at all been succour to Patroklos nor to all my
other comrades that have been slain by noble Hector, but I sit
beside my ships a profitless burden of the earth, I that in war am
such an one as is none else of the mail-clad Achaians, though in
council are others better – may strife perish utterly among gods and
men, and wrath that stirreth even a wise man to be vexed, wrath
that far sweeter than trickling honey waxeth like smoke in the
breasts of men, even as I was wroth even now against Agamemnon
king of men. But bygones will we let be, for all our pain, curbing
the heart in our breasts under necessity. Now go I forth, that I may
light on the destroyer of him I loved, on Hector: then will I accept
my death whensoever Zeus willeth to accomplish it and the other
immortal gods. For not even the mighty Herakles escaped death,
albeit most dear to Kronian Zeus the king, but Fate overcame him
and Hera's cruel wrath. So also shall I, if my fate hath been fashioned likewise, lie low when I am dead. But now let me Will high
renown, let me set some Trojan woman, some deep-bosomed
daughter of Dardanos, staunching with both hands the tears upon
her tender cheeks and wailing bitterly; yea, let them know that I am
come back, though I tarried long from the war. Hold not me then
from the battle in thy love, for thou shalt not prevail with me.'

Then Thetis the silver-footed goddess answered him saying: 'Yea
verily, my child, no blame is in this, that thou ward sheer destruction from thy comrades in their distress. Put thy fair glittering
armour of bronze is held among the Trojans. Hector of the glancing helm beareth it on his shoulders in triumph, yet not for long, I
ween, shall he glory therein, for death is hard anigh him. But thou
go not yet down into the mellay of war until thou see me with thine
eyes come hither. In the morning will I return, at the coming up of
the sun, bearing fair armour from the king Hephaistos.'

Thus spake she and turned to go from her son, and as she turned she spake among her sisters of the sea: 'Ye now go down within the wide bosom of the deep, to visit the Ancient One of the Sea and our father's house, and tell him all. I am going to high Olympus to Hephaistos of noble skill, if haply he will give unto my son noble armour shining gloriously.'

Thus spake she, and they forthwith went down beneath the surge of the sea. And the silver-footed goddess Thetis went on to Olympus that she might bring noble armour to her son.

So her unto Olympus her feet bore. But the Achaians with terrible cries were fleeing before man-slaying Hector till they came to the ships and to the Hellespont. Nor might the well-greaved Achaians drag the corpse of Patroklos Achilles' squire out of the darts, for now again overtook him the host and the horses of Troy, and Hector son of Priam, in might as it were a flame of fire. Thrice did glorious Hector seize him from behind by the feet, resolved to drag him away, and mightily called upon the men of Troy. Thrice did the two Aiantes, clothed on with impetuous might, beat him off from the dead man, but he nathless, trusting in his might, anon would charge into the press, anon would stand and cry aloud, but he gave ground never a whit. As when shepherds in the field avail no wise to chase a fiery lion in fierce hunger away from a carcase, so availed not the two warrior Aiantes to scare Hector son of Priam from the dead. And now would he have won the body and gained renown unspeakable, had not fleet wind-footed Iris come speeding from Olympus with a message to the son of Peleus to array him, unknown of Zeus and the other gods, for Hera sent her. And she stood anigh and spake to him winged words: 'Rouse thee, son of Peleus, of all men most redoubtable! Succour Patroklos, for whose body is terrible battle afoot before the ships. There slay they one another, these guarding the dead corpse, while the men of Troy are fierce to hale him unto windy Ilios, and chiefliest noble Hector is fain to drag him, and his heart biddeth him fix the head on the stakes of the wall when he hath sundered it from the tender neck. But arise, lie thus no longer! let awe enter thy heart to forbid that Patroklos become the sport of dogs of Troy. Thine were the shame if he go down mangled amid the dead.'

Then answered her fleet-footed noble Achilles: 'Goddess Iris, what god sent thee a messenger unto me?'

And to him again spake wind-footed fleet Iris: 'It was Hera that sent me, the wise wife of Zeus, nor knoweth the high-throned son of Kronos nor any other of the Immortals that on snowy Olympus have their dwelling-place.'

And Achilles fleet of foot made answer to her and said: 'And how may I go into the fray? The Trojans hold my arms; and my dear mother bade me forbear to array me until I behold her with my eyes returned, for she promised to bring fair armour from Hephaistos. Other man know I none whose noble armour I might put on, save it were the shield of Aias Telamon's son. But himself, I ween, is in the fore-front of the press, dealing death with his spear around Patroklos dead.'

Then again spake unto him wind-footed fleet Iris: 'Well are we also aware that thy noble armour is held from thee. But go forth unto the trench as thou art and show thyself to the men of Troy, if haply they will shrink back and refrain them from battle, and the warlike sons of the Achaians take breath [amid their toil, for small breathing-time is in the thick of fight].'

Thus spake fleet-footed Iris and went her way. But Achilles dear to Zeus arose, and around his strong shoulders Athene cast her tasselled aegis, and around his head the bright goddess set a crown of a golden cloud, and kindled therefrom a blazing flame. And as when a smoke issueth from a city and riseth up into the upper air, from an island afar off that foes beleaguer, while the others[1] from their city fight all day in hateful war, – but with the going down of the sun blaze out the beacon-fires in line, and high aloft rusheth up the glare for dwellers round about to behold, if haply they may come with ships to help in need – thus from the head of Achilles soared that blaze toward the heavens. And he went and stood beyond the wall beside the trench, yet mingled not among the Achaians, for he minded the wise bidding of his mother. There stood he and shouted aloud, and afar off Pallas Athene uttered her voice, and spread terror unspeakable among the men of Troy. Clear as the voice of a clarion when it soundeth by reason of slaughterous foemen that beleaguer a city, so clear rang forth the voice of Aiakides. And when they heard the brazen voice of Aiakides, the souls of all of them were dismayed, and the horses of goodly manes were fain to turn the chariots backward, for they boded anguish in their hearts. And the charioteers were amazed when they saw the unwearying fire blaze fierce on the head of the great-hearted son of Peleus, for the bright-eyed goddess Athene made it blaze. Thrice from over the trench shouted mightily noble Achilles, and thrice were the men of

[1] Reading οἱ δε for οἵ τε.

Troy confounded and their proud allies. Yea there and then perished twelve men of their best by their own chariot wheels and
spears. But the Achaians with joy drew Patroklos forth of the darts
and laid him on a litter, and his dear comrades stood around
lamenting him; and among them followed fleet-footed Achilles,
shedding hot tears, for his true comrade he saw lying on the bier,
mangled by the keen bronze. Him sent he forth with chariot and
horses unto the battle, but home again welcomed never more.

Then Hera the ox-eyed queen sent down the unwearying Sun to
be gone unwillingly unto the streams of Ocean. So the Sun set, and
the noble Achaians made pause from the stress of battle and the
hazardous war.

Now the men of Troy on their side when they were come back
out of the violent fray loosed their swift horses from the chariots
and gathered themselves in assembly or ever they would sup. Upon
their feet they stood in the assembly, neither had any man heart to
sit, for fear was fallen upon all because Achilles was come forth,
after long ceasing from fell battle. Then began to speak among
them wise Polydamas, son of Panthoos, for he alone saw before and
after. Comrade of Hector was he, and in the same night were both
born, but the one in speech was far the best, the other with the
spear. So with good intent toward them he made harangue and
spake: 'Take good heed on both sides, O my friends; for my part I
would have ye go up now to the city, not wait for bright morning
on the plain beside the ships, for we are far off from the wall. So
long as this man was wroth with noble Agamemnon, so long were
the Achaians easier to fight against, ay and I too rejoiced when I
couched nigh their swift ships, trusting that we should seize the
curved ships for a prey. But now am I sore afraid of the fleet son of
Peleus; so exceeding fierce is his heart, he will not choose to abide
in the plain where Trojans and Achaians both in the midst share the
spirit of war, but the prize he doeth battle for will be our city and
our wives. Now go we up to our fastness; hearken unto me, for thus
will it be. Now hath divine night stayed the fleet son of Peleus, but
if to-morrow fullarmed for the onset he shall light upon us abiding
here, well shall each know that it is he, for gladly will whosoever
fleeth win to sacred Ilios, and many of the men of Troy shall dogs
and vultures devour – far be that from my ear. But if, though loth,
we hearken unto my words, this night in counsel we shall possess
our strength, and the city shall be guarded of her towers and high
gates and tall well-polished doors that fit thereon close-shut. But at
dawn of day in armour harnessed will we take our stand along the

towers. Ill will he fare if he come forth from the ships to fight with us for our wall. Back to his ships shall he betake him when in vain chase he hath given his strong-necked horses their fill of hasting everywhither beneath the town. But within it never will he have heart to force his way, nor ever lay it waste; ere then shall he be devoured of swift dogs.'

Then with stern gaze spake unto him Hector of the glancing helm: 'Polydamas, no longer to my liking dost thou speak now, in that thou biddest us go back and be pent within the town. Have ye not had your fill already of being pent behind the towers? Of old time all mortal men would tell of this city of Priam for the much gold and bronze thereof, but now are its goodly treasures perished out of its dwellings, and much goods are sold away to Phrygia and pleasant Maionia, since mighty Zeus dealt evilly with us. But now when the son of crooked-counselling Kronos hath given me to win glory at the ships and to pen the Achaians beside the sea, no longer, fond man, put forth such counsels among the folk. No man of Troy will hearken unto thee, I will not suffer it. But come let us all be persuaded as I shall say. Sup now in your ranks throughout the host, and keep good ward, and each watch in his place. And whoso of the Trojans is grieved beyond measure for his goods, let him gather them together and give them to the people to consume in common, for it is better they have joy thereof than the Achaians. Then at dawn of day in armour harnessed at the hollow ships we will arouse keen war. What though in very truth noble Achilles be arisen beside the ships, ill shall he fare, if he will have it so. I at least will not flee from him out of the dread-sounding war, but full facing him will I stand, to try whether he win great victory, or haply I. The war-god is alike to all and a slayer of him that would slay.'

Thus Hector spake, and the men of Troy applauded with fond hearts, for Pallas Athene bereft them of their wit. And they gave assent to the ill advising of Hector, but none hearkened to Polydamas who devised good counsel. Then they supped throughout the host; but the Achaians all night made moan in lamentation for Patroklos. And first of them in the loud lamentation was the son of Peleus, laying upon the breast of his comrade his man-slaying hands and moaning very sore, even as a deep-bearded lion whose whelps some stag-hunter hath snatched away out of a deep wood; and the lion coming afterward grieveth, and through many glens he rangeth on the track of the footsteps of the man, if anywhere he might find him, for most bitter anger seizeth him; – thus Achilles moaning heavily spake among the Myrmidons: 'Ay me, vain verily was the word I uttered on that day when I cheered the hero Menoitios in his halls and said that I would bring back to Opoeis his son in glory from the sack of Ilios with the share of spoil that should fall unto him. Not all the purposes of men doth Zeus accomplish for them. It is as pointed that both of us redden the same earth with our blood here in Troy-land, for neither shall the old knight Peleus welcome me back home within his halls, nor my mother Thetis, but even here shall earth keep hold on me. Yet now, O Patroklos, since I follow thee under earth, I will not hold thy funeral till I have brought hither the armour and the head of Hector, thy high-hearted slayer,[1] and before thy pyre I will cut the throats of twelve noble sons of the men of Troy, for mine anger thou art slain. Till then beside the beaked ships shalt thou lie as thou art, and around thee deep-bosomed women, Trojan and Dardanian, shall mourn thee weeping night and day, even they whom we toiled to win by our strength and our long spears when we sacked rich cities of mortal men.'

Thus spake noble Achilles, and bade his comrades set a great tripod on the fire, that with all speed they might wash from Patroklos the bloody gore. So they set a tripod of ablution on the burning fire, and poured therein water and took wood and kindled it beneath; and the fire wrapped the belly of the tripod, and the water grew hot. And when the water boiled in the bright bronze, then washed they him and anointed with olive oil, and filled his wounds with fresh ointment, and laid him on a bier an

covered him with soft cloth from head to foot, and thereover a white robe. Then all night around Achilles fleet of foot the Myrmidons made lament and moan for Patroklos.

Meanwhile Zeus spake unto Hera his sister and wife: 'Thou hast accomplished this, O Hera, ox-eyed queen, thou hast aroused Achilles fleet of foot. Verily of thine own children must the flowing-haired Achaians be.'

Then answered unto him Hera the ox-eyed queen: 'Most dread son of Kronos, what is this word thou hast said? Truly even a man, I ween, is to accomplish what he may for another man, albeit he is mortal and hath not wisdom as we. How then was I who avow me the first of goddesses both by birth and for that I am called thy wife, and thou art king among all Immortals – how was I not in mine anger to devise evil against the men of Troy?'

So debated they on this wise with one another. But Thetis of the

[1] Or, reading σεῖο, 'slayer of thee the high-hearted.'

silver feet carne unto the house of Hephaistos, imperishable, star-
like, far seen among the dwellings of Immortals, a house of bronze,
wrought by the crook-footed god himself Him found she sweating
in toil and busy about his bellows, for he was forging tripods twenty
in all to stand around the wall of his stablished hall, and beneath the
base of each he had set golden wheels, that of their own motion
they might enter the assembly of the gods and again return unto his
house, a marvel to look upon. Thus much were they finished that
not yet were the ears of cunning work set thereon; these was he
making ready, and welding chains. While hereat he was labouring
with wise intent, then drew nigh unto him Thetis, goddess of the
silver feet. And Charis went forward and beheld her, fair Charis of
the shining chaplet whom the renowned lame god had wedded. And
she clasped her hand in hers and spake and called her by her name:
'Wherefore, long-robed Thetis, comest thou to our house, honoured that thou art and dear? No frequent comer art thou hitherto.
But come onward with me that I may set guest cheer before thee.'

Thus spake the bright goddess and led her on. Then set she her
on a silver-studded throne, goodly, of cunning work, and a footstool
was beneath her feet; and she called to Hephaistos, the famed artificer, and said unto him: 'Hephaistos, come forth hither, Thetis hath
need of thee.'

And the renowned lame god made answer to her: 'Verily a dread
and honoured goddess in my sight is she that is within, seeing that
she delivered me when pain came upon me from my great fall
though the ill-will of my shameless mother who would fain have hid
me away, for that I was lame. Then had I suffered anguish of heart
had not Eurynome and Thetis taken me into their bosom –
Eurynome daughter of Ocean that floweth back ever upon himself
Nine years with them I wrought much cunning work of bronze,
brooches and spiral arm-bands and cups and necklaces, in the
hollow cave, while around me the stream of Ocean with murmuring
foam flowed infinite. Neither knew thereof any other of gods or of
mortal men, save only Thetis and Eurynome who dc livered me.
And now cometh Thetis to our house; where fore behoveth it me
verily in all wise to repay fair-tressed Thetis for the saving of my
life. But do thou now set beside her fair entertainment, while I put
away my bellows and all my gear.'

He said, and from the anvil rose limping, a huge bulk, but under
him his slender legs moved nimbly. The bellows he set away from
the fire, and gathered all his gear wherewith he worked into a silver
chest; and with a sponge he wiped his face and hands and sturdy

neck and shaggy breast, and did on his doublet, and took a stout staff and went forth limping; but there were handmaidens of gold that moved to help their lord, the semblances of living maids. In them is understanding at their hearts, in them are voice and strength, and they have skill of the immortal gods. These moved beneath their lord, and he gat him haltingly near to where Thetis was, and set him on a bright seat, and clasped her hand in his and spake and called her by her name: Wherefore, long-robed Thetis, comest thou to our house, honoured that thou art and dear? No frequent comer art thou hitherto. Speak what thou hast at heart; my soul is fain to accomplish it, if accomplish it I can, and if it be appointed for accomplishment.'

Then answered unto him Thetis shedding tears: 'Hephaistos, hath there verily been any of all goddesses in Olympus that hath endured so many grievous sorrows at heart as are the woes that Kronian Zeus hath laid upon me above all others? He chose me from among the sisters o the sea to enthrall me to a man, even Peleus Aiakos' son, and with a man I endured wedlock sore against my will. Now lieth he in his halls forspent with grievous age, but other griefs are mine. A son he gave me to bear and nourish, the chief of heroes, and he shot up like a young branch. Like a plant in a very fruitful field I reared him and sent him forth on beaked ships to Ilios to fight against the men of Troy, but never again shall I welcome him back to his home within the house of Peleus. And while he yet liveth in my sight and beholdeth the light of the sun, he sorroweth, neither can I help him any whit though I go unto him. The maiden whom the sons of the Achaians chose out to be his prize, her hath the lord Agamemnon taken back out of his hands. In grief for her wasted he his heart; while the men of Troy were driving the Achaians on their ships, nor suffered them to come forth. And the elders of the Argives entreated him, and told over many noble gifts Then albeit himself he refused to ward destruction from them, he put his armour on Patroklos and sent him to the war, and much people with him. All day they fought around the Skaian gates and that same day had sacked the town, but that when now Menoitios' valiant son had wrought much harm, Apollo slew him in the forefront of the battle, and gave glory unto Hector. Therefore now come I a suppliant unto thy knees, if haply thou be willing to give my short-lived son shield and helmet, and goodly greaves fitted with ankle-pieces, and cuirass. For the armour that he had erst, his trusty comrade lost when he fell beneath the men of Troy; and my son lieth on the earth with anguish in his soul.'

Then made answer unto her the lame god of great renown: 'Be of good courage, let not these things trouble thy heart. Would that so might I avail to hide him far from dolorous death, when dread fate cometh upon him, as surely shall goodly armour be at his need, such as all men afterward shall marvel at, whosoever may behold.'

Thus saying he left her there and went unto his bellows and turned them upon the fire and bade them work. And the bellows, twenty in all, blew on the crucibles, sending deft blasts on every side, now to aid his labour and now anon howsoever Hephaistos willed and the work went on. And he threw bronze that weareth not into the fire, and tin and precious gold and silver, and next he set on an anvil-stand a great anvil, and took in his hand a sturdy hammer, and in the other he took the tongs.

First fashioned he a shield great and strong, adorning it all over, and set thereto a shining rim, triple, bright-glancing, and therefrom a silver baldrick. Five were the folds of the shield itself; and therein fashioned he much cunning work from his wise heart.

There wrought he the earth, and the heavens, and the sea, and the unwearying sun, and the moon waxing to the full, and the signs every one wherewith the heavens are crowned, Pleiads and Hyads and Orion's might, and the Bear that men call also the Wain, her that turneth in her place and watcheth Orion, and alone hath no part in the baths of Ocean.

Also he fashioned therein two fair cities of mortal men. In the one were espousals and marriage feasts, and beneath the blaze of torches they were leading the brides from their chambers through the city, and loud arose the bridal song. And young men were whirling in the dance, and among them flutes and viols sounded high; and the women standing each at her door were marvelling. But the folk were gathered in the assembly place; for there a strife was arisen, two men striving about the blood-price of a man slain; the one claimed to pay full atonement, expounding to the people, but the other denied him and would take naught; and both were fain to receive arbitrament at the hand of a daysman. And the folk were cheering both, as they took part on either side. And heralds kept order among the folk, while the elders on polished stones were sitting in the sacred circle, and holding in their hands staves from the loud-voiced heralds. Then before the people they rose up and gave judgment each in turn. And in the midst lay two talents of gold, to be given unto him who should plead among them most righteously.[1]

But around the other city were two armies in siege with glittering

_____

[1]Or rather, 'should utter among them the most righteous doom.'

arms. And two counsels found favour among them, either to sack the town or to share all with the towns folk[1] even whatsoever substance the fair city held within. But the besieged were not yet yielding, but arming for an ambushment. On the wall there stood to guard it their dear wives and infant children, and with these the old men; but the rest went forth, and their leaders were Ares and Pallas Athene, both wrought in gold, and golden was the vesture they had on. Goodly and great were they in their armour, even as gods, far seen around, and the folk at their feet were smaller. And when they came where it seemed good to them to lay ambush, in a river bed where there was a common watering-place of herds, there they set them, clad in glittering bronze. And two scouts were posted by them afar off to spy the coming of flocks and of oxen with crooked horns. And presently came the cattle, and with them two herdsmen playing on pipes, that took no thought of the guile. Then the others when they beheld these ran upon them and quickly cut off the herds of oxen and fair flocks of white sheep, and slew the shepherds withal. But the besiegers, as they sat before the speech-places[2] and heard much din among the oxen, mounted forthwith behind their high-stepping horses, and came up with speed. Then they arrayed their battle and fought beside the river banks, and smote one another with bronze-shod spears. And among them mingled Strife and Tumult, and fell Death, grasping one man alive fresh-wounded, another without wound, and dragging another dead through the mellay by the feet; and the raiment on her shoulders was red with the blood of men. Like living mortals they hurled together and fought, and haled the corpses each of the other's slain.

Furthermore he set in the shield a soft fresh-ploughed field, rich tilth and wide, the third time ploughed; and many ploughers therein drave their yokes to and fro as they wheeled about. Whensoever they came to the boundary of the field and turned, then would a man come to each and give into his hands a goblet of sweet wine, while others would be turning back along the furrows, fain to reach the boundary of the deep tilth. And the field grew black behind and seemed as it were a-ploughing, albeit of gold, for this was the great marvel of the work.

Furthermore he set therein the demesne-land of a king, where

---

[1]This must be the meaning in xxii. 120-121, where the same words are repeated. But here it might also be 'share all (exactly) between the two armies' (forbidding promiscuous plunder).

[2]From which the orators spoke. (Aristarchos.)

hinds were reaping with sharp sickles in their hands. Some armfuls along the swathe were falling in rows to the earth, whilst others the sheaf-binders were binding in twisted bands of straw. Three sheaf-binders stood over them, while behind boys gathering corn and bearing it in their arms gave it constantly to the binders; and among them the king in silence was standing at the swathe with his staff, rejoicing in his heart. And henchmen apart beneath an oak were making ready a feast, and preparing a great ox they had sacrificed; while the women were strewing much white barley to be a supper for the hinds.

Also he set therein a vineyard teeming plenteously with clusters, wrought fair in gold; black were the grapes, but the vines hung throughout on silver poles. And around it he ran a ditch of cyanus, and round that a fence of tin; and one single pathway led to it, whereby the vintagers might go when they should gather the vintage. And maidens and striplings in childish glee bare the sweet fruit in plaited baskets. And in the midst of them a boy made pleasant music on a clear-toned viol, and sang thereto a sweet Linos-song[1] with delicate voice; while the rest with feet falling together kept time with the music and song.

Also he wrought therein a herd of kine with upright horns, and the kine were fashioned of gold and tin, and with lowing they hurried from the byre to pasture beside a murmuring river, beside the waving reed. And herdsmen of gold were following with the kine, four of them, and nine dogs fleet of foot came after them. But two terrible lions among the foremost kine had seized a loud-roaring bull that bellowed mightily as they haled him, and the dogs and the young men sped after him. The lions rending the great bull's hide were devouring his vitals and his black blood; while the herdsmen in vain tarred on their fleet dogs to set on, for they shrank from biting the lions but stood hard by and barked and swerved away.

Also the glorious lame god wrought therein a pasture in a fair glen, a great pasture of white sheep, and a steading, and roofed huts, and folds.

Also did the glorious Lame god devise a dancing-place like unto that which once in wide Knosos Daidalos wrought for Ariadne of the lovely tresses. There were youths dancing and maidens of costly wooing, their hands upon one another's wrists. Fine linen the maidens had on, and the youths well-woven doublets faintly glistening with oil. Fair wreaths had the maidens, and the youths daggers of gold hanging from silver baldrics. And now would they run round with deft feet exceeding lightly, as when a potter sitting by his wheel that fitteth between his hands maketh trial of it whether it run: and now anon they would run in lines to meet each other. And a great company stood round the lovely dance in joy; [and among them a divine minstrel was making music on his lyre,] and through the midst of them, leading the measure, two tumblers whirled.

Also he set therein the great might of the River of Ocean around the uttermost rim of the cunningly-fashioned shield.

Now when he had wrought the shield great and strong, then wrought he him a corslet brighter than a flame of fire, and he wrought him a massive helmet to fit his brows goodly and graven, and set thereon a crest of gold, and he wrought him greaves of pliant tin.

So when the renowned lame god had finished all the armour, he took and laid it before the mother of Achilles. Then she like a falcon sprang down from snowy Olympus, bearing from Hephaistos the glittering arms.

BOOK XIX

How Achilles and Agamemnon were reconciled before the assembly of the Achaians, and Achilles went forth with them to battle.

NOW MORNING saffron-robed arose from the streams of Ocean to bring light to gods and men, and Thetis came to the ships, bearing his gift from the god. Her dear son she found fallen about Patroklos and uttering loud lament; and round him many of his company made moan. And the bright goddess stood beside him in their midst, and clasped her hand in his and spake and called upon his name: 'My child, him who lieth here we must let be, for all our pain, for by the will of gods from the beginning was he brought low. But thou take from Hephaistos arms of pride, arms passing goodly, such as no man on his shoulders yet hath borne.'

Thus spake the goddess and in front of Achilles laid the arms, and they rang all again in their glory. And awe fell on all the Myrmidons, nor dared any to gaze thereon, for they were awe-stricken. But when Achilles looked thereon, then came fury upon him the more, and his eyes blazed terribly forth as it were a flame beneath their lids: glad was he as he held in his hands that splendid gift of a god. But when he had satisfied his soul in gazing on the glory of the arms, straightway to his mother spake he winged words: 'My mother, the arms the god has given are suck as it beseemeth that the work of Immortals should be, and that no mortal man should have wrought. Now therefore will I arm me in them, but I have grievous fear lest meantime on the gashed wounds of Menoitios' valiant son flies light and breed worms therein, and defile his corpse – for the life is slain out of him – and so all his flesh shall rot.'

Then answered him Thetis, goddess of the silver feet: 'Child, have no care for this within thy mind. I will see to ward from him the cruel tribes of flies which prey on men slain in fight: for even though he lie till a whole year's course be run, yet his flesh shall be sound continually, or better even than now. But call thou the Achaian warriors to the place of assembly, and unsay thy wrath against Agamemnon shepherd of the host, and then arm swiftly for battle, and clothe thee with thy strength.'

Thus saying she filled him with adventurous might, while on

Patroklos she shed ambrosia and red nectar through his nostrils, that his flesh might abide the same continually.

But noble Achilles went down the beach of the sea, crying his terrible cry, and roused the Achaian warriors. And they who before were wont to abide in the circle of the ships, and they who were helmsmen and kept the steerage of the ships, or were stewards there and dealt out food, even these came then to the place of assembly, because Achilles was come forth, after long ceasing from grievous war. Limping came two of Ares' company, Tydeus' son staunch in fight and noble Odysseus, each leaning on his spear, for their wounds were grievous still; and they went and sate them down in the forefront of the assembly. And last came Agamemnon king of men, with his wound upon him, for him too in the stress of battle Koön Antenor's son had wounded with his bronze-tipped spear. But when all the Achaians were gathered, then uprose fleet-footed Achilles and spake in their midst: 'Son of Atreus, was this in any wise the better way for both thee and me, what time with grief at our hearts we waxed fierce in soul-devouring strife for the sake of a girl? Would that Artemis had slain her with her arrow at the ships, on the day whereon I took her to me, when I had spoiled Lyrnessos; so should not then so many Achaians have bitten the wide earth beneath their enemies' hands, by reason of my exceeding wrath. It hath been well for Hector and the Trojans, but the Achaians I think shall long remember the strife that was betwixt thee and me. But bygones will we let be, for all our pain, and curb under necessity the spirit within our breasts. I now will stay my anger: it beseems me not implacably for ever to be wroth; but come rouse speedily to the fight the flowing-haired Achaians, that I may go forth against the men of Troy and put them yet again to the proof, if they be fain to couch hard by the ships. Methinks that some among them shall be glad to rest their knees when they are fled out of the fierceness of the battle, and from before our spear.'

He spake, and the well-greaved Achaians rejoiced that the great-hearted son of Peleus had made renouncement of his wrath. Then among them spake Agamemnon king of men, speaking from the place where he sat, not arisen to stand forth in their midst: 'O Danaan friends and heroes, men of Ares' company, seemly is it to listen to him who standeth up to speak, nor behoveth it to break in upon his words: even toward a skilled man that were hard. For amid the uproar of many men how should one listen, or yet speak? even the clearest-voiced speech is marred. To the son of Peleus I will declare myself, but ye other Argives give heed, and each mark well my word. Oft have the Achaians spoken thus to me, and upbraided me; but it is not I who am the cause, but Zeus and Destiny and Erinys that walketh in the darkness, who put into my soul fierce madness on the day when in the assembly I, even I, bereft Achilles of his meed. What could I do? it is God who accomplisheth all. Eldest daughter of Zeus is Ate who blindeth all, a power of bane: delicate are her feet, for not upon earth she goeth, but walketh over the heads of men, making men to fall; and entangleth this one or that. Yea even Zeus was blinded upon a time, he who they say is greatest among gods and men; yet even him Hera with female wile deceived, on the day when Alkmene in fair-crowned Thebes was to bring forth the strength of Herakles. For then proclaimed he solemnly among all the gods: "Hear me ye all, both gods and goddesses, while I utter the counsel of my soul within my heart. This day shall Eileithuia, the help of travailing women, bring to the light a man who shall be lord over all that dwell round about, among the race of men who are sprung of me by blood." And to him in subtlety queen Hera spake: "Thou wilt play the cheat and not accomplish thy word. Come now, Olympian, swear me a firm oath that verily and indeed shall that man be lord over all that dwell round about, who this day shall fall between a woman's feet, even he among all men who are of the lineage of thy blood." So spake she, and Zeus no wise perceived her subtlety, but sware a mighty oath, and therewith was he sore blinded. For Hera darted from Olympus' peak, and came swiftly to Achaian Argos, where she knew was the stately wife of Sthenelos son of Perseus, who also was great with child, and her seventh month was come. Her son Hera brought to the light, though his tale of months was untold, but she stayed Alkmene's bearing and kept the Eileithuiai from her aid. Then she brought the tidings herself and to Kronos' son Zeus she spake: "Father Zeus of the bright lightning, a word will I speak to thee for thy heed. To-day is born a man of valour who shall rule among the Argives, Eurystheus, son of Sthenelos the son of Perseus, of thy lineage; not unmeet is it that he be lord among Argives." She said, but sharp pain smote him in the depths of his soul, and straightway he seized Ate by her bright-haired head in the anger of his soul, and sware a mighty oath that never again to Olympus and the starry heaven should Ate come, who blindeth all alike. He said, and whirling her in his hand flung her from the starry heaven, and quickly came she down among the works of men. Yet ever he groaned against her when he beheld his beloved son in cruel travail at Eurystheus' hest. Thus also I, what time great Hector of the glancing helm was slaying Argives at the sterns of our ships, could not be unmindful of Ate, who blinded me at the first. But since thus blinded was I, and Zeus bereft me of my wit, fain am I to make amends, and recompense manifold for the wrong. Only arise thou to the battle and rouse the rest of the host. Gifts am I ready to offer, even all that noble Odysseus went yesterday to promise in thy hut. So, if thou wilt, stay a while, though eager, from battle, and squires shall take the gifts from my ship and carry them to thee, that thou mayest see that what I give sufficeth thee.'

Then answered him Achilles swift of foot: 'Most noble son of Atreus, Agamemnon king of men, for the gifts, to give them as it beseemeth, if so thou wilt, or to withhold, is in thy choice. But now let us bethink us of battle with all speed; this is no time to dally here with subtleties, for a great work is yet undone. Once more must Achilles be seen in the forefront of the battle, laying waste with his brazen spear the battalions of the men of Troy. Thereof let each of you think as he fighteth with his man.'

Then Odysseus of many counsels answered him and said: 'Nay yet, for all thy valour, godlike Achilles, not against Ilios lead thou the sons of Achaians fasting to fight the men of Troy, since not of short spell shall the battle be, when once the ranks of men are met, and God shall breathe valour into both. But bid the Achaians taste at the swift ships food and wine; for thence is vigour and might. For no man fasting from food shall be able to fight with the foe all day till the going down of the sun; for though his spirit be eager for battle yet his limbs unaware grow weary, and thirst besetteth him, and hunger, and his knees in his going fail. But the man who having his fill of food and wine fighteth thus all day against the enemy, his heart is of good cheer within him, nor anywise tire his limbs, ere all give back from the battle. So come, disperse the host and bid them make ready their meal. And the gifts let Agamemnon king of men bring forth into the midst of the assembly, that all Achaians may behold them with their eyes, and thou be glad at heart. And let him swear to thee an oath, standing in the midst of the Argives, that he hath never gone up into the damsel's bed or lain with her, [O prince, as is the wont of man with woman]; and let thine own spirit be placable within thy breast. Then let him make thee a rich feast of reconcilement in his hut, that thou have nothing lacking of thy right. And thou, son of Atreus, toward others also shalt be more righteous hereafter; for no shame it is that a man that is a king should make amends if he have been the first to deal violently.'

Then to him spake Agamemnon king of men: 'Son of Laertes, I

rejoice to listen to thy speech; for rightfully hast thou told over all. And the oath I am willing to swear, yea my heart biddeth it, nor will I forswear myself before God. Let Achilles abide for a space, eager for battle though he be, and all ye others abide together, until the gifts come forth from my hut, and we make faithful oath with sacrifice. But thee thyself I thus charge and bid. Choose thee young men, princes of the Achaian folk, and bear my gifts from my ship, even all that we promised yesterday to Achilles, and take with thee the women. And let Talthybios speedily make me ready a boarswine in the midst of the wide Achaian host, to sacrifice to Zeus and to the Sun.'

And to him in answer swift-footed Achilles spake: 'Most noble son of Atreus, Agamemnon king of men, at some other time were it even better ye should be busied thus, when haply there shall be some pause of war, and the spirit within my breast shall be less fierce. But now they lie mangled on the field – even they whom Hector son of Priam slew, when Zeus gave him glory – and ye call men to their food. Verily for my part I would bid the sons of the Achaians to fight now unfed and fasting, and with the setting sun make ready a mighty meal, when we shall have avenged the shame. Till then down my throat at least nor food nor drink shall go, since my comrade is dead, who in my hut is lying mangled by the sharp spear, with his feet toward the door, and round him our comrades mourn; wherefore in my heart is no thought of those matters, but of slaying, and blood, and grievous moans of men.'

Then answered him Odysseus of many counsels: 'O Achilles, Peleus' son, mightiest of Achaians far, better and mightier not a little art thou than I with the spear, but in counsel I may surpass thee greatly, since I was born first and know more things: wherefore let thy heart endure to listen to my speech. Quickly have men surfeit of battle, of that wherein the sword streweth most straw yet is the harvest scantiest,[1] when Zeus inclineth his balance, who is disposer of the wars of men. But it cannot be that the Achaians fast to mourn a corpse; for exceeding many and thick fall such on every day; when then should there be rest from toil? Nay, it behoveth to bury him who is dead, steeling our hearts, when once we have wept him for a day; but such as are left alive from hateful war must take thought of meat and drink, that yet more against our foes we may fight relentlessly ever, clad in unyielding bronze. Then let none of

---

[1] i.e. in a pitched battle there is little plunder, the hope of which might help to sustain men's efforts in storming a town.

the host hold back awaiting other summons; this is the summons, and ill shall it be for whoso is left behind at the Argive ships; but all together as one we will rouse against the horse-taming Trojans the fury of war.'

He spoke, and took with him the sons of noble Nestor, and Meges son of Phyleus, and Thoas, and Meriones, and Lykomedes son of Kreiontes, and Melanippos. And they went on their way to the hut of Agamemnon, Atreus' son. Forthwith as the word was spoken so was the deed done. Seven tripods they bare from the hut, as he promised him, and twenty bright caldrons, and twelve horses, and anon they led forth women skilled in goodly arts, seven, and the eighth was fair-faced Briseis. Then Odysseus, having weighed ten talents of gold in all, led the way, and with him young men of the Achaians bare the gifts. These they set in the midst of the place of assembly, and Agamemnon rose up, and beside that shepherd of the host stood Talthybios, whose voice was like a god's, and held a boar between his hands. And the son of Atreus drawing with his hands his knife, which ever hung beside the mighty scabbard of his sword, cut off the first hairs from the boar, and lifting up his hands he prayed to Zeus, and all the Argives sat silent in their places, duly hearkening to the king. And he prayed aloud, looking up to the wide heaven: 'Be Zeus before all witness, highest and best of gods, and Earth, and Sun, and Erinyes, who under earth take vengeance upon men, whosoever forsweareth himself, that never have I laid hand on the damsel Briseis, neither to lie with her nor anywise else, but she has abode untouched within my huts. And if aught that I swear be false, may the gods give me all sorrows manifold, that they send on him who sinneth against them in his oath.'

He said, and cut the boar's throat with the pitiless knife. And the body Talthybios whirled and threw into the great wash of the hoary sea, to be the food of fishes; but Achilles arose up and spake in the midst of the warrior Argives: 'Father Zeus, sore madness dealest thou verily to men. Never could the son of Atreus have stirred the soul within my breast, nor led off the damsel implacably against my will, had not Zeus willed that on many of the Achaians death should come. But now go forth to your meal, that we may join battle there-upon.'

Thus he spake and dispersed the assembly with all speed. The rest were scattered each to his own ship, but the great hearted Myr-midons took up the gifts, and bare them to the ship of godlike Achilles. And they laid them in the huts and set the women there, and gallant squires drave the horses among their troop.

But Briseis that was like unto golden Aphrodite, when she beheld Patroklos mangled by the keen spear, fell about him and made shrill lament, and tore with her hands her breast and tender neck, and beautiful face. And she spake amid her weeping, that woman like unto goddesses: 'Patroklos, dearest to my hapless heart, alive I left thee when I left this hut, but now, O prince of the people, I am come back to find thee dead; thus evil ever followeth evil in my lot. My husband, unto whom my father and lady mother gave me, I beheld before our city mangled with the keen spear, and my three brothers whom my own mother bore, my near and dear, who all met their day of doom. But thou, when swift Achilles slew my husband and wasted godlike Mynes' city, wouldst ever that I should not even weep, and saidest that thou wouldst make me godlike Achilles' wedded wife, and that ye would take me in your ships to Phthia and make me a marriage feast among the Myrmidons. Therefore with all my soul I mourn thy death, for thou wert ever kind.'

Thus spake she weeping, and thereon the women wailed, in semblance for Patroklos, but each for her own woe. But round Achilles gathered the elders of the Achaians, praying him that he would eat; but he denied them with a groan: 'I pray you, if any kind comrade will hearken to me, bid me not sate my heart with meat and drink, since terrible grief is come upon me. Till the sun go down I will abide, and endure continually until then.'

He spoke, and his speech made the other chiefs depart, but the two sons of Atreus stayed, and noble Odysseus, and Nestor and Idomeneus and Phoinix, ancient knight, soothing him in his exceeding sorrow, but he could no whit be soothed until he had entered the mouth of bloody war. And bethinking him he sighed very heavily and spake aloud: 'Thou too, O hapless, dearest of my friends, thyself wouldst verily of yore set forth in our hut with ready speed a savoury meal, what time the Achaians hasted to wage against the horse-taming Trojans dolorous war. But now thou liest mangled, and my heart will none of meat and drink, that stand within, for desire of thee. Nought worse than this could I endure, not though I should hear of my father's death, who now I ween in Phthia is shedding big tears for lack of a son so dear, even me that in an alien land for sake of baleful Helen do battle with the men of Troy; nor though it were my beloved son who is reared for me in Skyros (if still at least is godlike Neoptolemos alive). For hitherto had my soul within me trusted that I alone should perish far from horse-pasturing Argos, here in the Trojan land, but that thou shouldst return to Phthia, so that thou mightest take me the child in thy swift black ship from Skyros and show him everything – my substance and servants, and high-roofed mighty hall. For Peleus I ween already must be dead and gone, or else in feeble life he hath sorrow of hateful age, and of waiting ever for bitter news of me, till he hear that I am dead.'

Thus spake he weeping, and the elders mourned with him, bethinking them what each had left at home. And when the son of Kronos beheld them sorrowing he pitied them, and forthwith to Athene spake he winged words: 'My child, thou hast then left utterly the man of thy heart. Hath Achilles then no longer a place within thy thought? He before the steep-prowed ships sits mourning his dear comrade; the rest are gone to their meal, but he is fasting and unfed. But go, distil into his breast nectar and pleasant ambrosia, that no pains of hunger come on him.'

Thus saying he sped forward Athene who before was fain. And she, like a falcon wide-winged and shrill-voiced, hurled herself forth from heaven through the upper air. So while the Achaians were arming presently throughout the camp, she in Achilles' breast distilled nectar and pleasant ambrosia, that grievous hunger might not assail his knees, and then herself was gone to the firm house of her mighty father. Then the Achaians poured forth from the swift ships. As when thick snowflakes flutter down from Zeus, chill beneath the blast of Boreas born in the upper air, so thick from the ships streamed forth bright glittering helms and bossy shields, strong-plated cuirasses and ashen spears. And the sheen thereof went up to heaven and all the earth around laughed in the flash of bronze, and there went a sound beneath the feet of the men, and in the midst of them noble Achilles harnessed him. His teeth gnashed together, and his eyes blazed as it were the flame of a fire, for into his heart was intolerable anguish entered in. Thus wroth against the men of Troy he put on the gift of the god, which Hephaistos wrought him by his art. First on his legs he set the fair greaves fitted with silver ankle-pieces, and next he donned the cuirass about his breast. Then round his shoulders he slung the bronze sword silver-studded; then lastly he took the great and strong shield, and its brightness shone afar off as the moon's. Or as when over the sea there appeareth to sailors the brightness of a burning fire, and it burneth on high among the mountains in some lonely steading sailors whom storm-blasts bear unwilling over the sea, the home of fishes, afar from them they love: – so from Achilles' goodly well-dight shield the brightness thereof shot up toward heaven. And he lifted the stout helmet and set it on his head, and like a star it shone, the horse-hair crested helmet, and around it waved plumes of gold that Hephaistos had set thick about the crest. Then noble Achilles proved him in his armour to know whether it fitted unto him, and whether his glorious limbs ran free; and it became to him as it were wings, and buoyed up the shepherd of hosts.

And forth from its stand he drew his father's spear, heavy and great and strong: that spear could none other of the Achaians wield, but Achilles alone awaited to wield it, the Pelian ashen spear that Cheiron gave to his father dear, from a peak of Pelion, to be the death of warriors. And Automedon and Alkimos went about to yoke the horses, and put on them fair breast-straps, and bits within their jaws, and stretched the reins behind to the firm-built chariot. Then Automedon took the bright lash, fitted to his hand, and sprang up behind the horses, and after him mounted Achilles armed, effulgent in his armour like bright Hyperion. And terribly he called upon the horses of his sire: 'Xanthos and Balios, famed children of Podarge, in other sort take heed to bring your charioteer safe back to the Danaan host, when we have done with battle, and leave him not as ye left Patroklos to lie there dead.'

Then the horse Xanthos of glancing feet made answer unto him from beneath the yoke; – and he bowed with his head, and all his mane fell from the yoke-cushion beside the yoke and touched the ground; – for the white-armed goddess Hera gave him speech: 'Yea verily for this hour, dread Achilles, we will still bear thee safe, yet is thy deathday nigh at hand, neither shall we be cause thereof, but a mighty god, and forceful Fate. For not through sloth or heedlessness of ours did the men of Troy from Patroklos' shoulders strip his arms, but the best of the gods, whom bright-haired Leto bore, slew him in the forefront of the battle, and to Hector gave renown. We even with the wind of Zephyr, swiftest, they say, of all winds, well might run; nathless to thee thyself it is appointed to be slain in fight by a god and by a man.'

Now when he had thus spoken the Erinyes stayed his voice. And sore troubled did fleet-footed Achilles answer him: 'Xanthos, why prophesiest thou my death? no wise behoveth it thee. Well know I of myself that it is appointed me to perish here, far from my father dear and mother; howbeit anywise I will not refrain till I give the Trojans surfeit of war.'

He said, and with a cry among the foremost held on his whole-hooved steeds.

BOOK XX

How Achilles made havoc among the men of Troy.

So BY THE BEAKED SHIPS around thee, son of Peleus, hungry for war, the Achaians armed; and over against them the men of Troy, upon the high ground of the plain.

But Zeus bade Themis call the gods to council from many-folded Olympus' brow; and she ranged all about and made them to the house of Zeus. There was no River came not up, save only Ocean, nor any nymph, of all that haunt fair thickets and springs of rivers and grassy water-meadows. And they came to the house of Zeus who gathereth the clouds, and sat them down in the polished colonnades which Hephaistos in the cunning of his heart had wrought for father Zeus.

Thus gathered they within the doors of Zeus; nor was the Earthshaker heedless of the goddess' call, but from the salt sea came up after the rest, and set him in the midst, and inquired concerning the purpose of Zeus: 'Wherefore, O Lord of the bright lightning, hast thou called the gods again to council? Say, ponderest thou somewhat concerning the Trojans and Achaians? for lo, the war and the fighting of them are kindled very nigh'

And Zeus, who gathereth the clouds answered him, saying: 'Thou knowest, O Earthshaker, the purpose within my breast? wherefor I gathered you hither; even in their perishing have I regard unto them. But for me I will abide here, sitting within a fold of Olympus, where I will gladden my heart with gazing; but go all ye forth that ye come among the Trojans and Achaians and succour these or those, howsoever each of you hath a mind. For if Achilles alone shall fight against the Trojans, not even a little while shall they hold back the son of Peleus, the fleet of foot. Nay, but even aforetime they trembled when they looked upon him; now therefore that his wrath for his friend is waxen terrible I fear me lest he overleap the bound of fate, and storm the wall.'

Thus spake the son of Kronos, and roused unabating war. For on this side and on that the gods went forth to war: to the company of the ships went Hera, and Pallas Athene, and Poseidon, Earthenfolder, and the Helper Hermes, pre-eminent in subtle thoughts;

and with these went Hephaistos in the greatness of his strength, halting, but his shrunk legs moved nimbly under him: but to the Trojans went Ares of the glancing helm, and with him Phoebus of the unshorn hair, and archer Artemis, and Leto and Xanthos and laughter-loving Aphrodite.

Now for so long as gods were afar from mortal men, so long waxed the Achaians glorious, for that Achilles was come forth among them, and his long ceasing from grim battle was at an end. And the Trojans were smitten with sore trembling in the limbs of every one of them, in terror when they beheld the son of Peleus, fleet of foot, blazing in his arms, peer of man-slaying Ares. But when among the mellay of men the Olympians were come down, then leapt up in her might Strife, rouser of hosts, then sent forth Athene a cry, now standing by the hollowed trench without the wall, and now on the echoing shores she shouted aloud And a shout uttered Ares against her, terrible as the blackness of the storm, now from the height of the city to the Trojans calling clear, or again along Simois shore over Kallikolonë he sped.[1]

So urged the blessed gods both hosts to battle, then themselves burst into fierce war. And terribly thundered the father of gods and men from heaven above; and from beneath Poseidon made the vast earth shake and the steep mountain tops. Then trembled all the spurs of many-fountained Ida, and all her crests, and the city of the Trojans, and the ships of the Achaians. And the Lord of the Underworld, Aïdoneus, had terror in hell, and leapt from his throne in that terror and cried aloud, lest the world be cloven above him by Poseidon, Shaker of earth, and his dwelling-place be laid bare to mortals and immortals – grim halls, and vast, and lothly to the gods. So loud the roar rose of that battle of gods. For against King Poseidon stood Phoebus Apollo with his winged arrows, and against Enyalios stood Athene, bright-eyed goddess, and against Hera she of the golden shafts and echoing chase, even archer Artemis, sister of the Far-darter; and against Leto the strong Helper Hermes, and against Hephaistos the great deep-eddying River, whom gods call Xanthos and men Skamandros.

Thus gods with gods were matched. Meanwhile Achilles yearned above all to meet Hector, son of Priam, in the fray; for with that blood chiefliest his spirit bade him sate Ares, stubborn lord of war. But straightway Apollo, rouser of hosts, moved Aineias to go to meet the son of Peleus, and filled him with brave spirit: and he

[1] Reading θέων.

made his own voice like the voice of Lykaon the son of Priam; in his semblance spake Apollo, son of Zeus: 'Aineias, counsellor of Trojans, where now are thy threats wherewith thou didst boast to the Trojan lords over thy wine, saying thou wouldest stand up in battle against Achilles, Peleus' son?'

And to him Aineias answered and said: 'Son of Priam, why biddest thou me thus face the fierce son of Peleus in battle, though I be not fain thereto? Not for the first time now shall I match me with Achilles, fleet of foot; once before drave he me with his spear from Ida, when he harried our kine and wasted Lyrnessos and Pedasos; but Zeus delivered me out of his hand and put strength into my knees that they were swift. Else had I fallen beneath the hands of Achilles, and of Athene who went before and gave him light, and urged him to slay Leleges and Trojans with his spear of bronze. Therefore it is impossible for man to face Achilles in fight, for that ever some god is at his side to ward off death. Ay, and at any time his spear flieth straight. neither ceaseth till it have pierced through flesh of man. But if God once give us fair field of battle, not lightly shall he overcome me, not though he boast him made of bronze throughout.'

And to him in answer spake Apollo son of Zeus: 'Yea, hero, pray thou too to the everliving gods; for thou too, men say, wast born of Aphrodite daughter of Zeus, and Achilles' mother is of less degree among the gods. For thy mother is child of Zeus, his but of the Ancient One of the Sea Come, bear up thy unwearying spear against him, let him no wise turn thee back with revilings and bitter words.'

He said, and breathed high spirit into the shepherd of the host, and he went onward through the forefront of the fighting, harnessed in flashing bronze. But white-armed Hera failed not to discern Anchises' son as he went through the press of men to meet the son of Peleus, and gathering the gods about her she spake among them thus: 'Consider ye twain, Poseidon and Athene, within your hearts, what shall come of these things that are done. Here is Aineias gone forth harnessed in flashing bronze, to meet the son of Peleus, and it is Phoebus Apollo that hath sent him. Come then, be it ours to turn him back straightway; or else let some one of us stand likewise beside Achilles and give him mighty power, so that he fail not in his spirit, but know that they who love him are the best of the Immortals, and that they who from of old ward war and fighting from the Trojans are vain as wind. All we from Olympus are come down to mingle in this fight that he take no hurt among the Trojans on this day – afterward he shall suffer whatsoever things Fate span for him with her thread, at his beginning, when his mother bare him. If Achilles learn not this from voice divine, then shall he be afraid when some god shall come against him in the battle; for gods revealed are hard to look upon.'

Then to her made answer Poseidon, Shaker of the earth:

era, be not fierce beyond wisdom; it behoveth thee not. Not fain am I at least to match gods with gods in strife.[1] Let us go now into some high place apart and seat us there to watch, and battle shall be left to men. Only if Ares or Phoebus Apollo fall to fighting, or put constraint upon Achilles and hinder him from fight, then straightway among us too shall go up the battle-cry of strife; right soon, methinks, shall they hie them from the issue of the fray back to Olympus to the company of the gods, overcome by the force of our hands.'

Thus spake the blue-haired god, and led the way to the mounded wall of heaven-sprung Herakles, that lofty wall built him by the Trojans and Pallas Athene, that he might escape the monster and be safe from him, what time he should make his onset from the beach to the plain.[2] There sate them down Poseidon and the other gods, and clothed their shoulders with impenetrable cloud. And they of the other part sat down on the brows of Kallikolonë around thee, Archer Phoebus, and Ares waster of cities. Thus they on either side sat devising counsels, but shrank all from falling to grievous war, and Zeus from his high seat commanded them.

Meanwhile the whole plain was filled with men and horses, and ablaze with bronze; and the earth rang with the feet of them as they rushed together in the fray. Two men far better than the rest were meeting in the midst between the hosts, eager for battle, Aineias, Anchises' son, and noble Achilles. First came on Aineias threateningly, tossing his strong helm; his rapid shield he held before his breast, and brandished his bronze spear. And on the other side the son of Peleus rushed to meet him, like a lion, a ravaging lion whom men desire to slay, a whole tribe assembled: and first he goeth his way unheeding, but when some warrior youth hath smitten him with a spear, then he gathereth him self open-mouthed, and foam cometh forth about his teeth, and his stout spirit groaneth in his heart, and with his tail he scourgeth either side his ribs and flanks and goadeth himself on to fight, and glaring is borne straight on

[1] Omitting line 135.
[2] Note 4.

them by his passion, to try whether he shall slay some man of them, or whether himself shall perish in the forefront of the throng: thus was Achilles driven of his passion and valiant spirit to go forth to meet Aineias great of heart. And when they were come near against each other, then first to Aineias spake fleet-footed noble Achilles: 'Aineias, wherefore hast thou so far come forward from the crowd to stand against me: doth thy heart bid thee fight with me in hope of holding Priam's honour and lordship among the horse-taming Trojans? Nay, though thou slay me, not for that will Priam lay his kingdom in thy hands, for he hath sons, and is sound and of unshaken mind Or have the Trojans allotted thee some lot of ground more choice than all the rest, fair land of tilth and orchard, that thou mayest dwell therein, if thou slay me? But methinks thou wilt find the slaying hard; for once before, I ween, have I made thee flee before my spear. Hast thou forgotten the day when thou wert alone with the kine, and I made thee run swift-footed down Ida's steeps in haste? – then didst thou not look behind thee in thy flight. Thence fleddest thou to Lernessos, but I wasted it, having fought against it with the help of Athene and of father Zeus, and carried away women captive, bereaving them of their day of freedom: only thee Zeus shielded, and other gods. But not this time, methinks, shall they shield thee, as thou imaginest in thy heart: therefore I bid thee go back into the throng and come not forth against me, while as yet thou art unhurt – after the event even a fool is wise.'

Then to him in answer again Aineias spake; 'Son of Peleus, think not with words to affright me as a child, since I too well know myself how to speak taunts and unjust speech. We know each other's race and lineage in that we have heard the fame proclaimed by mortal men, but never hast thou set eyes on my parents, or I on thine. Thou, they say, art son of noble Peleus, and of Thetis of the fair tresses, the daughter of the sea: the sire I boast is Anchises great of heart, and my mother is Aphrodite. Of these shall one pair or the other mourn their dear son to-day; for verily not with idle words shall we two satisfy our strife and depart out of the battle. But, if thou wilt, learn also this, that thou mayest well know our lineage, known to full many men: First Zeus the cloud-gatherer begat Dardanos, and he stablished Dardania for not yet was holy Ilios built upon the plain to be a city of mortal men, but still they dwelt on slopes of many-fountained Ida Then Dardanos begat a son, king Erichthonios, who became richest of mortal men. Three thousand mares had he that pastured along the marsh meadow, rejoicing in their tender foals. Of them was Boreas enamoured as they grazed, and in semblance of a dark-maned horse he covered them: then they having conceived bare twelve fillies. These when they bounded over Earth the grain-giver would run upon the topmost ripened ears of corn and break them not; and when they bounded over the broad backs of the sea they would run upon the crests of the breakers of the hoary brine. Then Erichthonios begat Tros to be lord over the Trojans, and to Tros three noble sons were born, Ilos and Assarakos and godlike Ganymedes, who became the most beautiful of mortal men. Him the gods caught up to be cupbearer to Zeus, for sake of his beauty, that he might dwell among immortals. Then Ilos again begat a son, noble Laomedon, and Laomedon begat Tithonos and Priam and Lampos and Klytios and Hiketaon, of the stock of Ares. And Assarakos begat Kapys, and Kapys Anchises, and Anchises me; but Priam begat the goodly Hector.

'Lo then of this blood and lineage declare I myself unto thee. But for valour, Zeus increaseth it in men or minisheth it according as he will, for he is lord of all. But come, let us talk thus together no longer like children, standing in mid onset of war. For there are revilings in plenty for both of us to utter – a hundred-thwarted ship would not suffice for the load of them. Glib is the tongue of man, and many words are therein of every kind, and wide is the range of his speech hither and thither. whatsoever word thou speaks such wilt thou hear in answer. But what need that we should bandy strife and wrangling each against each, like women, who when they wax wroth for some heart-wasting quarrel go forth into the mid street and wrangle each against each with words true and false; for these too anger bids them speak. But not by speech shalt thou turn me from the battle that I desire, until we have fought together, point to point: come then, and straightway we will each try the other with bronze-headed spears.'

He said, and against that other's dread and mighty shield hurled his great spear, and the shield rang loud beneath the spear-point. And the son of Peleus held away the shield from him with his stout hand, in fear, for he thought that the far-shadowing spear of Aineias great of heart would lightly pierce it through – fond man, and knew not in his mind and heart that not lightly do the glorious gifts of gods yield to force of mortal men. So did not the great spear of wise Aineias pierce that shield, for the gold resisted it, even the gift of the god. Yet through two folds he drave it, but three remained, for five folds had the lame god welded, two bronze, and two inside of tin, and one of gold; therein was stayed the ashen spear.

Then Achilles in his turn hurled his far-shadowing spear, and smote upon the circle of the shield of Aineias, beneath the edge of the rim, where the bronze ran thinnest round, and the bull-hide was thinnest thereon; and right through sped the Pelian ashen spear, and the shield cracked under it. And Aineias crouched and held up the shield away from him in dread; and the spear flew over his back and fixed itself in the earth, having divided asunder the two circles of the sheltering shield. And having escaped the long spear he stood still, and a vast anguish drowned his eyes, affrighted that the spear was planted by him so nigh. But Achilles drew his sharp sword and furiously made at him, crying his terrible cry: then Aineias grasped in his hand a stone (a mighty deed) such as two men, as men now are, would not avail to lift, but he with ease wielded it all alone. Then would Aineias have smitten him with the stone as he charged, either on helm or shield, which had warded from him bitter death, and then would the son of Peleus have closed and slain him with his sword, had not Poseidon, Shaker of earth, marked it with speed, and straightway spoken among the immortal gods: 'Alas, woe is me for Aineias great of heart, who quickly will go down to Hades slain by the son of Peleus, for that he will obey the words of Apollo the far-darter, fond man, but nowise shall the god help him from grievous death. But wherefore now is he to suffer ill in his innocence, cause-lessly for others' wickedness,[1] yet welcome ever are his offerings to the gods who inhabit the spacious heaven? Come, let us guide him out of death's way, lest the son of Kronos be wroth, if Achilles slay him; for it is appointed to him to escape, that the race of Dardanos perish not without seed or sign, even Dardanos whom the son of Kronos loved above all the children born to him from the daughters of men. For the race of Priam hath Zeus already hated. But thus shall the might of Aineias reign among the Trojans, and his chil-dren's children, who shall be born in the aftertime.'

And him then answered Hera the ox-eyed queen: 'Shaker of earth, thyself with thine own mind take counsel, whether thou wilt save Aineias, or leave him [to be slain, brave though he be, by Achilles, Peleus' son]. For by many oaths among all the Immortals have we two sworn, even Pallas Athene and I, never to help the Trojans from their evil day, not even when all Troy shall burn in the burning of fierce fire, and they that burn her shall be the warlike sons of the Achaians.'

Now when Poseidon Shaker of earth heard that, he went up amid the battle and the clash of spears, and came where Aineias and

[1]Reading ἀτέων.

renowned Achilles were. Then presently he shed mist over the eyes of Achilles, Peleus' son, and drew the bronze-headed ashen spear from the shield of Aineias great of heart, and set it before Achilles' feet, and lifted Aineias and swung him high from off the earth. Over many ranks of warriors, of horses many, sprang Aineias soaring in the hand of the god, and lighted at the farthest verge of the battle of many onsets, where the Kaukones were arraying them for the fight. Then hard beside him came Poseidon, Shaker of earth, and spake aloud to him winged words: 'Aineias, what god is it that biddeth thee fight infatuate against Peleus' vehement son, who is both a better man than thou and dearer to Immortals? Rather withdraw thee whensoever thou fallest in with him, lest even contrary to thy fate thou enter the house of Hades. But when Achilles shall have met his death and doom, then be thou of good courage to fight among the foremost, for there shall none other of the Achaians slay thee.'

He spoke, and left him there, when he had shown him all these things. Then quickly from Achilles' eyes he purged the magic mist; and he stared with wide eyes, and in trouble spake unto his proud soul: 'Ha! verily a great marvel behold I here with mine eyes. My spear lieth here upon the ground, nor can I anywise see the man at whom I hurled it with intent to slay him. Truly then is Aineias likewise dear to the immortal gods, howbeit I deemed that his boasting thereof was altogether vanity. Away with him! not again will he find heart to make trial of me, now that once more he has escaped death to his joy. But come, I will call on the warlike Danaans and go forth to make trial of some other Trojan face to face.'

He said, and leapt along the lines, and called upon each man: 'No longer stand afar from the men of Troy, noble Achaians, but come let man match man and throw his soul into the fight. Hard is it for me, though I be strong, to assail so vast a folk and fight them all: not even Ares, though an immortal god, nor Athene, could plunge into the jaws of such a fray and toil therein. But to my utmost power with hands and feet and strength no whit, I say, will I be slack, nay, never so little, but right through their line will I go forward, nor deem I that any Trojan shall be glad who shall come nigh my spear.'

Thus spake he urging them. But to the Trojans glorious Hector called aloud, and proclaimed that he would go forth against Achilles: 'High-hearted Trojans, fear not Peleus son. I too in words could fight even Immortals, but with the spear it were hard, for they are stronger far. Neither shall Achilles accomplish all his talk, but part thereof he is to accomplish, and part to break asunder in the midst. And against him will I go forth, though the hands of him be even as fire, yea though his hands be as fire and his fierceness as the flashing steel.'

Thus spake he urging them, and the Trojans raised their spears for battle; and their fierceness was mingled confusedly, and the battle-cry arose. Then Phoebus Apollo stood by Hector and spake to him: 'Hector, no longer challenge Achilles at all before the lines, but in the throng await him and from amid the roar of the battle, lest haply he spear thee or come near and smite thee with his sword.'

Thus spake he, and Hector again fell back into the crowd of men, for he was amazed when he heard the sound of a god's voice.

But Achilles sprang in among the Trojans, his heart clothed with strength, crying his terrible cry, and first he took Iphition, Otrynteus' valiant son, a leader of much people, born of a Naiad nymph to Otrynteus waster of cities, beneath snowy Tmolos, in Hyde's rich domain. Him as be came right on did goodly Achilles smite with his hurled spear, down through the midst of his head, and it was rent asunder utterly. And he fell with a crash, and goodly Achilles exulted over him: 'Low liest thou, son of Otrynteus, most redoubtable of men; here is thy death, thy birth was on the Gygaian lake, where is thy sire's demesne, by Hyllos rich in fish and eddying Hermos.'

Thus spake he exultant, but darkness fell upon the eyes of Iphition: him the chariots of the Achaians clave with their tires asunder in the forefront of the battle, and over him Achilles pierced in the temples, through his bronze-cheeked helmet, Demoleon, brave stemmer of battle, Antenor's son. No stop made the bronze helmet, but therethrough sped the spear-head and clave the bone, and the brain within was all scattered: that stroke made ending of his zeal. Then Hippodamas, as he leapt from his chariot and fled before him, Achilles wounded in the back with his spear: and he breathed forth his spirit with a roar, as when a dragged bull roareth that the young men drag to the altar of the Lord of Helike; for in such hath the Earthshaker his delight: thus roared Hippodamas as from his bones fled forth his haughty spirit. But Achilles with his spear went on after godlike Polydoros, Priam's son. Him would his sire continually forbid to fight, for that among his children he was youngest born and best beloved, and overcame all in fleetness of foot. Just then in boyish folly, displaying the swiftness of his feet, he was rushing through the forefighters, until he lost his life. Him in the midst did fleet-footed noble Achilles smite with a javelin, in his back as he darted by, where his belt's golden buckles clasped, and the breast and back plates overlapped: and right through beside the navel went the spear-head, and he fell on his knee with a cry, and dark cloud covered him round about, and he clasped his bowels to him with his hands as he sank.

Then when Hector saw his brother Polydoros clasping his bowels with his hands, and sinking to the earth, a mist fell over his eyes, nor longer might he endure to range so far apart, but he came up against Achilles brandishing his sharp spear, and like a flame of fire. And Achilles when he saw him, sprang up, and spake exultingly: 'Behold the man who hath deepest stricken into my soul, who slew my dear-prized friend; not long shall we now shrink from each other along the highways of the war.'

He said, and looking grimly spake unto goodly Hector: 'Come thou near, that the sooner thou mayest arrive at the goal of death.'

Then to him, unterrified, said Hector of the glancing helm: 'Son of Peleus, think not with words to affright me as a child, since I too know myself how to speak taunts and unjust speech. And I know that thou art a man of might, and a far better man than I. Yet doth this issue lie in the lap of the gods, whether I though weaker shall take thy life with my hurled spear, for mine too hath been found keen ere now.'

He said, and poised his spear and hurled it, and Athene with a breath turned it back from glorious Achilles, breathing very lightly; and it carne back to goodly Hector, and fell there before his feet. Then Achilles set fiercely upon him, eager to slay him, crying his terrible cry. But Apollo caught Hector up, very easily, as a god may, and hid him in thick mist. Thrice then did fleet-footed noble Achilles make onset with his spear of bronze, and thrice smote the thick mist. [But when the fourth time he had come godlike on,] then with dread shout he spake to him winged words: 'Dog, thou art now again escaped from death; yet came ill very nigh thee; but now hath Phoebus Apollo saved thee, to whom thou must surely pray when thou goest forth amid the clash of spears. Verily I will slay thee yet when I meet thee hereafter, if any god is helper of me too. Now will I make after the rest, whomsoever I may seize.'

Thus speaking he pierced Dryops in the midst of his neck with his spear, and he fell down before his feet. But he left him where he lay, and hurled at Demuchos Philetor's son, a good man and a tall, and stayed him with a stroke upon his knees; then smote him with his mighty sword and reft him of life. Then springing on Laogonos and Dardanos, sons of Bias, he thrust both from their chariot to the ground, one with a spear-cast smiting and the other in close battle with his sword. Then Tros, Alastor's son – he came and clasped his knees to pray him to spare him, and let him go alive, and slay him not, having compassion on his like age, fond fool, and knew not that he might not gain his prayers; for nowise soft of heart or tender was that man, but of fierce mood – with his hands he touched Achilles' knees, eager to entreat him, but he smote him in the liver with his sword, and his liver fell from him, and black blood therefrom filled his bosom, and he swooned, and darkness covered his eyes. Then Achilles came near and struck Mulios in the ear, and right through the other ear went the bronze spear-head. Then he smote Agenor's son Echeklos on the midst of the head with his hilted sword, and all the sword grew hot thereat with blood; and dark death seized his eyes, and forceful fate. Then next Deukalion, just where the sinews of the elbow join, there pierced he him through the forearm with his bronze spear-head; so abode he with his arm weighed down, beholding death before him; and Achilles smiting the neck with his sword swept far both head and helm, and the marrow rose out of the backbone, and the corpse lay stretched upon the earth. Then went he onward after Peires' noble son, Rhigmos, who had come from deep-soiled Thrace: him in the midst he smote with his hurled javelin, and the point fixed in his lung, and he fell forth of his chariot. And Areïthoös his squire, as he turned the horses round, he pierced in the back with his sharp spear, and thrust him from the car, and the horses ran wild with fear.

As through deep glens rageth fierce fire on some parched mountain-side, and the deep forest burneth, and the wind driving it whirleth every way the flame, so raged he every way with his spear, as it had been a god, pressing hard on the men he slew; and the black earth ran with blood. For even as when one yoketh wide-browed bulls to tread white barley in a stablèd threshing-floor, and quickly is it trodden out beneath the feet of the loud-lowing bulls, thus beneath great-hearted Achilles his whole-hooved horses trampled corpses and shields together; and with blood all the axle-tree below was sprinkled and the rims that ran around the car, for blood-drops from the horses' hooves splashed them, and blood-drops from the tires of the wheels. But the son of Peleus pressed on to win him glory, flecking with gore his Irresistible hands.

BOOK XXI

How Achilles fought with the River, and chased the men of Troy within their gates.

BUT WHEN NOW they came unto the ford of the fair-flowing river, even eddying Xanthos, whom immortal Zeus begat, there sundering them he chased the one part to the plain toward the city, even where the Achaians were flying in affright the day before, when glorious Hector was in his fury – thither poured some in flight, and Hera spread before them thick mist to hinder them: – but half were pent into the deep-flowing silver-eddied river, and fell therein with a mighty noise, and the steep channel sounded, and the banks around rang loudly; for with shouting they swam therein hither and thither, whirled round the eddies. And as when at the rush of fire locusts take wing to fly unto a river, and the unwearying fire flameth forth on them with sudden onset, and they huddle in the water; so before Achilles was the stream of deep-eddying Xanthos filled with the roar and the throng of horses and men.

Then the seed of Zeus left behind him his spear upon the bank, leant against tamarisk bushes, and leapt in, as it were a god, keeping his sword alone, and devised grim work at heart, and smote as he turned him every way about: and their groaning went up ghastly as they were stricken by the sword, and the water reddened with blood. As before a dolphin of huge maw fly other fish and fill the nooks of some fair-havened bay, in terror, for he devoureth amain whichsoever of them he may catch; so along the channels of that dread stream the Trojans crouched beneath the precipitous sides. And when his hands were weary of slaughter he chose twelve young men alive out of the river, an atonement for Patroklos Menoitios' son that was dead. These brought he forth amazed like fawns, and bound behind them their hands with well-cut thongs, which they themselves wore on their pliant doublets, and gave them to his comrades to lead down to the hollow ships Then again he made his onset, athirst for slaying.

There met he a son of Dardanid Priam, in flight out of the river, Lykaon, whom once himself he took and brought unwilling out of his father's orchard, in a night assault; he was cutting with keen bronze young shoots of a wild fig tree, to be hand-rails of a chariot; but to him an unlooked-for bane came goodly Achilles. And at that time he sold him into well-peopled Lemnos, sending him on ship board, and the son of Jason gave a price for him; and thence a guest friend freed him with a great ransom, Eetion of Imbros, and sent him to goodly Arisbe; whence flying secretly he came to his father's house. Eleven days he rejoiced among his friends after he was come from Lemnos, but on the twelfth once more God brought him into the hands of Achilles, who was to send him to the house of Hades though nowise fain to go. Him when fleet-footed noble Achilles saw bare of helm and shield, neither had he a spear, but had thrown all to the ground; for he sweated grievously as he tried to flee out of the river, and his knees were failing him for weariness: then in wrath spake Achilles to his great heart: 'Ha! verily great marvel is this that I behold with my eyes. Surely then will the proud Trojans whom I have slain rise up again from beneath the murky gloom, since thus hath this man come back escaped from his pitiless fate, though sold into goodly Lemnos, neither hath the deep of the hoary sea stayed him, that holdeth many against their will. But come then, of our spear's point shall he taste, that I may see and learn in my mind whether likewise he shall come back even from beneath, or whether the life-giving Earth shall hold him down, she that holdeth so even the strong.'

Thus pondered he in his place; but the other came near amazed, fain to touch his knees, for his soul longed exceedingly to flee from evil death and black destruction. Then goodly Achilles lifted his long spear with intent to smite him, but he stooped and ran under it and caught his knees; and the spear went over his back and stood in the ground, hungering for flesh of men. Then Lykaon besought him, with one hand holding his knees, while with the other he held the sharp spear and loosed it not, and spake to him winged words: 'I cry thee mercy, Achilles; have thou regard and pity for me: to thee, O fosterling of Zeus, am I in the bonds of suppliantship. For at thy table first I tasted meal of Demeter on the day when thou didst take me captive in the well-ordered orchard, and didst sell me away from my father and my friends unto goodly Lemnos, and I fetched thee the price of a hundred oxen. And now have I been ransomed for thrice that, and this is my twelfth morn since I came to Ilios after much pain. Now once again hath ruinous fate delivered me into thy hands; surely I must be hated of father Zeus, that he hath given me a second time unto thee; and to short life my mother bare me, Laothoë, old Altes' daughter – Altes who ruleth among the war-loving Leleges, holding steep Pedasos on the Satnioeis. His daughter Priam had to wife, with many others, and of her were we two born, and thou wilt butcher both. Him among the foremost of the foot-soldiers didst thou lay low, even godlike Polydoros, when thou smotest him with thy sharp spear: and now will it go hard with me here, for no hope have I to escape thy hands, since God hath delivered me thereunto. Yet one thing will I tell thee, and do thou lay it to heart: slay me not, since I am not of the same mother as Hector, who slew thy comrade the gentle and brave.'

Thus spake to him the noble son of Priam, beseeching him with words, but he heard a voice implacable: 'Fond fool, proffer me no ransom, nor these words. Until Patroklos met his fated day, then was it welcomer to my soul to spare the men of Troy, and many I took alive and sold beyond the sea: but now there is none shall escape death, whomsoever before Ilios God shall deliver into my hands – yea, even among all Trojans, but chiefest among Priam's sons. Ay, friend, thou too must die: why thus lamentest thou? Patroklos too is dead, who was better far than thou. Seest thou not also what manner of man am I for might and goodliness? and a good man was my father, and a goddess mother bare me. Yet over me too hang death and forceful fate. There cometh morn or eve or some noonday when my life too some man shall take in battle, whether with spear he smite or arrow from the string.'

Thus spake he, and the other's knees and heart were unstrung. He let go Achilles' spear, and sat with both hands outspread. But Achilles drew his sharp sword and smote on the collar-bone beside the neck, and all the two-edged sword sank into him, and he lay stretched prone upon the earth, and blood flowed dark from him and soaked the earth Him seized Achilles by the foot and sent him down the stream, and over him exulting spake winged words: 'There lie thou among the fishes, which shall lick off thy wound's blood heedlessly, nor shall thy mother lay thee on a bed and mourn for thee, but Skamandros shall bear thee on his eddies into the broad bosom of the sea Leaping along the wave shall many a fish dart up to the dark ripple to eat of the white flesh of Lykaon. So perish all, until we reach the citadel of sacred Ilios, ye flying and I behind destroying. Nor even the River, fair-flowing, silver-eddied, shall avail you, to whom long time forsooth ye sacrifice many bulls, and among his eddies throw whole-hooved horses down alive. For all this yet shall ye die the death, until ye pay all for Patroklos' slaying and the slaughter of Achaians whom at the swift ships ye slew while I tarried afar.'

Thus spake he, but the River waxed ever more wroth in his heart, and sought in his soul how he should stay goodly Achilles from his work, and ward destruction from the Trojans. Meanwhile the son of Peleus with his far-shadowing spear leapt, fain to slay him, upon Asteropaios son of Pelegon, whom wide-flowing Axios begat of Periboia eldest of the daughters of Akessamenos, for with her lay that deep-eddying River. Upon him set Achilles, and Asteropaios stood against him from the river, holding two spears; for Xanthos put courage into his heart, being angered for the slaughtered youths whom Achilles was slaughtering along the stream and had no pity on them. Then when the twain were come nigh in onset on each other, unto him first spake fleet-footed noble Achilles: 'Who and whence art thou of men, that darest to come against me? Ill-fated are they whose children match them with my might.'

And to him made answer Pelegon's noble son: 'High-hearted son of Peleus, why askest thou my lineage? I come from deep-soiled Paionia, a land far off, leading Paionian men with their long spears, and this now is the eleventh morn since I am come to Ilios. My lineage is of wide-flowing Axios. who begat Pelegon famous with the spear, and he, men say, was my father.[1] Now fight we, noble Achilles!'

Thus spake he in defiance, and goodly Achilles lifted the Pelian ash: but the warrior Asteropaios hurled with both spears together, for he could use both hands alike, and with the one spear smote the shield, but pierced it not right through, for the gold stayed it, the gift of a god; and with the other he grazed the elbow of Achilles' right arm, and there leapt forth dark blood, but the point beyond him fixed itself in the earth, eager to batten on flesh. Then in his turn Achilles hurled on Asteropaios his straight-flying ash, fain to have slain him, but missed the man and struck the high bank, and quivering half its length in the bank he left the ashen spear. Then the son of Peleus drew his sharp sword from his thigh and leapt fiercely at him, and he availed not to draw with his stout hand Achilles' ashen shah from the steep bank. Thrice shook he it striving to draw it forth, and thrice gave up the strain, but the fourth time he was fain to bend and break the ashen spear of the seed of Aiakos, but ere that Achilles closing on him reft him of life with his sword. For in the belly he smote him beside the navel, and all his bowels gushed out to the earth, and darkness covered his eyes as he lay gasping. Then Achilles trampling on his breast stripped off his

[1] Omitting line 158, with the best MSS.

armour and spake exultingly: 'Lie there! It is hard to strive against children of Kronos' mighty son, even though one be sprung from a River-god. Thou truly declarest thyself the seed of a wideflowing River, but I avow me of the lineage of great Zeus. My sire is a man ruling many Myrmidons, Peleus the son of Aiakos, and Aiakos was begotten of Zeus. As Zeus is mightier than seaward-murmuring rivers, so is the seed of Zeus made mightier than the seed of a river. Nay, there is hard beside thee a great river, if he may anywise avail; but against Zeus the son of Kronos it is not possible to fight. For him not even king Acheloïos is match, nor yet the great strength of deep-flowing Ocean, from whom all rivers flow and every sea, and all springs and deep wells: yea, even he hath fear of the lightning of great Zeus and his dread thunder, when it pealeth out of heaven.'

He said, and from the steep bank drew his bronze spear, and left there Asteropaios whom he had slain, lying in the sands, and the dark water flooded him. Around him eels and fishes swarmed, tearing and gnawing the fat about his kidneys. But Achilles went on after the charioted Paiones who still along the eddying river huddled in fear, when they saw their best man in the stress of battle slain violently by the hands and the sword of the son of Peleus. There slew he Thersilochos and Mydon and Astypylos and Mnesos and Thrasios and Ainios and Ophelestes; and more yet of the Paiones would swift Achilles have slain, had not the deepeddying River called unto him in wrath, in semblance of a man, and from an eddy's depth sent forth a voice: 'O Achilles, thy might and thy evil work are beyond the measure of men; for gods themselves are ever helping thee. If indeed the son of Kronos hath delivered thee all the Trojans to destroy, at least drive them forth from me and do thy grim deeds on the plain, for filled with dead men is my pleasant bed, nor can I pour my stream to the great sea, being choked with dead, and thou slayest ruthlessly. Come then, let be; I am astonied, O captain of hosts.'

And to him answered Achilles fleet of foot: 'So be it, heaven-sprung Skamandros, even as thou biddest. But the proud Trojans I will not cease from slaying until I have driven them into their city, and have made trial with Hector face to face whether he is to vanquish me or I him.'

Thus saying, he set upon the Trojans, like a god. Then unto Apollo spake the deepeddying River: 'Out on it, lord of the silver bow, child of Zeus, thou hast not kept the ordinance of Kronos' son, who charged thee straitly to stand by the Trojans and to help them, until eve come with light late-setting, and darken the deep-soiled earth.'

He said, and spear-famed Achilles sprang from the bank and leapt into his midst; but he rushed on him in a furious wave, and stirred up all his streams in tumult, and swept down the many dead who lay thick in him, slain by Achilles; these out to land he cast with bellowing like a bull, and saved the living under his fair streams, hiding them within eddies deep and wide. But terribly around Achilles arose his tumultuous wave, and the stream smote violently against his shield, nor availed he to stand firm upon his feet. Then he grasped a tall fair-grown elm, and it fell uprooted and tore away ail the bank, and reached over the fair river bed with its thick shoots, and stemmed the River himself, falling all within him: and Achilles, struggling out of the eddy, made haste to fly over the plain with his swift feet, for he was afraid. But the great god ceased not, but arose upon him with darkness on his crest, that he might stay noble Achilles from slaughter, and ward destruction from the men of Troy. And the son of Peleus rushed away a spear's throw, with the swoop of a black eagle, the mighty hunter, strongest at once and swiftest of winged birds. Like him he sped, and on his breast the bronze rang terribly as he fled from beneath the onset, and behind him the River rushed on with a mighty roar. As when a field-waterer from a dark spring leadeth water along a bed through crops and garden grounds, a mattock in his hands, casting forth hindrances from the ditch, and as it floweth all pebbles are swept down, and swiftly gliding it murmureth down a sloping place, and outrunneth him that is its guide: – thus ever the river wave caught up Achilles for all his speed; for gods are mightier than men. For whensoever fleet-footed noble Achilles struggled to stand against it, and know whether all immortals be upon him who inhabit spacious heaven, then would a great wave of the heaven-sprung River beat upon his shoulders from above, and he sprang upward with his feet, sore vexed at heart; and the River was wearying his knees with violent rush beneath, and devouring the earth from under his feet. Then the son of Peleus cried aloud, looking up to the broad heaven: 'Zeus, Father, how doth none of the gods take it on him in pity to save me from the River I after that let come to me what may. None other of the inhabitants of Heaven is chargeable so much, but only my dear mother, who beguiled me with false words, saying that under the wall of the mail-clad men of Troy I must die by the swift arrows of Apollo. Would that Hector had slain me, the best of men bred here: then brave had been the slayer, and a brave man had he slain. But now by a sorry death am I doomed to die, pent in this mighty river, like a swineherd boy whom a torrent sweepeth down as he essayeth to cross it in a storm.'

Thus spake he, and quickly Poseidon and Athene came near and stood beside him, in the likeness of men, and taking his hands in theirs pledged him in words. And the first that spake was Poseidon, Shaker of the earth: 'Son of Peleus, tremble not, neither be afraid; such helpers of thee are we from the gods, approved of Zeus, even Pallas Athene and I, for to be vanquished of a river is not appointed thee, but he will soon give back, and thou wilt thyself perceive it: but we will give thee wise counsel, if thou wilt obey it; hold not thy hand from hazardous battle until within Ilios' famous walls thou have pent the Trojan host, even all that flee before thee. But do thou, when thou hast taken the life of Hector, go back unto the ships; this glory we give unto thee to win.'

They having thus spoken departed to the immortals, but he toward the plain – for the bidding of gods was strong upon him – went onward; and all the plain was filled with water-flood, and many beautiful arms and corpses of slain youths were drifting there. So upward sprang his knees as he rushed against the stream right on, nor stayed him the wide-flowing River, for Athene put great strength in him. Neither did Skamandros slacken his fierceness, but yet more raged against the son of Peleus, and he curled crestwise the billow of his stream, lifting himself on high, and on Simoeis he called with a shout: 'Dear brother, the strength of this man let us both join to stay, since quickly he will lay waste the great city of king Priam, and the Trojans abide not in the battle. Help me with speed, and fill thy streams with water from thy springs, and urge on all thy torrents, and raise up a great wave, and stir huge roaring of tree-stumps and stones, that we may stay the fierce man who now is lording it, and deeming himself match for gods. For neither, I ween, will strength avail him, nor comeliness anywise, nor that armour beautiful, which deep beneath the flood shall be o'erlaid with slime, and himself I will wrap him in my sands and pour round him countless shingle without stint, nor shall the Achaians know where to gather his bones, so vast a shroud of silt will I heap over them. Where he dieth there shall be his tomb, neither shall he have need of any barrow to be raised, when the Achaians make his funeral.'

He said, and rushed in tumult on Achilles, raging from on high, thundering with foam and blood and bodies of dead men. Then did a dark wave of the heaven-sprung River stand towering up and would overwhelm the son of Peleus. But Hera cried aloud in terror for Achilles, lest the great deep-eddying River sweep him away, and straightway she called to Hephaistos, her dear son: 'Rise, lame god, O my son; it was against thee we thought that eddying Xanthos was matched in fight. Help with all speed, put forth large blast of flame. Then will I go to raise a strong storm out of the sea of the west wind and the white south which shall utterly consume the dead Trojans and their armour, blowing the angry flame. Thou along Xanthos' banks bum up his trees and wrap himself in fire, nor let him anywise turn thee back by soft words or by threat, nor stay thy rage – only when I cry to thee with my voice, then hold the unwearying fire.'

Thus spake she, and Hephaistos made ready fierceblazing fire. First on the plain fire blazed, and burnt the many dead who lay there thick, slain by Achilles; and all the plain was parched and the bright water stayed And as when in late summer the north wind swiftly parcheth a new watered orchard, and he that tilleth it is glad, thus was the whole plain parched, and Hephaistos consumed the dead; then against the river he turned his gleaming flame. Elms burnt and willow-trees and tamarisks, and lotos burnt and rush and galingale, which round the fair streams of the river grew in multitude. And the eels and fishes beneath the eddies were afflicted, which through the fair streams tumbled this way and that, in anguish at the blast of crafty Hephaistos And the strong River bumed, and spake and called to him by name: 'Hephaistos, there is no god can match with thee, nor will I fight thee thus ablaze with fire. Cease strife, yea, let noble Achilles drive the Trojans forthwith out of their city; what have I to do with strife and succour?'

Thus spake he, burnt with fire, for his fair streams were bubbling. And as a caldron boileth within, beset with much fire, melting the lard of some fatted hog spurting up on all sides, and logs of firewood lie thereunder, – so burned his fair streams in the fire, and the water boiled. He had no mind to flow, but refrained him, for the breath of cunning Hephaistos violently afflicted him. Then unto Hera, earnestly beseeching her, he spake winged words: 'Hera, wherefore hath thy son assailed my stream to vex it above others? I am less chargeable than all the rest that are helpers of the Trojans. But lo, I will give over, if thou wilt, and let thy son give over too. And I further will swear even this, that never will I ward the day of evil from the Trojans, not even when all Troy is burning in the blaze of hungry fire, and the warlike sons of Achaians are the burners thereof.'

Then when the white-armed goddess Hera heard his speech, straightway she spake unto Hephaistos her dear son: 'Hephaistos, hold, famed son; it befitteth not thus for mortals' sake to do violence to an immortal god.'

Thus said she and Hephaistos quenched the fierce-blazing fire, and the wave once more rolled down the fair river-bed.

So when the rage of Xanthos was overcome, both ceased, for Hera stayed them, though in wrath. But among the other gods fell grievous bitter strife, and their hearts were carried diverse in their breasts. And they clashed together with a great noise, and the wide earth groaned, and the clarion of great Heaven rang around. Zeus heard as he sate upon Olympus, and his heart within him laughed pleasant]y when he beheld that strife of gods. Then no longer stood they asunder, for Ares piercer of shields began the battle and first made for Athene with his bronze spear, and spake a taunting word: 'Wherefore, O dogfly, dost thou match gods with gods in strife, with stormy daring, as thy great spirit moveth thee? Rememberest thou not how thou movedst Diomedes Tydeus' son to wound me, and thyself didst take a visible spear and thrust it straight at me and pierce through my fair skin? Therefore deem I now that thou shalt pay me for all that thou hast done.'

Thus saying he smote on the dread tasselled aegis that not even the lightning of Zeus can overcome – thereon smote bloodstained Ares with his long spear. But she, giving back, grasped with stout hand a stone that lay upon the plain, black, rugged, huge, which men of old time set to be the landmark of a field; this hurled she, and smote impetuous Ares on the neck, and unstrung his limbs. Seven roods he covered in his fall, and soiled his hair with dust, and his armour rang upon him. And Pallas Athene laughed, and spake to him winged words exultingly: 'Fool, not even yet hast thou learnt how far better than thou I claim to be, that thus thou matchest thy might with mine. Thus shalt thou satisfy thy mother's curses, who deviseth mischief against thee in her wrath, for that thou hast left the Achaians and givest the proud Trojans aid.'

Thus having said she turned from him her shining eyes. Him did Aphrodite daughter of Zeus take by the hand and lead away, groaning continually, for scarce gathered he his spirit back to him. But when the white-armed goddess Hera was aware of them, straightway she spake unto Athene winged words: 'Out on it, child of aegis-bearing Zeus, maiden invincible, lo there the dogfly is leading Ares destroyer of men out of the fray of battle down the throng – nay then, pursue her.'

She said, and Athene sped after her with heart exultant, and made at her and smote her with stout hand upon the breast, and straightway her knees and heart were unstrung. So they twain lay on the bounteous earth, and she spake winged words exultingly: 'Such let all be who give the Trojans aid when they fight against the mailed Argives. Be they even so bold and brave as Aphrodite when she came to succour Ares and defied my might. Then should we long ago have ceased from war, having laid waste the stablished citadel of Ilios.'

[She said, and the white-armed goddess Hera smiled.] Then to Apollo spake the earth-shaking lord: 'Phoebus, why stand we apart? It befitteth not after the rest have begun: that were the more shameful if without fighting we should go to Olympus to the bronze-thresholded house of Zeus. Begin, for thou art younger; it were not meet for me, since I was born first and know more. Fond god, how foolish is thy heart! Thou rememberest not all the ills we twain alone of gods endured at Ilios, when by ordinance of Zeus we came to proud Laomedon and served him through a year for promised recompense, and he laid on us his commands. I round their city built the Trojans a wall, wide and most fair, that the city might be unstormed, and thou, Phoebus, didst herd shambling crook-horned kine among the spurs of woody many-folded Ida. But when the joyous seasons were accomplishing the term of hire, then redoubtable Laomedon robbed us of all hire, and sent us off with threats. He threatened that he would bind together our feet and hands and sell us into far-off isles, and the ears of both of us he vowed to shear off with the sword. So we went home with angry hearts, wroth for the hire he promised and gave us not. To his folk now thou showest favour, nor essayest with us how the proud Trojans may be brought low and perish miserably with their children and noble wives.'

Then to him answered King Apollo the Far-darter: 'Shaker of the earth, of no sound mind wouldst thou repute me if I should fight against thee for the sake of pitiful mortals, who like unto leaves now live in glowing life, consuming the fruit of the earth, and now again pine into death. Let us with all speed cease from combat, and let them do battle by themselves.'

Thus saying he turned away, for he felt shame to deal in blows with his father's brother. But his sister upbraided him sore, the queen of wild beasts, huntress Artemis, and spake a taunting word: 'So then thou fleëst, Far-darter, and hast quite yielded to Poseidon the victory, and given him glory for naught! Fond god, why bearest thou an ineffectual bow in vain? Let me not hear thee again in the halls of our sire boast as before among the immortal gods that thou wouldst stand up to fight against Poseidon.'

Thus spake she, but far-darting Apollo answered her not. But angrily the noble spouse of Zeus [upbraided the Archer Queen with taunting words:] 'How now art thou fain, bold vixen, to set thyself against me? Hard were it for thee to match my might, bow-bearer though thou art, since against women Zeus made thee a lion, and giveth thee to slay whomso of them thou wilt. Truly it is better on the mountains to slay wild beasts and deer than to fight amain with mightier than thou. But if thou wilt, try war, that thou mayest know well how far stronger am I, since thou matchest thy might with mine.'

She said, and with her left hand caught both the other's hands by the wrist, and with her right took the bow from off her shoulders, and therewith, smiling, beat her on the ears as she turned this way and that; and the swift arrows fell out of her quiver. And weeping from before her the goddess fled like a dove that from before a falcon flieth to a hollow rock, a cleft – for she was not fated to be caught; – thus Artemis fled weeping, and left her bow and arrows where they lay. Then to Leto spake the Guide, the slayer of Argus: 'Leto, with thee will I no wise fight; a grievous thing it is to come to blows with wives of cloud-gathering Zeus; but boast to thy heart's content among the immortal gods that thou didst vanquish me by might and main.'

Thus said he, and Leto gathered up the curved bow and arrows fallen hither and thither amid the whirl of dust: so taking her daughter's bow she went back. And the maiden came to Olympus, to the bronze-thresholded house of Zeus, and weeping set herself on her father's knee, while round her her divine vesture quivered: and her father, Kronos' son, took her to him and asked of her, laughing gently: 'Who of the inhabitants of heaven, dear child, hath dealt with thee thus [hastily, as though thou hadst been doing some wrong thing openly]?'

And to him in answer spake the fair-crowned queen of the echoing chase: 'It was thy wife that buffeted me, father, the white-armed Hera, from whom are strife and contention come upon the immortals.'

Thus talked they unto one another. Then Phoebus Apollo entered into sacred Ilios, for he was troubled for the wall of the well-built city, lest the Danaans waste it before its hour upon that day. But the other ever-living gods went to Olympus, some angry and some greatly triumphing, and sat down beside Zeus who hideth himself in dark clouds.

Now Achilles was still slaying the Trojans, both themselves and their whole-hooved horses. And as when a smoke goeth up to the broad heaven, when a city burneth, kindled by the wrath of gods, and causeth toil to all, and griefs to many, thus caused Achilles toil and griefs to the Trojans. And the old man Priam stood on the sacred tower, and was aware of dread Achilles, how before him the Trojans thronged in rout, nor was any succour found of them. Then with a cry he went down from the tower, to rouse the gallant warders along the walls: 'Hold open the gates in your hands until the folk come to the city in their rout, for closely is Achilles chasing them – now trow I there will be deadly deeds. But when they are gathered within the wall and are taking breath, then again shut back the gate-wings firmly builded; for I fear lest that murderous man spring in within the wall.'

Thus spake he, and they opened the gates and thrust back the bolts; and the gates flung back gave safety. Then Apollo leapt forth to the front that he might ward destruction from the Trojans. They straight for the city and the high wall were fleeing, parched with thirst and dust-grimed from the plain, and Achilles chased them vehemently with his spear, for strong frenzy possessed his heart continually, and he thirsted to win him renown. Then would the sons of the Achaians have taken high-gated Troy, had not Phoebus Apollo aroused goodly Agenor, Antenor's son, a princely man and a strong. In his heart he put good courage, and himself stood by his side that he might ward off the grievous visitations of death, leaning against the oak, and he was shrouded in thick mist. So when Agenor was aware of Achilles waster of cities, he halted, and his heart much wavered as he stood; and in trouble he spake to his great heart: 'Ay me, if I flee before mighty Achilles, there where the rest are driven terror-struck, nathless will he overtake me and slaughter me as a coward. Or what if I leave these to be driven before Achilles the son of Peleus, and flee upon my feet from the wall by another way to the Ileian plain, until I come to the spurs of Ida, and hide me in the underwood? So then at evening, having bathed in the river and refreshed me of sweat, I might return to Ilios. Nay, why doth mg heart debate thus within me? Lest he might be aware of me as I get me from the city for the plain, and speeding after overtake me with swift feet; then will it no more be possible to avoid the visitation of death, for he is exceeding mighty above all mankind. What then if in front of the city I go forth to meet him? Surely his flesh too is penetrable by sharp bronze, and there is but one life within, and men say he is mortal, howbeit Zeus the son of Kronos giveth him renown.'

Thus saying, he gathered himself to await Achilles, and within him his stout heart was set to strive and fight. As a leopardess goeth forth from a deep thicket to affront a huntsman, nor is afraid at heart, nor fleeth when she heareth the bay of hounds; for albeit the man first smite her with thrust or throw, yet even pierced through with the spear she ceaseth not from her courage until she either grapple or be slain, so noble Antenor's son, goodly Agenor, refused to flee till he should put Achilles to the proof, but held before him the circle of his shield, and aimed at him with his spear, and cried aloud: 'Doubtless thou hopest in thy heart, noble Achilles, on this day to sack the city of the proud men of Troy. Fond man, there shall many woful things yet be wrought before it, for within it we are many men and staunch, who in front of our parents dear and wives and sons keep Ilios safe; but thou shalt here meet death, albeit so redoubtable and bold a man of war.'

He said, and hurled his sharp spear with weighty hand, and smote him on the leg beneath the knee, nor missed his mark, and the greave of new-wrought tin rang terribly on him; but the bronze bounded back from him it smote, nor pierced him, for the god's gift drave it back. Then the son of Peleus in his turn made at god-like Agenor, but Apollo suffered him not to win renown, but caught away Agenor, and shrouded him in thick mist, and sent him in peace to be gone out of the war. Then by wile he kept the son of Peleus away from the folk, for in complete semblance of Agenor himself he stood before the feet of Achilles, who hasted to run upon him and chase him. And while he chased him over the wheat-bearing plain, edging him toward the deepeddying river Skamandros, as he ran but a little in front of him (for by wile Apollo beguiled him that he kept ever hoping to overtake him in the race), meantime the other Trojans in common rout came gladly unto their fastness, and the city was filled with the throng of them. Neither had they heart to await one another outside the city and wall, and to know who might have escaped and who had perished in the fight, but impetuously they poured into the city, whomsoever of them his feet and knees might save.

BOOK XXII

How Achilles fought with Hector, and slew him, and brought
his body to the ships.

THUS THEY THROUGHOUT THE CITY, scared like fawns, were cooling their sweat and drinking and slaking their thirst, leaning on the fair battlements, while the Achaians drew near the wall, setting shields to shoulders. But Hector deadly fate bound to abide in his place, in front of Ilios and the Skaian gates. Then to the son of Peleus spake Phoebus Apollo: 'Wherefore, son of Peleus, pursuest thou me with swift feet, thyself being mortal and I a deathless god? Thou hast not even yet known me, that I am a god, but strivest vehemently. Truly thou regardest not thy task among the affliction of the Trojans whom thou affrightedst, who now are gathered into the city, while thou hast wandered hither. Me thou wilt never slay, for I am not subject unto death.'

Then mightily moved spake unto him Achilles fleet of foot: 'Thou hast baulked me, Far-darter, most mischievous of all the gods, in that thou hast turned me hither from the wall: else should full many yet have bitten the dust or ever within Ilios had they come. Now hast thou robbed me of great renown, and lightly hast saved them, because thou hadst no vengeance to fear thereafter. Verily I would avenge me on thee, had I but the power.'

Thus saying toward the city he was gone in pride of heart, rushing like some victorious horse in a chariot, that runneth lightly at full speed over the plain; so swiftly plied Achilles his feet and knees. Him the old man Priam first beheld as he sped across the plain, blazing as the star that cometh forth at harvest-time, and plain seen his rays shine forth amid the host of stars in the darkness of night, the star whose name men call Orion's Dog. Brightest of all is he, yet for an evil sign is he set, and bringeth much fever upon hapless men. Even so on Achilles' breast the bronze gleamed as he ran. And the old man cried aloud and beat upon his head with his hands, raising them on high, and with a cry called aloud beseeching his dear son; for he before the gates was standing, all hot for battle with Achilles. And the old man spake piteously unto him, stretching forth his hands: 'Hector, beloved son, I pray thee await not this man alone with none beside thee, lest thou quickly meet thy doom, slain by the son of Peleus, since he is mightier far, a merciless man. Would the gods loved him even as do I! then quickly would dogs and vultures devour him on the field – thereby would cruel pain go from my heart – the man who hath bereft me of many valiant sons, slaying them and selling them captive into far-off isles. Ay even now twain of my children, Lykaon and Polydoros, I cannot see among the Trojans that throng into the fastness, sons whom Laothoe bare me, a princess among women. If they be yet alive amid the enemy's host, then will we ransom them with bronze and gold, for there is store within, for much goods gave the old man famous Altes to his child. If they be dead, then even in the house of Hades[1] shall they be a sorrow to my soul and to their mother, even to us who gave them birth, but to the rest of the folk a briefer sorrow, if but thou die not by Achilles' hand. Nay, come within the wall, my child, that thou preserve the men and women of Troy, neither give great triumph to the son of Peleus, and be thyself bereft of sweet life. Have compassion also on me, the helpless one, who still can feel, ill-fated; whom the father, Kronos' son, will bring to nought by a grievous doom in the path of old age, having seen full many ills, his sons perishing and his daughters carried away captive, and his chambers laid waste and infant children hurled to the ground in terrible war, and his sons' wives dragged away by the ruinous hands of the Achaians. Myself then last of all at the street door will ravening dogs tear, when some one by stroke or throw of the sharp bronze hath bereft my limbs of life even the dogs I reared in my halls about my table and to guard my door, which then having drunk my blood, maddened at heart shall lie in the gateway. A young man all beseemeth, even to be slain in war, to be torn by the sharp bronze and lie on the field; though he be dead yet is all honourable to him, whate'er be seen: but when dogs defile the hoary head and hoary beard and the secret parts of an old man slain, this is the most piteous thing that cometh upon hapless men.'

Thus spake the old man, and grasped his hoary hairs, plucking them from his head, but he persuaded not Hector's soul. Then his mother in her turn wailed tearfully, loosening the folds of her robe, while with the other hand she showed her breast; and through her tears spake to him winged words: 'Hector, my child, have regard unto this bosom and pity me, if ever I gave thee consolation of my breast. Think of it, dear child, and from this side the wall drive back the foe, nor stand in front to meet him. He is merciless; if he slay thee it will not be on a bed that I or thy wife wooed with many gifts shall bewail thee, my own dear child, but far away from us by the ships of the Argives will swift dogs devour thee.'

Thus they with wailing spake to their dear son, beseeching him sore, yet they persuaded not Hector's soul, but he stood awaiting Achilles as he drew nigh in giant might. As a serpent of the mountains upon his den awaiteth a man, having fed on evil poisons, and fell wrath hath entered into him, and terribly he glareth as he coileth himself about his den, so Hector with courage unquenchable gave not back, leaning his shining shield against a jutting tower. Then sore troubled he spake to his great heart: 'Ay me, if I go within the gates and walls, Polydamas will be first to bring reproach against me, since he bade me lead the Trojans to the city during this ruinous night, when noble Achilles arose. But I regarded him not, yet surely it had been better far. And now that I have undone the host by my wantonness, I am ashamed before the men of Troy and women of trailing robes, lest at any time some worse man than I shall say: "Hector by trusting his own might undid the host." So will they speak; then to me would it be better far to face Achilles and either slay him and go home, or myself die gloriously before the city. Or what if I lay down my bossy shield and my stout helm, and lean my spear against the wall, and go of myself to meet noble Achilles and promise him that Helen, and with her all possessions that Alexandros brought in hollow ships to Troy, the beginning of strife, we will give to the sons of Atreus to take away, and therewithal to divide in half with the Achaians all else that this city holdeth: and if thereafter I obtain from the Trojans an oath of the Elders that they will hide nothing but divide all in twain [whatever wealth the pleasant city hold within]? But where fore doth my heart debate thus? I might come unto him and he would not pity or regard me at all, but presently slay me unarmed as it were but a woman, if I put off my armour. No time is it now to dally with him from oaktree or from rock, like youth with maiden, as youth and maiden hold dalliance one with another. Better is it to join battle with all speed: let us know upon which of us twain the Olympian shall bestow renown.'

Thus pondered he as he stood, but nigh on him came Achilles, peer of Enyalios warrior of the waving helm, brandishing from his right shoulder the Pelian ash, his terrible spear; and all around the bronze on him flashed like the gleam of blazing fire or of the Sun as he ariseth. And trembling seized Hector as he was aware of him, nor endured he to abide in his place, but left the gates behind him and fled in fear. And the son of Peleus darted after him, trusting in his swift feet. As a falcon upon the mountains, swiftest of winged things, swoopeth fleetly after a trembling dove; and she before him fleeth, while he with shrill screams hard at hand still darteth at her, for his heart urgeth him to seize her; so Achilles in hot haste flew straight for him, and Hector fled beneath the Trojans' wall, and plied swift knees. They past the watch-place and wind-waved wild figtree sped ever, away from under the wall, along the waggon-track, and came to the two fair-flowing springs, where two fountains rise that feed deep-eddying Skamandros. The one floweth with warm water, and smoke goeth up therefrom around as it were from a blazing fire, while the other even in summer floweth forth like cold hail or snow or ice that water formeth. And there beside the springs are broad washing-troughs hard by, fair troughs of stone, where wives and fair daughters of the men of Troy were wont to wash bright raiment, in the old time of peace, before the sons of the Achaians came. Thereby they ran, he flying, he pursuing. Valiant was the flier but far mightier he who fleetly pursued him. For not for beast of sacrifice or for an oxhide were they striving, such as are prizes for men's speed of foot, but for the life of horse-taming Hector was their race. And as when victorious wholehooved horses run rapidly round the turning-points, and some great prize lieth in sight, be it a tripod or a woman, in honour of a man that is dead, so thrice around Priam's city circled those twain with flying feet, and all the gods were gazing on them. Then among them spake first the father of gods and men: 'Ay me, a man beloved I see pursued around the wall. My heart is woe for Hector, who hath burnt for me many thighs of oxen amid the crests of many-folded Ida, and other times on the city-height; but now is goodly Achilles pursuing him with swift feet round Priam's town. Come, give your counsel, gods, and devise whether we shall save him from death or now at last slay him, valiant though he be, by the hand of Achilles Peleus' son.'

Then to him answered the bright-eyed goddess Athene: 'O Father, Lord of the bright lightning and the dark cloud, what is this thou hast said? A man that is a mortal, doomed long ago by fate, wouldst thou redeem back from ill-boding death? Do it, but not all we other gods approve.'

And unto her in answer spake cloud-gathering Zeus: 'Be of good cheer, Trito-born, dear child: not in full earnest speak I, and I would fain be kind to thee. Do as seemeth good to thy mind, and draw not back.'

Thus saying he roused Athene, that already was set thereon, and from the crests of Olympus she darted down.

But after Hector sped fleet Achilles chasing him vehemently. And as when on the mountains a hound hunteth the fawn of a deer, having started it from its covert, through glens and glades, and if it crouch to baffle him under a bush, yet scenting it out the hound runneth constantly until he find it; so Hector baffled not Peleus' fleet-footed son. Of, as he set himself to dart under the well built walls over against the Dardanian gates, if haply from above they might succour him with darts, so oft would Achilles gain on him and turn him toward the plain, while himself he sped ever on the cityside. And as in a dream one faileth in chase of a flying man – the one faileth in his flight and the other in his chase – so failed Achilles to overtake him in the race, and Hector to escape. And thus[1] would Hector have avoided the visitation of death, had not this time been utterly the last wherein Apollo came nigh to him, who nerved his strength and his swift knees. For to the host did noble Achilles sign with his head, and forbade them to hurl bitter darts against Hector, lest any smiting him should gain renown, and he himself come second. But when the fourth time they had reached the springs, then the Father hung his golden balances, and set therein two lots of dreary death, one of Achilles, one of horse-taming Hector, and held them by the midst and poised. Then Hector's fated day sank down, and fell to the house of Hades, and Phoebus Apollo left him. But to Peleus' son came the bright-eyed goddess Athene, and standing near spake to him winged words: 'Now verily, glorious Achilles dear to Zeus, I have hope that we twain shall carry off great glory to the ships for the Achaians, having slain Hector, for all his thirst for fight. No longer is it possible for him to escape us, not even though far-darting Apollo should travail sore, grovelling before the Father, aegis-bearing Zeus. But do thou now stand and take breath, and I will go and persuade this man to confront thee in fight.'

Thus spake Athene, and he obeyed, and was glad at heart, and stood leaning on his bronze-pointed ashen-spear. And she left him and came to noble Hector, like unto Deiphobos in shape and in strong voice, and standing near spake to him winged words: 'Dear brother, verily fleet Achilles doth thee violence, chasing thee round Priam's town with swift feet: but come let us make a stand and await him on our defence.'

Then answered her great Hector of the glancing helm: 'Deipho-

---

[1] Reading τώς, Düntzer's conjecture for τῶς of MSS.

bos, verily aforetime wert thou far dearest of my brothers, whom Hekabe and Priam gendered, but now methinks I shall honour thee even more, in that thou hast dared for my sake, when thou sawest me, to come forth of the wall, while the others tarry within.'

Then to him again spake the bright-eyed goddess Athene: 'Dear brother, of a truth my father and lady mother and my comrades around besought me much, entreating me in turn, to tarry there, so greatly do they all tremble before him; but my heart within was sore with dismal grief And now fight we with straight-set resolve and let there be no sparing of spears, that we may know whether Achilles is to slay us and carry our bloody spoils to the hollow ships, or whether he might be vanquished by thy spear.'

Thus saying Athene in her subtlety led him on. And when they were come nigh in onset on one another, to Achilles first spake great Hector of the glancing helm: 'No longer, son of Peleus, will I fly thee, as before I thrice ran round the great town of Priam, and endured not to await thy onset. Now my heart biddeth me stand up against thee; I will either slay or be slain. But come hither and let us pledge us by our gods, for they shall be best witnesses and beholders of covenants: I will entreat thee in no outrageous sort, if Zeus grant me to outstay thee, and if I take thy life, but when I have despoiled thee of thy glorious armour, O Achilles, I will give back thy dead body to the Achaians, and do thou the same.'

But unto him with grim gaze spake Achilles fleet of foot: 'Hector, talk not to me, thou madman, of covenants. As between men and lions there is no pledge of faith, nor wolves and sheep can be of one mind, but imagine evil continually against each other, so is it impossible for thee and me to be friends, neither shall be any pledge between us until one or other shall have fallen and glutted with blood Ares, the stubborn god of war. Bethink thee of all thy soldier-ship: now behoveth it thee to quit thee as a good spearman and valiant man of war. No longer is there way of escape for thee, but Pallas Athene will straightway subdue thee to my spear; and now in one hour shalt thou pay back for all my sorrows for my friends whom thou hast slain in the fury of thy spear.'

He said, and poised his far-shadowing spear and hurled. And noble Hector watched the coming thereof and avoided it; for with his eye on it he crouched, and the bronze spear flew over him, and fixed itself in the earth; but Pallas Athene caught it up and gave it back to Achilles, unknown of Hector shepherd of hosts. Then Hector spake unto the noble son of Peleus: 'Thou hast missed, so no wise yet, godlike Achilles, hast thou known from Zeus the hour of my doom, though thou thoughtest it. Cunning of tongue art thou and a deceiver in speech, that fearing thee I might forget my valour and strength. Not as I flee shalt thou plant thy spear in my reins, but drive it straight through my breast as I set on thee, if God hath given thee to do it. Now in thy turn avoid my spear of bronze. O that thou mightst take it all into thy flesh! Then would the war be lighter to the Trojans, if but thou wert dead, for thou art their greatest bane.'

He said, and poised his long-shadowed spear and hurled it, and smote the midst of the shield of Peleus' son, and missed him not: but far from the shield the spear leapt back. And Hector was wroth that his swift weapon had left his hand in vain, and he stood downcast, for he had no second ashen spear. And he called with a loud shout to Deiphobos of the white shield, and asked of him a long spear, but he was no wise nigh. Then Hector knew the truth in his heart, and spake and said: 'Ay me, now verily the gods have summoned me to death. I deemed the warrior Deiphobos was by my side, but he is within the wall, and it was Athene who played me false. Now therefore is evil death come very nigh me, not far off, nor is there way of escape. This then was from of old the pleasure of Zeus and of the far-darting son of Zeus, who yet before were fain to succour me: but now my fate hath found me. At least let me not die without a struggle or ingloriously, but in some great deed of arms whereof men yet to be born shall hear.'

Thus saying he drew his sharp sword that by his flank hung great and strong, and gathered himself and swooped like a soaring eagle that darteth to the plain through the dark clouds to seize a tender lamb or crouching hare. So Hector swooped, brandishing his sharp sword. And Achilles made at him, for his heart was filled with wild fierceness, and before his breast he made a covering with his fair graven shield, and tossed his bright four-plated helm; and round it waved fair golden plumes [that Hephaistos had set thick about the crest.] As a star goeth among stars in the darkness of night, Hesperos, fairest of all stars set in heaven, so flashed there forth a light from the keen spear Achilles poised in his right hand, devising mischief against noble Hector, eyeing his fair flesh to find the fittest place. Now for the rest of him his flesh was covered by the fair bronze armour he stripped from strong Patroklos when he slew him, but there was an opening where the collar bones coming from the shoulders clasp the neck, even at the gullet, where destruction of life cometh quickliest; there, as he came on, noble Achilles drave at him with his spear, and right through the tender neck went the point. Yet the bronze-weighted ashen spear clave not the windpipe, so that he might yet speak words of answer to his foe. And he fell down in the dust, and noble Achilles spake exultingly: 'Hector, thou thoughtest, whilst thou wert spoiling Patroklos, that thou wouldst be safe, and didst reck nothing of me who was afar, thou fool. But away among the hollow ships his comrade, a mightier far, even I, was left behind, who now have unstrung thy knees. Thee shall dogs and birds tear foully, but his funeral shall the Achaians make.'

Then with faint breath spake unto him Hector of the glancing helm: 'I pray thee by thy life and knees and parents leave me not for dogs of the Achaians to devour by the ships, but take good store of bronze and gold, gifts that my father and lady mother shall give to thee, and give them home my body back again, that the Trojans and Trojans' wives give me my due of fire after my death.'

But unto him with grim gaze spake Achilles fleet of foot: 'Entreat me not, dog, by knees or parents. Would that my heart's desire could so bid me myself to carve and eat raw thy flesh, for the evil thou hast wrought me, as surely is there none that shall keep the dogs from thee, not even should they bring ten or twenty fold ransom and here weigh it out, and promise even more, not even were Priam Dardanos' son to bid pay thy weight in gold, not even so shall thy lady mother lay thee on a bed to mourn her son, but dogs and birds shall devour thee utterly.'

Then dying spake unto him Hector of the glancing helm: 'Verily I know thee and behold thee as thou art, nor was I destined to persuade thee; truly thy heart is iron in thy breast. Take heed now lest I draw upon thee wrath of gods, in the day when Paris and Phoebus Apollo slay thee, for all thy valour, at the Skaian gate.'

He ended, and the shadow of death came down upon him, and his soul flew forth of his limbs and was gone to the house of Hades, wailing her fate, leaving her vigour and youth. Then to the dead man spake noble Achilles: 'Die: for my death, I will accept it whensoever Zeus and the other immortal gods are minded to accomplish it.'

He said, and from the corpse drew forth his bronze spear, and set it aside, and stripped the bloody armour from the shoulders. And other sons of Achaians ran up around, who gazed upon the stature and marvellous goodliness of Hector. Nor did any stand by but wounded him, and thus would many a man say looking toward his neighbour: 'Go to, of a truth far easier to handle is Hector now than when he burnt the ships with blazing fire.' Thus would many a man say, and wound him as he stood hard by. And when fleet noble

Achilles had despoiled him, he stood up among the Achaians and spake winged words: 'Friends, chiefs and counsellors of the Argives, since the gods have vouchsafed us to vanquish this man who hath done us more evil than all the rest together, come let us make trial in arms round about the city, that we may know somewhat of the Trojans' purpose, whether since he hath fallen they will forsake the citadel, or whether they are minded to abide, albeit Hector is no more. But wherefore doth my heart debate thus? There lieth by the ships a dead man unbewailed, unburied, Patroklos; him will I not forget, while I abide among the living and my knees can stir. Nay if even in the house of Hades the dead forget their dead, yet will I even there be mindful of my dear comrade. But come, ye sons of the Achaians, let us now, singing our song of victory, go back to the hollow ships and take with us our foe. Great glory have we won; we have slain the noble Hector, unto whom the Trojans prayed throughout their city, as he had been a god.'

He said, and devised foul entreatment of noble Hector. The tendons of both feet behind he slit from heel to anklejoint, and thrust therethrough thongs of ox-hide, and bound him to his chariot, leaving his head to trail. And when he had mounted the chariot and lifted therein the famous armour, he lashed his horses to speed, and they nothing loth flew on. And dust rose around him that was dragged, and his dark hair flowed loose on either side, and in the dust lay all his once fair head, for now had Zeus given him over to his foes to entreat foully in his own native land.

Thus was his head all grimed with dust. But his mother when she beheld her son, tore her hair and cast far from her her shining veil, and cried aloud with an exceeding bitter cry. And piteously moaned his father, and around them the folk fell to crying and moaning throughout the town. Most like it seemed as though all beetling Ilios were burning utterly in fire. Scarcely could the folk keep back the old man in his hot desire to get him forth of the Dardanian gates. For he besought them all, casting himself down in the mire, and calling on each man by his name: 'Hold, friends, and though you love me leave me to get me forth of the city alone and go unto the ships of the Achaians. Let me pray this accursed horror-working man, if haply he may feel shame before his age-fellows and pity an old man. He also hath a father such as I am, Peleus, who begat and reared him to be a bane of Trojans – and most of all to me hath he brought woe. So many sons of mine hath he slain in their flower – yet for all my sorrow for the rest I mourn them all less than this one alone, for whom my sharp grief will bring me down to the house of

Hades – even Hector. Would that he had died in my arms; then would we have wept and wailed our fill, his mother who bore him to her ill hap, and I myself.'

Thus spake he wailing, and all the men of the city made moan with him. And among the women of Troy, Hekabe led the wild lament: 'My child, ah, woe is me! wherefore should I live in my pain, now thou art dead, who night and day wert my boast through the city, and blessing to all, both men and women of Troy throughout the town, who hailed thee as a god, for verily an exceeding glory to them wert thou in thy life: – now death and fate have overtaken thee.'

Thus spake she wailing. But Hector's wife knew not as yet, for no true messenger had come to tell her how her husband abode without the gates, but in an inner chamber of the lofty house she was weaving a double purple web, and broidering therein manifold flowers. Then she called to her goodly-haired handmaids through the house to set a great tripod on the fire, that Hector might have warm washing when he came home out of the battle – fond heart, and was unaware how, far from all washings, bright-eyed Athene had slain him by the hand of Achilles. But she heard shrieks and groans from the battlements, and her limbs reeled, and the shuttle fell from her hands to earth. Then again among her goodly-haired maids she spake: 'Come two of ye this way with me that I may see what deeds are done. It was the voice of my husband's noble mother that I heard, and in my own breast my heart leapeth to my mouth and my knees are numbed beneath me: surely some evil thing is at band against the children of Priam. Would that such word might never reach my ear! yet terribly I dread lest noble Achilles have cut off bold Hector from the city by himself and chased him to the plain and ere this ended his perilous pride that possessed him, for never would he tarry among the throng of men but ran out before them far, yielding place to no man in his hardihood.'

Thus saying she sped through the chamber like one mad, with beating heart, and with her went her handmaidens. But when she came to the battlements and the throng of men, she stood still upon the wall and gazed, and beheld him dragged before the city: – swift horses dragged him recklessly toward the hollow ships of the Achaians. Then dark night came on her eyes and shrouded her, and she fell backward and gasped forth her spirit. From off her head she shook the bright attiring thereof, frontlet and net and woven band, and veil, the veil that golden Aphrodite gave her on the day when Hector of the glancing helm led her forth of the house of Eetion, having given bride -gifts untold. And around her thronged her husband's sisters and his brothers' wives, who held her up among them, distraught even to death. But when at last she came to herself and her soul returned into her breast, then wailing with deep sobs she spake among the women of Troy: 'O Hector, woe is me! to one fate then were we both born, thou in Troy in the house of Priam, and I in Thebe under woody Plakos, in the house of Eetion, who reared me from a little one – ill-fated sire of cruel-fated child. Ah, would he had begotten me not. Now thou to the house of Hades beneath the secret places of the earth departest, and me in bitter mourning thou leavest a widow in thy halls: and thy son is but an infant child – son of unhappy parents, thee and me – nor shalt thou profit him, Hector, since thou art dead, neither he thee. For even if he escape the Achaians' woful war, yet shall labour and sorrow cleave unto him hereafter, for other men shall seize[1] his lands. The day of orphanage sundereth a child from his fellows, and his head is bowed down ever, and his cheeks are wet with tears. And in his need the child seeketh his father's friends, plucking this one by cloak and that by coat, and one of them that pity him holdeth his cup a little to his mouth, and moisteneth his lips, but his palate he moisteneth not. And some child unorphaned thrusteth him from the feast with blows and taunting words, "Out with thee! no father of thine is at our board." Then weeping to his widowed mother shall he return, even Astyanax, who erst upon his father's knee ate only marrow and fat flesh of sheep; and when sleep fell on him and he ceased from childish play, then in bed in his nurse's arms he would slumber softly nested, having satisfied his heart with good things; but now that he hath lost his father he will suffer many ills, Astyanax – that name the Trojans gave him, because thou only wert the defence of their gates and their long walls. But now by the beaked ships, far from thy parents, shall coiling worms devour thee when the dogs have had their fill, as thou liest naked; yet in these halls lieth raiment of thine, delicate and fair, wrought by the hands of women. But verily all these will I consume with burning fire – to thee no profit, since thou wilt never lie therein, yet that this be honour to thee from the men and the women of Troy.'

Thus spake she wailing, and the women joined their moan.

---

[1] Reading ἀπουρήσουσιν. With the alternative ἀπουρίσουσιν, the meaning is, 'shall remove his landmarks.'

BOOK XXIII

Of the funeral of Patroklos, and the funeral games.

THUS THEY THROUGHOUT the city made moan: but the Achaians when they were come to the ships and to the Hellespont were scattered each to his own ship: only the Myrmidons Achilles suffered not to be scattered, but spake among his comrades whose delight was in war: 'Fleet-horsed Myrmidons, my trusty comrades, let us not yet unyoke our whole-hooved steeds from their cars, but with horses and chariots let us go near and mourn Patroklos, for such is the honour of the dead. Then when we have our fill of grievous wailing, we will unyoke the horses and all sup here.'

He said, and they with one accord made lamentation, and Achilles led their mourning. So thrice around the dead they drave their well-maned steeds, moaning; and Thetis stirred among them desire of wailing. Bedewed were the sands with tears, bedewed the warriors' arms; so great a lord of fear they sorrowed for. And Peleus' son led their loud wail, laying his man-slaying hands on his comrade's breast: 'All hail, Patroklos, even in the house of Hades; for all that I promised thee before am I accomplishing, seeing I have dragged hither Hector to give raw unto dogs to devour, and twelve noble children of the Trojans to slaughter before thy pyre, because of mine anger at thy slaying.'

He said, and devised foul entreatment of noble Hector, stretching him prone in the dust beside the bier of Menoitios' son. And the rest put off each his glittering bronze arms, and unyoked their high-neighing horses, and sate them down numberless beside the ship of fleet-footed Aiakides, and he gave them ample funeral feast. Many sleek oxen were stretched out, their throats cut with steel, and many sheep and bleating goats, and many white-tusked boars well grown in fat were spitted to singe in the flame of Hephaistos; so on all sides round the corpse in cupfuls blood was flowing.

But the fleet-footed prince, the son of Peleus, was brought to noble Agamemnon by the Achaian chiefs, hardly persuading him thereto, for his heart was wroth for his comrade. And when they were come to Agamemnon's hut, forthwith they bade clear-voiced heralds set a great tripod on the fire, if haply they might persuade the son of Peleus to wash from him the bloody gore. But he denied them steadfastly, and sware moreover an oath: 'Nay, verily by Zeus, who is highest and best of gods, not lawful is it that water should come nigh my head or ever I shall have laid Patroklos on the fire, and heaped a barrow, and shaved my hair, since never again shall second grief thus reach my heart, while I remain among the living. Yet now for the present let us yield us to our mournful meal: but with the morning, O king of men Agamemnon, rouse the folk to bring wood and furnish all that it beseemeth a dead man to have when he goeth beneath the misty gloom, to the end that untiring fire may burn him quickly from sight, and the host betake them to their work.'

Thus spake he, and they listened readily to him and obeyed, and eagerly making ready each his meal they supped, and no lack had their soul of equal feast. But when they had put off from them the desire of meat and drink, the rest went down each man to his tent to take his rest, but the son of Peleus upon the beach of the sounding sea lay groaning heavily, amid the host of Myrmidons, in an open place, where waves were breaking on the shore. Now when sleep took hold on him, easing the cares of his heart, deep sleep that fell about him, (for sore tired were his glorious knees with onset upon Hector toward windy Ilios), then came there unto him the spirit of hapless Patroklos, in all things like his living self, in stature, and fair eyes, and voice, and the raiment of his body was the same; and he stood above Achilles' head and spake to him: 'Thou sleepest, and hast forgotten me, O Achilles. Not in my life wast thou ever unmindful of me, but in my death. Bury me with all speed, that I pass the gates of Hades. Far off the spirits banish me, the phantoms of men outworn, nor suffer me to mingle with them beyond the River, but vainly I wander along the wide-gated dwelling of Hades Now give me, I pray pitifully of thee, thy hand, for never more again shall I come back from Hades, when ye have given me my due of fire. Never among the living shall we sit apart from our dear comrades and take counsel together, but me hath the harsh fate swallowed up which was appointed me even from my birth. Yea and thou too thyself, Achilles peer of gods, beneath the wall of the noble Trojans art doomed to die. Yet one thing will I say, and charge thee, if haply thou wilt have regard thereto. Lay not my bones apart from thine, Achilles, but together, even as we were nurtured in your house, when Menoitios brought me yet a little one from Opoeis to your country by reason of a grievous man-slaying, on the day when I slew Amphidamas' son, not willing it, in childish wrath over the dice. Then took me the knight Peleus into his house and reared me kindly and named me thy squire: so therefore let one coffer hide our bones, [a golden coffer, two handled, thy lady mother's gift].'

Then made answer unto him Achilles fleet of foot: 'Wherefore, O my brother, hast thou come hither, and chargest me everything that I should do? Verily I will accomplish all, and have regard unto thy bidding. But stand more nigh me; for one moment let us throw our arms around each other, and take our fill of dolorous lament.'

He spake, and reached forth with his hands, but clasped him not; for like a vapour the spirit was gone beneath the earth with a faint shriek. And Achilles sprang up marvelling, and smote his hands together, and spake a word of woe: 'Ay me, there remaineth then even in the house of Hades a spirit and phantom of the dead, albeit the life be not anywise therein: for all night long hath the spirit of hapless Patroklos stood over me, wailing and making moan, and charged me everything that I should do, and wondrous like his living self it seemed.'

Thus said he, and stirred in all of them yearning to make lament; and rosy-fingered Morn shone forth on them while they still made moan around the piteous corpse. Then lord Agamemnon sped mules and men from all the huts to fetch wood; and a man of valour watched thereover, even Meriones, squire of kindly Idomeneus. And they went forth with wood-cutting axes in their hands and well-woven ropes, and before them went the mules, and uphill and down-hill and sideways and across they went. But when they came to the spurs of many-fountained Ida, straightway they set them lustily to hew high-foliaged oaks with the long-edged bronze, and with loud noise fell the trees. Then splitting them asunder the Achaians bound them behind the mules, and they tore up the earth with their feet as they made for the plain through the thick underwood. And all the woodcutters bare logs; for thus bade Meriones, squire of kindly Idomeneus. And on the shore they threw them down in line, where Achilles purposed a mighty tomb for Patroklos and for himself.

Then when they had laid down all about great piles of wood, they sate them down all together and abode. Then straightway Achilles bade the warlike Myrmidons gird on their arms, and each yoke the horses to his chariot; and they arose and put their armour on, and mounted their chariots, both fighting men and charioteers. In front were the men in chariots, and a cloud of footmen followed after, numberless; and in the midst his comrades bare Patroklos. And they heaped all the corpse with their hair that they cut off and threw thereon; and behind did goodly Achilles bear the head, sorrowing;

for a noble comrade was he speeding forth unto the realm of Hades.

And when they came to the place where Achilles had bidden them, they set down the dead, and piled for him abundant wood. Then fleet-footed noble Achilles bethought him of one thing more: standing apart from the pyre he shore off a golden lock, the lock whose growth he nursed to offer unto the River Spercheios, and sore troubled spake he, looking forth over the wine-dark sea: 'Spercheios, in other wise vowed my father Peleus unto thee that I returning thither to my native land should shear my hair for thee and offer a holy hecatomb, and fifty rams should sacrifice there above thy springs, where is thy sacred close and altar burning spice. So vowed the old man, but thou hast not accomplished him his desire. And now since I return not to my dear native land, unto the hero Patroklos I may give this hair to take away.'

Thus saying he set the hair in the hands of his dear comrade, and stirred in all of them yearning to make lament And so would the light of the sun have gone down on their lamentation, had not Achilles said quickly to Agamemnon as he stood beside him: 'Son of Atreus – for to thy words most will the host of the Achaians have regard – of lamentation they may sate them to the full. But now disperse them from the burning and bid them make ready their meal, and we to whom the dead is dearest will take pains for these things; yet let the chiefs tarry nigh unto us.'

Then when Agamemnon king of men heard that, he forthwith dispersed the host among the trim ships, but the nearest to the dead tarried there and piled the wood, and made a pyre a hundred feet this way and that, and on the pyre's top set the corpse, with anguish at their hearts. And many lusty sheep and shambling crook-horned oxen they flayed and made ready before the pyre; and taking from all of them the fat, great-hearted Achilles wrapped the corpse therein from head to foot, and heaped the flayed bodies round. And he set therein two-handled jars of honey and oil, leaning them against the bier; and four strong-necked horses he threw swiftly on the pyre, and groaned aloud. Nine house-dogs had the dead chief: of them did Achilles slay twain and throw them on the pyre. And twelve valiant sons of great-hearted Trojans he slew with the sword – for he devised mischief in his heart – and he set to the merciless might of the fire, to feed thereon. Then moaned he aloud, and called on his dear comrade by his name: 'All hail to thee, O Patroklos, even in the house of Hades, for all that I promised thee before am I now accomplishing. Twelve valiant sons of great-hearted Trojans, behold these all in company with thee the fire devoureth: but

Hector son of Priam will I nowise give to the fire to feed upon, but to dogs.'

Thus spake he threatening, but no dogs might deal with Hector, for day and night Aphrodite daughter of Zeus kept off the dogs, and anointed him with rose-sweet oil ambrosial that Achilles might not tear him when he dragged him. And over him Phoebus Apollo brought a dark cloud from heaven to earth and covered all that place whereon the dead man lay, lest meanwhile the sun's strength shrivel his flesh round about upon his sinews and limbs.

But the pyre of dead Patroklos kindled not. Then fleet-footed noble Achilles had a further thought: standing aside from the pyre he prayed to the two Winds of North and West, and promised them fair offerings, and pouring large libations from a golden cup besought them to come, that the corpses might blaze up speedily in the fire, and the wood make haste to be enkindled. Then Iris, when she heard his prayer, went swiftly with the message to the Winds. They within the house of the gusty West Wind were feasting all together at meat, when Iris sped thither, and halted on the threshold of stone. And when they saw her with their eyes, they sprang up and called to her every one to sit by him. But she refused to sit, and spake her word: 'No seat for me; I must go back to the streams of Ocean, to the Ethiopians' land where they sacrifice hecatombs to the immortal gods, that I too may feast at their rites. But Achilles is praying the North Wind and the loud West to come, and promising them fair offerings, that ye may make the pyre be kindled whereon lieth Patroklos, for whom all the Achaians are making moan.'

She having thus said departed, and they arose with a mighty sound, rolling the clouds before them. And swiftly they came blowing over the sea, and the wave rose beneath their shrill blast; and they came to deep-soiled Troy, and fell upon the pile, and loudly roared the mighty fire. So all night drave they the flame of the pyre together, blowing shrill; and all night fleet Achilles, holding a two-handled cup, drew wine from a golden bowl, and poured it forth and drenched the earth, calling upon the spirit of hapless Patroklos. As a father waileth when he burneth the bones of his son, new-married, whose death is woe to his hapless parents, so wailed Achilles as he burnt the bones of his comrade, going heavily round the burning pile, with many moans.

But at the hour when the Morning Star goeth forth to herald light upon the earth, the star that saffron-mantled Dawn cometh after, and spreadeth over the salt sea, then grew the burning faint, and the flame died down. And the Winds went back again to betake them home over the Thracian main, and it roared with a violent swell. Then the son of Peleus turned away from the burning and lay down wearied, and sweet sleep leapt on him. But they who were with Atreus' son gathered all together, and the noise and clash of their approach aroused him; and he sate upright and spake a word to them: 'Son of Atreus and ye other chiefs of the Achaians, first quench with gleaming wine all the burning so far as the fire's strength hath reached, and then let us gather up the bones of Patroklos, Menoitios' son, singling them well, and easy are they to discern, for he lay in the middle of the pyre, while the rest apart at the edge burnt confusedly, horses and men. And his bones let us put within a golden urn, and double-folded fat, until that I myself be hidden in Hades. But no huge barrow I bid you toil to raise – a seemly one, no more: then afterward do ye Achaians build it broad and high, whosoever of you after I am gone may be left in the benched ships.'

Thus spake he, and they hearkened to the fleet-footed son of Peleus. First quenched they with gleaming wine the burning so far as the flame went, and the ash had settled deep: then with lamentation they gathered up the white bones of their gentle comrade into a golden urn and doublefolded fat, and placed the urn in the hut and covered it with a linen veil. And they marked the circle of the barrow, and set the foundations thereof around the pyre, and straightway heaped thereon a heap of earth. Then when they had heaped up the barrow they were for going back. But Achilles stayed the folk in that place, and made them sit in wide assembly, and from his ships he brought forth prizes, caldrons and tripods, and horses and mules and strong oxen, and fair-girdled women, and grey iron.

First for fleet chariot-racers he ordained a noble prize, a woman skilled in fair handiwork for the winner to lead home, and an eared tripod that held two-and-twenty measures; these for the first man; and for the second he ordained a six-year-old mare unbroke, with a mule foal in her womb; and for the third he gave a goodly caldron yet untouched by fire, holding four measures, bright as when first made; and for the fourth he ordained two talents of gold; and for the fifth a two-handled urn untouched of fire. Then he stood up and spake a word among the Argives: 'Son of Atreus and ye other well-greaved Achaians, for the chariot-racers these prizes lie await-ing them in the lists. If in some other's honour we Achaians were now holding our games, it would be I who should win the first prize and bear it to my hut; for ye know how far my pair of horses are first in excellence, for they are immortal, and Poseidon gave them to my father Peleus, and he again to me. But verily I will abide, I and my whole-hooved horses, so glorious a charioteer have they lost, and one so kind, who on their manes full often poured smooth oil, when he had washed them in clear water. For him they stand and mourn, and their manes are trailing on the ground, and there stand they with sorrow at their hearts. But ye others throughout the host get ye to your places, whosoever of the Achaians hath trust in his horses and firm jointed car.'

Thus spake the son of Peleus, and the fleet chariot-racers were gathered. First of all arose up Eumelos king of men, Admetos' son, a skilful charioteer; and next to him arose Tydeus' son, valiant Diomedes, and yoked his horses of the breed of Tros, which on a time he seized from Aineias, when Apollo saved their lord. And after him arose Atreus' son, fair-haired heaven-sprung Menelaos, and yoked him a swift pair, Aithe, Agamemnon's mare, and his own horse Podargos. Her unto Agamemnon did Anchises' son Echepolos give in fee, that he might escape from following him to windy Ilios and take his pleasure at home; for great wealth had Zeus given him, and he dwelt in Sikyon of spacious lawns: – so Menelaos yoked her, and she longed exceedingly for the race. And fourth, Antilochos made ready his fair-maned horses, even the noble son of Nestor, high-hearted king, who was the son of Neleus; and fleet horses bred at Pylos drew his car. And his father standing by his side spake counselling him to his profit, though himself was well advised: 'Antilochos, verily albeit thou art young, Zeus and Poseidon have loved thee and taught thee all skill with horses; wherefore to teach thee is no great need, for thou well knowest how to wheel round the post; yet are thy horses very slow in the race: therefore methinks there will be sad work for thee. For the horses of the others are fleeter, yet the men know not more cunning than thou hast. So come, dear son, store thy mind with all manner of cunning, that the prize escape thee not. By cunning is a woodman far better than by force; by cunning doth a helmsman on the wine-dark deep steer his swift ship buffeted by winds; by cunning hath charioteer the better of charioteer. For whoso trusting in his horses and car alone wheeleth heedlessly and wide at either end, his horses swerve on the course, and he keepeth them not in hand. But whoso is of crafty mind, though he drive worse horses, he ever keeping his eye upon the post turneth closely by it, neither is unaware how far at first to force his horses by the ox-hide reins, but holdeth them safe in hand and watcheth the leader in the race. Now will I tell thee a certain sign, and it shall not escape thee. A fathom's height above the ground standeth a withered stump, whether of oak or pine: it decayeth not in the rain, and two white stones on either side thereof are fixed at the joining of the track, and all round it is smooth driving ground. Whether it be a monument of some man dead long ago, or have been made their goal in the race by ancient men, this now is the mark fixed by fleet-footed goodly Achilles. Wherefore do thou drive close and bear thy horses and chariot hard thereon, and lean thy body on the well-knit car slightly to their left, and call upon the off-horse with voice and lash, and give him rein from thy hand. But let the near horse hug the post so that the nave of the well-wrought wheel seem to graze it – yet beware of touching the stone, lest thou wound the horses and break the chariot; so would that be triumph to the rest and reproach unto thyself. But, dear son, be wise and on thy guard; for if at the turning-post thou drive past the rest, there is none shall overtake thee from behind or pass thee by, not though he drave the goodly Arion in pursuit, the fleet horse of Adrastos, of divine descent, or the horses of Laomedon, best of all bred in this land.'

Thus spake Neleian Nestor and sate him down again in his place, when he had told his son the sum of every matter.

And Meriones was the fifth to make ready his sleekcoated steeds. Then went they up into their chariots, and cast in the lots: and Achilles shook them, and forth leapt the lot of Antilochos Nestor's son, and the next lot had lord Eumelos, and next to him the son of Atreus, spearfamed Menelaos, and next to him drew Meriones his place; then lastly Tydeides, far the best of all, drew his lot for his chariot's place. Then they stood side by side, and Achilles showed to them the turning-post, far off in the smooth plain; and beside it he placed an umpire, god-like Phoinix, his father's follower, that he might note the running and tell the truth thereof.

Then all together lifted the lash above their steeds, and smote them with the reins, and called on them eagerly with words: and they forthwith sped swiftly over the plain, leaving the ships behind; and beneath their breasts stood the rising dust like a cloud or whirlwind, and their manes waved on the blowing wind. And the chariots ran sometimes on the bounteous earth, and other whiles would bound into the air. And the drivers stood in the cars, and the heart of every man beat in desire of victory, and they called every man to his horses, that flew amid their- dust across the plain.

But when the fleet horses were now running the last part of the course, back toward the grey sea, then was manifest the prowess of each, and the horses strained in the race; and presently to the front rushed the fleet mares of Pheres' grandson, and next to them Diomedes' stallions of the breed of Tros, not far apart, but hard anigh, for they seemed ever as they would mount Eumelos' car, and with their breath his back was warm and his broad shoulders, for they bent their heads upon him as they flew along. Thus would Tydeus' son have either outstripped the other or made it a dead heat, had not Phoebus Apollo been wroth with him and smitten from his hand the shining lash. Then from his eyes ran tears of anger, for that he saw the mares still at speed, even swiftlier than before, while his own horses were thrown out, as running without spur. But Athene was not unaware of Apollo's guile against Tydeides, and presently sped after the shepherd of hosts, and gave him back the lash, and put spirit into his steeds. Then in wrath after the son of Admetos was the goddess gone, and brake his steeds' yoke, and the mares ran sideways off the course, and the pole was twisted to the ground. And Eumelos was hurled out of the car beside the wheel, and his elbows and mouth and nose were flayed, and his forehead bruised above his eyebrows; and his eyes filled with tears and his lusty voice was choked. Then Tydeides held his whole-hooved horses on one side, darting far out before the rest, for Athene put spirit into his steeds and shed glory on himself Now next after him came golden-haired Menelaos Atreus' son. But Antilochos called to his father's horses: 'Go ye too in, strain to your fleetest pace. Truly I nowise bid you strive with those, the horses of wise Tydeides, unto which Athene hath now given speed, and shed glory on their charioteer. But overtake Atreides' horses with all haste, and be not outstripped by them, lest Aithe that is but a mare pour scorn on you. Why are ye outstripped, brave steeds? Thus will I tell you, and verily it shall be brought to pass – ye will find no ten-dance with Nestor shepherd of hosts, but straightway he will slay you with the edge of the sword if through heedlessness we win but the worse prize. Have after them at your utmost speed, and I for my part will devise a plan to pass them in the strait part of the course, and this shall fail me not.'

Thus spake he, and they fearing the voice of the prince ran swift-lier some little while; and presently did the good warrior Antilochos espy a strait place in a sunk part of the way. There was a rift in the earth, where torrent water gathered and brake part of the track away, and hollowed all the place; there drave Menelaos, shunning the encounter of the wheels. But Antilochos turned his whole-hooved horses out of the track, and followed him a little at one side.

And the son of Atreus took alarm and shouted to Antilochos: 'Antilochos, thou art driving recklessly – hold in thy horses! The road is straitened, soon thou mayest pass me in a wider place, lest thou foul my chariot and undo us both.'

Thus spake he, but Antilochos drave even fiercelier than before, plying his lash, as though he heard him not. As far as is the range of a disk swung from the shoulder when a young man hurleth it, making trial of his force, even so far ran they on; then the mares of Atreus' son gave back, for he ceased of himself to urge them on, lest the whole-hooved steeds should encounter on the track, and overset the well-knit cars, and the drivers fall in the dust in their zeal for victory. So upbraiding Antilochos spake golden-haired Menelaos: 'Antilochos, no mortal man is more malicious than thou. Go thy mad way, since falsely have we Achaians called thee wise. Yet even so thou shalt not bear off the prize unchallenged to an oath.'

Thus saying he called aloud to his horses: 'Hold ye not back nor stand still with sorrow at heart. Their feet and knees will grow weary before yours, for they both lack youth.'

Thus spake he, and they fearing the voice of the prince sped faster on, and were quickly close upon the others.

Now the Argives sitting in concourse were gazing at the horses, and they came flying amid their dust over the plain. And the first aware of them was Idomeneus, chief of the Cretans, for he was sitting outside the concourse in the highest place of view, and when he heard the voice of one that shouted, though afar off, he knew it; and he was aware of a horse showing plainly in the front, a chestnut all the rest of him, but in the forehead marked with a white star round like the moon. And he stood upright and spoke among the Argives: 'Friends, chiefs, and counsellors of the Argives, is it I alone who see the horses, or do ye also? A new pair seem to me now to be in front, and a new charioteer appeareth; the mares which led in the outward course must have been thrown out there in the plain. For I saw them turning first the hither post, but now can see them nowhere, though my eyes are gazing everywhere along the Trojan plain. Did the reins escape the charioteer so that he could not drive aright round the post and failed in the turn? There, methinks, must he have been cast forth, and have broken his chariot, and the mares must have left the course, in the wildness of their heart. But stand up ye too and look, for myself I discern not certainly, but the first man seemeth to me one of Aitolian race, and he ruleth among Argives, the son of horse-taming Tydeus, stalwart Diomedes.'

Then fleet Aias Oileus' son rebuked him in unseemly sort:

'Idomeneus, why art thou a braggart of old? As yet far off the high-stepping mares are coursing over the wide plain. Neither art thou so far the youngest among the Argives; nor do thy eyes look so far the keenliest from thy head, yet continually braggest thou. It beseemeth thee not to be a braggart, for there are here better men. And the mares leading are they that led before, Eumelos' mares, and he standeth and holdeth the reins within the car.'

Then wrathfully in answer spake the chief of Cretans: 'Aias, master of railing, ill-counselled, in all else art thou behind other Argives, for thy mind is unfriendly Come then let us wager a tripod or caldron, and make Agamemnon Atreus' son our umpire, which mares are leading, that thou mayest pay and learn.'

Thus said he, and straightway fleet Aias Oileus' son arose angrily to answer with harsh words: and strife between the twain would have gone further, had not Achilles himself stood up and spake a word: 'No longer answer each other with harsh words, Aias and Idomeneus, ill words, for it beseemeth not. Surely ye are displeased with any other who should do thus. Sit ye in the concourse and keep your eyes upon the horses; soon they in zeal for victory will come hither, and then shall ye know each of you the Argives' horses, which follow, and which lead.'

He said, and the son of Tydeus came driving up, and with his lash smote now and again from the shoulder, and his horses were stepping high as they sped swiftly on their way. And sprinklings of dust smote ever the charioteer, and his chariot overlaid with gold and tin ran behind his fleet-footed steeds, and small trace was there of the wheel-tires behind in the fine dust, as they flew speeding on. Then he drew up in the mid concourse, and much sweat poured from the horses' heads and chests to the ground. And Diomedes leapt to earth from the shining car, and leant his lash against the yoke. Then stalwart Sthenelos tarried not, but promptly took the prize, and gave to his proud comrades the woman to lead and the eared tripod to bear away, and he loosed the horses from the yoke.

And next after him drave Neleian Antilochos his horses, by craft, not swiftness, having passed by Menelaos; yet even now Menelaos held his swift steeds hard anigh. As far as a horse is from the wheel, which draweth his master, straining with the car over the plain – his hindmost tail-hairs touch the tire, for the wheel runneth hard anigh nor is much space between, as he speedeth far over the plain – by so much was Menelaos behind high-born Antilochos, howbeit at first he was a whole disk-cast behind, but quickly he was catching Antilochos up, for the high mettle of Agamemnon's mare, sleek-coated Aithe, was rising in her. And if yet further both had had to run he would have passed his rival nor left it even a dead heat. But Meriones, stout squire of Idomeneus, came in a spear-throw behind famous Menelaos, for tardiest of all were his sleek-coated horses, and slowest he himself to drive a chariot in the race. Last of them all came Admetos' son, dragging his goodly car, driving his steeds in front. Him when fleet-footed noble Achilles beheld he pitied him, and he stood up and spake winged words among the Argives: 'Last driveth his whole-hooved horses the best man of them all. But come let us give him a prize, as is seemly, prize for the second place, but the first let the son of Tydeus take.'

Thus spake he, and all applauded that he bade. And he would have given him the mare, for the Achaians applauded, had not Antilochos, son of great-hearted Nestor, risen up and answered Peleïan Achilles on behalf of his right: 'O Achilles, I shall be sore angered with thee if thou accomplish this word, for thou art minded to take away my prize, because thou thinkest of how his chariot and fleet steeds miscarried, and himself withal, good man though he be. Nay, it behoved him to pray to the Immortals, then would he not have come in last of all in the race. But if thou pitiest him and he be dear to thy heart, there is much gold in thy hut, bronze is there and sheep, handmaids are there and whole-hooved horses. Thereof take thou and give unto him afterward even a richer prize, or even now at once, that the Achaians may applaud thee. But the mare I will not yield; for her let what man will essay the battle at my hands.'

Thus spake he, and fleet-footed noble Achilles smiled, pleased with Antilochos, for he was his dear comrade; and spake in answer to him winged words: 'Antilochos, if thou wouldst have me give Eumelos some other thing beside from out my house, that also will I do. I will give unto him a breast-plate that I took from Asteropaios, of bronze, whereon a casting of bright tin is overlaid, and of great worth will it be to him.' He said, and bade his dear comrade Automedon bring it from the hut, and he went and brought it. [Then he placed it in Eumelos' hands, and he received it gladly.]

But Menelaos also arose among them, sore at heart, angered exceedingly against Antilochos; and the herald set the staff in his hand, and called for silence among the Argives; then spake among them that godlike man: 'Antilochos, who once wert wise, what thing is this thou hast done? Thou hast shamed my skill and made my horses fail, thrusting thine own in front that are far worse. Come now, ye chiefs and counsellors of the Argives, give judgment between us both, and favour neither: lest some one of the mail-clad

Achaians say at any time: "By constraining Antilochos through false words hath Menelaos gone off with the mare, for his horses were far worse, howbeit he hath advantage in rank and power." Nay, I myself will bring the issue about, and I deem that none other of the Danaans shall reproach me, for the trial shall be just. Antilochos, fosterling of Zeus, come thou hither and as it is ordained stand up before thy horses and chariot and take in thy hand the pliant lash wherewith thou dravest erst, and touching thy horses swear by the Enfolder and Shaker of the earth that not wilfully didst thou hinder my chariot by guile.'

Then answered him wise Antilochos: 'Bear with me now, for far younger am I than thou, king Menelaos, and thou art before me and my better. Thou knowest how a young man's trangressions come about, for his mind is hastier and his counsel shallow. So let thy heart suffer me, and I will of myself give to thee the mare I have taken. Yea, if thou shouldst ask some other greater thing from my house, I were fain to give it thee straightway, rather than fall for ever from my place in thy heart, O fosterling of Zeus, and become a sinner against the gods.'

Thus spake great-hearted Nestor's son, and brought the mare and put her in the hand of Menelaos. And his heart was gladdened as when the dew cometh upon the ears of ripening harvest-corn, what time the fields are bristling. So gladdened was thy soul, Menelaos, within thy heart. And he spake unto Antilochos and uttered winged words: 'Antilochos, now will I of myself put away mine anger against thee, since no wise formerly wert thou flighty or light-minded, howbeit now thy reason was overcome of youthfulness. Another time be loth to outwit better men. Not easily should another of the Achaians have persuaded me, but thou hast suffered and toiled greatly, and thy brave father and brother, for my sake: therefore will I hearken to thy prayer, and will even give unto thee the mare, though she is mine, that these also may know that my heart was never overweening or implacable.'

He said, and gave the mare to Noëmon Antilochos' comrade to lead away, and then took the shining caldron. And Meriones took up the two talents of gold in the fourth place, as he had come in. So the fifth prize was left unclaimed, a two-handled cup; to Nestor gave Achilles this, bearing it to him through the concourse of Argives, and stood by him and said: 'Lo now for thee too, old man, be this a treasure, a memorial of Patroklos' burying; for no more shalt thou behold him among the Argives. Now give I thee this prize unwon, for not in boxing shalt thou strive, neither wrestle, nor enter on the javelin match, nor race with thy feet; for grim old age already weigheth on thee.'

Thus saying he placed it in his hand, and Nestor received it gladly, and spake unto him winged words: 'Ay, truly all this, my son, thou hast meetly said; for no longer are my limbs, friend, firm, nor my feet, nor do my arms at all swing lightly from my shoulders either side. Would that my youth were such and my force so firm as when the Epeians were burying lord Amarynkes at Buprasion, and his sons held the king's funeral games. Then was no man found like me, neither of the Epeians nor of the Pylians themselves or the great-hearted Aitolians. In boxing I overcame Klytomedes, son of Enops, and in wrestling Ankaios of Pleuron, who stood up against me, and in the foot-race I outran Iphiklos, a right good man, and with the spear outthrew Phyleus and Polydoros; only in the chariot-race the two sons of Aktor beat me [by crowding their horses in front of me, jealous for victory, because the chief prizes were left at home.][1] Now they were twins – one ever held the reins, the reins he ever held, the other called on the horses with the lash. Thus was I once, but now let younger men join in such feats; I must bend to grievous age, but then was I of mark among heroes. But come hold funeral for thy comrade too with games. This gift do I accept with gladness, and my heart rejoiceth that thou rememberest ever my friendship to thee – (nor forget I thee) – and the honour[2] wherewith it is meet that I be honoured among the Achaians. And may the gods for this grant thee due grace.'

Thus spake he, and Peleides was gone down the full concourse of Achaians, when he had hearkened to all the thanks of Neleus' son. Then he ordained prizes of the violent boxing match; a sturdy mule he led forth and tethered amid the assembly, a six-year mule unbroken, hardest of all to break; and for the loser set a two-handled cup. Then he stood up and spake a word among the Argives: 'Son of Atreus and ye other well-greaved Achaians, for these rewards we summon two men of the best to lift up their hands to box amain. He to whom Apollo shall grant endurance to the end, and all the Achaians acknowledge it, let him take the sturdy mule and return with her to his hut; and the loser shall take with him the two-handled cup.'

Thus spake he, and forthwith arose a man great and valiant and

---

[1]It seems impossible to obtain a satisfactory meaning from this couplet, especially the word πλήθει.

[2]Reading τιμῆς θ'

skilled in boxing, Epeios son of Panopeus, and laid his hand on the sturdy mule and said aloud: 'Let one come nigh to bear off the two-handled cup; the mule I say none other of the Achaians shall take for victory with his fists, for I claim to be the best man here. Sufficeth it not that I fall short of you in battle? Not possible is it that in all arts a man be skilled. Thus proclaim I, and it shall be accomplished: I will utterly bruise mine adversary's flesh and break his bones, so let his friends abide together here to bear him forth when vanquished by my hands.'

Thus spake he, and they all kept deep silence. And alone arose against him Euryalos, a godlike man, son of king Mekisteus the son of Talaos, Mekisteus, who came on a time to Thebes when Oedipus had fallen, to his burial, and there he overcame all the sons of Kadmos. Thus Tydeides famous with the spear made ready Euryalos for the fight, cheering him with speech, and greatly desired for him victory. And first he cast about him a girdle, and next gave him well-cut thongs of the hide of an ox of the field. And the two boxers being girt went into the midst of the ring, and both lifting up their stalwart hands fell to, and their hands joined battle grievously. Then was there terrible grinding of teeth, and sweat flowed from all their limbs. And noble Epeios came on, and as the other spied for an opening, smote him on the cheek, nor could he much more stand, for his fair limbs failed straightway under him. And as when beneath the North Wind's ripple a fish leapeth on a tangle-covered beach, and then the black wave hideth it, so leapt up Euryalos at that blow. But great-hearted Epeios took him in his hands and set him upright, and his dear comrades stood around him, and led him through the ring with trailing feet, spitting out clotted blood, drooping his head awry, and they set him down in his swoon among them and themselves went forth and fetched the two-handled cup.

Then Peleus' son ordained straightway the prizes for a third contest, offering them to the Danaans, for the grievous wrestling match: for the winner a great tripod for standing on the fire, prized by the Achaians among them at twelve oxen's worth; and for the loser he brought a woman into the midst, skilled in manifold work, and they prized her at four oxen. And he stood up and spake a word among the Argives: 'Rise, ye who will essay this match.'

Thus said he, and there arose great Aias son of Telamon, and Odysseus of many wiles stood up, the crafty-minded. And the twain being girt went into the midst of the ring, and clasped each the other in his arms with stalwart hands, like gable rafters of a lofty house which some famed craftsman joineth, that he may baffle the

wind's force. And their backs creaked, gripped firmly under the vig-
orous hands, and sweat ran down in streams, and frequent weals
along their ribs and shoulders sprang up, red with blood, while ever
they strove amain for victory, to win the wrought tripod. Neither
could Odysseus trip Aias and bear him to the ground, nor Aias him,
for Odysseus' strength withheld him. But when they began to irk
the well-greaved Achaians, then said to Odysseus great Aias, Telamon's son: 'Heaven-sprung son of Laertes, Odysseus of many wiles,
or lift thou me, or I will thee, and the issue shall be with Zeus.'

Having thus said he lifted him, but Odysseus was not unmindful
of his craft. He smote deftly from behind the hollow of Aias' knee,
and loosed his limbs, and threw him down backward, and Odysseus
fell upon his chest, and the folk gazed and marvelled. Then in his
turn much-enduring noble Odysseus tried to lift, and moved him a
little from the ground, but lifted him not, so he crooked his knee
within the other's, and both fell on the ground nigh to each other,
and were soiled with dust. And now starting up again a third time
would they have wrestled, had not Achilles himself arisen and held
them back: 'No longer press each the other, nor wear you out with
pain. Victory is with both; take equal prizes and depart, that other
Achaians may contend.'

Thus spake he, and they were fain to hear and to obey, and wiped
the dust from them and put their doublets on.

Then straightway the son of Peleus set forth other prizes for
fleetness of foot; a mixing-bowl of silver, chased; six measures it
held, and in beauty it was far the best in all the earth, for artificers
of Sidon wrought it cunningly, and men of the Phoenicians brought
it over the misty sea, and landed it in harbour, and gave it a gift to
Thoas; and Euneos son of Jason gave it to the hero Patroklos a
ransom for Lykaon Priam's son. Now this cup did Achilles set forth
as a prize in honour of his friend, for whoso should be fleetest in
speed of foot. For the second he set an ox great and very fat, and for
the last prize half a talent of gold. And he stood up and spake a
word among the Argives: 'Rise, ye who will essay this match.'

Thus spake he, and straightway arose fleet Aias Oïleus' son, and
Odysseus of many wiles, and after them Nestor's son Antilochos,
for he was best of all the youth in the footrace. Then they stood side
by side, and Achilles showed to them the goal. Right eager was the
running from the start, but Oïleus' son forthwith shot to the front,
and close behind him came noble Odysseus, as close as is a weaving-
rod to a fair-girdled woman's breast when she pulleth it deftly with
her hands, drawing the spool along the warp, and holdeth the rod

nigh her breast – so close ran Odysseus behind Aias and trod in his footsteps or ever the dust had settled there, and on his head fell the breath of noble Odysseus as he ran ever lightly on, and all the Achaians applauded his struggle for the victory and called on him as he laboured hard. But when they were running the last part of the course, forthwith Odysseus prayed in his soul to bright-eyed Athene: 'Hearken, goddess, come thou a good helper of my feet.'

Thus prayed he, and Pallas Athene hearkened to him, and made his limbs feel light, both feet and hands. But when they were now nigh darting on the prize, then Aias slipped as he ran, for Athene marred his race, where filth was strewn from the slaughter of loud-bellowing oxen that fleet Achilles slew in honour of Patroklos: and Aias' mouth and nostrils were filled with that filth of oxen. So much-enduring noble Odysseus, as he came in first, took up the mixing-bowl, and famous Aias took the ox. And he stood holding in his hand the horn of the ox of the field, sputtering away the filth, and spake among the Argives: 'Out on it, it was the goddess who marred my running, she who from of old like a mother standeth by Odysseus' side and helpeth him.'

So spake he, but they all laughed pleasantly to behold him. Then Antilochos smiling bore off the last prize, and spake his word among the Argives: 'Friends, ye will all bear me witness when I say that even herein also the immortals favour elder men. For Aias is a little older than I, but Odysseus of an earlier generation and earlier race of men. A green old age is his, they say, and hard were it for any Achaian to rival him in speed, save only Achilles.'

Thus spake he, and gave honour to the fleet son of Peleus. And Achilles answered him and said: 'Antilochos, not unheeded shall thy praise be given; a half-talent of gold I will give thee over and above.' He said, and set it in his hands, and Antilochos received it gladly.

[[1]Then Peleus' son brought a long-shadowed spear into the ring and laid it there, and a shield and helmet, the arms of Sarpedon whereof Patroklos spoiled him. And he stood up and spake a word among the Argives: 'To win these arms we bid two warriors of the best put on their armour and take flesh-cleaving bronze to make

[1]'There can be little doubt that from 798 to 883 is a late interpolation. The following contests seem to have no place in the Homeric gymnasium, and are not hinted at by Achilles in 621-3. In the second only one prize is offered, contrary to the otherwise courteous practice of Achilles, the descriptions lose their vigour, often becoming grotesque and impossible, and the actors are reduced to mere lay figures, instead of being living Homeric heroes of flesh and blood.' – Pratt and Leaf's *Story of Achilles*, p. 455

trial of each other before the host whether of the two shall first reach the other's fair flesh and touch the inward parts through armour and dark blood. To him will I give this silver-studded sword, a goodly Thracian sword that I took from Asteropaios; and these arms let both bear away to hold in common, and a fair feast will we set before them in the huts.'

Thus spake he, and then arose Telamon's son great Aias, and up rose Tydeus' son, stalwart Diomedes. So when on either side the assembly they had armed them, they met together in the midst eager for battle, with terrible gaze; and wonder fell on all the Achaians. But when they were now nigh in onset on each other, thrice they came on and thrice drew nigh to smite. Then Aias smote on the round shield, but pierced not to the flesh, for the breast-plate within kept off the spear. But the son of Tydeus over his great shield kept ever aiming at the neck with the point of his bright spear. Then fearing for Aias the Achaians bade them cease and each take equal prize. But to Tydeus' son the hero gave the great sword, bringing it with its scabbard and wellcut belt.

Then the son of Peleus set an unwrought metal mass which anciently the mighty Eetion was wont to whirl; but him fleet noble Achilles slew, and brought the mass in his ships with his other possessions. And he stood up and spake a word among the Argives: 'Rise, ye who will essay this match. The winner of this, even though his rich fields be very far remote, will have it for use five rolling years, for his shepherd or ploughman will not for want of iron have to go into the town, but this will give it them.'

Thus said he, and then arose warlike Polypoites, and the valiant strength of godlike Leonteus, and Aias son of Telamon and noble Epeios. And they stood in order, and noble Epeios took the weight, and whirled and flung it; and all the Achaians laughed to see it. Then next Leonteus, of the stock of Ares, threw; and thirdly great Aias Telamon's son hurled it from his stalwart hand, and overpassed the marks of all. But when warlike Polypoites took the mass he flung it as far as a herdsman flingeth his staff, when it flieth whirling through herds of kine; – so far cast he beyond all the space, and the people shouted aloud. And the comrades of strong Polypoites arose and bare the king's prize to the hollow ships.

Then for the archers he set a prize of dark iron – ten double-headed axes he set, and ten single; and set up the mast of a dark-prowed ship far off in the sands, and bound a pigeon thereto by the foot with a fine cord, and bade shoot thereat: – 'Whosoever shall hit the pigeon let him take all the double axes home with him, and whoso shall miss the bird but hit the cord, he shall take the single, since his shot is worse.'

Thus spake he, and then arose the strength of the chief Teukros, and Meriones arose, Idomeneus' brave brother in arms. And they took lots and shook them in a brazen helm, and Teukros drew the first place by lot. Forthwith he shot an arrow with power, but made no vow to offer a famous hecatomb of firstling lambs to the Lord of archery. The bird he missed – Apollo grudged him that – but struck the cord beside its foot, where the bird was tied, and the keen dart cut the cord clean away. Then the bird shot up toward heaven, and the cord hung loose toward earth; and the Achaians shouted. Then Meriones made haste and took from Teukros' hand the bow, – an arrow he had ready, while the other aimed – and vowed withal to far-darting Apollo a famous hecatomb of firstling lambs. High up under the clouds he saw the pigeon; there, as she circled round, he struck her in the midst beneath her wing, and right through her went the dart, and fell back and fixed itself in the ground before Meriones' foot; but the bird lighting on the mast of the dark-prowed ship hung down her neck, and her feathered pinions drooped. And quickly life fled from her limbs, and she fell far down from the mast; and the folk looked on and marvelled. And Meriones took up all the ten double axes, and Teukros bare the single to the hollow ships.]

Then Peleus' son brought and set in the ring a farshadowing spear and a caldron that knew not the fire, an ox's worth, embossed with flowers; and men that were casters of the javelin arose up. There rose Atreus' son wide-ruling Agamemnon, and Meriones, Idomeneus' brave squire. And swift-footed noble Achilles spake among them: 'Son of Atreus, for that we know how far thou excellest all, and how far the first thou art in the might of thy throw, take thou this prize with thee to the hollow ships, and to the hero Meriones let us give the spear, if thou art willing in thy heart: thus I at least advise.'

Thus spake he, nor disregarded him Agamemnon king of men. So to Meriones he gave the spear of bronze, but to the herald Talthybios the hero gave the goodliest prize.

BOOK XXIV

How the body of Hector was ransomed, and of his funeral.

THEN THE ASSEMBLY was broken up, and the tribes were scattered to betake them each to their own swift ships. The rest bethought them of supper and sweet sleep to have joy thereof; hut Achilles wept, remembering his dear comrade, nor did sleep that conquereth all take hold on him, but he kept turning him to this side and to that, yearning for Patroklos' manhood and excellent valour, and all the toils he achieved with him and the woes he bare, cleaving the battles of men and the grievous waves. As he thought thereon he shed big tears, now lying on his side, now on his back, now on his face; and then anon he would arise upon his feet and roam wildly beside the beach of the salt sea. Nor would he be unaware of the Dawn when she arose over the sea and shores. But when he had yoked the swift steeds to his car he would bind Hector behind his chariot to drag him withal; and having thrice drawn him round the barrow of the dead son of Menoitios he rested again in his hut, and left Hector lying stretched on his face in the dust. But Apollo kept away all defacement from his flesh, for he had pity on him even in death, and covered him all with his golden aegis, that Achilles might not tear him when he dragged him.

Thus Achilles in his anger entreated noble Hector shamefully; but the blessed gods when they beheld him pitied him, and urged the clear-sighted slayer of Argus to steal the corpse away. So to all the others seemed it good, yet not to Hera or Poseidon or the bright-eyed Maiden, but they continued as when at the beginning sacred Ilios became hateful to them, and Priam and his people, by reason of the sin of Alexandros in that he contemned those goddesses w hen they came to his steading, and preferred her who brought him deadly lustfulness. But when the twelfth morn from that day arose, then spake among the Immortals Phoebus Apollo: 'Hard of heart are ye, O gods, and cruel. Hath Hector never burnt for you thigh-bones of unblemished bulls and goats? Now have ye not taken heart to rescue even his corpse for his wife to look upon and his mother and his child and his father Priam and his people, who speedily would burn him in the fire and make his funeral. But

fell Achilles, O gods, ye are fain to abet, whose mind is nowise just
nor the purpose in his breast to be turned away, but he is cruelly
minded as a lion that in great strength and at the bidding *of* his
proud heart goeth forth against men's flocks to make his meal; even
thus Achilles hath cast out pity, neither hath he shame, that doth
both harm and profit men greatly. It must be that many a man lose
even some dearer one than was this, a brother of the same womb
born or perchance a son; yet bringeth he his wailing and lamentation to an end, for an enduring soul have the Fates given unto men.
But Achilles after bereaving noble Hector of his life bindeth him
behind his horses and draggeth him around the tomb of his dear
comrade: not, verily, is that more honourable or better for him. Let
him take heed lest we wax wroth with him, good man though he be,
for in his fury he is entreating shamefully the senseless clay.'

Then in anger spake unto him white-armed Hera: 'Even thus
mightest thou speak, O Lord of the silver bow, if ye are to give
equal honour to Achilles and to Hector. Hector is but a mortal and
was suckled at a woman's breast, but Achilles is child of a goddess
whom I myself bred up and reared and gave to a man to be his wife,
even to Peleus who was dearest of all men to the Immortals' heart.
And all ye gods came to her bridal, and thou among them wert
feasting with thy lyre, o lover of ill company, faithless ever.'

Then to her in answer spake Zeus who gathereth the clouds:
'Hera, be not wroth utterly with the gods: for these men's honour is
not to be the same, yet Hector also was dearest to the gods of all
mortals that are in Ilios. So was he to me at least, for nowise failed
he in the gifts I loved. Never did my altar lack seemly feast, drink-
offering and the steam of sacrifice, even the honour that falleth to
our due. But verily we will say no more of stealing away brave
Hector, for it cannot be hidden from Achilles, for his mother
abideth ever nigh to him night and day. But I were fain that some
one of the gods would call Thetis to come near to me, that I may
speak unto her a wise word, so that Achilles may take gifts from
Priam and give Hector back.'

Thus spake he, and airy-footed Iris sped forth upon the errand
and between Samothrace and rocky Imbros leapt into the black sea,
and the waters closed above her with a noise. And she sped to the
bottom like a weight of lead that mounted on horn of a field-ox
goeth down bearing death to ravenous fishes. And she found Thetis
in a hollow cave; about her sat gathered other goddesses of the sea,
and she in their midst was wailing for the fate of her noble son who
must perish in deep-soiled Troy, far from his native land. And

standing near, fleet-footed Iris spake to her: 'Rise, Thetis; Zeus of immortal counsels calleth thee.'

And to her made answer Thetis the silver-footed goddess: 'Wherefore biddeth me that mighty god? I shrink from mingling among the Immortals, for I have countless woes at heart. Yet go I, nor shall his word be in vain, whatsoever he saith.'

Thus having said the noble goddess took to her a darkhued robe, no blacker raiment was there found than that. Then she went forth, and wind-footed swift Iris led the way before her, and around them the surge of the sea was sundered. And when they had come forth upon the shore they sped up to heaven, and found the far-seeing son of Kronos, and round him sat gathered all the other blessed gods that are for ever. Then she sat down beside father Zeus, and Athene gave her place. And Hera set a fair golden cup in her hand and cheered her with words, and Thetis drank, and gave back the cup. Then began speech to them the father of gods and men: 'Thou art come to Olympus, divine Thetis, in thy sorrow, with violent grief at thy heart; I know it of myself. Nevertheless will I tell thee wherefore I called thee hither. Nine days hath dispute arisen among the Immortals concerning the corpse of Hector and Achilles waster of cities. Fain are they to send clear-sighted Argeïphontes to steal the body away, but now hear what glory I accord herein to Achilles, that I may keep through times to come thy honour and good will. Go with all speed to the host and bear to thy son my bidding. Say to him that the gods are displeased at him, and that I above all Immortals am wroth, because with furious heart he holdeth Hector at the beaked ships and hath not given him back, if haply he may fear me and give Hector back. But I will send Iris to great-hearted Priam to bid him go to the ships of the Achaians to ransom his dear son, and carry gifts to Achilles that may gladden his heart.'

Thus spake he, and Thetis the silver-footed goddess was not disobedient to his word, and sped darting upon her way down from the peaks of Olympus. And she came to her son's hut; there found she him making grievous moan, and his dear comrades round were swiftly making ready and furnishing their early meal, and a sheep great and fleecy was being sacrificed in the hut. Then his ladymother sate her down close beside him, and stroked him with her hand and spake to him by his name: 'My child, how long with lamentation and woe wilt thou devour thine heart, taking thought of neither food nor rest? good were even a woman's embrace, for not long shalt thou be left alive to me; already death and forceful fate are standing nigh thee. But hearken forthwith unto me, for I am the messenger of Zeus to thee. He saith that the gods are displeased at thee, and that himself above all Immortals is wroth, because with furious heart thou holdest Hector at the beaked ships and hast not given him back. But come restore him, and take ransom for the dead.'

Then to her in answer spake fleet-footed Achilles: 'So be it: whoso bringeth ransom let him take back the dead, if verily with heart's intent the Olympian biddeth it himself'

So they in the assembly of the ships, mother and son, spake to each other many winged words. But the son of Kronos thus bade Iris go to holy Ilios: 'Go forth, fleet Iris, leave the abode of Olympus and bear my message within Ilios to great-hearted Priam that he go to the ships of the Achaians and ransom his dear son and carry gifts to Achilles that may gladden his heart; let him go alone, and no other man of the Trojans go with him. Only let some elder herald attend on him to guide the mules and smooth-wheeled waggon and carry back to the city the dead man whom noble Achilles slew. Let not death be in his thought nor any fear; such guide will we give unto him, even the slayer of Argus, who shall lead him until his leading bring him to Achilles. And when he shall have led him within the hut, neither shall Achilles himself slay him nor suffer any other herein, for not senseless is he or unforeseeing or wicked, but with all courtesy he will spare a suppliant man.'

Thus spake he, and airy-footed Iris sped forth upon the errand. And she came to the house of Priam, and found therein crying and moan. His children sitting around their father within the court were bedewing their raiment with their tears, and the old man in their midst was close wrapped all over in his cloak; and on his head and neck was much mire that he had gathered in his hands as he grovelled upon the earth. And his daughters and his sons' wives were wailing throughout the house, bethinking them of all those valiant men who had lost their lives at the hands of the Argives and were lying low. And the messenger of Zeus stood beside Priam and spake softly unto him, and trembling came upon his limbs: 'Be of good cheer in thy heart, O Priam son of Dardanos, and be not dismayed for anything, for no evil come I hither to forebode to thee, but with good will. I am the messenger of Zeus to thee, who, though he be afar off, hath great care and pity for thee. The Olympian biddeth thee ransom noble Hector and carry gifts to Achilles that may gladden his heart: go thou alone, let none other of the Trojans go with thee. Only let some elder herald attend on thee to guide the mules and the smooth-wheeled waggon to carry back to the city the dead man whom noble Achilles slew. Let not death be in thy thought, nor any fear; such guide shall go with thee, even the slayer of Argus, who shall lead thee until his leading bring thee to Achilles. And when he shall have led thee into the hut, neither shall Achilles himself slay thee nor suffer any other herein, for not senseless is he or unforeseeing or wicked, but with all courtesy he will spare a suppliant man.'

Thus having spoken fleet Iris departed from him; and he bade his sons make ready the smooth-wheeled mule waggon, and bind the wicker carriage thereon. And himself he went down to his fragrant chamber, of cedar wood, highroofed, that held full many jewels: and to Hekabe his wife he called and spake: 'Lady, from Zeus hath an Olympian messenger come to me, that I go to the ships of the Achaians and ransom my dear son, and carry gifts to Achilles that may gladden his heart. Come tell me how seemeth it to thy mind, for of myself at least my desire and heart bid me mightily to go thither to the ships and enter the wide camp of the Achaians.'

Thus spake he, but his wife lamented aloud and made answer unto him: 'Woe is me, whither is gone thy mind whereby aforetime thou wert famous among stranger men and among them thou rulest? How art thou fain to go alone to the ships of the Achaians, to meet the eyes of the man who hath slain full many of thy brave sons? of iron verily is thy heart. For if he light on thee and behold thee with his eyes, a savage and ill-trusted man is this, and he will not pity thee, neither reverence thee at all. Nay, now let us sit in the hall and make lament afar off. Even thus did forceful Fate erst spin for Hector with her thread at his beginning, when I bare him, even I, that he should glut fleet-footed dogs, far from his parents, in the dwelling of a violent man whose inmost vitals I were fain to fasten and feed upon; then would his deeds against my son be paid again to him, for not playing the coward was he slain of him, but championing the men and deep-bosomed women of Troy, neither bethought he him of shelter or of flight.'

Then to her in answer spake the old man godlike Priam: 'Shy me not, for I am fain to go, neither be thyself a bird of ill boding in my halls, for thou wilt not change my mind. Were it some other and a child of earth that bade me this, whether some seer or of the priests that divine from sacrifice, then would we declare it false and have no part therein; but now, since I have heard the voice of the goddess myself and looked upon her face, I will go forth, and her word shall not be void. And if it be my fate to die by the ships of the mail-clad Achaians, so would I have it; let Achilles slay me with all speed, when once I have taken in my arms my son, and have satisfied my desire with moan.'

He spake, and opened fair lids of chests wherefrom he chose twelve very goodly women's robes and twelve cloaks of single fold and of coverlets a like number and of fair sheets, and of doublets thereupon. And he weighed and brought forth talents of gold ten in all, and two shining tripods and four caldrons, and a goblet exceeding fair that men of Thrace had given him when he went thither on an embassy, a chattel of great price, yet not that even did the old man grudge from his halls, for he was exceeding fain at heart to ransom his dear son. Then he drave out all the Trojans from the colonnade, chiding them with words of rebuke: 'Begone, ye that dishonour and do me shame! Have ye no mourning of your own at home that ye come to vex me here? Think ye it a small thing that Zeus Kronos' son hath given me this sorrow, to lose him that was the best man of my sons? Nay, but ye too shall feel it, for easier far shall ye be to the Achaians to slay now he is dead. But for me, ere I behold with mine eyes the city sacked and wasted, let me go down into the house of Hades.'

He said, and with his staff chased forth the men, and they went forth before the old man in his haste. Then he called unto his sons, chiding Helenos and Paris and noble Agathon and Pammon and Antiphonos, and Polites of the loud war-cry, and Deiphobos and Hippothoos and proud Dios; nine were they whom the old man called and bade unto him: 'Haste ye, ill sons, my shame; would that ye all in Hector's stead had been slain at the swift ships! Woe is me all unblest, since I begat sons the best men in wide Troy-land, but none of them is left for me to claim, neither godlike Mestor, nor Troilos with his chariot of war, nor Hector who was a god among men, neither seemed he as the son of a mortal man but of a god: – all these hath Ares slain, and here are my shames all left to me, false-tongued, light-heeled, the heroes of the dance, plunderers of your own people's sheep and kids. Will ye not make me ready a wain with all speed, and lay all these thereon, that we get us forward on our way?'

Thus spake he, and they fearing their father's voice brought forth the smooth-running mule chariot, fair and new, and bound the body thereof on the frame; and from its peg they took down the mule yoke, a boxwood yoke with knob well fitted with guiding-rings; and they brought forth the yoke-band of nine cubits with the yoke. The yoke they set firmly on the polished pole on the rest at the end thereof, and slipped the ring over the upright pin, which with three turns of the band they lashed to the knob, and then belayed it close round the pole and turned the tongue thereunder. Then they brought from the chamber and heaped on the polished wain the countless ransom of Hector's head, and yoked strong-hooved harness. mules, which on a time the Mysians gave to Priam, a splendid gift. But to Priam's car they yoked the horses that the old man kept for his use and reared at the polished crib.

Thus in the high palace were Priam and the herald letting yoke their cars, with wise thoughts at their hearts, when nigh them came Hekabe sore at heart, with honey sweet wine in her right hand in a golden cup that they might make libation ere they went. And she stood before the horses and spake a word to Priam by name: 'Lo now make libation to father Zeus and pray that thou mayest come back home from among the enemy, since thy heart speedeth thee forth to the ships, though fain were I thou wentest not. And next pray to Kronion of the Storm-cloud, the god of Ida, that beholdeth all Troy-land beneath, and ask of him a bird of omen, even the swift messenger that is dearest of all birds to him and of mightiest strength, to appear upon thy right, that seeing the sign with thine own eyes thou mayest go in trust thereto unto the ships of the fleet-horsed Danaans. But if far-seeing Zeus shall not grant unto thee his messenger, I at least shall not bid thee on to go among the ships of the Achaians how fain soever thou mayest be.'

Then answered and spake unto her godlike Priam: 'Lady I will not disregard this hest of thine, for good it is to lift up hands to Zeus, if haply he will have pity.'

Thus spake the old man, and bade a house-dame that served him pour pure water on his hands; and she came near to serve him with water in a ewer to wash withal. And when he had washed his hands he took a goblet from his wife: then he stood in the midst of the court and prayed and poured forth wine as he looked up to heaven, and spake a word aloud: 'Father Zeus that bearest sway from Ida, most glorious and most great, grant that I find welcome and pity under Achilles' roof, and send a bird of omen, even the swift mes-senger that is dearest of all birds to thee and of mightiest strength, to appear upon the right, that seeing this sign with mine own eyes I may go trusting therein unto the ships of the fleet-horsed Danaans.'

Thus spake he praying, and Zeus of wise counsels hearkened unto him, and straightway sent forth an eagle, surest omen of winged birds, the dusky hunter called of men the Black Eagle. Wide as the door, well locking, fitted close, of some rich man's high-roofed hall, so wide were his wings either way; and he appeared to them speeding on the right hand above the city. And when they saw the eagle they rejoiced and all their hearts were glad within their breasts.

Then the old man made haste to go up into his car, and drave forth from the doorway and the echoing portico. In front the mules drew the four-wheeled wain, and wise Idaios drave them; behind came the horses which the old man urged with the lash at speed along the city: and his friends all followed lamenting loud as though he were faring to his death. And when they were come down from the city and were now on the plain, then went back again to Ilios his sons and marriage kin. But the two coming forth upon the plain were not unbeheld of far-seeing Zeus. But he looked upon the old man and had compassion on him, and straightway spake unto Hermes his dear son: 'Hermes, since unto thee especially is it dear to companion men, and thou hearest whomsoever thou wilt, go forth and so guide Priam to the hollow ships of the Achaians that no man behold or be aware of him, among all the Danaans' host, until he come to the son of Peleus.'

Thus spake he, and the Messenger, the slayer of Argus, was not disobedient unto his word. Straightway beneath his feet he bound on his fair sandals, golden, divine, that bare him over the wet sea and over the boundless land with the breathings of the wind. And he took up his wand wherewith he entranceth the eyes of such men as he will, and others he likewise waketh out of sleep: this did the strong slayer of Argus take in his hand, and flew. And quickly came he to Troy-land and the Hellespont, and went on his way in semblance as a young man that is a prince, with the new down on his chin, as when the youth of men is the comeliest.

Now the others, when they had driven beyond the great barrow of Ilos, halted the mules and horses at the river to drink; for darkness was come down over the earth. Then the herald beheld Hermes from hard by, and marked him, and spake and said to Priam: 'Consider, son of Dardanos; this is matter of prudent thought. I see a man, methinks we shall full soon be rent in pieces. Come, let us flee in our chariot, or else at least touch his knees and entreat him that he have mercy on us.'

Thus spake he, and the old man was confounded, and he was dismayed exceedingly, and the hair on his pliant limbs stood up, and he stood still amazed. But the Helper came nigh of himself and took the old man's hand, and spake and questioned him: 'Whither, father, dost thou thus guide these horses and mules through the divine night, when other mortals are asleep? Hadst thou no fear of the fierce-breathing Achaians, thy bitter foes that are hard anigh thee? If one of them should espy thee carrying such treasures through the swift black night, what then would be thy thought? Neither art thou young thyself, and thy companion here is old, that ye should make defence against a man that should assail thee first. But I will no wise harm thee, yea I will keep any other from thy hurt: for the similitude of my dear father I see in thee.'

And to him in answer spake the old man, godlike Priam: 'Even so, kind son, are all these things as thou sayest. Nevertheless hath some god stretched forth his hand even over me in that he hath sent a wayfarer such as thou to meet me, a bearer of good luck, by the nobleness of thy form and semblance; and thou art wise of heart and of blessed parents art thou sprung.'

And to him again spake the Messenger, the slayer of Argus: 'All this, old sire, hast thou verily spoken aright. But come say this and tell me truly whether thou art taking forth a great and goodly treasure unto alien men, where it may abide for thee in safety, or whether by this ye are all forsaking holy Ilios in fear; so far the best man among you hath perished, even thy son; for of battle with the Achaians abated he never a jot.'

And to him in answer spake the old man, godlike Priam: 'Who art thou, noble sir, and of whom art born? For meetly hast thou spoken of the fate of my hapless son.'

And to him again spake the Messenger, the slayer of Argus: 'Thou art proving me, old sire, in asking me of noble Hector. Him have I full oft seen with mine eyes in glorious battle, and when at the ships he was slaying the Argives he drave thither, piercing them with the keen bronze, and we stood still and marvelled thereat, for Achilles suffered us not to fight, being wroth against Atreus' son. His squire am I, and came in the same well-wrought ship. From the Myrmidons I come, and my father is Polyktor. Wealthy is he, and an old man even as thou, and six other sons hath he, and I am his seventh. With the others I cast lots, and it fell to me to fare hither with the host. And now am I come from the ships to the plain, for at day-break the glancing-eyed Achaians will set the battle in array around the town. For it chafeth them to be sitting here, nor can the Achaian lords hold in their fury for the fray.'

And the old man, godlike Priam, answered him, saying: 'If verily thou art a squire of Achilles Peleus' son, come tell me all the truth, whether still my son is by the ships, or whether ere now Achilles hath riven him limb from limb and cast him to the dogs.'

Then to him again spake the Messenger the slayer of Argus: 'Old sire, not yet have dogs or birds devoured him, but there lieth he still by Achilles' ship, even as he fell, among the huts, and the twelfth morn now hath risen upon him, nor doth his flesh corrupt at all, neither worms consume it, such as devour men slain in war. Truly Achilles draggeth him recklessly around the barrow of his dear comrade so oft as divine day dawneth, yet marreth he him not; thou wouldst marvel if thou couldst go see thyself how dewy fresh he lieth, and is washed clean of blood, nor anywhere defiled; and all his wounds wherewith he was stricken are closed; howbeit many plunged their points in him. So careful are the blessed gods of thy son, though he be but a dead corpse, for they held him dear at heart.'

Thus spake he, and the old man rejoiced, and answered him, saying: 'My son, it is verily a good thing to give due offerings withal to the Immortals, for never did my child – if that child indeed I had – forget in our halls the gods who inhabit Olympus. Therefore have they remembered this for him, albeit his portion is death. But come now take from me this goodly goblet, and guard me myself and guide me, under Heaven, that I may come unto the hut of Peleus' son.'

Then spake unto him again the Messenger the slayer of Argus: 'Thou art proving me, old sire, who am younger than thou, but thou wilt not prevail upon me, in that thou biddest me take gifts from thee without Achilles' privity. I were afraid and shamed at heart to defraud him, lest some evil come to pass on me hereafter. But as thy guide I would go even unto famous Argos, accompanying thee courteously in swift ship or on foot. Not from scorn of thy guide would any assail thee then.'

Thus spake the Helper, and leaping on the chariot behind the horses he swiftly took lash and reins into his hand, and breathed brave spirit into horses and mules. But when they were come to the towers and trench of the ships, there were the sentinels just busying them about their supper. Then the Messenger, the slayer of Argus, shed sleep upon them all and straightway opened the gates and thrust back the bars, and brought within Priam and the splendid gifts upon his wain. And they came to the lofty hut of the son of Peleus, which the Myrmidons made for their king and hewed there-for timber of the pine, and thatched it with downy thatching-rush that they mowed in the meadows, and around it made for him their lord a great court with close-set palisades; and the door was barred by a single bolt of pine that three Achaians wont to drive home, and three drew back that mighty bar – three of the rest, but Achilles by himself would drive it home. Then opened the Helper Hermes the door for the old man, and brought in the splendid gifts for Peleus' fleet-footed son, and descended from the chariot to the earth and spake aloud: 'Old sire, I that have come to thee am an immortal god, even Hermes, for my father sent me to companion thee on thy way. But now will I depart from thee nor come within Achilles' sight; it were cause of wrath that an immortal god should thus show favour openly unto mortals. But thou go in and clasp the knees of Peleus' son and entreat him for his father's sake and his mother's of the lovely hair and for his child's sake that thou mayest move his soul.'

Thus Hermes spake, and departed unto high Olympus. But Priam leapt from the car to the earth, and left Idaios in his place; he stayed to mind the horses and mules; but the old man made straight for the house where Achilles dear to Zeus was wont to sit. And therein he found the man himself, and his comrades sate apart: two only, the hero Automedon and Alkimos, of the stock of Ares, were busy in attendance; and he was lately ceased from meat, even from eating and drinking: and still the table stood beside him. But they were unaware of great Priam as he came in, and so stood he anigh and clasped in his hands the knees of Achilles, and kissed his hands, terrible, man-slaying, that slew many of Priam's sons. And as when a grievous curse cometh upon a man who in his own country hath slain another and escapeth to a land of strangers, to the house of some rich man, and wonder possesseth them that look on him – so Achilles wondered when he saw godlike Priam, and the rest wondered likewise, and looked upon one another. Then Priam spake and entreated him, saying: 'Bethink thee, O Achilles like to gods, of thy father that is of like years with me, on the grievous pathway of old age. Him haply are the dwellers round about entreating evilly, nor is there any to ward from him ruin and bane. Nevertheless while he heareth of thee as yet alive he rejoiceth in his heart, and hopeth withal day after day that he shall see his dear son returning from Troy-land. But I, I am utterly unblest, since I begat sons the best men in wide Troy-land, but declare unto thee that none of them is left. Fifty I had, when the sons of the Achaians came; nineteen were born to me of one mother, and concubines bare the rest within my halls. Now of the more part had impetuous Ares unstrung the knees, and he who was yet left and guarded city and men, him slewest thou but now as he fought for his country, even Hector. For his sake come I unto the ships of the Achaians that I may win him back from thee, and I bring with me untold ransom. Yea, fear thou the gods, Achilles, and have compassion on me, even me, bethinking thee of thy father. Lo, I am yet more piteous than he, and have braved what none other man on earth hath braved before, to stretch forth my hand toward the face of the slayer of my sons.'

Thus spake he, and stirred within Achilles desire to make lament for his father. And he touched the old man's hand and gently moved him back. And as they both bethought them of their dead, so Priam for man-slaying Hector wept sore as he was fallen before Achilles' feet, and Achilles wept for his own father, and now again for Patroklos, and their moan went up throughout the house. But when noble Achilles had satisfied him with lament, and the desire thereof departed from his heart and limbs, straightway he sprang from his seat and raised the old man by his hand, pitying his hoary head and hoary beard, and spake unto him winged words and said: 'Ah hapless! many ill things verily thou hast endured in thy heart. How durst thou come alone to the ships of the Achaians and to meet the eyes of the man who hath slain full many of thy brave sons? of iron verily is thy heart. But come then set thee on a seat, and we will let our sorrows lie quiet in our hearts, for all our pain, for no avail cometh of chill lament. This is the lot the gods have spun for miserable men, that they should live in pain; yet themselves are sorrowless. For two urns stand upon the floor of Zeus filled with his evil gifts, and one with blessings. To whomsoever Zeus whose joy is in the lightning dealeth a mingled lot, that man chanceth now upon ill and now again on good, but to whom he giveth but of the bad kind him he bringeth to scorn, and evil famine chaseth him over the goodly earth, and he is a wanderer honoured of neither gods nor men. Even thus to Peleus gave the gods splendid gifts from his birth, for he excelled all men in good fortune and wealth, and was king of the Myrmidons1 and mortal though he was the gods gave him a goddess to be his bride. Yet even on him God brought evil, seeing that there arose to him no offspring of princely sons in his halls, save that he begat one son to an untimely death. Neither may I tend him as he groweth old, since very far from my country I am dwelling in Troy-land, to vex thee and thy children. And of thee, old sire, we have heard how of old time thou wert happy, even how of all that Lesbos, seat of Makar, boundeth to the north thereof and Phrygia farther up and the vast Hellespont – of all these folk, men say, thou wert the richest in wealth and in sons, but after that the Powers of Heaven brought this bane on thee, ever are battles and manslayings around thy city. Keep courage, and lament not unabatingly in thy heart. For nothing wilt thou avail by grieving for thy son, neither shalt thou bring him back to life or ever some new evil come upon thee.'

Then made answer unto him the old man, godlike Priam: 'Bid me not to a seat, O fosterling of Zeus, so long as Hector lieth uncared for at the huts, but straightway give him back that I may behold him with mine eyes; and accept thou the great ransom that we bring. So mayest thou have pleasure thereof, and come unto thy native land, since thou hast spared me from the first.'[1]

Then fleet-footed Achilles looked sternly upon him and said: 'No longer chafe me, old sire; of myself am I minded to give Hector back to thee, for there came to me a messenger from Zeus, even my mother who bare me, daughter of the Ancient One of the Sea And I know, O Priam, in my mind, nor am unaware that some god it is that hath guided thee to the swift ships of the Achaians. For no mortal man, even though in prime of youth, would dare to come among the host, for neither could he escape the watch, nor easily thrust back the bolt of our doors. Therefore now stir my heart no more amid my troubles, lest I leave not even thee in peace, old sire, within my hut, albeit thou art my suppliant, and lest I transgress the commandment of Zeus.'

Thus spake he, and the old man feared, and obeyed his word. And the son of Peleus leapt like a lion through the door of the house, not alone, for with him went two squires, the hero Automedon and Alkimos, they whom above all his comrades Achilles honoured, save only Patroklos that was dead. They then loosed from under the yoke the horses and mules, and led in the old man's crier-herald and set him on a chair, and from the wain of goodly felloes they took the countless ransom set on Hector's head. But they left two robes and a well-spun doublet, that Achilles might wrap the dead therein when he gave him to be carried home. And he called forth handmaids and bade them wash and anoint him when they had borne him apart, so that Priam should not look upon his son, lest he should not refrain the wrath at his sorrowing heart when he should look upon his son, and lest Achilles' heart be vexed thereat and he slay him and transgress the commandment of Zeus. So when the handmaids had washed the body and anointed it with oil, and had thrown over it a fair robe and a doublet, then Achilles himself lifted it and laid it on a bier, and his comrades with him lifted it onto the polished waggon. Then he groaned aloud and called on his dear comrade by his name: 'Patroklos, be not vexed with me if thou

---

[1] Omitting line 558, which was unknown to Aristarchos, and even to Herodianos.

hear even in the house of Hades that I have given back noble
Hector unto his dear father, for not unworthy is the ransom he hath
given me, whereof I will deal to thee again thy rightful share.'

Thus spake noble Achilles, and went back into the hut, and sate
him down on the cunningly-wrought couch whence he had arisen
by the opposite wall, and spake a word to Priam: 'Thy son, old sire,
is given back as thou wouldest and lieth on a bier, and with the
break of day thou shalt see him thy. self as thou carriest him. But
now bethink we us of supper. For even faired-haired Niobe
bethought her of meat, she whose twelve children perished in her
halls, six daughters and six lusty sons. The sons Apollo, in his anger
against Niobe, slew with arrows from his silver bow, and the daughters archer Artemis, for that Niobe matched herself against
faircheeked Leto, saying that the goddess bare but twain but herself
many children: so they though they were but twain destroyed the
others all. Nine days they lay in their blood, nor was there any to
bury them, for Kronion turned the folk to stones. Yet on the tenth
day the gods of heaven buried them, and she then bethought her of
meat, when she was wearied out with weeping tears. And somewhere now among the cliffs, on the lonely mountains, even on Sipy-
los, where they say are the couching-places of nymphs that dance
around Acheloös, there she, albeit a stone, broodeth still over her
troubles from the gods. But come let us too, noble father, take
thought of meat, and afterward thou shalt mourn over thy dear son
as thou carriest him to Ilios; and many tears shall be his due.'

Thus spake fleet Achilles, and sprang up, and slew a pure white
sheep, and his comrades skinned and made it ready in seemly fashion, and divided it cunningly and pierced it with spits, and roasted it
carefully and drew all off. And Automedon took bread and served it
on a table in fair baskets, while Achilles dealt out the flesh. And they
stretched forth their hands to the good cheer lying ready before
them. But when they had put off the desire of meat and drink, then
Priam son of Dardanos marvelled at Achilles to see how great he
was and how goodly, for he was like a god to look upon. And
Achilles marvelled at Priam son of Dardanos, beholding his noble
aspect and hearkening to his words. But when they had gazed their
fill upon one other, then first spake the old man, godlike Priam, to
Achilles: 'Now presently give me whereon to lie, fosterling of Zeus,
that of sweet sleep also we may now take our fill at rest: for never
yet have mine eyes closed beneath their lids since at thy hands my
son lost his life, but I continually mourn and brood over countless
griefs, grovelling in the courtyard-close amid the mire. Now at last

have I tasted bread and poured bright wine down my throat, but till now I had tasted nought.'

He said, and Achilles bade his comrades and handmaids to set a bedstead beneath the portico, and to cast thereon fair shining rugs and spread coverlets above and thereon to lay thick mantles to be a clothing over all. And the maids went forth from the inner hall with torches in their hands, and quickly spread two beds in haste. Then with bitter meaning[1] said fleet-footed Achilles unto Priam: 'Lie thou without, dear sire, lest there come hither one of the counsellors of the Achaians, such as ever take counsel with me by my side, as custom is. If any of such should behold thee through the swift black night, forthwith he might haply tell it to Agamemnon shepherd of the host, and thus would there be delay in giving back the dead. But come say this to me and tell it true, how many days' space thou art fain to make funeral for noble Hector, so that for so long I may myself abide and may keep back the host.'

And the old man, godlike Priam, answered him saying: 'If thou art verily willing that I accomplish noble Hector's funeral, by doing as thou sayest, O Achilles, thou wilt do me grace. For thou knowest how we are pent within the city, and wood from the mountain is far to fetch, and the Trojans are much in fear. Nine days will we make moan for him in our halls, and on the tenth we will hold funeral and the folk shall feast, and on the eleventh we will make a barrow over him, and on the twelfth we will do battle if need be.'

Then again spake the fleet noble Achilles unto him saying: 'All this, O ancient Priam, shall be as thou biddest; for I will hold back the battle even so long a time as thou tellest me.'

Thus speaking he clasped the old man's right hand at the wrist, lest he should be anywise afraid at heart. So they in the forepart of the house laid them down, Priam and the herald, with wise thoughts at their hearts, but Achilles slept in a recess of the firm-wrought hut, and beside him lay faircheeked Briseis.

Now all other gods and warriors lords of chariots slumbered all night, by soft sleep overcome. But not on the Helper Hermes did sleep take hold as he sought within his heart how he should guide forth king Priam from the ships unespied of the trusty sentinels. And he stood above his head and spake a word to him: 'Old sire, no thought then hast thou of any evil, seeing thou yet sleepest among men that are thine enemies, for that Achilles spared thee. Truly now hast thou won back thy dear son, and at great price But for thy

[1] In his reference to Agamemnon.

life will thy sons thou hast left behind be offering threefold ransom, if but Agamemnon Atreus' son be aware of thee, and aware be all the Achaians.'

Thus spake he, and the old man feared, and roused the herald. And Hermes yoked the horses and mules for them, and himself drave them lightly through the camp, and none was aware of them.

But when they came to the ford of the fair-flowing river, [even eddying Xanthos, begotten of immortal Zeus,] then Hermes departed up to high Olympus, and Morning of the saffron robe spread over all the earth. And they with wail and moan drave the horses to the city, and the mules drew the dead. Nor marked them any man or fair-girdled woman until Kassandra, peer of golden Aphrodite, having gone up upon Pergamos, was aware of her dear father as he stood in the car, and the herald that was crier to the town. Then beheld she him that lay upon the bier behind the mules, and thereat she wailed and cried aloud throughout all the town: 'O men and women of Troy, come ye hither and look upon Hector, if ever while he was alive ye rejoiced when he came back from battle, since great joy was he to the city and all the folk.'

Thus spake she, nor was man or woman left within the city, for upon all came unendurable grief And near the gates they met Priam bringing home the dead. First bewailed him his dear wife and lady mother, as they cast them on the fair-wheeled wain and touched his head; and around them stood the throng and wept. So all day long unto the setting of the sun they had lamented Hector in tears without the gate, had not the old man spoken from the car among the folk: 'Give me place for the mules to pass through; hereafter ye shall have your fill of wailing, when I have brought him unto his home.'

Thus spake he, and they parted asunder and gave place to the wain. And the others when they had brought him to the famous house, laid him on a fretted bed, and set beside him minstrels leaders of the dirge, who wailed a mournful lay, while the women made moan with them. And among the women white-armed Andromache led the lamentation, while in her hands she held the head of Hector slayer of men: 'Husband, thou art gone young from life, and leavest me a widow in thy halls. And the child is yet but a little one, child of ill-fated parents, thee and me; nor methinks shall he grow up to manhood, for ere then shall this city be utterly destroyed. For thou art verily perished who didst watch over it, who guardedst it and keptest safe its noble wives and infant little ones. These soon shall be voyaging in the hollow ships, yea and I too with them, and thou, my child, shalt either go with me unto a place where thou shalt toil at unseemly tasks, labouring before the face of some harsh lord, or else some Achaian will take thee by the arm and hurl thee from the battlement, a grievous death, for that he is wroth because Hector slew his brother or father or son, since full many of the Achaians at Hector's hands have bitten the firm earth. For no light hand had thy father in the grievous fray. Therefore the folk lament him throughout the city, and woe unspeakable[1] and mourning hast thou left to thy parents, Hector, but with me chiefliest shall grievous pain abide. For neither didst thou stretch thy hands to me from a bed in thy death, neither didst speak to me some memorable word that I might have thought on evermore as my tears fall night and day.'

Thus spake she wailing, and the women joined their moan. And among them Hekabe again led the loud lament: 'Hector, of all my children far dearest to my heart, verily while thou wert alive dear wert thou to the gods, and even in thy doom of death have they had care for thee. For other sons of mine whom he took captive would fleet Achilles sell beyond the unvintaged sea unto Samos and Imbros and smoking Lemnos,[2] but when with keen-edged bronze he had bereft thee of thy life he was fain to drag thee oft around the tomb of his comrade, even Patroklos whom thou slewest, yet might he not raise him up thereby. But now all dewy and fresh thou liest in our halls, like one on whom Apollo, lord of the silver bow, hath descended and slain him with his gentle darts.'

Thus spake she wailing, and stirred unending moan. Then thirdly Helen led their sore lament: 'Hector, of all my brethren of Troy far dearest to my heart! Truly my lord is godlike Alexandros who brought me to Troy-land – would I had died ere then. For this is now the twentieth year since I went thence and am gone from my own native land, but never yet heard I evil or despiteful word from thee: nay, if any other haply upbraided me in the palace-halls, whether brother or sister of thine or brother's fair-robed wife, or thy mother – but thy father is ever kind to me as he were my own – then wouldst thou soothe such with words and refrain them, by the gentleness of thy spirit and by thy gentle words. Therefore bewail I thee with pain at heart, and my hapless self with thee, for no more is any left in wide Troy-land to be my friend and kind to me, but all men shudder at me.'

Thus spake she wailing, and therewith the great multitude of the people groaned. But the old man Priam spake a word among the

[1] Reading ἄρρητον.
[2] A volcanic island

folk: 'Bring wood, men of Troy, unto the city, and be not anywise afraid at heart of a crafty ambush of the Achaians; for this message Achilles gave me when he sent me from the black ships, that they should do us no hurt until the twelfth morn arise.'

Thus spake he, and they yoked oxen and mules to wains, and quickly then they flocked before the city. So nine days they gathered great store of wood. But when the tenth morn rose with light for men, then bare they forth brave Hector, weeping tears, and on a lofty pyre they laid the dead man, and thereon cast fire.

But when the daughter of Dawn, rosy-fingered Morning, shone forth, then gathered the folk around glorious Hector's pyre.[1] First quenched they with bright wine all the burning, so far as the fire's strength went, and then his brethren and comrades gathered his white bones lamenting, and big tears flowed down their cheeks. And the bones they took and laid in a golden urn, shrouding them in soft purple robes, and straightway laid the urn in a hollow grave and piled thereon great close-set stones, and heaped with speed a barrow, while watchers were set everywhere around, lest the well-greaved Achaians should make onset before the time. And when they had heaped the barrow they went back, and gathered them together and feasted right well in noble feast at the palace of Priam, Zeus-fostered king.

Thus held they funeral for Hector tamer of horses.

NOTES.

NOTE 1, p. 40; Book II, 628.

THE STORY OF PHYLEUS.

Phyleus was the son of Augeias, and sought a new home in Duli chion because he had borne witness against his father before Herakles, concerning the hire which Augeias had promised for the cleansing of his stables.

NOTE 2, p. 177; Book IX, 529.

THE STORY OF MELEAGROS.

[1] Omitting, with almost all the best MSS., the superfluous line 790.

Oineus the Aitolian King of Kalydon having wedded Althaia daughter of Thestias King of the Kuretes, the two peoples combined to slay the wild boar that savaged Kalydon, but fell out over the spoils; for Meleagros, son of Oineus, wished to give them to Atalanta, who helped in the chase. But the sons of Thestias, indignant, had taken them from her: for which Meleagros slew them, and was therefore cursed by his mother Althaia, their sister.

NOTE 3, p. 178; Book IX, 50

SHE STORY OF KLEOPATRA.

Idas son of Aphareus carried off Marpessa from her father Euenos; and Apollo wished lo take her from Idas. So the two came to fighting, until Zeus separated them, and bade Marpessa choose which she would have. And she chose the mortal, fearing least the god should prove faithless.

NOTE 4, p. 403; Book XX, 145.

Apollo, hsving been commznded by Zeus to serve Lsomedon king of Troy for hire, builded him z wall for a certain reward, but Laomedon brake the osths and the covenant, and drave them away without their wsge. Whereon Poseidon, being wroth, sent a seabeast against the land, and the people perished, and the f uits. So Laomedon sought to the oracle, that bade him sacrifice his daughter, Hesione, to the monster, wherefore he exposed her, but offered a reward, namely the immortal horses of Zeus, to him thst would slay the thing. So Herakles was fain to achieve this adrenture, and Athena builded him a wall, whence he might sally out against the sea-besst. Then Herakles lesped down the mouth aud into the belly of the beast, and tore its flanks, and so it died. But Laomedon gave none but mortal steeds to Herakles, who, in his wrath, destroyed Ilios utterly, and seized the horses. *The story is in Hellanilos.*

> ABOVE THE DIN OF SLAYERS AND OF SLAIN
>   AND DIAPASON OF THE WAR-GOD'S CRY;
>   BEHIND THE DAZZLE AND STRESS OF CHIVALRY
> AND GLOW MERIDIAN OF THE ILIAN PLAIN,
> THE FINER EAR DISCERNED A SECRET STRAIN,
>   A VISION PIERCED TO THE DIVINER EYE;
>   THE FAR-OFF ECHO OF A WOMAN'S SIGH,
> WEAKNESS MADE PERFECT UNTO STRENGTH IN PAIN.
> BEFORE THE THRONE OF GREAT ACHILLES SEE
>   THE BROCKEN KING KISSING THE DEADLY HANDS
>   WHEREBY HIS HOUSE IS LEFT HIM DESOLATE;
>   AND IN THE SHADOW OF THE SKAIAN GATE,
>   HER BABE FOREDOOMED UPON HER BOSOM, STANDS
> SMILING AMID HER TEARS, ANDROMACHE.
>   W. L.

WORDSWORTH CLASSICS

REQUESTS FOR INSPECTION COPIES Lecturers wishing to obtain copies of Wordsworth Classics, Wordsworth Poetry Library or Wordsworth Classics of World Literature titles for inspection are invited to contact: Dennis Hart, Wordsworth Editions Ltd, Crib Street, Ware, Herts SG12 9ET; E-mail: dennis.hart@wordsworth-editions.com. Please quote the author, title and ISBN of the books in which you are interested, together with your name, academic address, E-mail address, the course on which the books will be used and the expected enrolment.

Teachers wishing to inspect specific core titles for GCSE or A-level courses are also invited to contact Wordsworth Editions at the above address.

Inspection copies are sent solely at the discretion of Wordsworth Editions Ltd.